ANDRASTE'S BLADE

By

Andrew Richardson

Dark Realm Press
A Division of Gate Way Publishers

Vallejo, California

For information, contact Dark Realm Press, a division of Gate Way Publishers, 2801 Redwood Parkway, #219, Vallejo, California 94591 USA. Visit us on the World Wide Web at www.darkrealmpress.com.

ISBN: 0-9752645-6-7

Cover Artwork by Gate Way Publishers
Book design by DigitalWrite. www.digitalwrite.com

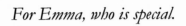

For Emma, who is special.

Preface

I am not evil.

I have felt the pains of birth. I am no more malevolent than the tormenting pangs of labour. Is the cold of winter that takes the lives of the weak and the young, evil? Is the spear that rips through flesh sated with evil? Is the plague, which takes the people at random, young and old, king or bondsman, evil? No, these are mere instruments of destruction, unable to avoid the anguish they cause. Like me, they are judged on the all consuming suffering which follows them, a suffering over which they have no control.

I feast upon mortal bodies and souls because of the way I was created, not because I have been granted a choice. Am I evil because I take what is essential for my survival? Maybe I should starve myself of what I need, and experience a slow lingering death as I become weak and emancipated. That would save many lives.

But do not condemn me because I lack the courage to die.

And power?

Who does not yearn for power? Throughout history countless usurpers have taken kingship for themselves. Given noble birth and a keen warband would you not stake a claim for leadership? I want nothing that any mortal would not grasp with both hands.

I wish only to satisfy my needs and desires.

No. I am not evil.

Prologue

Archdruid Bran fell to his knees. His ageing eyes scanned the water for a vision.

Although he gazed long and hard from beneath bushed brows, the sacred pool would reveal no secrets. He saw only his own knotted features frowning back at him, and the reflections of lofty peaks peering over his shoulder.

A weathered hand gently caressed his greying beard as he concentrated.

His senses, finely tuned by years of experience, searched for omens in the nature around him: a shift in the breeze; a cloud crossing the summer sun; a change in the birdsong or in the laughter of the small stream dancing along the valley.

But there was nothing. No portents of the future to ease or curse his troubled mind. He took a berry of mistletoe from a pouch at the belt of his white robe and placed it in his mouth. He hoped the magical fruit would ease his passage into the realms of prophecy.

His lips trembled as he made a plea to the gods. "Give me a sign! Give me a sign I can present to the Warrior Queen!"

His pulse quickened as he remembered her words. "Go to your Sacred Pool in the Western Mountains," she had ordered. "Find me a portent of defeat or victory. Let me take the advice of the gods." Her eyes had gleamed with the passion of fire, matching her long red hair, her face hardened into a mask of determination. He stroked his beard once more.

For Boudicca, Warrior Queen of the Iceni, did not accept failure.

And still the Druid gained no response from the sacred water. He knew, with a sense of fear, that he needed more strength to reach the gods. He must risk his soul and call upon the ancient power of the earth to help him.

He dared not return to his queen empty handed.

His staff helped him to his feet and he took the few determined paces to the circle of stones, erected at a time in the primeval past, long before legends or heroes were born. He knelt in the centre of the ancient enclosure.

Beyond the stones his eyes met a burial mound, as aged as the megaliths surrounding him, and maybe even erected by the same hands. As always, he was grateful that the massive slab guarding the entrance remained sealed. He had no wish to meet the horrors lying inside the resting place of the ancestors.

He closed his eyes and passed into the realms of blackness. The mistletoe had cleared his mind to a blank, but his body consumed the fear that had been wiped from his consciousness. It did not take a soul to tell flesh and bone of the danger to come.

Apprehension coiled within Archdruid Bran as the ancient power of the circle coursed through him, over him, around him, like a river trying to drown him with the force of the earth's energies. A powerful wind pounded his eardrums with the ferocity of a winter's gale. The gods permitted the power to sting him like the pricks of a thousand needles as it entered his pores. He took the pain, knowing he was being invigorated with a potency to help him reach the future. He let the strength reach his soul until his body was numbed.

His eyes remained closed; he felt, rather than saw, the thick white mist embracing him. Was it his imagination, or were the ancestors calling him, telling him it was time to enter the mound and join them in the Otherworld? He recognised the voices, some close by and whispering in his ear, others distant, as if echoes reaching him from beyond the mountains. Their words held a musical beauty to rival the finest harp, bringing joy with the merest whisper. Some belonged to long dead parents or grandparents. Other voices were of childhood friends, long forgotten but now dragged from the recesses of his mind.

He hesitated. Tears filled his eyes as the voices reminded him of a contented youth; lost days fishing with his father, or playing with friends in buttercup-strewn meadows. Every part of his body ached to pull away the stone blocking the entrance to the tomb, to join the people he loved in the shadows beyond. His fingers tightened around his staff as he prepared to stand and take the few steps to paradise.

"NO. YOU ARE NOTHING BUT A DREAM SENT TO HAUNT ME. I WILL NOT BE TEMPTED," he shouted with ferocity to dispel the sounds from his mind and send them back to the Otherworld.

He opened his eyes.

As quickly as it had come, the mist dissipated. The wind stilled. The energy of the stones subsided. Nothing remained of his experience except a hastily beating heart, a mild ache in his forehead, and the unnatural silence in the valley.

He had passed the test.

He raised his arms upwards, towards the gods.

"Give me a sign! I have endured and overcome your test. Give me a sign! I, Bran, Archdruid of Britain, demand of you, reveal the outcome of our strife. Will Boudicca throw the yoke of oppression from the shoulders of Britain? ARE THE EAGLES OF ROME DESTINED TO TIGHTEN THEIR TALONS AROUND OUR THROATS?" His voice had risen to a roar, echoing around the valley as the mountains trapped it between their grey walls.

A sudden touch of colour pulled his gaze to the ancient tomb. He gasped as blood seeped from around the entrance stone, at first no more than a couple of drops, but increasing in force until within a few heartbeats the red trickle had become a steady scarlet torrent. A puddle quickly formed. He blinked, but the blood remained. He watched in eerie fascination, a lifetime of training forcing fear to the recesses of his mind.

More movement caught the corner of his vision, and he turned his head around the circle of stones. Each was bleeding with equal intensity. His brows knotted as a red stream formed. It soon became a river which emptied itself into his sacred pool and tainted it scarlet. He raised himself up and knelt at the pool's edge.

In the pool, faces downward and bloated in death, floated naked bodies, each baring the open wounds of battle. Most were men, but women had not been spared the slaughter. And purveying the area, the stench of flesh in the first stages of decay. Flies busied themselves on the bloated corpses, looking for a break in the skin in which to bury their larvae. Despite his training, the Archdruid put his mouth to his face in disgust, fighting back the urge to gag as the sight and stench of death hit his senses. He must interpret the sight with the impartiality of one schooled to look for signs, he remembered.

Each carcass had the swarthy, naturally tanned skin of the Roman invaders. Well-manicured nails and fastidiously styled hair served only to confirm their origin, contrasting with the light colouring and blond, restless locks of Bran's fellow Celt.

A sigh of relief escaped his lips. "It is victory for Britain. Boudicca will triumph," he whispered to himself.

"But blood will flow."

At that same moment, two lambs appeared bounding down the hillside, seemingly from nowhere but the steep walls of slate. Their wool, the colour of milk, was unnatural in a way Bran couldn't place, reflecting the sun's rays as they made their way to the pool. The Archdruid expected them to turn away on seeing death floating in the water, but instead the animals quenched themselves on a drink of barely diluted blood. After filling their bellies, they took their reddened muzzles from the water and started on a meal of Roman corpses, gnawing eagerly as flesh and bones mangled between their teeth. One lamb looked up and saw the other enjoying a particularly succulent piece of thigh from the leg of a well-tuned warrior. A fight over the morsel followed, with both animals screaming, kicking and biting. They appeared ready to tear each other apart in their anger, their pure wool becoming scarlet cloaks. The Druid watched the fight in horrified fascination, until one lamb finally gained a grip on the other's windpipe, and bit and thrashed the other unfortunate animal from side to side until it convulsed in the throes of death.

"What malicious force could corrupt the most gentle of creatures?" the Druid asked himself, cursing the quiver in his voice.

The vision became misty and indistinct as it faded into the atmosphere, taking blood, corpses and feasting lamb with it.

But Archdruid Bran knew he had seen something more than certain victory. There was something else stabbing at his heart. Something evil, something just beyond the reach of his interpretation, which the gods, as if goading him, had taken back as his mind had been about to reach and grab it.

He was bought back to the mortal world by the sound of Majestic whinnying anxiously beyond the small rise. Something was worrying his horse. The priest climbed to his feet.

The sun angered his eyes, but a shiver ran through him. A sudden breeze scuttled past, caressing his skin with an icy breath. Then in an instant it was gone. The summer warmth returned, but Bran shivered again. It had been no ordinary eddy of wind caught between the mountains. Malevolence had touched past him. Something evil had been summoned by his vision.

The Druid quickened his pace.

"It's all right, girl. Bran's back now. You felt it too, did you?" He reassured his pure white mount with a calmness he didn't feel. The horse stamped the ground and tossed her head.

Bran would normally have spent the night on the rise. He enjoyed feeling at one with the gods and looked forward to seeing friends at the fortress of Tre'r Ceiri, the City of Stones, tomorrow. But he wouldn't stay here tonight. There was a presence around him. He would beg shelter with the shepherds whose summer dwellings lay at the entrance to the valley.

For the first time in his life, Bran feared solitude.

The Archdruid yearned to look back at his lonely grove, tucked away from prying eyes in a corner of the remote valley. He always bade farewell, not knowing when his duties would allow his return. His life had made him a wanderer; this place of peace was the nearest he had to a home.

But this time he didn't turn around. He kept his gaze firmly on the rocky path before him. His experienced mind knew something had manifested itself. Something he didn't want his eyes to encounter.

Despite the chill inside his body, the sweat on Archdruid's hands made handling Majestic's reins difficult.

He reached out to pat the horse's flank. "Good girl. We're leaving it behind," he said, half to his horse, and half to himself. "So it is to be victory for Britain. But at the cost of an evil I have not yet even been allowed to imagine."

As he rode down the valley, his gaze strayed from the ground only once. He raised his head in response to the call of a raven, the bringer of death, taunting him as it circled the skies above.

Chapter 1

Above the lofty fortress, high among the eagles, mother moon illuminated the way with a sweep of her silver arm. A light breeze rippled through the maiden's coal black hair and refreshed her after the heat of the day. The fragrance of crushed plants with which she had scented herself drifted across the fort, giving her confidence in the power of her own body. She breathed long and deep, taking the night into her lungs. The air was pure here in the western mountains. The wind carried no stench of Rome.

She grasped her long black dress in one hand to keep the hem free of the dew; her other arm was delicately outstretched to maintain her balance over the uneven ground. The damp earth caressed her toes and muffled her footfall as she glided across the heather with a grace other women could only dream of.

She passed through the stone ramparts unseen. The skulls hanging from the gateway as a warning to enemies glistened in the moonlight, but would not unnerve her, nor deflect her from her task.

Once inside the defences, the town of Tre'r Ceiri, the City of Stones, lay stretched out before her like a long, slender finger, hugging the high ridge. Slate huts huddled beneath the walls, seeking warmth and shelter from the defences, as well as protection from intruders.

A wide path ran through the centre of the citadel, and she had no trouble picking her way among the thatched roofs as she searched out *his* hut. There was no telling which were occupied and which were empty, for sleep had taken the citizens of Tre'r Ceiri, capital of the Ordovices, and silence reigned tonight.

She turned in response to a sudden noise, but it was merely an owl breaking the stillness to warn of her approach.

She picked out King Caswallon's hut part by instinct, part by the low light flickering from within. In a land where the people slept from dusk to dawn, only the greatest could afford a candle.

Her knock was firm but distinctly feminine.

There was movement from inside, and after a few heartbeats the king's wooden door opened just a crack. In the moonlight she could see a pair of cautious eyes peering back at her. At first they were impassive and clouded by fatigue, but as they focussed upon her they became two burning beacons of light. Caswallon relaxed and opened the wooden door wider, obviously not considering that one so demure and comely could pose a threat to his safety.

She had made sure she was beautiful for the king. Long, black hair flowed over her shoulders and down her back like a river of night as it shimmered in the full moon. Her simple black dress was loose enough to ripple delicately around her in the evening breeze, but at the same time tight enough to show off her curves, and low cut enough to betray a hint of her breasts. Her soft eyes were large, dark and deep enough for any man to drown in, complimenting her black hair but contrasting with her delicate skin and full lips. She wore no jewellery; not even a discreet bracelet adorned her long, slender arms. She needed no trinkets.

Yes, she thought. *My needs will be satisfied tonight.*

"May I come in?" she asked, her voice little more than a sensual whisper.

Caswallon just stood at the doorway, mouth agape in surprise as if trying to understand the vision of beauty before him. Eventually he replied with a strangled "Yes, of course," paying no heed to the possibility of an assassin's dagger beneath her dress. Questions flashed across his features, but they remained unasked. She would not give him answers. Not until she had conquered the recesses of his soul. He must depend on her, need her, first. That was the way to control a man.

Caswallon did not look a king, although his tunic, dyed in yellow saffron to ward off lice, was a fine piece of clothing. He was tall enough to have a presence, but his seventeen-year-old bones had still to gain the muscular coating of manhood. A mane of uncombed red hair arranged itself around his shoulders, but his moustache had still to thicken, leaving him looking an immature caricature of a Celtic warrior. Above the downy upper lip a long, thin ridge of a nose rose, separating two blue eyes whose youthful sparkle had been submerged by the pressures of kingship. Fingernails bitten to the quick and the nervous twitch of a neck muscle provided further evidence of the anxieties that responsibility had thrust upon him.

Here was a man with little bearing or inner strength. A man for whom kingship was a curse, not a blessing.

Just the sort of man she needed.

It was always so easy, she thought as she stepped across the threshold. All men shared the same weaknesses. Any woman who offered beauty and power could hold a man in her spell for eternity.

King Caswallon's hut was little different from the other circular huts in Tre'r Ceiri. She had to step down into the single room, which was partly below the level of the ground as further defence against winter's winds. To the height of a man's waist the walls were of stone, providing solid foundations. Above that, the thatched roof gave adequate protection against all but the heaviest storms.

Inside the hut were clues of its occupant's position. His fine, imported robe of Roman purple lay carelessly tossed over a small stool, while rich armour and an exquisitely decorated shield sat propped up against the stone wall of the interior. A small bench groaned under the weight of other rich trinkets: an enamelled tankard; a silver brooch for his cloak; an imported comb of whalebone and other goods only king could hope to possess. A beeswax candle fought to banish the shadows from the far side of the hut as two moths danced around it. The only other furniture was a simple bed of straw.

"Not sleeping, King Caswallon?" she purred, nodding in the direction of the candle.

"I couldn't sleep. The light helps me think." He paused and looked pensive. "Who are you, lady?"

"I am a woman who has travelled far to meet you."

A frown of only semi-belief darkened his forehead. "How old are you, lady? Seventeen, eighteen summers?" She didn't respond, so he continued. "Why is a woman as beautiful as you not already providing a warleader with heirs?" He spread his hands to emphasise the questions.

"Why do you fear one who merely wants to know you as a man, not a king?" she asked, changing the subject.

His brows rose sharply, but his surprise was understandable. Caswallon was not a handsome man. It was unlikely that any woman had ever sought him out for anything more than his royal powers.

His eyes shot to the door; he was obviously thinking of discovery. "My slaves! If anyone should find you here..."

"Would you be ashamed to be found with me?" she asked casually before lowering her tone. "We are safe from discovery, my king."

"They'll call Novax, my Druid, if they catch you. He'll have had you killed."

She gave a light laugh. The king couldn't know they would not be caught. "What danger is a woman to a warrior as great as Caswallon?"

Both knew the answer. A woman was as unwelcome in a king's bedchamber as a hungry wolf. Bastard children on the king's knee, the results of casual liaisons, clouded too many issues of succession.

The time for talking was over, she decided. Despite his shyness, the way the king let his eyes caress her left no doubt what he wanted.

She put a finger over his lips, then raised herself onto her toes to give him a soft, lingering kiss before gently pulling away. As he watched, his eyes wide open, she lifted her dress off her shoulders and let it glide gently down her body to the floor to reveal a supple body, firm breasts, and long, slender limbs.

She put her arms around his neck and kissed him again, but he was too inhibited to hold her. She took his hand and led him towards the bed. He had only known her for a few minutes, but already he was becoming powerless to resist.

Soon Caswallon, too, was undressed, and she sat above him on the bed of straw. He was inexperienced and shy, but she knew how to calm his nerves and put him at ease. As she moved backwards and forwards her long black hair brushed his chest, giving a sensation too soft to be anything more than a gentle caress. Expertly, she ran her fingers down his flanks, sometimes lightly, sometimes vigorously. She gently massaged his shoulders, but still he was too shy to reach out for her until she took his hands and cupped them against her breasts.

She needed him to enjoy her. She could almost feel her dominance, feel the life force draining from his body as she sapped it from him. But she mustn't be greedy, she remembered. She must take only enough to leave him dependent on her. He was a weak man; she needed him healthy.

For now.

She felt the king stirring inside her, saw him clenching his fists and eyelids as he prepared to fully respond. She found her own body answering his call.

As she felt their pleasure becoming more intense, she took away the physical satisfaction and replaced it with a vision. She showed Caswallon flying, free as a bird, over a land of green meadows and woods, of dramatic but beautiful mountain peaks, of bountiful pastures. A land where blue ribbons of water gurgled between the fat legs of contented cattle. A land of plenty, where even the poor had honey to sweeten their food, where mead flowed like water in the drinking mugs of victorious warriors. She showed him a land where men raced their horses and engaged in sport every day, cheered on by their delighted women. A land where crops grew strong and proud towards the golden sun, where all babies had enough milk, and where no mother was left to mourn her child in even the harshest winter.

His eyes glinted with a hint of fear, but his voice was high pitched with wonder. "What magic is this? What tricks are you playing on me? Have you taken me to the Otherworld?"

She put a finger to his lip. "Silence, my king," she whispered. "There is more to see." She needed him ensnared in her dream. She would take him down the path she had set until he had travelled too far to turn back.

He had seen the beauty of the country. Now she moved the vision on to show him true power. They flew together over Tara, instantly recognisable as the semi-enchanted seat of the High Kings of Ireland. They flew closer to the great feasting hall, its thatch thick and shining in the reflection of the warm sun. She showed him the sacred circles and stones which surrounded the palace. She showed him a mighty army at the disposal of the High King, a man who, in this vision, ruled not only Ireland, but Britain as well. The greatest king the Celtic world had known.

She looked into his eyes. He was staring back, captivated, but whether by her beauty or by what she was showing him, she couldn't tell.

They descended into the Great Hall.

Two long rows of tables were lined by warriors celebrating a famous victory over the eagle standards of the Roman legions. The men, as one, turned to the massive oak table at the far end of the hall where the famous High King and his lady sat, their identities obscured by wisps of smoke from the hearth. She made sure Caswallon would recognise some of the great names: Segovax, his own personal champion; Bran, the Archdruid of Britain; all were there, paying their respects to their great, bountiful High King and his beautiful wife. Warriors of the past and future sat intermingled; Cuchulain, Hound of Ulster; Niall of the Hostages; Finn McCool; Brian Boru. Even Arthur, the greatest Celtic warrior who would ever live, praised the High King.

In one corner sat three bards, singing silken voiced praises on delicately tuned harps of the finest gold. Around the throng, serving wenches drawn from among the most beautiful women in the world happily served unceasing supplies of mead and beef to the drunken warriors, willingly joining in the bawdy repartee and arranging trysts with drunken fighters. There were as many women serving as there were men to serve; no warrior would be alone in a cold bed this night!

At the High King's feet, prisoners of war, once proud warriors of the Roman legions, but now grovelling captives, begged to be allowed a quick dagger to the heart rather than one of the imaginative deaths demanded by the gods.

Finally, a pile of treasure, greater than any Caswallon could ever have known existed, lay in a pile at the centre of the hall. Golden torques, solid necklaces as thick as a man's wrist; bejewelled goblets from Rome herself; rings encrusted with gems of every sort; startlingly coloured and decorated clothes of the finest silk from the semi-mythical land men called Arabia.

And, hanging safely at the king's waist, in a scabbard of expertly tanned leather and enamelled in highly decorated gold and silver, was Caladchlog, the magical Rainbow Sword of Fergus mac Roy. Its hilt gave off its low light, almost daring the foolhardy to challenge the High King of Britain and Ireland.

At that moment a breeze drifted through the vision and wafted the hearth-smoke to one side. The identities of the High King and his woman were revealed: Caswallon and she, sharing the Celtic world between them.

The vision faded as their bodies relaxed. The king breathed a deep sigh of contentment as, more confident now, he reached out to hold her.

"Who are you?"

"I am every dream you ever had." She let herself melt into his arms, but although her body was calming her mind remained sharp and focussed upon the task in hand. "May I see you again, my king?"

"I couldn't live without the thought of your return." He kissed her forehead as if to emphasise the point.

She lifted herself up onto an elbow, partly to look into his eyes, partly to remind him of her beauty. His face was soft. That was good. His mind, too, would be relaxing and ready for her next move. "You would soon come to think of me as little more than a common whore to be cast aside when you tire of me."

"NO, NEVER!" The words were almost shouted. Arms flailed in random directions, like sparks escaping an anvil.

"How do I know you mean it?"

"Name a gift. You shall have anything within my powers."

She threw her eyes around the hut, pretending to look for a suitable present, but in truth there was only one thing she wanted. But her gift was constantly guarded by a dozen of the Ordovices' finest warriors.

She wanted Caladcholg, the Rainbow Sword.

No, more than that. She *needed* it. And she would make it hers.

Caladchlog's blade of iron was as tough as any in Britain and Ireland. It had been expertly wrought by the finest smiths nearly two thousand years ago, at the instruction of Govannon, the Smithgod, in the days when the working of iron ore was unknown to mortals. The hardened weapon easily outfought the bronze swords of the Fomorians at the battle of Moytura, the great battle of which the bards still sang. Later, only a century ago, it had been owned by Fergus mac Roy, champion to the great King Conor of Ulster. In the time of Caswallon's father it had found its way to Britain by conquest after falling into evil hands. The Ordovices, as the custodians of Ynys Mon, the Sacred Island, had been chosen by the Council of Druids to keep the sword safe until it was needed.

The jewels encrusting the hilt had been imported from foreign lands the other side even of the Roman Empire, and worked into the gilded hilt. The red and green gems would reflect the light of leaping flames, but even when away from the glare of a fire they glowed in their own energy. In the hands of a man who would use the sword for the good of Britain the green emeralds would radiate their coloured light. But when held by one willing to weaken the land to advance his own ends, the legends said, the rubies burned a bright red warning of the bloodshed to follow. When swung in battle it would form circles of colour like the bands of a rainbow as it cut down the enemy with little help from the wielder.

She smiled to herself. In future she would harness the power of the sword. It would be hers as she claimed Britain for herself.

After brushing a playful moth from her face she spoke. "The Ordovices have many rich treasures."

"And you, my sweet, may name the one which shall be yours to carry with you as a token of my love."

Her body tingled with tension. It was time to stake her claim. "Caladchlog. I want the sword."

The king's features tightened. "No. Not the sword. Choose anything but the sword." His threw his arms towards the roof.

"Why not the sword?"

"It is not mine. The Ordovices merely safeguard it for Britain. If Novax... "

"To the Otherworld with Novax," she cut in. "Are you the sort of king who cannot make decisions without hiding behind a Druid's robe?"

"Of course not," Caswallon defended himself. "But the sword is magic. Britain needs it to free itself from the Eagles of Rome."

This was proving harder than she had expected. She gently picked a chaff of straw from his eyebrow and kissed his forehead to relax him again, showing him once more the vision of a perfect Celtic world. "Do you not want to lead Britain to victory against the Eagles?" she asked, putting a slight pout in her voice. "Do you want the vision I showed you to come to pass?"

Powerlust glinted in his eyes. "Boudicca leads us to war, not me."

"Who leads an army into war is important, I grant you. But it is the man who leads an army from the final battle who will be remembered. Boudicca isn't a queen, merely a regent for two young girls. What experience of war does she have? Let a real king lead us, I say!"

Caswallon smiled as she massaged her words into his ego. He would not, could not, fight her.

Somewhere in the distance a baby screamed for its mother's breast.

"Take the sword. It is yours."

"Your word! I need your word."

"You have it. The sword is yours."

"I cannot take it. It must be freely given."

He made to sit up as if to fetch the weapon from its guards immediately, but a gentle hand stopped him.

"No. In the way that befits my station. At a Sacred Pool."

Caswallon stared back, almost blankly. "But these are the places where the gods receive our gifts."

She smiled back, a sickly sweet leer of triumph. Her heart pounded in celebration. "I know. And remember, Caswallon, I have your word."

His face reddened with anger and fear. She merely laughed in his face, and within a heartbeat had disappeared. The hut was filled with the flapping of vile, black wings and the triumphant clucking of a raven. The candle cast her shadows onto the wall behind the king, causing the image of the bird to be inflated to the size of an eagle. The feathers around her neck bristled proudly as she celebrated victory, and the stench of death filled the small room, replacing the gentle perfume of crushed flowers. The bird gave one final rasping laugh at the king before pushing her way through the door and becoming as one with the darkness. She left Caswallon with wide eyes a mouth silenced by fear.

The skulls guarding Tre'r Ceiri's gateway grinned with malicious approval as she soared overhead. But still they did not unnerve her, for night was her shadow and death her companion.

The fortress of Tre'r Ceiri was immediately a cauldron of activity. "NOVAX! GUARDS! TO ME!" The king had found his voice, and his panic-stricken cries fading into the distance were the last sounds she heard as she faded into the night.

Chapter 2

The midday sun hit Peter Davis as soon as he walked out through the front door. He paused to enjoy the view over Snowdonia before turning to his young brother.

"How would you like to live here, Johnny? With Daddy and Lucy and me."

The six-year-old paused for a moment. "It's very nice, Peetie. But I'll miss Swindon."

Peter ruffled the youngster's hair. "And what's so good about Swindon?"

"There's lots of play areas."

"But just look at this." Peter swept his hands towards the mountains. "You've got one whole play area here. We can take Tipsy for long walks, or go fishing. And we're nearer the sea than in Swindon. And the doctor says the fresh air will help your chest. You'll be able to run and play with all the new friends you'll make here."

Johnny looked doubtful. "That's what Daddy says too. I'll go and ask Lucy what she thinks."

As Johnny trotted off at a pace which wouldn't provoke a wheeze from his lungs, Peter's gaze flicked beyond him to Lucy. His brow knotted into a frown; his sister was chatting to Mr. Griffiths, the young—too young, Peter thought—Estate Agent. Or more specifically his eyes, which seemed to be resting a few inches below the crucifix their mother had given Lucy shortly before her death. She continued to chat happily though, giving off an occasional low giggle from behind a demurely cupped hand, or tossing her blonde pigtail. But she had obviously noticed Griffiths's straying gaze, and paused to do up another button of her blouse.

His rather emerged from the doorway behind Peter. "We'll have it," he announced. He pushed his spectacles up his nose and grinned at his three children.

"You won't regret it, Mister Davis," Toby Griffiths drawled in a confident Welsh lilt. He strode over to Alun Davis to shake on the deal. "The owner wants the property occupied as soon as possible, so I'll have the rental agreements drawn up this afternoon. As you saw, the house is furnished, so if they can be signed today you could even be in by this evening."

"This evening?" Young Johnny cheered and jumped in excitement, joined playfully by his older siblings. His mop of blond hair bounced with him. "We're going to live in the mountains, we're going to live in the mountains," he sang happily. Even Tipsy yapped enthusiastically in typical terrier fashion.

Peter grimaced and broke off from his childish show of enthusiasm as he caught Griffiths's eyes sparkling, as if already calculating his commission.

Lucy moved closer to Peter. "You don't like him, do you?" she whispered.

"Not really. He's a bit false," Peter replied.

"He seems fine to me."

"I might have guessed you'd think so. You girls fall over for the pretentious look. And what does he need to stink of after shave for? He hasn't seen a razor for days."

"It's called designer stubble. And stop rubbing your chin," she chided. "Only pensioners do that. It makes you look a pillock."

"Humph. I don't look as big a pillock as him," he said, nodding towards Griffiths. "He's called *Tobias*, for God's sake."

"You're just jealous, bruv. And anyway, he's shortened it to Toby, which I think is sweet. You took one look at his personalised numberplate and decided to hate him." She grinned. "He's been very pleasant to me. Thinks it great that I'm at university. He's always wanted to study Roman Britain himself."

"Humph. He just fancies you. He probably wouldn't know Julius Caesar from Adolf Hitler."

"And he thinks I should take up modelling. He says I look a natural."

"Humph. He definitely fancies you."

"And he's got a cute bum."

Peter raised his eyes to the heavens. "'I can't be blamed for caring about my little sister." He put a protective arm around her shoulder. "Can't we talk about something else?"

"Like your chances of getting a girlfriend?"'

He sighed. "Not that old chestnut again. Please."

"Well, as long as you know that now we're living in Wales I'm going to make it my mission to find you a nice homely sheep farmer's daughter. Someone to bring you out of your shell." She broke into a sly grin, and freed herself from her brother's arm. "I want reassurance that you're not a raving poofter."

Peter managed to keep annoyance from his tone, knowing his sister was only teasing. "I can assure you I'm one hundred per cent heterosexual."

"It's a shame you never gave the decent looking Swindon lasses a chance to find out. You only go out with dogs."

"How do you know? I might have been Mister Stud the moment your back was turned."

"Yeah? I didn't hear about anyone having to lock up their daughters because Peter 'Sew Your Oats' Davis was on the prowl. You're always too busy painting to practice flirting."

Peter decided to back down while the mood was still upbeat. "Can't we change the subject again? Don't you think the house is great?"

"So you don't like the salesman, but you're willing to take his goods," teased Lucy.

"I love it," he admitted. He paused to roll up his shirtsleeves, and looked around him to admire the views again. There were countless scenes of dramatic beauty for him to reproduce on canvas. Walls of rock rose dramatically on three sides around him, and on the fourth side a stream gurgled happily down the valley toward the village of Nantbran. He looked upwards, where a few white tufts hugged the higher peaks.

His mind contrasted the place with Swindon. He thought of the town, grasping at its railway heritage amid characterless blue-collar office blocks. And of the terraced housing broken only by graffiti-strewn back alleys.

There was no competition. The prospect of escaping to a mountain range almost had his mouth watering. Especially to a house this remote.

For a building so far from anywhere—the drive was at least five hundred yards long, and Nantbran nearly a mile away—it was remarkably modern looking and in good condition. Griffiths had told them the bulk of the house was over a hundred years old, and that it had been extended some twenty years ago when the owners had taken the opportunity to modernise it.

Although aged, the walls and tiles of locally mined slate were clean, having been scrubbed of lichen recently—as Griffiths had taken great pains to point out. Despite the antiseptic look of dirt-free stone and the mock traditional double glazed windows, it retained a homely appearance. Possibly it was because there was no formal garden. Weeds peered through the large gravel parking area in front, but elsewhere there was just a mass of green, interrupted by half-buried rocks strewn erratically across the ground, like pebbles dropped from a giant hand. In some places marsh grass grew to untidy tufts, in others the uneven lawn hugged the broken contours of the ground, helped in places by the constant attentions of sheep escaping through a collapsing dry-stone boundary.

"No need to mow the grass. Maybe I could be happy here after all!" laughed Lucy, her mood lightening. Peter was pleased to see sparkle returning to her blue eyes.

"This is heaven," agreed Peter. "The house seems to be asking to be lived in. I almost feel is if I've settled here already."

"I still think I'd prefer Swindon." Lucy gave a sigh of resignation.

"But Johnny's so much better already. And you men outvote me three to one…"

Peter couldn't help notice how her nose screwed upwards in the centre of a light scowl. He put a comforting hand on her shoulder. "Don't worry, sis. We'll have great fun here."

She pulled away, tossing her pigtail. "I suppose so. I know it's for Johnny's health, but…" her voice trailed off.

"… but there's nothing to do?" Peter smiled, finishing off the sentence.

"Yeah, that's right. Make fun. But the cinemas and things are all miles away. It'll cost loads by taxis, and I can't expect you and dad to drive me everywhere." She chewed her bottom lip thoughtfully before giving a shrug. "Anyway, I'll be back at university in a few weeks. Then I'll get a job based who knows where, so it won't be for long. I'll just miss Swindon and all my mates, that's all."

"I know. We all appreciate you making the sacrifice. Maybe you'll be able to get a job in the Cultural Capital of the South when you graduate."

She smiled weakly as Peter teased her with a patronising pat on the head. He gave an exaggerated wince as her friendly punch found its mark.

Lucy pilled a pack of cigarettes from a rear pocket of her jeans, lit one and inhaled deeply. Peter caught Alun's disapproving frown.

"Dad doesn't like you doing that," Peter warned.

"Humph. Tell me something I don't know. But I only smoke outside or in my room. He can't complain about that. Anyway, he'd really have something to say if he knew what we smoked in our digs."

"Yes, and I remember your reaction when he nearly found out," teased Peter. "I've never seen such a look of genuine panic."

"Yeah, well. Everyone knows you shouldn't pay a surprise visit on a student."

"It could have been worse, though. You could have been stark naked and copulating with some hairy ecology undergraduate when we arrived."

"If that had been the case it would only have taken a few seconds to get some clothes on. I'm just grateful you knocked on the door while dad was parking. At least we had a couple of minutes to try and hide the smell."

"Yeah. And you had dad wondering if you'd gone bonkers, having all the windows open in the middle of a gale." Peter couldn't stop himself laughing. He was pleased to see his sister joining in.

"And I don't copulate," she said defensively.

"No?"

"No. I make meaningful love."

Alun's enthusiastic voice interrupted the brother-sister secret. "Hey, kids! Mr Griffiths says there's something interesting around the back!"

With a squeal of delight and obviously looking forward to having more to explore, Johnny ran to the rear of the building. Tipsy, yapping happily, followed closely. Peter followed at a more sedate pace, pausing to pull his sweaty shirt from his back and brush a sticky strand of brown hair from his forehead.

At the back of the house Peter paused as he reached the modest stream, but everyone, even Johnny, managed to jump it without difficulty. A small, eroded gully showed the size the brook could expand to in the winter months. Johnny squealed about the delights of having a stream in his garden, and babbled enthusiastically about making dams and pools.

Peter looked around for his sister, and his buoyant mood was disturbed as he saw her bringing up the rear with Toby Griffiths.

"Bring back memories, dad?" he asked, falling in step alongside his father.

"I've never been in this valley before, but, yes, it's good to be back in the mountains again. Snowdonia's just as beautiful as I remember it," confided Alan as he pushed his glasses up his nose. "My Aunt Gwyn only lived five or six miles away." He changed the subject to speak to his younger son. "Johnny, would you really like to sleep here tonight?"

"Yeah, dad! This place is really cool!" The six-year-old jumped about with enthusiasm, blond hair untidy and eyes glistening emerald green.

"I know it's great, sonny, I know." A gentle smile played with the corner of Alun's lips as he watched his son bounding across the ground.

"He's looking better already," observed Peter.

"I know. And we've only been in the mountains a few days. Just think how he'll be after a month. Or even a year."

"It's hard to think he's the same child who could hardly breathe a week ago. I never thought fresher air would make this difference. And he's really looking forward to living here. I just hope I haven't oversold Snowdonia to him—he thinks it'll be constant fishing, walking, and all the other things he hasn't been able to do up to now."

"Look at this," said their father, unable to hide his excitement as he spread his hands towards the pile of fallen stones they had reached, shaped into a rough rectangle on the crown of a small rise. Lichen and tufts of grass peering through the rocks showed that the ruin had been undisturbed for some time. "We've got real history on our doorstep. Mister Griffiths says it's the remains of a church."

"An old church dating back centuries, so the locals believe," Toby said woodenly, as if reciting a rehearsed speech. His voice certainly showed no enthusiasm for the subject. "They reckon there's been churches here since the Dark Ages, all dedicated to Saint Bran. That's how they think Nantbran, or Bran's Brook in English, got its name. Nant Bran is the stream which runs across the property. It comes out of the ground over there." He waved his arm in the general direction of where the water emerged from the hillside; a small hollow boasting a couple of struggling oaks and a few rocks. "It's a bit more of a stream once it reaches the village," he added apologetically.

Peter stepped inside the ruin. The rectangular outline was still recognisable, but the fallen walls stood to no more than a foot or so high. He wondered if some of the stones had been plundered to build the farmhouse. Although the remains weren't much to look at, the thought of history on his doorstep set his palms tingling with excitement. "Do you know who Saint Bran was?" he asked, his interest aroused.

Toby shrugged in obvious disinterest, but Peter was becoming oblivious to everything except the stones. His mind turned to the people who worshipped on the ground beneath his feet over the centuries. He could almost see some of them; the preacher in his starched white collar warning of the perils of sin with threats of fire and brimstone; the simple farmers and slate miners believing every word with fearful ears; the bored young boys, to whom the terrors of damnation seemed an eternity away, fidgeting at the back. The same scenes must have been replayed countless times over the years. The church was surely full of life at one stage, much more so than the deserted pile of rubble which remained. Peter felt humbled and almost guilty, as if by just being there he was invading the privacy of generations of worshippers.

He resolved to make the place resound with happiness. That would be a fitting tribute to the dignity of these people who had shaped the mountains, but whose descendants had been forced to leave by poverty and the need to find jobs.

Words cut into Peter's daydream. "There's some other remains over there," Toby said, nodding in the direction of Nant Bran's source. "A standing stone by the spring, and a cairn just beyond it."

"Let's go and see them," screeched Johnny, already bounding off.

"Woah, hold your horses sonny," said Alun. "We need to get the papers signed if we're going to be in by tonight. There'll be plenty of time for exploring when we're living here."

"LET'S GO TO THE CAIRN FIRST," shouted Johnny in wide-eyed eagerness to fully explore his new home. Within seconds he had reached what looked like a mound of football-sized stones and one massive slab, almost his height, which obviously blocked an entrance.

"I want to know what's behind that rock," said Johnny.

"Bones and bodies," teased Alun, tapping at the entrance stone, which suddenly shifted as he touched it, leaving the entrance slightly open. Johnny giggled as his father flinched in surprise.

"Oh. Dad!" teased Lucy. "It's been like this for thousands of years. But it can't survive the ravishes of the Davis Clan! Look Johnny. It's opening for you," she continued. "Do you want to go and see if you can go and find the bones in the darkness?"

"'No!" Johnny took a step back.

But Peter didn't want to join in the laughter. He could feel something. Something making him shiver, despite the warmth of the day. He looked into the blackness beyond the massive slab, and took an involuntary step back.

He remembered his experience at the church. The more he looked into the dark space, the more sure he was that he could imagine the scenes at a burial; skin clad barbarians chanting primitive spells to the pounding of a pigskin drum as they appease the spirits. He pictured the slab being heaved back into place, while the mourners left the sacred place hastily, looking behind to ensure the dead were safely sleeping.

"I'll find the standing stone now," Johnny enthused, ignoring his father, jogging ahead towards the trees with Tipsy in hot pursuit.

Alun shrugged his shoulders. "I suppose a few more minutes won't hurt," he conceded.

"I'M HERE FIRST! I'M HERE FIRST!" Johnny shouted gleefully, his face a picture of triumph as he found the stone in the undergrowth. He tried to climb the rock, which stood to about his height, but failed dismally as he slipped on years of accumulated algae. Peter couldn't help a laugh at his brother's misfortune, and drew a grimace from the boy who stuck his tongue out as well for good measure. When he had caught up, Peter gave Johnny's hair a friendly ruffle and placed a hand on the stone to inspect it more closely.

Something cut through him as he touched the monolith. Something like an electric shock, rushing up his arm and through his body, until he withdrew his fingers.

He looked up.

The sky was bleeding!

Chapter 3

In an instant the sky darkened as if welcoming a storm, and his mind became filled with images of blood. Blood everywhere, dripping down the stone and from the broad leaves of the oaks. Blood flowing like water from the spring. The thick, angry clouds above him had their bellies ripped apart by the sharp, jagged mountain peaks cutting through their deep, grey flesh. Their gaping wounds dropped dark red blood. Peter struggled to breath, with the oxygen torn from the atmosphere and replaced by blood. Thick, dark, cloying blood forced its way into his mouth as he opened it, flowing into his lungs and invading his airways.

He looked around for his family, and when his eyes found them gave out a contorted scream of terror.

Alun, Lucy and Johnny were around him, each naked and tied to a boulder of rock which formed a circle. Peter was in the centre. Lucy's body hung limply from her bonds, and her blond hair lay streaked red and plastered around her face as the bloody rain fell from the sky. Peter felt a shudder of revulsion run through him as he noticed semen running down the inside of her thigh. Although the blood-rain drenched her skin, the bruising around her thighs and breasts was obvious, and showed she had not been a willing participant in the act.

He tried for a second to work out why she was staring straight through him with bulging, unseeing eyes.

Until the awful truth bored through him. She's dead. The welts around her neck, her bulging eyes, and the way her tongue reached her chin showed how she had met her death. Peter wondered if she had been raped before, during, or after strangulation. He hoped she had not suffered the indignity while she still breathed.

Alun raised his head to look at his daughter, his eyes moist with tears of pain and pity. As Alun moved slightly a gash sliced across his stomach opened like a grotesque mouth. Silently, an intestine appeared over the lip of the hole in caricature of a tongue, before sliding out further and eventually falling to the ground around his bare feet, followed with a sickening squelch as the rest of his insides fell from his body. He gave out a groan of resignation and stared blankly down at his ruined torso. He looked Peter in the eye. "You could have stopped this," he accused before his chin fell limply to his chest.

Peter's breath caught. His father was right. It was his fault. But he didn't know why.

At that moment, Johnny, who had been silent, loosed a long, loud, hysterical scream and gave a panic-stricken fight against his unyielding bonds.

Peter made to lurch forward to help his family.

But he couldn't move. He wasn't just pinned down—he realised he was lying on the blood-streaked grass—but paralysed, and a new fear surged through him.

Tipsy trotted into the stone circle and rubbed himself around Johnny's legs as if trying to comfort the child, but Peter's brother refused to be calmed and continued his shrieks of terror. Tipsy stopped and tensed, staring at something outside the circle. With a struggle against his neck muscles, Peter turned his head. Two pure white lambs were trotting towards the circle. Struggling to recall the sight from the depths of his memory, Peter tried to remember where he's seen them before. But his mind was blank. He noticed their wool; not only was it untouched by the torrents of blood falling from the sky, but it seemed almost to glisten, as if reflecting the rays of the hidden sun.

Despite their outward look of innocence, there was something in the sheep that scared Peter. He knew he should be able to recall why, but the reason lay hidden beyond his grasp.

Tipsy started to growl. The dog, too, seemed to know the animals were evil. One of the lambs curled its lips back into a snarl and fell into a crouch before flinging itself at the terrier. Tipsy tried to evade, but the lamb displayed strength and tenacity as it clamped its jaws around her throat and thrashed from side to side as if the family pet were a rag doll.

Tipsy soon stopped struggling, but the lamb, in a state of frenzy and bloodlust, kept throwing the limp body around as it played out its grotesque game.

The other lamb had paused to watch, but seemed to lose interest as the life drained from the dog's life and into the grass. Instead, as Tipsy died, it turned its attention to Johnny. The child tried to kick the lamb away, but it was too strong for him. As the boy screamed in agony the animal tore a mouthful of meat from his thigh and gulped it down in a single mouthful before returning for more.

His father reached out a hand towards Johnny in a pathetic attempt to help his son, but his arm fell away as Alun finally joined Lucy in death.

Peter made one more concerted effort to rise, forcing every muscle in his body to move in response to his brother's screams. But it was still useless. He could just about move his head, but the rest of him was still struck down and paralysed.

And the lamb which had murdered Tipsy, it's muzzle awash with blood, was trotting purposefully towards him...

"You all right, Pete?"

Everything was still and quiet again. Lucy's voice had broken the moment. She and Alun were leaning over him, their brows knotted.

Relief flooded through him. "You're okay?" he asked.

"*We're* okay?" asked Alun incredulously. "What about you? You're the one who's been out cold."

Peter wondered how long he's been lying on the ground. *An hour or so? Or only a few seconds?* "I'm okay now." The blood was gone. The sky was clear; there were no blood-baring clouds. "I just came over... I don't know... when I touched the stone..."

"We thought you'd fainted," said Alun, helping him to his feet.

"I'm okay now," repeated Peter with a bravery he didn't feel. He shrugged his shoulders and tried to dismiss the experience, especially when he saw Johnny and Tipsy playing happily by the stream.

But he couldn't stop shaking. He looked hard at the stone. It seemed so peaceful, standing undisturbed in the ground, in the same place where it had observed the world for millennia.

And there was something nagging at the back of his mind. Something asking why the gory deaths he had imagined for his family had been his fault.

I could have done something to stop them dying like that, he realised. His heart lurched as a sheep's call drifted from a nearby hillside.

But he had no idea what he could, or should, have done.

"Well, what do you think of having a church and a standing stone in the back garden," Alun asked Johnny, changing the subject.

"And a cairn," Peter reminded him. "But it's a circle of stones, not a single stone."

He bit his lip as what he had just said sunk in.

His father looked at him warily. "What makes you say it's a circle? There's only one stone here," he asked.

"I... I don't know. I just felt that there's more stones." Peter caressed his chin as he remembered all too vividly, the sight of his family dying in the stone circle.

"Well, let's see," said his father.

A brief search revealed five more stones, which, as Peter had predicted, had once formed a rough circle. All had fallen over the centuries, and lay embedded in the soft earth and covered in years of moss and lichen. But they were definitely there.

"Maybe they're just rocks, like all the others," Peter offered, sweeping his arm around at the boulders lying randomly on the ground.

"I don't think so," said Alun. "I'm no archaeologist, but look. They're all rectangular. Too regular in shape to be like this naturally. They're a bit worn, but were definitely cut to shape and put here on purpose. I think you're right. Are you sure you don't know how you knew?"

Peter shrugged his shoulders and lied. "I've no idea. Like I said, I just knew. I felt really strange for a few seconds, then I just knew. Anyway, shouldn't we be going off to get the papers signed?" he asked, wanting to get away. "Where's Tipsy?"

They all looked round. The dog was standing some distance off, staring at them.

"Tipsy, boy. Over here," encouraged Johnny.

The animal small took a few paces closer, but would not enter the hollow. He gave a growl when Peter tried to coax him nearer.

Toby and Lucy headed off back towards the drive and the cars. Alun, Peter and Johnny followed a discreet distance behind.

"Looks like Lucy's found herself a friend," said Peter. "Hopefully that'll make her feel more relaxed about coming here. I don't think she's happy about moving, but she's putting on a brave face for you and Johnny".

"Yes," was the only, icy response Peter got as his father turned his head to look. A shadow of disapproval flickered across Alun's features.

Toby made his excuses as they reached the cars. "I hope you'll don't mind: the sooner I get back to the office the sooner I can have the paperwork drawn up." He shook each of the Davis family—even little Johnny—by the hand before departing, with his false smile broadening to a grin when he came to Lucy.

"Well, as the lease will be in my name I'll go over later and sign it," said Alun when Toby's four-wheel drive was nothing more than a distant hum breaking the summer silence. "You kids might as well start back to the hotel in Pete's car and start packing. I'll follow you later."

Lucy surprised them all. "I'd prefer to come with you, dad. There might be something I can do."

"Like get Toby Griffiths's telephone number?" teased Peter.

"Oh, no," grinned Lucy through one of her characteristic giggles as she waved a small piece of paper. "I've already got it!"

Her father extended the thumb and little finger of his right hand as a pretend telephone, then spoke into it. "Yes, this is Alun Davis. Yes, Toby, I'll see if I can find Lucinda."

"You wouldn't dare!" She glared at the use of her hated full name. Only a select few knew what she considered the embarrassing contents of her birth certificate.

"What's it worth?" Alun laughed, playfully hugging his daughter as reassurance that he was only teasing.

Peter put his own mouth to an imaginary telephone and mimicked a feminine voice. "Hello, Lucinda here… oh, *yes,* Tobias. Meaningful love would be *wonderful.*"

Lucy gave her older brother a playful swipe, and shot an embarrassed sideways glance at her father.

The family broke into fits of laughter, but as they shared the joke, Peter found himself looking nervously back at the ancient remains, remembering what he had seen at the stones. And he wondered why he felt the vision of death had been his fault.

The hollow would be a place to avoid, he decided.

****

Deep within the cairn, there was silent movement. Something—no, someone—had awoken her. Someone important.

Someone she knew.

Sleep had overcome her all those years ago, when there had been no reason to remain awake. But she knew she would be summoned again, and had let the flame of hope warm her subconscious while she endured her rest. Her slumbers had been broken only by dreams of triumph, interspersed with nightmare visions of failure which left cold fingers of fear caressing her spine.

For two millennia those very people who had once worshipped her had cast her aside like offal. The same men, woman and children who had thrust their blood, gold and prayers upon her as they begged her favour. The very same who had pleaded for triumph over their enemies, or for deliverance from evil. In those days she had been able to either enslave or free entire kingdoms depending upon her mood, or upon how pleasing the mortal's gifts had been. She had been able to lighten men's hearts with her radiant beauty, or send them rigid with fear by appearing as a malevolent terror from the recesses of their minds.

Generations ago, men had heard the name 'Andraste'. And they had been afraid.

But the Romans had said she was evil. They had ordered her banished from her peoples' minds, and had cleansed with swords and fire the bodies of those who had been unable to forget.

But now destiny was calling. Something was telling her that her day had come. And the lust for power consumed her with a passion undiminished by centuries of sleep. Ambition burned within her like the heat from the summer sun, but at the same time the prospect of power chilled her very soul like the iciest of winds.

And this time she had the sword. Lovingly, shaking the weariness from her stiff, jaded joints, she ran a delicate finger down the blade. Even after two thousand years the weapon remained keen, and she thrilled at the feel of her warm blood trickling across her hand. Instinctively she sucked the wound and felt alive at its sweet taste. The sword glowed a low red in response.

The tomb was ready to relinquish its captive. The hollow cavern of stone, with its massive boulder across the entrance, had been her prison while she rested. Her eyes blinked as a shaft of light forced its way into her resting-place. The entrance had been disturbed, and nothing barred her way to freedom. For centuries her only company had been the dark creatures; spiders, worms and other crawling beings. These animals were her friends, and while she had eaten when she had needed to they had provided little sustenance during her incarceration.

She needed mortal *souls.*

But the fates had permitted her only two mortal guises. She must ensure he would not recognise her.

This time she was ready. This time Andraste would be victorious.

Chapter 4

Bran, Archdruid of Britain, caressed his beard and looked wearily at the towering slopes. He had travelled since dawn and although the sun had passed its zenith, the ascent to Tre'r Ceiri would be a warm and challenging one.

He had not been to the citadel of the Ordovices since the Beltane festival the previous year. It was comforting to see that the same, familiar activities still taking place on the few slopes, which were not either prohibitively precipitous, or too buried in scree, to be safe. Slaves filled leather flasks with water from the springs which erupted part way down the hill; craftsmen ascended with logs or bundles of straw to re-roof a house; and children collected heather petals, which would be crushed and used to make a yellow-brown dye for woollen clothing. A couple of kestrels scudded the scree, enjoying the sunlight while searching out careless rodents.

The familiar sights relaxed Bran. He still thought of yesterday's vision by his Sacred Pool, but at sun-splashed Tre'r Ceiri the feeling of malevolence lifted itself from his shoulders.

The hill was too steep to attempt on horseback, so Bran left Majestic and a couple of coins in the corral along with the other horses and the king's brightly decorated chariots. Then, with a tired sigh and a prayer to Lugh he leaned on his oaken staff, shouldered his leather bag, and started the climb. He doubted, though, that even the Great God could restore the youthful vigour to his legs. He was just grateful that the Goddess Boann had held off the rains and kept the winding path free of mud.

Word soon spread. A man with the front of his head shaven in the Druid's manner and wearing the white cloak of his office would be a newsworthy arrival. One or two people waved as his approach became known, but others, possibly in awe of an Archdruid's presence, ran for the safety of the ramparts.

But there was one figure Bran scanned the skyline for more than any other, and he was soon smiling to himself as the dark-haired figure of the king's bard bounded down the scree towards him.

"Dermot! It does my heart good to see you again. Your shoulders get wider and your moustache thicker each time I see you!"

"And your waist gets broader and your beard greyer," laughed the young man as they embraced. Dermot took the Druid's bag as the two started the slow climb to the summit.

"This hill gets higher and steeper every time I climb it," groaned Bran, rubbing a twinge in his back. "How are Kyra and the babe? I expect she's grateful not to be carrying him around in her belly any more."

Dermot's deep brown eyes spread wide open in amazement. "How did you know it was a him?"

"Never ask a Druid how he knows anything," replied Bran with a smile.

"Apologies... The Sight. Kyra and Conor are both fine. Conor—I expect The Sight told you we called him Conor—is healthy. He has the lungs of a banshee!"

"He'll be a bard like his father," said Bran before changing the subject. "How is your king?"

Dermot stiffened slightly. "You know about Caswallon? It's all over Tre'r Ceiri, but you must have some special gift to arrive here the following day!"

"What about the king?" Bran's step faltered. Something between unease and fear braced itself in the pit of his stomach. "I've come to discuss the future of Caladchlog with him, nothing more."

"Ah, the Rainbow Sword. But you're too late. They say last night he bedded a raven and promised it the sword."

"By the fires of Bel! Will the young fool never learn?" Bran's jaw dropped as he raised his eyes to the heavens. A feeling of evil settled on his shoulders. "And what does Novax have to say of it?"

"Him?" spat Dermot. "The Human Weasel holds his counsel. But doubtless he will work the whole business into his favour."

"Doubtless."

"He should have been a politician, not a Druid. He's got a politician's guile without a Druid's wisdom. But he is dying, Bran. And the pain increases his bitterness." He put a warning hand on Bran's arm. "Be careful. He is a dangerous enemy. And he *is* your enemy... isn't he?"

Bran didn't answer. Instead, as they ascended the step slopes, he pressed for fuller details of the king's night. By the time they reached the ramparts, he had heard all the bard could tell him.

A large informal welcoming party had gathered inside the wall, but at a distance, which showed the respect—and the suspicion—a powerful Druid was accorded.

A smaller, more formal group waited just inside the gate. King Caswallon, of course, was there, avoiding the gaze of anybody who cared to look in his direction, his cheeks deepened to the colour of Roman wine. He evidently understood the magnitude of his night's actions. Novax, Caswallon's personal Druid, stood beside his king, displaying yellowed teeth through a forced smile. As always, his long pointed nose seemed to sniff its way between two small beady, cunning eyes, and he continually rubbed his hands together as if kneading a small portion of bread. His once white Druidical robes hung from a body which was even more drawn than Bran remembered it.

Making up the party was Sergovax, the King's Champion, a wild looking man with swarthy skin and thick grey-streaked black hair. He stood proudly next to Caswallon, as if daring anyone to criticise the actions of his benefactor.

"Archdruid Bran. A pleasure," said Novax in a tone which suggested the opposite. His thin mouth formed a tight, frosty line as he chewed pain-relieving willow leaves. He winced and held his stomach. A sign of his illness, Bran supposed.

"And what about you, King Caswallon? Have you a welcome for me?"

Sergovax answered for his lord with a tact unusual in a warrior. "The Ordovices are always proud to welcome Britain's Archdruid to Tre'r Ceiri." His face was the friendliest of the three. "Let us feast to celebrate your coming."

There was a murmur of approval from the warriors among the crowd, but a few frowns from the bondsmen who would be expected to prepare the small hall for revelry.

"A warrior is always too ready to drink," retorted Novax, spitting out an overchewed mouthful of willow. "We have not thought to ask what business brings our guest to this corner of Britain. Doubtless there are things my brother Druid wishes to discuss. Let the feast wait until tomorrow."

Bran raised an arm for silence. "Gentlemen, I am grateful for your welcome," he said because courtesy, not the warmth of his reception, demanded it. "However, I am too tired to feast, and the news I have heard needs thought before I can discuss it." He shot his eyes to the king, who fidgeted his fingers and looked to the ground. "I will enjoy a bard's company tonight—if he will allow me to share his home."

Dermot gave a smile of approval and ignored Novax's icy glare. "Kyra and I would be offended if you were to make any other arrangement," he enthused.

Bran put an arm around Dermot's shoulders. "Come then. Let me meet young Conor."

* * * *

The hut Dermot shared with his wife and young son was no bigger than any of the others in Tre'r Ceiri. The position of bard was an honoured one, though, and his home showed the trappings of wealth. Kyra's cooking pots bore the designs of Roman craftsmen, rather than the crude motifs of inexperienced local potters. Her cloak, hanging by the door, was noticeably, if not richly, embroidered and was fastened by a silver brooch. The one bed had a covering of sheep fleeces as well as rushes and straw. The sweet aroma of Roman wine pleased Bran's palate, although it fought with little success against the nostril-cloying stench of the peat hearth, which lay thick in every upland house in Britain. In a position of honour on a low table sat Dermot's harp. *Not the finest in Britain, perhaps*, thought Bran. It wasn't inlaid with gold. It was maybe a generation or two old. But it was still a good harp. Dermot had the gift of voice; any instrument would sound like a gift from the gods with Caswallon's bard to accompany it.

And, of course, wrapped in white swaddling clothes, and sleeping soundly in a small pallet of straw, was Conor, white skinned and cherubic. Bran reached out to touch his delicate, perfect fingers, but thought better of it. He didn't want to risk waking the mite.

Finally, there was Kyra, momentarily unbent from the hearth. When she saw Bran step over the threshold, she gave a look, which, even with The Sight, he didn't know how to interpret.

Bran had always liked Kyra, although he had never been sure of her feelings towards him. She was never beautiful, perhaps on the pretty side of plain, he thought to himself. And she had put on weight since he had last seen her, too, although she couldn't be blamed for that. Childbearing often left its mark around the waist. But she had a happy face, and anyone could see that she and Dermot were deeply in love.

That, supposed Bran, *was all that mattered.* Had Dermot asked his approval of the match, the Archdruid would have given it without hesitation.

"Kyra, look who's here," opened Dermot.

"Yes," she replied, without sounding welcoming. "The arrival of the Archdruid has overtaken the king's bed as today's big news."

"Forgive my wife," said Dermot. "She is pleased to see you, but is suspicious of magic."

"Please don't think me rude, Archdruid. You have always been kind to us, but..." Bran opened his palms in a gesture to encourage her to bare her concerns. "But... I don't feel safe sheltering a man who has enemies here."

"Novax," Bran mused as his brow knotted. "Yes, Druid Novax and I have known each other for many years. I assume he has poisoned the king against me?"

"He has tried," admitted Dermot. "But Sergovax is a sensible man— for a warrior. He keeps the king's mind balanced. I don't need to tell you that Sergovax was once a fine soldier. He keeps himself fit and ready for war, but his reflexes have slowed with age. He needs to keep the king's favour."

Bran nodded knowingly as he felt a twinge in his back.

Dermot continued. "Sergovax fears the new generation of warriors, and more importantly Caswallon's friends. There are a score of impetuous youths ready to stake a claim for the Champion's portion at the feasting table—young Guthor is a hothead, but he's already building a reputation. One or two of them may soon even be good enough to challenge Sergovax. Certainly Sergovax and Novax vie for the king's attention. Caswallon must sometimes think he's being pulled in two directions at once!" Dermot's eyes narrowed as his voice fell to a whisper. His face became hard, and he looked directly into the Archdruid's eyes, as if searching for something in his soul. "But tell me, Bran. Why does Novax hate you? He seems to be undertaking his own personal war against you. There's something deeper than a dispute over policy between you. Isn't there?"

Bran sighed. "I suppose there's no harm in telling you. It started before you were born, my boy. We both wanted the same woman. Beautiful, she was. Beautiful." His voice threatened to trail off as his mind filled with the past. "I was so fortunate that she chose me, but Novax couldn't take the rejection." He paused to take a swig from the mug of wine Kyra handed him before continuing. "Then, when the position of Archdruid became vacant a few years later, we were both nominated. There were several other candidates, but he seemed to take my election as a personal slight." Bran came back to the present as there was first movement and then crying from the small bed. "I've probably said enough. Let me meet Conor." He tried to ignore notice the knowing look in Dermot's eyes.

Kyra bent down to pick up the baby who gurgled happily at her touch while Dermot looked on proudly. Bran cradled his arms as Conor was gently placed in them, and the Druid cooed bubbles and looked fondly down into his face. Bran imagined there was something of both mother and father in that small, warm bundle of flesh and linen. And was there something of himself there as well? An emotion began to well up inside his heart. He threw his mind back to a similar small bundle; wrinkled and helpless in his arms. A bundle now grown to manhood and standing proudly beside him.

Bran wished for the chance to rectify the past. But even a Druid couldn't unlock the passage of time.

"Dermot, reach inside my bag, will you? I have a gift."

The bard did as he was asked, and withdrew a linen likeness of a man stuffed with duck's down. It was obviously Roman, wearing a toga with its dark hair cut short in the manner of the invaders. "This?"

"Ah, yes. My gift to the little one." Bran took the present and waved it in front of Conor, who gurgled laughter as he reached out two miniature arms.

"It's lovely," broke in Kyra. "Where did you get it?"

"I was in the lands of the Iceni during the last moon. I visited Camulodunum as part of Queen Boudicca's delegation. A Centurion there had a rotten tooth which I pulled. How he whimpered!" Bran noticed Dermot's smile at the mention of a Roman soldier in discomfort. "When he offered payment I asked him to take me around the market to look for something for the baby. I chose the doll."

"A generous gift," thanked Dermot. "Tell me, Bran, do you think young Conor will have The Sight?"

Kyra scowled.

Bran was slightly taken aback by the bluntness of the question. "I think you know the answer to that. The Sight is often passed from father to son. Do you have the sight?"

Dermot bit his lip. "Sometimes. I have a friend, Ardac, who lives at Dun Dinille, half a day's walk along the coast."

Bran nodded. He knew the fort.

"Ardac is a fisherman. I got to know him through his father, who organises trade between Dinas Dinille and Tre'r Ceiri. You may know him? Dafyd mac Gallas?"

Bran nodded again. He couldn't recall the man's face—an Archdruid met many people in the course of his travels—but the name was familiar.

Dermot continued. "I hadn't seen him for a while, but during the first frosts I had a feeling. A strong, bad, feeling about Ardac. Then in a dream I saw him swimming, struggling for breath and far from shore, the last of his strength being sapped from him as the waters finally filled his lungs and converged over his head. On the shore watching him drown was a travelling craftsman, wearing Roman clothes, and holding the reins of a horse laden with the tools of his trade." He pursed his lips thoughtfully. "At the time I dismissed my vision as the guilty dream of one who is not maintaining a good friendship, but the following day Caswallon asked me to sing for a guest of honour. That guest was the Roman craftsman I had seen in my vision; I knew his arrival signalled that the events I had seen were imminent."

"I stayed sober throughout the feast, but my singing was below the standard I have set for myself. I was thinking of my friend all the time. Eventually, though, the feast ended. I was tired, but fortunately there was a good moon. I scrambled down the scree as quickly as any mountain goat, took the first horse I could find, and rode like the wind to Dinas Dinille."

"And what did you find there?"

"I found Ardac, asleep in his bed, resting before he and other fishermen set out in their coracles the next morning. I begged and pleaded with him not to go. When he had finished moaning at me for depriving him of his sleep he called me for a fool, not wishing to miss out on a day's catch. But I begged and pleaded with him, and told him about my dream, and eventually his wife talked him around. "What's a day's catch, husband, if you are not here to share it?" she asked him, and eventually he relented."

"Two days later he visited me here. He told me his friends had set out in their coracles without him, laughing at him for listening to the warnings of a mere songsmith. But they never returned. How Ardac thanked me for saving his life!"

"Yes," mused Bran, partly to himself. "You certainly have The Sight."

"Please, let's talk of something else," Kyra butted in as she put three bowls on the low table. She had remained quiet to that point, but her face was shadowed. Talk of things she didn't understand was obviously unnerving her. Bran happily changed the subject, and he sat to eat his meaty stew with genuine relish. Kyra was a good cook. He could feel his muscles and his mind unknot as he relaxed.

They talked of everything and nothing over their meal; the exceptionally good weather; who was marrying who; their hopes for Conor; rumours of rebellion. Everything, in Kyra's hearing, except the Rainbow Sword and the king's indiscretion the previous night.

When the meal was over, Bran and Conor remained at the table and settled down into a session of the board game *phwyll*. Kyra made her excuses and took Conor to discuss baby matters with friends in a neighbouring hut.

"So," said Bran thoughtfully as he slowly moved a piece across the board. "Last time I was here I put a proposition to you. Have you given it thought?"

Dermot gave a long, deep breath. Bran almost wondered whether the bard had heard, but at length Dermot spoke. "I've thought long and hard, but there is only one answer I can give. You know as well as I do how Kyra thinks about anything... well, unearthly. Turning down the chance to become a Druid isn't something a man does lightly, but I can't risk losing her."

"You're turning it down because of Kyra?"

"Yes. I haven't even discussed it with her. I love her more than anything, and I didn't want it to drive a wedge between us. And anyway, even if she'd been happy, it would mean years of study. I would be away from my family for moons at a time. I don't want to miss Conor growing up." He looked over to the empty cot.

Bran thought back to a time, many years ago, when he had made the choice between the priesthood and the woman he loved.

He envied Dermot.

Dermot was making the right choice.

"Anyway, Bran, I have everything I need right here, in Tre'r Ceiri. I can sing. I can watch Conor grow up. I can support my family. I am excused the duties of war." His face screwed up, as it always did, at the notion of violence. "I'm happy. Why do I need to change anything?"

"Why indeed? Please understand, Dermot, that it was my duty to offer you the chance. There is a Druid inside you. You have wisdom. You have the personality. But most of all you have The Sight. That is a precious gift, lad." He stroked his beard gently. "But you are right to turn it down if it is not for you. Other things in are important as well." *As I know from experience*, Bran stopped himself from continuing.

Dermot returned his attention to the game and Bran gave an inward sigh of relief. The discussion had brought back too many painful memories, so Dermot's sudden, uncharacteristically blunt question caught him unprepared.

"You have said The Sight can be passed from father to son. My mother always refused to speak of my father. But how many men did she know who had The Sight?"

Bran shifted uncomfortably. The lad's questions were getting to near to the truth. He pretended to study the board to buy himself time to think. "I don't know." He slid a piece across the board thoughtfully to avoid the other's gaze. "Maybe she knew one or two. I don't know." He risked looking up and met Dermot's hard frown. There was no denying the penetrating gaze. His son knew.

Dermot moved a piece. "I win. There are no more moves left open to you."

Bran smiled his congratulations. The lad was right in more ways than one. He was manoeuvred into a corner. His heart pounded. "You know? How?"

"Part good guesswork. Partly The Sight. Why did you never acknowledge me?"

"Your mother and I could never be together. And the woman you thought of as your mother… she was a willing wetnurse and widow whose agreed to take you only if she could bring you up as her own. By the time she died it was too late to have the truth thrust upon you. The secret ached, but I judged it best to remain in my soul."

No more words were needed. With tears in their eyes, the two men stood and embraced as father and son for the first time. A great surge of relief swept through Bran. The secret which had pinched his heart had at last been spilled.

Their reunion was broken by urgent sounds outside. A man, his breath caught by his climb and his voice broken by emotion, shouted for attention in short gasps.

"THE ROMANS! THE ROMANS ARE COMING. THE EAGLES

MARCH ON THE ORDOVICES!"

Bran tensed as the feeling of dread returned. He remembered the dead, bloated bodies and bloodthirsty sheep from his vision.

"It has started," he muttered into his beard.

* * * *

Peter Davis awoke with a start. Darkness enveloped him, and for a second panic took his mind as he tried to place his surroundings. Familiar, and yet unfamiliar. He calmed as he remembered. Nantbran. His first night in the perfect home in the mountains.

But it had been a strange dream. Unlike the form of any dream he had before. Most dreams were fuzzy at the edges, struggling to be remembered even immediately after waking.

Not this one, though. It wasn't like a dream. It was almost like a memory, he thought to himself. *No, not a memory, it was more vivid even than that. It was like an* experience. *As if I had been Bran.* He had never been to Tre'r Ceiri before, although he had heard of the hillfort, among those memories which lay half forgotten, to be brought out again when needed.

But he had never heard of Bran, Kyra, Conor, King Caswallon or any of the other characters who had emerged during his sleep. Yet they seemed as real as anyone he had ever met. He found himself fearing for these people, with the Roman legions advancing on North Wales, and was unable to slowly shake the emotions off as he would have with any other dream.

Something pinched him as he thought of the lambs. Pictures of violent white lambs had appeared in Bran's memory, a dozen or so hours after he had first thought he remembered them.

The mountain night was cool, and his window open, but Peter sweated. He rolled over to look at the luminous number on his clock: three twenty-seven. He tried to fall back to sleep, but his dream—no, his experience—left him lying awake, his mind too alive to return to its rest until sheer fatigue defeated his mind.

His remaining sleep was filled with nightmare visions of slaughter and violent lambs.

Chapter 5

Peter blinked into his illuminated alarm clock.

Five forty-two.

After an hour wrestling with his pillow he gave up any thoughts of more sleep, so turned his light on but found no relaxation with his favourite author. He eventually rose at dawn, after hearing the muffled sounds of someone else stirring.

The day showed early promise, with sunlight already burning through the fingers of mist. With luck, he thought, it would be a good day for putting paint to canvas.

But his dream kept cutting into him.

He tried to shake it off. *It was only a dream.*

But it had been very real.

"You're up early, Pete," said his father as he looked up from some papers scattered around the kitchen table. "Kettle's just boiled. Please." He waved an empty mug.

"Couldn't sleep." Peter took the hint and prepared two coffees. "I thought I'd get out early and do some painting. What about you?"

"Doing the paperwork for the computer. If I get some freelance work I'll need to be connected to the Web and have an e-mail address." He nodded his thanks and took a sip from his drink. "Also, we need to start thinking about childcare for Johnny. I thought I might go into the village this morning and put some feelers out in the shop. Perhaps they'll put a card in the window for us."

The pyjama-clad object of the conversation bounded in. "Hello Peetie. Hello Daddy. What are we doing today?"

Peter shrugged. "How do you fancy coming with me while I paint? You can bring Tipsy to play with, and your bike, or —"

"'I'll come with you. I'll bring Tipsy. We'll like it."

The terrier appeared from nowhere to yap his agreement.

"What about Lucy?" asked Peter. "And Johnny—you won't be going anywhere with me if you don't get some clothes on."

"Don't ask about your sister," laughed Alun. "It's not term time, so she probably won't get up until our bed time."

Peter took a deep breath. Now was the time. "Dad?"

"Hmm?" Alun was engrossed in his paperwork again.

"Have you ever heard of a place called Tre'r Ceiri?"

Alun pushed his spectacles up his nose. "That's a name that takes me back a few years! It's an old hillfort near the coast, a few miles down from Caernarfon. Why?"

Peter shrugged with forced nonchalance. "I just vaguely heard about it. I thought I'd take a trip up there sometime. Johnny might like to come."

"Yes. A hillfort! Let's go to the hillfort," enthused Johnny.

"It's a wonderful place," Alun enthused. "Can we leave it a few days so I can join you when I'm all set up here?" He swept an arm toward the computer and accompanying paperwork. "I went there with Aunt Gwyn. It must have been... thirty years ago. There's dramatic views as far as Anglesey, and the slate ramparts and hut walls still stand." He breathed out. "Incredible."

"Oh." Peter remembered the slate ramparts and hut walls of his dream.

* * * *

The morning was crisp and dry. Peter set with his easel and canvas under one arm and a folding chair under the other. Johnny, holding his brother's brushes and palette like bone china, trudged carefully behind. Tipsy loudly expressed his contentment as he contorted around their legs to Peter's chosen spot. A large, wide bank separated their land from a rugged footpath running upward to the mountains. As well as giving a good view of the house, the bank would let him keep an eye on Johnny no matter which side of it the youngster chose to play. He was soon painting happily.

The old church was between the house and Peter's vantage point. He felt a bond with the place of worship and wanted to make the ruin, as much as the house, a central part of his work. After his experience, he felt a little less well disposed towards the cairn and the hollow containing the stones and oaks, but decided to make the area look as attractive and inviting as possible.

He didn't know how long he had been caught up in his hobby; he was enjoying the fresh air, the morning sun on his face, and the sound of Johnny playing with Tipsy. The canvas succumbed to sweeping, flamboyant brushstrokes, reflecting his mood.

Until he remembered last night.

Peter brushed away a minor mistake as he thought back to his dream. He would normally have expected daylight to fade the memory to the point where it became lost, but this dream had stayed as crisp and fresh as the morning around him.

As soon as possible, he would get to Tre'r Ceiri. Johnny and Tipsy would enjoy a walk around a hillfort. And maybe it would lay his dream to rest.

His thoughts and concentration were broken by a worried call from his brother.

"Tipsy! Tipsy! What is it? Come here boy! PETER! Tipsy's run away."

"Where?" Peter asked without too much concern as he rested his brush. The dog would come back when he wanted to. "Oh, Johnny. I hope you weren't teasing him."

"No, I wasn't," snapped Johnny. "We were playing and then he just started growling and ran off over there." He pointed towards a marshy gully and fought back a sob.

"I don't fancy looking for him in that water. It's all stagnant. Don't worry. He'll come home when he's ready." Peter stood to put a reassuring hand the boy's shoulder. "If he was hurt or anything we'd hear him bark. But it doesn't look dangerous, does it?" He strained his neck, hoping to catch a flash of the dog's white coat among the rocks and marsh grass.

Tears began to form in the corner of Johnny's eyes as they both turned in response to a noise along the path. But it wasn't Tipsy. It was a walker with her own animal.

Peter did a double take as he saw the dog. It was a massive, strange looking brute, he thought, although sleek and well groomed. He guessed it was something like a cross between a Labrador and a German Shepherd. It was the animal's colouring that unnerved Peter—it was white all over—white enough to be an albino, were it not for its brown eyes and red ears.

At first he thought the animal's deep red ears were covered in blood, but as the dog came nearer, it soon became obvious that this was its natural colouring. The eyes unnerved him, too—brooding and angry, as if the animal had been brought up to fend for itself.

He was thankful it was on a lead. He wouldn't have wanted to face it on equal terms, even with its owner to control the situation.

In fact, it was only as a second glance that he looked at its owner. And he had trouble looking away.

She was beautiful. Even hidden away behind sunglasses, beauty radiated from her as, despite having only a pair of flimsy black plimsolls on her feet, she moved effortlessly down the rough path. Long, dark hair fluttered in the breeze. A plain and simple night-black dress looked exquisite, caressing her body as she moved. She had something about her, an unidentifiable magnetism making the description 'sex appeal' seem insignificant. That was even before she was close enough even for him to make out her cutely dimpled cheeks, slender neck and a smile that quickened his heart.

"Hello. Everything all right?" she asked in a voice as smooth as warm honey, but with a gentle accent Peter couldn't quite place. Her head turned towards Johnny, who had stopped his sobbing to take in the stranger and her awe-inspiring dog.

"Our dog's run off," Peter responded, nodding in the direction of the gully. "I'm sure he'll come back when he's hungry though."

She turned towards Johnny and lowered herself to his level. "Don't worry. My dog's always doing things like that. They enjoy exploring. Think of all the fun he's having finding out what's over there."

To Peter's surprise, Johnny seemed reassured. "Yes, Miss," he said almost reverently.

"I'm sure he'll be back in a minute." Then, turning to Peter but nodding in the direction of the house, "You must be the new people. We've heard all about you. Gossip spreads fast in a place like Nantbran."

"I'm sure it does. We expected to provide a few comments. I'm Peter Davis; this is my brother Johnny. We've moved up from Swindon."

"Morgan," she replied simply, extending a hand.

"An unusual name," flirted Peter. It was a clumsy chat up line, but he couldn't think of anything better. He enjoyed the feel of her soft, warm hand in his, and found himself holding it for a second or so longer than was polite.

"I'm half Irish. Morgan's an Irish name," she explained, either not minding or not noticing Peter's extended handshake, before turning her attention back to Johnny. "How do you like living in the mountains?"

"I like it. There's things to do here." The youngster looked at her in wide-eyed awe.

A competitor for me! Peter thought to himself flippantly. He flicked his eyes to her left hand, and breathed an inward sigh of relief when he saw nothing adorning her slender ring finger.

Morgan was still talking with Johnny. "Do you want to stroke the dog? His name's Owain. After Owain Glyndwr. Have you heard of him?" she continued when Johnny shook his head. "He was a great Welshman who fought the English."

At the word 'English' Owain gave a low growl.

"I'm half English," said Johnny, taking a wary step back.

"But half Welsh, too," added Peter.

"Well, I think you'll be safe from Owain, then," she teased. "But seriously, it's a good thing you've got Welsh blood. Snowdonia's suffered a lot at the hands of the English over the centuries. They're not too popular. I'd stress 'half Welsh' rather than 'half English' if I were you."

"I'll remember that," Peter agreed, not mentioning that his father had already passed on a similar warning to his children.

Morgan turned back to her dog, encouraging Johnny to pet the animal which seemed to be enjoying the attention. Peter admired the way such a brute could be controlled by one so demure, and took the opportunity to admire her more fully. Her sleek black hair fell forward across her chest as she leaned forward to speak, leaving exposed her slim neck, with its skin as smooth and unblemished as ivory. Her small mouth was surrounded by full, red lips, and Peter couldn't help noticing how they remained slightly parted even when she wasn't talking. He found himself wondering what it would be like to kiss that perfect mouth.

"He's a nice kid," Morgan said to Peter when she finally turned her attention back to him. She took off her sunglasses as she spoke, swinging them delicately between two fingers in a gesture both casual and alluring at the same time. Peter couldn't help a gasp as he looked into her eyes for the first time. Eyes soft and gentle as a doe's, he thought to himself as he studied them beneath their long, dark lashes.

But those deep, dark eyes held something more. *Something unnerving.*

Something, which added an adrenaline-pumping danger to her beauty, not something detracting from it. Something hinting at a strong, unconquerable spirit beneath the feminine exterior.

"Yeah. Like all youngsters he has his moments, but, yes, he's generally okay."

"I've always wanted to work with kids." There was a hint of the dreamer in her voice.

"I would have thought you'd be able to get a job. If Johnny's anything to go by you're a natural with youngsters."

"It's difficult somewhere as remote as this. I love the mountains and would never move away, but there's no jobs around here. North Wales has one of the highest unemployment rates in the UK. It's certainly rare to find a family where both parents work, so there's no call for childminders, and even those in work can't afford nurseries. My family have tilled the soil for generations, all for little reward."

"How about teaching?"

She shrugged. "Never fancied it. I think a classroom would be a bit too enclosed for me. I prefer my life a little less structured."

Peter's mind raced. "Well, we've been thinking about some childcare for Johnny. I'd have to ask dad, but—"

"I'd love to," she butted in, before biting her lower lip and looking coyly at the ground. "I'm sorry. I shouldn't be so forward. But if you're after a childminder I'd certainly be interested."

Peter smiled back, resisting the urge to put a reassuring arm around her. "I'll speak to dad," he promised.

Morgan's big eyes looked up into his. "I'd certainly appreciate it. I bring Owain here for his walk most mornings—don't I boy?—so we'll probably meet again."

"I'll be painting here again tomorrow," said Peter. "If you're passing we can discuss it again."

"What about your mum? Won't she want a say?"

Peter shrugged. "'She died," he said simply.

"I... I'm sorry. I didn't realise."

"That's okay. It was six months ago. Cancer. She was in a lot of pain."

"So how did you end up in Snowdonia?" she asked.

Peter was grateful for the change of subject. "The mortgage had a life assurance policy attached, so it got paid off when mum died. Then dad's firm was looking to cut numbers, and he was offered a good redundancy package. Johnny's got problems with his lungs, so as we could afford to sell up we decided to take his doctor's advice and move somewhere with clearer air. He seems to be benefiting already," Peter smiled as he glanced down at his brother. "Everything seems to be turning out okay."

"So you're rich?" Her voice carried a hint of a tease.

"Hardly. We're comfortable, but we need some sort of extra income. Dad's hoping to do some consultancy work, and I'm going to try and sell some paintings." He swept an arm towards his canvas.

"Can I see?" she asked, turning her attention to Peter's work.

"It's the house," Peter replied nervously. "I thought my first in Wales should be of where we're living." His breath locked in his throat as Morgan followed him up the bank to examine the half-finished work. At that moment, her opinion mattered more than anything else.

The corners of her mouth lifted into a half-smile that enchanted Peter. "I like it," she announced, and he felt his stomach give a churn of relief. Then, for a few too short minutes they chatted lightly before Morgan made her excuses.

"Here, Owain. Bye Peter, bye Johnny. Johnny: would you like us to see more of each other?"

"Yes please. Can I see Owain too?"

"Yes, I should think so. Let's hope your father lets me come round to look after you." She turned her head to smile a goodbye.

That same half-smile which had held Peter in its power only seconds before. But with those powerful, expressionless eyes that gave her whole being an edge. *Yes*, he thought. *Let's hope father lets you come round.* He watched as she continued into the distance, letting his eyes rest on her. Nothing would stop him being here again this time tomorrow.

He was bought back to the present by a familiar yapping.

"Tipsy!" squealed Johnny, opening his arms for a hug as his pet frolicked towards him.

"Oh Johnny, you're filthy," laughed Peter, after the dog had covered the youngster in foul smelling marsh water. "You're both going to have to go home for a bath."

Tipsy took a look towards Morgan and her own dog disappearing into the distance, and at once he stiffened, before yapping after them as they disappeared out of sight. "Oi! Tipsy, calm down," ordered Peter. "I know the dog's a bit bigger than you, but his mistress is okay."

"Peter, why doesn't Tipsy like Morgan and Owain?"

"He's probably afraid of Owain. He must seem like a giant dog to Tipsy."

"Peter?"

"Yes?"

"I can't give him a bath on my own. He'll run away."

"Get your sister to help.'

"She'll still be in bed. She won't like being woken."

"Call her Lucinda. She'll soon get out of bed then." Peter couldn't resist a smile at the look of horror on his brother's face.

"I can't call her that. She'll kill me." Johnny paused for a second, finger on lip, before announcing, "I know! I'll tell her you've got a new girlfriend," and before Peter could object Johnny was tearing past the church to the house, with Tipsy in hot pursuit, shouting, "PETER'S GOT A GIRLFRIEND! PETER'S GOT A GIRLFRIEND!" At the top of his voice.

Peter wondered, anxiously for a second, if Johnny's chant was being carried on the breeze down the path to Morgan. But he decided it couldn't do any harm for her to know he'd fallen for her.

He turned back to his picture, but Morgan, not his work, was consumed his thoughts.

* * * *

Peter yawned, not knowing how long he'd been painting. But only the finishing touches of his Snowdonian vista remained.

The sun was high. He glanced at his wrist, and tutted to himself when he realised he'd forgotten to put his watch on. But he knew from the position of the sun that it must have been about noon.

The day had turned out warm. Too warm for painting, he told himself. The masterpiece could wait.

He stepped down from his easel and sat on the bank, enjoying the serenity of the house, dwarfed on three sides by slopes of emerald green. The ground was warm and he found himself lying on his back, eyes closed, as he enjoyed the solitude which was broken only by the occasional bleat of a distant sheep or birds chattering overhead.

Forty winks wouldn't hurt, he decided.

Chapter 6

Despite the efforts of the morning sun, war hung like a pall over the Sacred Isle.

Bran snorted in an attempt to blot out the cloying stench of forthcoming death, trying to replace it with the smells of seaweed and salt air.

Bran caressed his beard as he contemplated the ritual goat's blood congealing on his robe. He cursed The Sight. Sometimes it showed a man things best not seen.

At the demand of his ageing legs he shifted position. The sand invaded his sandals and caressed his toes. The dune was high, and the Druid grouping could look down upon the battlefield and almost enjoy the view of a raven.

At the thought of the bird of death Bran made a secret prayer to Bel.

The Archdruid shielded his eyes from the sun as he looked along the beach to his front, where the Ordovices prepared for battle. Some men sharpened their swords on handily placed rocks. Others prayed to whichever god they trusted in, murmuring a wish to see a lover or child again, or roaring for a heroic death to take them to the eternal feasts of the Otherworld. Nobles encouraged their men with promises of victory. Some warriors belched back mead; a double edged weapon which would provide courage, but also deaden the reactions and leave a warrior open to the sudden thrust of a Roman blade. Others emptied nervous bladders or bowels. Yet more men merely sat, either in silence or paining sacred swirls on their bared chest with blue dye from the woad plant.

But not all those begging for deliverance would find the gods were good listeners. Bran caressed his beard, knowing those men praying for an Otherworldly feast would be thanking the gods tonight.

On the other side of the strait, only a couple of hundred paces away, the army of the Eagles stood alert to their hastily constructed rafts, awaiting low tide and the order to cross the water. Armour glinted from the regular lines of drilled legionaries, but individuals were too far away for Bran's aged eyes to identify, although he had no doubt that the same rituals were being carried out on the mainland.

He looked around at the other sullen-faced Druids. They looked to the front anxiously, their brows knotted in anticipation. One or two looked to Bran as if for guidance, but quickly turned away. Bran wondered if his own features mirrored their concern.

He turned, watching the ridge above a small wood to the north, to the north of the beach to look out for his son. As a bard, Dermot would not take part in the fighting, but he had escorted civilians to the relative safety of Aberffraw, the king's winter palace on the west coast. Here Caswallon and his warriors would make merry during the cold months, knowing that the storms would protect the Ordovices from Irish raiders. The rugged, cold security of Tre'r Ceiri was not needed during the winter moons. Bran remembered many happy winters spent in the safety of Aberffraw's blazing hearths.

"Well, Bran, what hope do you give the Ordovices?" The voice belonged to Novax, the question an oblique sneer.

"The Ordovices are surprised," replied Bran calmly. "We have had only one night to ready ourselves. The Eagles have had time to prepare." Bran sighed. The last thing he needed was an interruption to his spiritual tasks. Or his earthly worries.

"I agree it's been a surprise to our army. But it doesn't take The Sight to notice an army caught unprepared," sneered Novax. As usual, a leaf of pain-relieving willow muffled his voice. "Just what did you see in the slaughtered goat?"

Bran sighed again. He had tried to drive the goat from his mind, but its dying stains on his white robe reminded the Archdruid of the warning from the Otherworld. "I told the army the omens were of victory."

"You are not the only Druid versed in divining. I grant you, the animal was healthy. But it fought. I wondered you weren't hurt by its struggles." Novax's yellow eyes gleamed with triumph, despite the portents of a British defeat and the pain slowly eating away at his belly.

Bran found himself on the defensive. "The goat was healthy. What was I to tell the warriors? That the animal's struggles were a sign of defeat? With a blow to morale like that the battle would have been lost before we started anyway." A knot of unease tightened itself in his stomach as he contemplated defeat, and the prospect of friends slaughtered or enslaved.

But here was Dermot, returning on one of the small, sturdy ponies indigenous to the mountains. Bran raised an arm to gain his attention, and was surprised when the greeting was not returned.

There was something wrong. Even from a hundred paces away Bran could see Dermot's head and shoulders bowed, and his hands lankly holding onto the reins. Bran made to meet his son.

"Dermot?" Bran asked as they met.

"Bran? Father?" The words were said without emotion. Bran looked upwards into his son's eyes for a clue to his spirit, and was nearly broken by what he saw. The blank face. The dead eyes. The straight, thin line of a mouth. It was Dermot's face, yet it wasn't Dermot's face. Gone was the sparkling optimism.

Instead Bran saw the mask of death; the look of a man who had lost hope; who knew he was about to die. The Archdruid had encountered it countless times. On condemned criminals; or on warriors who could see the swordblade cutting the air towards their unprotected flesh.

The face of despair.

But why on Dermot? The battle wasn't even fought. And Dermot wouldn't know of the omens—would he?

The Sight...

He helped his son dismount. "Dermot. Tell me, what is wrong? Is it The Sight? Have you seen defeat?"

"Yes," he said bitterly. "It is the curse of The Sight. But I don't know whether the army will win or fall."

"Then why have you lost hope? What have you seen?"

"I have felt death, Bran. As I felt my adopted mother's death all those years ago, I feel it again, yet stronger. I can feel the walls of life closing in around me. I can feel the breath being squeezed from my body. The Ordovices may win or lose, but the stench of death on the breeze is overpowering. Such strength of feeling can only mean my own end will arrive today."

Bran nodded slowly. He, too, had smelled death this morning. But he did not know how it felt for a man to see of his own end. He held his son, trying and failing to think of comforting words.

Dermot pulled away from his father's embrace. "Since I am to die then I might at least take some Romans with me." His voice, only a matter of heartbeats ago limp and passionless, was becoming steely and resolved. "Let me take a spare sword and shield from the slaves and die serving my tribe!" As he looked into Bran's face the familiar fire returned to his eyes.

"Farewell, Dermot,'" Bran said simply, knowing better than to question The Sight. "I am old; it will not be long before we meet again."

A brief flicker of emotion flashed across Dermot's face as a thought entered his mind. "Kyra? Conor?"

"Do not worry about your family. They are my family. While there is breath in my body they will have my protection. And I will not let Conor forget his father's harp."

A smile briefly danced around the corner of Dermot's mouth. He clasped his father's hand, and then in an instant was scurrying toward the battle line, shouting for weapons and a chariot.

Bran's heart thumped solemnly, bringing a heavy hollow to the pit of his stomach as he watched his son melt into the mass of warriors.

There was a noise behind Bran. Everyone, warrior, priest, or slave, turned behind them to see, from the north, a purple cloud of awesome proportions. Thunder roared from its belly as it filled the sky, roaring at the assembled battle hosts and darkening the morning. Bran knew the time had come to address the throng. The wild eyes of men preparing for battle fell on him as he spoke, and he raised his hands to the heavens as the advancing cloud silenced.

"Warriors of Britain! See the cloud which comes to envelop the field of battle! See how it comes from the north to drive the stifling heat of drought from us! Like the Ordovices who, after the battle, like a refreshing thunderstorm will drive the Eagles southwards and back to the gutters of Rome. The omens have been set. Let the battle commence!"

There was a scream of response from the warriors of the Ordovices.

The sky darkened as the threatening cloud hovered to the edge of the battlefield, expanding to fill almost the whole sky as it spread its menace across the heavens. The dawn was blotted out as day threatened to revert to night.

But his mind was dragged from his son to the matter of war by an Otherworldly screaming.

The noise of wild women, piercing and terrifying to match the wails of a banshee appeared from nowhere, as if bursting froth from a portal to the Otherworld.

The witches.

Wild women from the fringes of the Sacred Isle who lived alone to tone their supernatural powers with savage acts of devotion to their chosen deity. Their unkempt appearance and fearsome, magical personalities helped them maintain their solitude, for they were treated with fear. However, Bran knew that when battle was joined they would play a part as important and brave as any woad-splattered warriors.

The women burst toward the battle line, screaming anti-Roman obscenities like the madwomen some considered them to be before jerking a primeval dance between the ranks. Their hair, in some naturally black, in others dyed by the unwashed years of dirt, escaped from their heads like lice infested cobwebs, around faces made ugly by open sores and hate-twisted their features. Unkempt clothes hung like rags from their emancipated bodies.

But most of all it was the fires. The witches had lit themselves faggots of wood from a source of flames Bran was unsure of, giving an almost Otherworldly vision as they danced in the halflight from the hands of dishevelled, wild-eyes witches.

Their actions had the desired effect as the Ordovices took up their cries of abuse to the legions standing within earshot on the other side of the narrow strait.

And Bran, with his gift, could feel the Eagles' fear. Their dread was almost visible, advancing over the water like a blanket of fog, choking the willingness for battle like an executioner's thong.

But then, he mused to himself, *who would not be frightened by a screaming, angry mob of warriors, roused to a frenzy by fearless hags whose faces were thrown into grotesque contortions by flames in the fading light?*

But Bran was not Archdruid of Britain for no reason. With his years of training he knew there was something missing. True, there were omens aplenty for Druid and Roman priest to make of what they would. But there was something more. Instinctively Bran searched the heavens.

Where were the gods?

Few mortal men could sense their presence although, of course, no man doubted their existence — for the evidence of their work was all around. In the hills and valleys of Britain the sheer power of the mountains was a testament to the age-old work of the Immortals. The gentle breeze, soothing like the breath of a lover, was a sign of their pleasure, while the storms of the winter moons was their reminder of what could befall should man desert their worship.

But the gods of the Ordivices were not on the field of battle today.

Where was Andraste, the supreme Goddess of War?

Where were Neimen, Badbe and Macha, her lieutenants?

The deities of war should be helping the Britons in adversity, taking raven form above the battlefield. The gods should be encouraging men to wreak havoc and urge them and provide a bath of blood, flesh and mangled bones for their feasts, for death and souls were the foods of the Lady of War and Death. And where better to find death aplenty than on the battlefield? And what better source of flesh and souls than the Eagle invaders? Bran winced as his teeth pinched his lower lip. *Surely the Goddess should be here, today of all days, when the future of her worship hung in the balance?*

So where were the gods?

He caressed his beard.

Bran thrust thoughts of Dermot to the back of his mind as his eyes dropped to the battlelines, searching out Caswallon. His gaze eventually found the king's chariot in the gathering gloom. The boy never had a king's countenance, Bran thought, and he was a world away from displaying it now. The king of the Ordovices hid his fear behind a mask of lime-streaked hair and confident whorls of woad jumping from his body like demons. By his side, as always, was the loyal Sergovax. Bran was pleased the king had the veteran warrior as his champion. The old, experienced swordsman would lead the Ordovices where the king feared to tread.

But the Archdruid had a greater interest in Caswallon than the king's strength of mind. Bran was looking out for Caladchlog, the Rainbow Sword. His old eyes found the blade resting in the king's right hand.

But there was no low green glow emanating from the weapon. Not even the flash of a reflection from the witches' firebrands. He would have expected it to begin shining by now as a beacon of confidence for the British army, and a warning of death for the legions. Without its glow, Caladchlog would be no more useful in battle than any one of the countless weapons clasped in British hands.

A cold, piercing chill of helplessness enveloped Bran.

The gods have deserted the Ordovices.

And the Eagles seemed to know instinctively. A roar rose from the other side of the strait as centurions and tribunes urged their men on. The rank and file took up the shout. Even in the halflight Roman swords seemed to glint as men leapt onto rafts and paddled towards the British host.

"We'll take them as they disembark. We'll charge into the shallows and take them before they have time to form! It will be victory for Britain!" Novax's nasal voice was triumphant.

Bran ran a hand across his beard. "Hold your optimism, Novax. Why would the Eagles throw themselves upon our swords in such a manner? There's something wrong."

Novax rubbed his hands together in glee, as if he were a child receiving a carved plaything. "The Sacred Isle is safe from the ravishes of Rome. We'll be sacrificing Latin whelps on the alters tonight!"

"Anticipating turning your robes scarlet in the sacred groves, eh? The gods don't demand human sacrifice just for the sake of it. Better that any prisoners are given useful role to play—let them be tasked with slavery."

"Pah! The gods want respect. There's only respect through blood."

"The Sight tells you, does it?"

Novax's jaw slackened as if Bran's response had been a physical blow. His face reddened as he descended into silence, but he still found the dignity to spit a chewed willow leaf at the sand between Bran's feet.

But although Novax was not blessed with The Sight, Bran knew he was right. It did seem that the Eagles were throwing themselves towards the Ordovices like lambs to the slaughter.

Why? Why did The Sight taunt him with only glimpses of the truth?

The rafts were only paces from the shore now; British warriors, all anxious to have their name sung by the bards for taking the first enemy head, had to be restrained by their warleaders from rushing headlong into the waves. Better a mass charge at the right moment than allow the Eagles to pick off individuals in a chaotic battle in the surf.

Instead it was the wild women who charged into the water, screaming like furies until they were only a spearthrust from the iron-clad enemy, spitting into their faces and hurling barbed abuse. Javelins punctured a couple of the hags as they taunted the enemy, but the witches refused to fall. Instead, with their spirit increased and pain dulled by their breakfast of power-giving hazel berries, they ignored the wounds and withdrew from the enemy, waving firebrands in Roman faces as they did so.

A shiver passed through Bran as the reason for Roman confidence came to him.

Cavalry! Where was the Roman cavalry?

The answer was immediate. He turned in response to a thundering beyond a ridge to the east. Hooves. Horses' hooves. As he turned the first of the mail clad riders appeared on the ridge, followed by a moving sea of uncountable horsemen.

And they were heading for the rear of the British host.

And Bran and the rest of the Druid grouping were standing in their way.

As one, the entire British army responded to the noise of screaming beasts and riders with stunned inactivity. Warriors, some knee deep in seawater, stood rooted to the spot by the unexpected assault to the rear, mouths open and swords hanging limply from numbed hands.

The legions in their rafts had reached the beach.

The Ordovices, who only heartbeats before were contemplating a slaughter of their enemies, now dropped back as one. Event he witches fell sullen, their firebrands dulling along with their spirits. It was the Romans' turn to look forward to slaughter. The stomach for the fight had gone from the beach.

Bran's eyes left the carnage which was surely to come. He had charging horsemen to contend with.

"Down here! A gully!" a terrified voice quivered from behind Bran. As one, the white-clad group, forgetting the decorum demanded of their status, ran for the shelter of a small stream. The parching summer had left only a small trickle; the gully was about three paces wide and half that deep.

The Druids jumped in, flattening themselves against the overhanging side where tufts of grass held the muddy sand together. Someone dropped on top of him, but with the thunder of hooves nearly upon him, Bran didn't care who was above him, or about the discomfort of an elbow or knee in his ribs. The only things that mattered were the murderous sharp hooves which shook the earth as they came nearer, nearer, so loud that the noise might almost have been inside him. The earth shook, bouncing him against the gully sides. Dislodged sand and earth fell on him, invading his mouth and nose. He wanted to spit it out; he wanted to scream, but terror forbade movement.

Then they were above him; launching themselves over the gully. One or two at first, then more and more until even with his eyes clamped shut Bran knew the world was blotted out by a wave of snorting, screaming horses and their battlecrazed riders.

One horse missed its footing and Bran felt the gully falling over him as he lay. There was a muffed scream from whoever lay above him, mingled with the sound of a horseshoe sinking into flesh and cracking bone.

Bran could hear the sound of death over the mind-numbing, roar of a thousand horses.

As soon as it arrived, the sound of hooves receded. The enemy continued on its way to hit the Ordovices in the back. There was screaming from the battleline as British warriors begged for mercy or divine help.

But neither mercy nor divine help was forthcoming.

Bran lay still, waiting for his body to calm before even venturing to open his eyes. His heart pounded against his ribs with the strength of a thousand fists.

He wiped the mixture of sand and blood from his face. But he kept his eyes closed. He could smell, taste and feel blood. Blood everywhere. His hand found something soft and sticky. Resisting the temptation to pull his fingers away, they found a mixture of flesh and brains.

He wondered whose body it was, with its head mangled. He risked a look, but the head was too mangled and bloody to be recognisable. He pulled his way out of the gully, and used a tuft of sand to wipe the worst of the blood from his hands.

"The woods! Make for the woods!" The voice belonged to another Druid, and Bran followed his lead, along with the remaining priests, making for the dubious safety of a nearby copse. His lungs, unused to panic and exertion, threatened to explode as Bran gasped for precious air. His aged legs ached.

"Bran!"

The Archdruid looked through the trees for the bearer of the voice.

"Bran! Over here!"

"Dermot? How have you avoided the slaughter?" Bran hugged his son with relief. He was ashamed that in his own danger he had forgotten Dermot was fighting in the front line.

The young man looked down ashamed. "I am no warrior. I held my sword and realised I couldn't kill. There didn't seem much point in fighting when I don't want to take life. I just grabbed a horse and made for the rear. I thought my prayers would be more use than my cowardice." He hung his head. "I'm sorry, father. I've let you down."

Bran took hold of his son's shoulder. He felt a pang at being called father as he looked into the boy's eyes. "Nonsense. I'm no killer either. The place for people like us is at the rear. We have The Sight. We're too important to waste in combat."

"The fight is over. By the gods, look at the carnage." The voice, in the verge of breaking, belonged to another Druid who had sought sanctuary in the wood. In response, Bran, Dermot and the rest peered out from between he branches.

The slaughter was as great as anything Bran had ever seen. The beach lay littered with bodies. Nearly all were British, most lying still or twitching their death throes in the scarlet-stained sand. A few moved or groaned, calling out in agony for the gods or for anyone who would use a sword to put an end to their suffering. And their ends would not be long in coming. Roman soldiers on the beach were despatching the wounded with professional competence.

"What are they doing?" One man pointed away from the battlefield, where the decisive force of Roman cavalry had split into small groups of perhaps half a dozen men and were heading off in seemingly random directions.

"They're searching out survivors," another commented. "The Romans don't consider a battle won until they've wiped out every living thing in the area; man, woman, child, or even animal. I saw even dogs and pigs slaughtered by the Eagles after the revolt of Caractacus. They won't stop until the Sacred Isle has been purged."

Bran and Dermot looked at each other in dread.

"Bran. I foresaw death. Then why am I still living?"

The knot Bran had become so familiar with retightened itself. "Are you sure it was *your* death you saw? Experience will show you the tricks The Sight plays on the inexperienced."

"Kyra! Conor!" Dermot's jaw slackened as an awful truth dawned on father and son.

Chapter 7

Archdruid Bran pulled himself awake and thanked the gods for sparing him the ravishes of war. Then, with a pang of guilt for thinking of he own safety first, words of prayer passed his lips.

"Hear me, Guardians of Britain and Warlords of the Otherworld. If it is not too late, help your innocent servants, Kyra and Conor. They are mere innocents amid the turmoil of conflict and should be spared. I, Bran, Archdruid of Britain, will hasten to my own place of sanctity on the morrow, to offer a tribute in exchange for their safety."

He reached into his belt to put a hazelnut to his mouth, so that his prayer may more easily cross the shadowy boundary to the gods.

But he felt only the pocket of his jeans.

Peter Davis sighed.

It had been a dream.

But his heart pounded against his ribs. His body shook and sweated as he lay beneath the clear sky.

Like his dream about Ter'r Ceiri, this one had been real. *Felt* real. Like an *experience*. He wiped a trickling bead from his brow. He wondered what time it was, and looked at his left wrist.

No watch.

He guessed. The sun had definitely moved since he had fallen asleep. *Three o'clock?*

He sat up. Panic hit him. Had he made his prayer to the gods in his sleep? *Had anyone heard? How Lucy would enjoy that! And Morgan would think...*

He looked desperately down the path, realising he was caressing his chin as he did so. He pulled his hand away.

The path was empty.

But the memories of his encounter with Morgan softened the powerful emotions of his dream.

He turned his eyes to the house at the sound of a car's engine breaking the mountain silence.

To his surprise, not one but two cars snaked up the long drive, pushing memories of Morgan's delicate features fell from his mind. Alun's car pulled level with Peter's, but he felt his forehead knot as he focussed on the battered white van, it's paint splattered with rust and mud, which stopped behind.

Puzzled, Peter picked up his paintbrush and watched his father get out.

Nothing unexpected in that.

The door of the van opened, and Peter was surprised to see a woman get out. The distance was too great to be able to make out her features, but her shoulder length brown hair and reasonable figure were obvious. Her blue T-shirt, tucked into brown Bermuda shorts, hugged a decent figure.

Certainly not a good as Morgan's. And I'll bet she hasn't got Morgan's challenging eyes, either.

Deciding it was unfair on both women to compare them, he shook the thoughts from his head.

He returned his attention to the battered van, and watched with growing surprise as the woman opened a rear door and a young boy, perhaps Johnny's age, jumped out.

If Peter was puzzled by the presence of this possibly attractive woman, he was particularly perplexed by the body language displayed by both her and his father. The way Alun confidently spread his arms indicated he was at ease with her. And the way she gestured to her son—Peter assumed it was her son—that he should go inside, without asking Alun's permission first, showed she was equally confident and comfortable.

Maybe she's dad's lover?

Peter laughed quietly.

Before disappearing inside, Alun paused to wave. The woman stopped as Alun appeared to say something, and she raised a friendly hand in Peter's direction.

Peter could feel puzzlement knotting his brow as he returned the gesture. Then she and Alun disappeared inside.

Peter wondered what Lucy would make of this.

He returned to his canvas, but after meeting Morgan, and seeing the stranger arrive with his father, his concentration and enthusiasm were drained. And experience had taught him that quality work wouldn't be forced.

With a sigh, he pulled his equipment together and paused one final time to admire his work before, wishing he had an extra pair of hands, he carried everything clumsily back to the house.

He set his gear down in the hallway, picture leaning against the staircase. The painted side was turned towards the stairs, hidden from prying eyes. It would be safe there. His family knew better than to take an uninvited preview of one of his creations.

"Dad?" His voice was cautious, knowing there was a stranger in the house.

"Ah, Peter!" exclaimed Alun. "Come in, come in. There's someone here I'd like you to meet."

He followed his father's voice into the kitchen, still wondering who the 'someone' was.

The scene that met him surprised Peter. The mystery woman was sitting with Alun and Lucy, all three at ease around the kitchen table. He shot her a quick glance.

Brunette. Shoulder length hair. Green eyes. A splattering of freckles. About thirty, maybe. *Quite pretty*, Peter decided. *But not a pretty as Morgan*, he couldn't stop himself thinking. *No. More than that. Paling into insignificance next to the animal magnetism of Morgan... Morgan what?* he asked himself, wanting to kick himself for not grabbing her full name.

Alun spoke. "Peter. You remember Rhiannon? Rhiannon Jones, now."

"Hi!" Her voice was relaxed, her smile genuine. "Pleased to meet you again."

"Hello." *Again?* He still couldn't place her, but he recognised the lilt of a local accent.

"Aunt Gwyn's granddaughter," prodded Alun.

Dim memories from childhood holidays fought to be recalled. He vaguely remembered an older girl, throwing snowballs with him and Lucy in the back yard of Aunt Gwyn's terrace house. "Yes, of course," he said. "I'm sorry. I didn't recognise you without your pigtails."

She laughed lightly, green eyes sparkling. "Heck, is it that long since I saw you? I ditched the pigtails before I left school. I had it cut really short and purple during my rebellious phase. That's before I decided on shoulder length." She ran her fingers through it. "You used to be about four-foot high and in short trousers. I remember you were quite sweet... for a boy."

"No he wasn't," Lucy interrupted.

Rhiannon gave a quick smile before continuing. "You came up just before Christmas. Lucy was in a bad mood."

"Wasn't."

"Yes you were. Peter told you there'd been a terrible sleigh crash and Father Christmas and Rudolph had been killed."

"Humph. I never believed in Father Christmas."

"Anyway. I was saying to Uncle Alun and Lucy. We're cousins. Of sorts. Once removed? Or second or third cousins? I never know the difference. And I'm married with Bryn now." She nodded in the direction of the living room, and the youngster taking some action figures on a commando mission with Johnny.

"I think we can drop the 'Uncle' tab," said Alun. "I always intended to get in contact once we were settled. But I never expected to bump into family in the local shop."

"My fault for recognising you," she admitted with a grin. "I always was a bit forward."

Peter couldn't help noticing the way her nose screwed up when she smiled. He found he liked it as much as he had all those years ago. And the easy personality which hadn't been driven away by adulthood.

"Yeah. Rhiannon overheard me asking if I could put up a card. And the coincidence doesn't stop there."

Rhiannon continued the story. "I used to housekeep for the previous occupant here. Miss Morris. So I know my way around with my eyes closed. It's a lot livelier with the Davis family in residence, I can tell you! Anyway, I'd be able to keep and eye on Johnny and Bryn as I work." She hesitated for a second. "And I'd be doing two different jobs at once, so I'd be willing to be more... er... flexible about rates of pay than separate childminder and cleaners. But I've already discussed that with Uncle Alun." She put her hand to her mouth. "Oops! I mean just Alun."

"Well," began Peter. "If it means more money left in the kitty, young Lucy here will be all for it."

"I will?"

"Sure you will. More for the 'Lucy Davis Clothing Fund'."

Lucy spread her hands. "Why not? The best way for a father to keep his daughter quiet is with regular top-ups to her budget. How can I become one of Snowdonia's beautiful people on a budget of peanuts?"

"But, sister, you prefer to wear faded old jeans anyway."

Her reply was to give Peter a good view of her tongue.

"Don't worry, Bryn," interjected Johnny from the living room. "It's just Peter and Lucy fighting. They do it all the time."

"But you do most of your socialising by mobile or e-mail," cut in Alun. "Wouldn't some call time or a dedicated 'phone line be better than clothes?"

"I have to communicate remotely because I'm too ashamed of all my old gear," she argued with a grin. "And anyway, the computer's not set up yet, and mobile 'phone reception in the mountains is a bit poor —"

"'A bit poor' wasn't the phrase you used when we talked about it a couple of days ago," Peter reminded her. "You used one very short word instead."

Lucy frowned and glanced anxiously at her father before continuing. "Anyway, with no computer yet and mobiles being... er... *dodgey*. I can see I'm going to go out and meet my public face-to-face. I men, how's a girl to arrange her social life with just an ordinary *wall-mounted* telephone?"

"How indeed. I don't know how my generation managed to cope with such obsolete technology," said Alun.

There was a squeal from the hall, and Bryn burst in, closely followed by Tipsy. "Mummy, mummy," he burst out excitedly. "Johnny's got a dog."

"So they have." She leaned down to fuss Tipsy. "He's nice... or she's nice."

"He. Tipsy," advised Lucy.

"Tipsy? An unusual name."

Lucy smiled wistfully. "We got him from a home. He looked so sweet. He had something wrong with his ear and didn't have any balance. He looked drunk. And mum wouldn't let me call him 'Pissed'."

Peter felt a veil descend upon the room at the mention of his mother, drawing a new atmosphere into the room like a breath of melancholy.

There was a silence until Rhiannon's cautious voice changed the subject. Her grin has dissolved. "I've spoken with... er... Alun about working for you. Is there anything either of you want to ask me?"

"Only, when can you start?" said Lucy.

"Now's good for me. Peter?"

He paused. There seemed no practical reason why she shouldn't be hired. *But Morgan... it would be great if she could have the job.*

"Fine," he eventually replied. "Johnny seems to be getting along with Bryn, so if you know how to fire a bottle of cleaner I think the matter's settled." He hoped the disappointment was absent from his voice as he looked around the room, grasping for a sign of dissent. He found none until Johnny's voice sailed from the living room.

"What about your girlfriend?" asked his younger brother from the living room. "She wanted to look after me."

Disappointment threw itself across Rhiannon's face.

"Girlfriend, brother? I forgot Johnny mentioning it, what with all the excitement of seeing Rhiannon again. I think we need to hear more."

"Later."

"Yes, talk about it later," said Johnny. "You two get all yucky when you're in love. I don't want to listen."

"Yeah, later," agreed Peter quickly.

"But she was nice, wasn't she Peetie?"

"*Nice*, brother?"

"Pretty," added Johnny.

"Was she really, brother?"

"Yes. I suppose she is." *Absolutely stunning.*

Lucy turned to Rhiannon. "He usually pulls stuff that barks, does its business in the garden and needs a lead."

"They're not that bad."

"Yes they are." Lucy turned back to Rhiannon. "You should have seen the last one he had back in Swindon. Before we moved up here.

Even dad described her as plain. Didn't you, dad? And dad's known for his tact."

"I suppose she'd have been out of her depth in a beauty contest," Alun admitted. He shrugged helplessly in Peter's direction.

"She had a good personality," Peter argued.

"So did Hitler. At least, Eva Braun probably thought so. Or was it her willingness that was attractive?"

"Who, Eva's?"

"No, you pillock. Caroline's. Caroline Barker. An appropriate name if ever I heard one."

"Willing at what?" asked Bryn, his face a picture of innocence.

"Your father or I will explain when you're older," said Rhiannon.'

"Her name's Morgan," said Johnny. "We met her when we were painting this morning. She's got a massive dog." He stretched his arms out wide to emphasise the point.

"Does she live around here?" asked Rhiannon.

Peter wondered if his face was a red as it felt. "I thought you'd probably know her. She says she's a local. And there can't be too many Morgans around?"

She shook her head. "I don't know anyone called Morgan. You don't know her second name? I'd probably know her family."

Peter shrugged. He could have kicked himself for forgetting to ask.

"In a small place like Nantbran I'd expect to know her." Rhiannon paused thoughtfully. "There are some hippy types living in a few tents and caravans a couple of miles down the road, though. One of them might be called Morgan. They don't really mix with the locals. They just come to the village to shop and use the pub." She screwed her nose up in obvious distaste.

"I don't think so. She didn't seem a hippy type. Too wholesome. And I'm sure she mentioned her dad being a local farmer."

A puzzled frown caressed her brow. "Sorry. I've no idea. If her parents are farmers it doesn't sound like she's only just moved here. So I doubt she's an *immigrant*."

The last word was spat out, reminding Peter of his father's warning of Snowdonian attitudes towards newcomers. He found himself caressing his chin, and pulled his hand away. "You said you could start now? Lucy's not got a date tonight, but she may still want to spend a couple of hours in the bathroom later *trying* to beautify herself."

"Cheers, bruv. At least I come out of the bog looking passable. Caroline Barker would have looked better if she'd kept her face pack on."

Rhiannon ignored the sibling jibes, as if used to them already. She left her seat and leaned into the cupboard under the sink. "The cleaning stuff used to be kept in here... oh, great!... Some bast... I mean some *idiot's* shoved it all to the back. I can only just reach it."

Peter looked down, watching her disappear into the cupboard. He couldn't help noticing the way her Bermuda shorts tightened against her rear.

He caught his sister's gaze. She flicked her eyes to the ceiling. "Pervert!" She mouthed.

Peter grinned. "I know," he mouthed back.

Chapter 8

Bran and Dermot rode as if driven by demons, continually encouraging their mounts to greater efforts. Time was waning. Finding and calming two animals after exposure to the carnage of war had cost valuable time.

The sky dimmed from the east. Bran's mount flared its nostrils, exertion drooling from its mouth. He wished he knew the animal's name. Having something to call the beast would make it easier to control and encourage. His hands gripped the reigns tightly—he wondered where Majestic was—but he was hopeful of reaching Abberffraw before the sun slid into the western ocean.

He realised he hadn't yet wondered how Caswallon had fared.

"Dermot! In front. Dismount!" Bran had seen the dust betraying a mounted force on the track ahead. He stalled the horse and led it into the woods. Dermot did the same, although his gestures showed frustration at the delay.

"Can't we just ride off the roads? This is the third time we've had to stop for Romans."

"No." Bran ran a hand through this beard. The other stroked his horse's mane, gently quieting it. "You know well there are marshes and soft sand all along this stretch of coast. Better arrive careful than be swallowed by a bog on the way."

The young man sighed. His hands fidgeted. The rattle of hooves was nearing, and the two Britons clamped their horses' mouths.

As the riders neared their hiding place Bran counted five riders, but his head snapped round in response to a sound further into the woods. "Sshh! What was that?"

"A deer. Over there," whispered Dermot, pointing to a doe. "Scared by the noise."

Bran nodded once as he saw the animal. The animal stood still as a stone, sniffing at the air before bolting in wide-eyed panic.

Heading straight for the road.

The leading Roman yelled in triumph as the doe emerged only a few paces in front of his horse. It froze as terror took its legs. The Roman spurred his mount on, raised a sword, and thrust it into the animal's neck.

Blood flowed. The horseman yelled in triumph, but although Bran knew the Latin tongue the words were lost in turmoil. The animal fell to its knees, but before it could die with its dignity intact the four remaining Romans had joined the attack, thrusting and slashing. Even when it had fallen lifeless to the ground the bloodcrazed cavalrymen dismounted to continue their work.

It wasn't until the animal was lying in pieces that they remounted, laughing and boasting at their bravery, before leaving the carcass for carrion to pick clean.

"It is no wonder the Iceni plan revolt," said Dermot incredulously. "What manner of men could resort to such butchery?"

"The sort of men from whom your family are in danger," reminded Bran. "Come, let us remount and ride to Abberffraw."

The horses objected to the renewed exercise, but Bran and Dermot showed no mercy, stopping only to inspect from the saddle a roadside grove mutilated by the Eagles. Bran shook his head at the sight of trees and stones, which had stood for generations, ripped down and defiled with blood of animals whose remains the Romans had left to rot.

He mouthed a silent prayer for the safety of his own sacred pool.

Eventually, father and son reached the summit of a low ridge. The king's winter hall and the dependent settlement were laid out before them, and Bran's eyes were immediately drawn to the thatch burning beaconlike in the dying light.

"By the gods, Bran, they've got here first. Let's go!"

Bran urged caution, but Dermot forced his horse on the open road, ignoring the threat of Roman patrols. The night was silent but for the crackling of flames hooves pounding the earthen track.

But the settlement was free of the Eagles.

Indeed, devoid of all life. Not the bustling town he knew, with men labouring, women gossiping and children whooping.

Where were the women and children of the Ordovices? A knot of dread formed in Bran's stomach. It didn't take The Sight to know something was wrong.

"By the fires, Bran, they've beaten us here." Dermot's words called through the dark. The Archdruid paused to pull a burning plank from the King's hall as a makeshift torch. The flames threw shadows across his son's already drawn features tinted his colouring. The corners of his mouth had fallen slack. Bran lifted the torch over the scene of devastation.

Bodies lay scattered around Abberffaw. Men had been slaughtered where they stood, makeshift weapons in their hands as they fought against overwhelming odds to ward off their attackers.

"Where are our women? KYRA?" There was panic in Dermot's voice now. He called his wife's name over and over, but received no response. He ran from building to building, stepping over bodies of friends to search out evidence of his family. Bran followed, trying to restrain his son.

"Dermot! Dermot! Calm yourself. Panicking isn't going to help. We need—" the sight that lay beyond his son, just within the flames' grasp, strangled his voice.

Dermot turned to follow his father's gaze. He stiffened.

"Wait there." Bran wanted to spare his son any agony. He held the torch before him and stepped forward to investigate the scattering of female bodies. He managed to put one foot before the other, despite everything inside him telling him to turn around and flee. Far better, his mind and soul told him, not to find what he knew must be there: the find that would destroy his son's life.

A disturbed rat scuttled from its meal of flesh.

Bran felt his jaw quiver, his legs weakening with every step. The bodies were still and silent except for the occasional flutter of a linen dress in the breeze. That same breeze which refused to cool Bran's fear-induced sweat.

He reached the bodies and looked back. Dermot was still as a statue, silhouetted against the burning hall. His arms hung limply at his side. Bran was glad his son's face was hidden by darkness.

He knelt, surrounded by carnage. A dozen or so women lay face down, the earth around each of them stained dark with blood. With trembling hands, Bran rolled one of the corpses onto its back.

He breathed a sigh of relief. He didn't recognise the woman, but stopped to mumble a prayer on her behalf.

The next woman was Brigit, an aged, overweight battleaxe and cousin of Novax. Bran knew he would have to break the news of her death to his enemy.

If Novax was still alive.

He took his torch over to the next corpse. Bile rose in his throat at the sight of a familiar cloak. The instantly recognisable, richly embroidered cloak Kyra was so proud of. Familiar long brown hair streamed from her head.

There was no doubting whose body he had found, but gently he rolled the corpse over, hoping against hope that he was wrong, praying to Bel that she had lent her cloak to another woman.

But it wasn't to be. Kyra's sightless eyes looked up at him, her contorted face a deathmask of terror and pain. He gently dignified her by closing her eyes to the world before looking down at her body. Her blood covered his hands and almost without thinking he wiped his fingers on his cloak.

His breath locked. The upper portion of her skirt was stained with blood. He looked away, trying not to imagine the mutilation between her legs. "By the fires, I pray that they did this to her when she was dead," he whispered through taut lips. But he knew from the agony in her staring eyes his prayer was in vain.

"What is it, Bran? What have you found?" Dermot's voice was strained, as if he already knew the answer.

"Stay away, lad, stay away."

But Dermot stepped forward. "Why? What is it? For the sake of the earth! No!" He fell to the ground and swept the body into his arms before breaking into sobs. "I saw death, Bran." He looked up, his face anguished. "I saw her death and thought it was my own. I thought *I* was to die. Why didn't I know? Why didn't I do something?"

Bran couldn't answer. For the first time in years he wanted to vomit. A stream a few paces away was revealed by the jumping light of the flames; dropping the firebrand he leaned over and emptied his breakfast into the waters.

As Bran wiped his lips on a tuft of grass, something downstream caught the edge of his sight. A white bundle of rags caught in the reeds. Feeling slightly better for his sickness, he stood to investigate.

As he picked the bundle up, he wished he hadn't. It was too heavy to be rags. Something was wrapped up in it. Bran knew it was a baby.

And, even before he pulled a stray piece of material away from its face, he knew whose baby.

"Conor," he whispered at the lifeless child. "Oh that Dermot should be spared this too. What sort of animals are these Romans that they throw away a helpless babe to drown?"

But death had a final trick to play on the Archdruid. Conor's arm slumped forward, his hand outstretched towards Bran as if in a pitiful plea for help.

Tears moistened Bran's cheeks.

Only heartbeats later a scream rent the night air as Dermot grieved for a son as well as a wife.

Bran left his son to mourn in peace. He took himself to one of the few unburned huts, a small but comfortable single roomed dwelling. A recent coat of mud and straw protected the stone walls against sea breezes. It had belonged to a craftsman. *What had been his name? Maelmur? Yes that was it. Maelmur. A fastidious man,* Bran remembered; tweezers and a small hammer were among the tools carefully placed in an open container before the man had fled or become one of the corpses outside. And the floor had been newly swept. The man's wife, whose name escaped even the finely tuned memory of a Druid, had been the perfect, fussy partner for him.

Bran chided his mind for wandering to the owners of an insignificant hut. *There was a crisis surrounding the Ordovices.* The desperate situation should be in his thoughts. *The tribe is devastated, the groves of the Sacred Isle destroyed around me. The king may or may not be dead.*

And Caladchlog, the Rainbow Sword. Bran ran a hand over his beard.

What had become of the Rainbow Sword, the hope for British freedom? Why had the Gods deserted it?

It was then that he heard the groan. Hope leaped to his throat. He eased himself into a standing position as quickly as his tired body would allow, and shuffled to the workshop at the rear of the hut. Darkness dimmed his eyes, but he heard the groan again. A man's voice. Then some words to accompany the voice.

And Bran's heart fell to his stomach.

The man spoke in Latin.

A Roman!

Maybe this was one of the men who had tortured and defiled Kyra before she died. Maybe it had been this man who had sliced a sword across her throat.

Maybe this was the man who had thrown the defenceless Conor into the water to drown. Bran chilled at the thought.

As his eyes adjusted to the light he saw the wounded man clearly. He wore the segmented armour and red tunic of the Eagles. His red shield, emblazoned with golden lightning strikes, lay discarded beside him. The soldier bled from a wound which had nearly severed his foot from his shin.

The man had obviously seen Bran; his short but deadly legionary sword pointed towards him, protecting a face that wore an expression mixing fear, pain and Latin pride. Bran raised his hands slowly, palms towards the foreigner, who visibly relaxed on seeing Bran was unarmed.

The Druid cupped a hand and made a drinking motion. The man nodded. Bran backed out of the workshop, hands still raised.

He took one of Maelmur's moulds as a makeshift cup and made for the stream.

"Bran?" Dermot looked up from his grieving, the dirt on his face streaked with tears. "How can you work at a time like this?"

"I found a wounded man in the craftsman's workshop. He's asked for water." Bran held out the small container he was carrying to emphasise the point.

"A Briton? Does he say what happened here? Did he fight valiantly? Is he well enough to tell us?"

Bran wished he'd bitten his tongue. But he had gone too far to lie. He sighed. "No. Not a Briton. The man is Roman."

"A warrior of the Eagles?"

Bran nodded reluctantly.

Dermot's eyes sharpened in the firelight like a newly wrought sword. His face displayed hatred, an emotion Bran had never before seen his son. "Take me to him."

"Dermot, listen to me. It would do no good. He cannot speak our language. He couldn't tell you what happened."

"By the gods, I don't want to talk to him," Dermot said bitterly. "My wife and child have been butchered and one of the men responsible lies only a few paces away. I claim him, Bran. Do not stand in my way." He paused for a second to give emphasis to his next sentence. "I claim his death for my own. By Ordovician law, I have a right to vengeance on the man who killed my wife."

As his son pushed past him, Bran pleaded for the Roman. "Make it swift and sure, Dermot. The Eagle is dying anyway. There has been enough suffering on the Sacred Isle for one day."

Dermot lifted the terrified and crippled Roman, keeping his sword against the man's throat. Paying little heed as he the soldier whimpered in pain, Dermot forced him up one of the low hills overlooking Abberffraw and the bay beyond. Atop the ridge, standing beaconlike on the horizon stood a single, ancient standing stone. He stripped the man of his armour and clothes before ripping his tunic into shreds and tying him in a standing position to the megalith.

Bran followed close behind, his fingers clasping a makeshift torch.

"Look into my eyes," whispered Dermot.

The Roman stared incomprehensibly back, eyes wide open in terror. As if knowing he was to die.

"Interpret, Bran. Tell him what I'm saying."

The Archdruid did as he was bid.

"I want the last thing he sees to be the face of a ruined husband and father. Tell him, Bran. Tell him about Kyra and Conor."

As Bran finished relating his son's grief, Dermot grabbed the Roman's close-cropped hair and held his head steady. The soldier tried to twist away, begging for mercy in his own tongue. Dermot ignored his pleas, spitting into the Latin face before slowly and deliberately levelling the sword and sinking the blade into the soldier's eye.

A scream mingled with blood in the night air.

"Make it quick, Dermot. His screams will draw patrols."

"I want this to be slow," Dermot whispered as he edged the red-tinted sword towards the legionary's other eye. "If his Roman friends show I'll fall on my sword. What have I got to live for anyway, other than revenge?"

* * * *

Peter Davis turned in his sleep, his body wet with sweat.

I watched a man's eye taken out!

His breaths came in short, sharp bursts. Vomit rose in his throat.

Gotta get out of here. Don't want to watch.

* * * *

Bran shook his head and returned to Aberffraw, wondering why the slaughter revolted him. As a Druid he had killed for the gods more than once.

But he found himself revolted by the sight of freely flowing blood.

The Roman's agony rent the evening air as it was carried to the sea on the breeze. The sounds of suffering continued into the night, at some times a single, long scream, at others a low groan. Using all his training, Bran blotted the sounds from his mind, hoping they wouldn't attract the attention of a Roman patrol.

To keep his mind occupied he washed the blood from Kyra's body.

Eventually the air went quiet and Dermot returned. Satisfaction was etched across his tired features.

"Is it over?" Bran asked.

"It is."

There was silence between father and son.

* * * *

"Let us bury them now," Bran suggested as the morning peered over the hill, silhouetting the slumped body still tied to the ancient stone. He laid a hand on Dermot's shoulder. "There won't be time for the usual ceremony. But I'm sure Arawn of the Otherworld will look favourably upon the souls of two such innocent creatures."

Dermot's nodded his assent and Bran scooped up Kyra's limp body. Although her skin was clean, blood still stained her blue cloak. Dermot followed his father up the slope towards the stone with Conor cradled in his arms, one hand also clumsily grasping his harp.

"Here?" asked Dermot.

"Here. The megalith will focus the earth's energies on them. Their souls will be safe."

Dermot nodded vaguely before unsheathing his sword and cutting the bonds from the dead Roman. He pushed the naked body down the slope for the carrion. Bran noticed the skilfully wrought wounds on the dead man's flesh, and remembered the screams carrying through the night. *Dermot's blade has done an expert's job*, he thought to himself again.

Bran wondered where his son had learned the skills of death.

They dug. Dermot used his sword to loosen the soil while Bran pulled the ground away with his bare hands. The fertile earth of the Sacred Isle came away easily, for which Bran silently praised the gods.

- 71 -

Bran took a sharp stone from the earth, and despite its edges cutting into his fingers, carved four short marks into the standing rock.

'K' for Kyra, in ogham, the written tongue of the Druids. And another, beneath, for Conor.

Bran lifted Kyra's body again and placed her in her resting-place. Dermot put his son in the grave soon after, arranging the bodies so that Kyra lay with her arms around their son. Then he placed his harp, his most treasured possession, on top of their chests.

"I have no wish to sing anymore. My songs go with them."

"What will you do?"

"I will be a Druid. That is the way I may best help drive the Eagles from Britain."

Bran frowned. "Don't use Druidism for revenge, Dermot." He turned and retreated down the hill, leaving the lad alone once more to grieve.

"What could I have done to avoid such bloodshed?" he asked the gods.

His flesh tingled as he earned a response.

"The sword. Cadalachelog, the Rainbow Sword of Fergus mac Roy. Give me the sword and Britain's troubles will end."

Bran looked around him. He couldn't tell from which direction the words had come; indeed, they seemed to come from all around, from the air itself.

After seeing no one except Dermot, grieving in the middle distance, Bran looked skyward. A raven screeched as it circled above him.

The Archdruid shivered.

* * * *

Peter Davis awoke. He was used to the sweat and strained muscles his dreams imposed upon him. But his time there was a new emotion.

Elation.

I did it! I controlled Bran! I got away from the torture.

He calmed as a thought swept across him.

Does that mean I am Bran?

Chapter 9

Peter looked up from his easel. "Hello, hello. This is some surprise. It's only eight o'clock!"

Lucy stuck out her tongue and struggled to drag a deck chair up the bank. "You could help."

"Bit early for you, sis?"

"Sorry. No teasing until I've had a coffee." She gesticulated at Johnny's brightly coloured rucksack which clung precariously to her back. "I don't think my body's cut out for getting up at a time when it should be going to bed. Christ." Letting the chair fall, she gave a long breath and parked herself next to Peter, arms clasped around her knees.

"So why *are* you up so early?"

She pulled a strand of uncombed hair from her eyes. "To keep an eye on my brother."

"Huh?"

"To supervise your painting."

"You've never been the least bit interested in watching me before."

"You've never needed to support the family before. You'll get that picture finished today if I have to stand over you with a horsewhip."

"Yeah. The quicker I get the production line up and running, the sooner you'll be able to hit the shopping malls of Caernarfon."

"Humph. You think shopping's hit North Wales?" She put on a mock town crier voice. "Oyez! Oyez! Read all abaht it! Wheel invented. Chariot showroom now opened. Mammoth-fur mini-skirts now in stock!" Her tone changed. "I *don't* think so. It's catalogue shopping for me from now on. Unless you fancy taking me on a day trip to Chester?" Her eyebrows rose hopefully.

"But you need me back here, churning out the masterpieces to fund your shopping habits. Remember?"

"We could take Morgan. The poor yokel has probably never seen a *real* shop."

Peter felt his face crack into a grin. "I know the reason you're here, hassling me at eight o'clock in the morning."

"You do?"

"You want to run an eye over her, don't you?"

She pouted indignantly, but with smiling eyes. "Who?"

"Morgan. And don't act all innocent."

"Oh, brother dearest! You know me. I wouldn't *dream* of interfering in your love life. But, seeing as how you've put the idea in my head, I suppose it wouldn't do any harm to meet her."

"Don't you dare! Go away!"

"You can't mean it? I'll put in a good word for you. We all know you're too shy to put a good one in for yourself."

"I certainly can mean it."

"Pig!"

"Bitch! Please sis. Keep out of this. For me?"

"Humph." She stood and folded her arms across her chest. "I only want to reassure myself she's good enough for you. I'll go and sit over by the old church."

"Okay. As long as it keeps you quiet."

"Moi? On one condition."

"Name it."

"*You* carry the deckchair. I'm shagged."

"Lucky you."

Lucy muttered under her breath as she traipsed behind Peter. "Are you *sure* you don't want me to stay and…"

"Yes. Perfectly sure. Or else I'll introduce you as Lucinda."

"You wouldn't."

"I would. See you later."

"Humph."

Peter returned to his easel and settled down. Unlike yesterday, though, his hobby was no comforting escape from the confines of reality. He was pleased this was a morning for finishing touches. The passion had been needed for the basic structure of yesterday's work. His mind kept wandering to the Sacred Isle—*no, Anglesey*—he reminded himself, and the carnage at Abberffraw. And the loss he had felt as Bran; the loss he was still feeling, with tears of anguish waiting to bubble to the surface.

He forced himself back to his picture.

Nearly finished.

The low mound with its moss-stippled bricks stood proudly in the foreground of his scene. Peter had added a wooden cross, fallen at an angle, to mark the rough rectangle as a place or worship.

The ancient circle had been re-erected so that the stones stood once more. He had removed the years from their flesh, so they gleamed like marble in the noonday sun. The copse of oaks spread healthy green boughs over the circle, as if protecting the monoliths from the forces of evil.

A few paces away his painting had transformed the marshy hollow into a sun-reflecting pond of blue, with the brook gurgling happily as it escaped down the valley. Contented cows drank lazily from its edge.

The friendly old house hardly needed embellishment in Peter's eyes. All he had added was a homely wisp of smoke spiralling skyward from the chimney.

He had not included the cairn in his picture. He preferred to shut out memories of whatever it was he had felt escape from the mound.

He looked towards Lucy. A puff of cigarette smoke shrouded her head for an instant before dissipating.

His mind stayed away from his work and to Morgan. He looked anxiously up the path, waiting, willing her to appear. But some of him hoped she wouldn't be walking Owain today.

A childish fear stoked itself inside him, as he panicked at the prospect of meeting her again. He caressed his chin as he thought about trying to impress her, and hoping to find the right words to say. Despite the cool of the morning, his hands slipped with nervous sweat. He had to wipe them on a brush-cleaning rag before he could continue.

The painting's nearly finished, he thought. *I can add the final touches inside. If I was in the house I wouldn't have to worry about meeting Morgan.*

Christ! I'd do that just to avoid saying "hello" to her? I'd regret it for ever!

But while he though about packing up his decision was made for him. There was a dog's bark from along the track. Not the bark of any dog, but a low, guttural warning to anything even thinking about challenging him.

The sound of a dog which could only be Owian.

Only seconds later Morgan and her animal came into view.

Peter's nervousness gained a new edge as Owain bounded along the path, until his mistress gave the most delicate of hand gestures and the brute fell into step at her side.

Peter rose, his breath coming in shallow gasps. His heart pounded. His hands sweated again.

Morgan!

He looked toward his sister, who responded with a reassuring raised thumb, obviously having heard Owain's bark.

Hoping his legs wouldn't collapse, he jumped down the bank towards Morgan, trying to remember his carefully rehearsed speech. But his mind was too fuddled. He knew it would be a major effort to get any sound from his lips.

She was wearing exactly the same clothes as yesterday, he noted. Her black dress swirled around her, following her movements, as it had done at their previous meeting.

"Hello, Morgan," he said, forcing his voice level. He wished she'd take off her sunglasses. He wanted to peer into her passive, deep hazel gaze once more.

"Hello, Peter. How's the painting going?" She hitched up her dress up a few inches to climb the bank, looking around coyly as Peter tried not to let the gentle movements of her body draw his gaze.

He scrambled up after her. "I wish I could climb as easily as you."

She smiled at the compliment and nodded towards the picture. "It's coming on. Is it finished?"

"Should be finished sometime today. I've hit a bit of Painter's Block this morning, though."

"Painter's Block?"

"It's like Writer's Block, only it happens to painters." He hoped the joke didn't sound limp.

Her grin reassured him. "Hmm. It's still looking fine to me. No Johnny and Tipsy today?"

"No. But my sister's here."

"Yes. Lucy." She raised a hand and the gesture was returned.

"Johnny's gone into Caernarfon with dad to buy some clothes. Now his health's improving, touch wood," he laid a finger on a paintbrush handle. "We've realised he hasn't got any tough clothes to play outside in. He's never needed them."

"Poor mite. It must have been so hard for all of you." Her jawline softened.

There was a purr from the distance. Morgan's brow furrowed as she watched Rhiannon's van navigate the long gravel drive. She chewed her lower lip, not looking away from the van until it stopped and Rhiannon jumped out with Bryn. Lucy rose and entered the house with them. The soft tone of girlish giggles carried on the breeze; Peter had no doubt he and Morgan were the objects of the conversation.

Morgan's arm rose theatrically as she extended an accusing finger in the direction of Peter's relatives.

"Who is that woman?"

"Er, yeah. That's Rhiannon. Rhiannon Jones. She's a cousin. And Bryn's her son."

She turned to face him and ripped her sunglasses from her face. Her eyes, at last, showed emotion. Suspicious and untrusting.

"*Cousin?* You told me you were new to the mountains. Now you tell me you have kin here?"

The ferocity of her voice threw Peter on the defensive. "I told me we were half Welsh. But what does it matter?"

"What does it matter? *What does it matter?* You told me you were new. For centuries *immigrants* have made pacts with the Celtic people with words of peace, but with swords concealed behind their backs. And I thought you might be different. Centuries ago your sort would have been good only as food for the gods."

"I'm sorry, but dad bumped into her in the shop. And she was looking for some childminding. And her son's about Johnny's age. And..." He trailed off, aware that his words were beginning to flow uncontrolled. Morgan's intensity had taken him aback.

"But you said *I* could look after Johnny."

"I said I'd try. I said I'd speak to dad... I'm really sorry."

"Pah! You let that... that *harlot* and her bastard son into your household? Liar!" Her face hardened into a contortion of pure hatred. Her beautiful yet ferocious features contained... contained... *evil?*

Peter found himself stepping away from her.

"I should have known! For all your flowery words and finery. You *immigrants* are all the same. You come here over the ages and take our land and our liberty. And now you...you even give Celtic jobs to *witches.*" She spat between Peter's feet. "May the forces of the Earth strike you and your family down."

Glaring at Peter, her eyes finally sparkled into life. As if they were made to hate. As if her whole being enjoyed hating.

"Morgan! Hold off a second. It's not that big a deal."

"*Not that big a deal,*" she mimicked. "You wouldn't say that if *your* people were facing the yoke. You've already ignored one warning."

Peter winced as Owain snarled. Morgan let the animal threaten for a moment before clicking her fingers, when the dog silenced. But Owain's eyes never left Peter's face, glaring at him as if only just able to prevent himself from pouncing.

With a short glare over her shoulder, Morgan led her pet down the path toward the village of Nantbran.

"Howd'it go?"

"Huh?" Peter turned as Lucy bounded down the bank. He slumped into a sitting position, resting his twisting stomach.

"How did it go? With Morgan?" She paused. "Not too well, I take it? I missed the show when Rhiannon arrived. Didn't catch a sodding word."

"She... she just went mad. Exploded."

"Why? Oh Peter. You didn't?"

"Didn't what?"

"Make an... er... *suggestion?* Shit. It'll be all over Nantbran. My brother, the sex pervert."

Peter felt himself snap. "For Christ's sake, Lucy, grow up! I'm not in the mood." He took a breath to steady himself. "If you must know she just went loopy when I told her dad had already asked Rhiannon to babysit Johnny."

Lucy looked mildly disappointed. "Is that all? No scandal?"

"Nope. Nothing. She just went like a madman."

"Mad*woman* you mean."

"For Christ's sake. Like I told you. She just went loopy. She threatened me… us… the family, you know?"

Lucy's grin folded. "What sort of threats? Dad warned us about people around here not liking the English. Firebombs through letterboxes and that. Shit. We can do without that."

"No. Nothing like that."

"What then?"

"Just weird. Like she was *cursing* us. And she said I'd already had one warning." He caressed his chin. "I don't remember any warning."

Lucy looked relieved. "Look, bruv. I know you liked her and she's pretty and all that, but if she's just going to fuck you about and make stupid threats you're better off without her. She sounds unbalanced."

"Yeah."

"Honest, Pete. I'm a bit of a bitch with blokes myself. I know what I'm talking about."

"Yeah." But his eyes traced the path down the slope, holding out the faint hope that Morgan would reappear over the horizon to ask for his forgiveness. But he knew it wasn't going to happen. "And another thing."

"What?"

"She knew your name."

"So?"

"I don't think I've told her your name."

"Humph. I'm that unimportant to you, am I? She probably heard it in the village."

"Yeah," he reluctantly agreed.

"Peter?"

"Yeah?"

"Come on. Let's get the painting inside." She looked away in an obvious attempt not to see Peter's work.

But he didn't care whether she looked at it or not.

* * * *

The evening was pushed out of the house by an electric light as Peter finally finished his painting and, having let it dry to the touch, draped his red 'Unveiling Silk' over it.

He was ready to show his family. The excitement drove Morgan from his mind.

For a few seconds.

"DAD! LUCY! JOHNNY! IT'S READY," he shouted to the rest of the house. He was answered by whoops from Johnny, an "At last," from Lucy, and barking from Tipsy. Peter knew his father would be eager to see the picture too, but would retain a dignified silence before saying how much he liked it.

Soon the family was crowded around Peter's easel, with the red silk covering the picture. He cleared his throat theatrically. "Ladies and gentleman…"

"You mean *lady* and gentleman…"

"Oh heck, he's going to wade through a speech…"

"As I was saying, *lady* and gentleman…"

"There's no lady here…"

"Can *I* take your Unveiling Silk off? Can I, Peetie? Please?"

He raised his hand to quieten the room. "As I was saying…"

"…Before you were so *rudely* interrupted…"

"Just get on with it…"

"As I was saying. *Lady* and gentlemen, we are gathered here today to witness my first painting in our new home. I call it…"

"Can I take the Unveiling Silk off now, Peetie?"

"I call it 'View of Nantbran'," Peter smiled, enjoying the family banter.

"Can I do it now, Peetie?"

"Okay, Johnny. You can unveil it now."

With a sweep of his hand belying his young age, Johnny pulled the red silk from the canvas.

There was momentarily silence.

Until Johnny screamed and ran from the room.

Alun shook his head and glared at Peter before following his youngest son.

"Fuckin' hell, Pete. That's sick," swore Lucy, shaking her head and storming out, closely followed by a yapping Tipsy.

Peter collapsed back onto his painting stool, his eyes drawn to the scene in front of him.

"I didn't paint this," he gasped to himself.

In front of him the scene had changed from the one he had covered with silk only minutes earlier. At least, the scene was the same. It was still the view of the farmhouse from the bank. But gone was the sunshine and carefree attitude of his creation.

Instead the picture was a tribute to death and suffering. Black clouds hung from the mountains like palls from a thousand funeral pyres. Day gave way to night, with the silver glow from the moon somehow finding a way through the smoke.

But the scene it illuminated was one Peter would rather have had hidden. Wolves scoured the plain around the house looking for scraps among thorns and stark boulders. The pool had been replaced by a swamp, from which creatures emerged to enjoy the cover of the night. Peter's eyes widened as they were drawn to the stones, where his family were tied, naked, to the monoliths which stood beneath oaks whose boughs seemed to want to reach out to strangle them.

This is just like the vision I had. When we first arrived.

"I DIDN'T PAINT THIS," Peter shouted. He ran to the door. "LUCY! JOHNNY! DAD! I DIDN'T PAINT THIS. IT WASN'T ME. IT...IT'S...A *WARNING?*"

He remembered Morgan's words. *"You've already ignored one warning."*

Is this a warning? What of? And does it have to do with Bran and the dreams?

He slumped back onto his stool. But the scene of evil had gone.

The picture was as he had finished it.

Perfect.

Chapter 10

Archdruid Bran paced the Feasting hall of Tre'r Ceiri as he spoke. "…but, my Lord, we must please the gods…" He would have continued addressing the Council of the Ordovices, but his voice was drowned by another roar of thunder. He paused and raised his eyes to the sodden thatch, watching raindrops all from the rafters to the earthen floor. He lamented the loss of the master thatcher at the slaughter of the Sacred Isle.

He suppressed a shiver and pulled his white cloak tightly around him. The rains made his joints ache.

King Caswallon looked troubled in his robe of Roman purple. Beside him, Druid Novax rose to speak. He cleared his throat as the gods' roar faded into the distance. "And which god would you have us appease, Archdruid?"

"My Lord, the rains fall incessantly upon the crops of the Ordovices." Bran's hand gestured towards the leaking roof. "In the days of your ancestors there was land to grow corn and raise cattle. The rains came only in moderation, and in the planting season. Now the Goddess Boann sends waters to threaten the very existence of the Ordovices. The rivers overflow."

Novax snorted.

"The rains are ceaseless," continued Bran. "The Sacred Isle was the Breadbasket of Cambria, but her fields are now nothing more than bogs. The Ordovices have barely enough food to feed themselves, even before the depredations of Roman plunder." He sat down. His ageing legs had stood long enough. "Let the Lady Boann, Mistress of the Waters, have the gift of the sword. Maybe then she will take the accursed rains from Britain…"

Novax interrupted. "What about the Romans? What about the revolt? Boudicca must have the sword to drive the Eagles from Britain."

Bran glared and continued. "Caswallon, I speak for peace. I cannot guarantee that the Romans would not come again, but let us have healthy land to defend should they choose to invade." He leaned back in his chair, aware that his words could keep the sword from the Warrior Queen. He would not—*could* not—allow Boudicca to tighten her fingers around the hilt of Caladchlog. *The Warrior Queen must not fall under Andraste's spell. The Lady of Battle must not be permitted to ally with a woman whose heart overflowed with bloodlust.*

Evil must not prevail.

Novax threw his hands towards the heavens, as if seeking an injunction from the Goddess herself. "But to give the sword to the waters would be madness! Already our friends in the east, the Iceni, plan revolt against the legions of Rome. How would Britain triumph in battle without the magic sword of Fergus mac Roy?" Fire momentarily shone from his dulled eyes as he faced the Archdruid. "The weapon must go to Andraste, Lady of War, so that she may lead us to victory."

"But there is greater magic than even The Shimmering Sword," explained Bran levelly. "Next to the power of the Goddess Boann, even the sword of Fergus is a blunt instrument. But it is the greatest gift any mortal could possess."

"So we agree on one point, Archdruid!"

"Let us give it to appease the Goddess of the Waters, so that she may use its immortal powers to keep the rains from Britain, so our crops may grow once more, and we can feed our children."

Novax spat a gob of chewed willow to the floor. "Pah! And how would our children eat when they are slaughtered by the legions? Give the sword to appease the Goddess of the Water, and she may well take the rains from Britain. Our cattle would grow healthy, and our corn would grow. But will healthy crops bear weapons against the Eagles? No! The Romans will still defeat Britain and inherit our wheat. Our well-fed children will be slaves or carrion food." He slammed his fist on the table. "No. The sword must go to Andraste, that we may drive the Romans from Britain."

"But Boudicca has revenge in her heart. Victory for Britain, lead by the Battlesword, would mean slaughter borne of hatred."

"…and we have seen the slaughter that the Romans will impose on the Ordovices if we allow ourselves to be defeated," broke in Novax.

"So," cut in Sergovax, his eyes flitting between the priests, as if unsure of his footing, "Could we give the sword to Boudicca instead of Andraste? The Warrior Queen leads Britain! Give her the sword of Fergus and the Eagles will fall before her! And, as the sword-giver, Caswallon will be owed a place of power in the new Britain!"

"No!" snapped Caswallon. "The sword belongs to the Ordovices. To give it away to another tribe would be madness. We cannot afford to lose a lever to power amongst the tribes."

Caswallon sighed. "So, my Council, I must choose. I can give the sword to the waters and consign Britain to the Romans. Or I may give the weapon to Andraste to push the Eagles from Britain, and watch our island drown." Fingers fidgeted with his hair. "Has any king ever had a choice as grim? The two Druids present are divided. Who else will speak?

Remember, my advisors, that I have met Andraste, Goddess of War and Death. How many here can claim to have spoken with a deity?"

Silence met the king's words. Even Bran, while not doubting the existence of the gods, had never found himself face-to-face with an immortal. The Archdruid turned to Sergovax. "Could we drive the Romans from Britain without appeasing Andraste?"

The king's champion spoke carefully. "Bran is right. A kingdom could muster the greatest of champions, but without the gods' favour... I wouldn't even fight a slave woman if Andraste frowned on me."

"So, we must give one goddess the sword. Perhaps the other would accept more gold in its place? Or more prisoners? Maybe one of the ladies wants more blood shed for her?" King Caswallon's voice was eager as a winter wind.

Bran let out a gentle sigh of frustration. "Maybe so. But yours is a rich kingdom. Your sacred springs already overflow with gold and corpses. What else have you to give other than the sword?" He calmed himself with a deep breath. "Would you give our free men instead of slaves or criminals? How would you console mothers whose children are taken from them for sacrifice? Can you be confident that the Ordovices would not rise against you? And how," he continued, lowering his voice, "How do you know that noble blood would not be demanded? Maybe one of the men in this room, or even their child, should give their life for the tribe?"

There was a silence around the hall, broken by the sound of rain on thatch. Bran could feel fear enveloping the Council: his words were swaying the argument. No man would risk the lives of his family. "No, we must give her something precious, but let us stop short of the lives of your people until we know nothing else is acceptable."

King Caswallon sat silent as he pondered the weight of decision. All eyes looked to him, unspeaking. His fingers fidgeted with his fluffy beard, picking at lice as he fought indecision.

Bran took the time to study the men around him. All sat stern, knowing the magnitude of the decision. *Which goddess would the Ordovices appease?*

He leaned back and emptied his mug. The mead warmed his aching bones.

Somewhere outside a woman scolded a lazy husband.

A crack of thunder split the silence. Novax chewed willow and looked towards.

Sergovax still studied the floor.

Other men concentrated on avoiding the dripping water, or concentrated their gaze on empty jugs. Some watched mice in the thatch. All refused to meet the eyes of king and Druids. Being asked for an opinion would incur the enmity of ruler or priest.

Novax lifted his head to glare at Bran, resentment and mucus seeping from his eyes.

Finally, Bran's gaze fell on the one other man in the hall.

Dermot.

The bard kept his own council, maybe writing music in his mind. *Probably a lament for the lost,* Bran reflected sadly.

Caswallon chewed a knuckle.

Novax snorted and looked around the Hall with pleading eyes. He broke the silence. "Do I alone speak for the tribe? Are we to become... what? The lackeys of an eastern queen? A *woman?*" The last word was spat from between clenched teeth. "Let us give the sword to Andraste, the Battle-Lady. With victory in war will the floods matter? Our neighbours will become our slaves. We can take what we want! Let the Ordovices drive out the Empire and her whores! Let us rule Britain!" He looked around the Hall once more. "Is no-one with me?"

There were cautious nods of agreement. But still silence.

Until Dermot rose.

Breath locked itself in Bran's throat as the young man gained his feet and looked nervously around the hall.

Novax sat straight in his chair and flicked his wrist as a gesture that gave the bard permission to speak.

"Council of the Ordovices," he began, "I beg to speak. As a man who is to undertake Druid training so that I may serve the tribe."

Bran's heart descended. He remembered his words to the lad as he tortured the Roman warrior on the Sacred Isle: *"Don't use Druidism for revenge, Dermot."*

But Caswallon nodded for Dermot to continue.

"Council of the Ordovices, I am two men. One man is to become a Druid. The second is as a man whose future has been taken."

There were nods around the Hall. All knew of the deaths of Kyra and Conor.

And Bran found the image of baby Conor, hand reaching out to him in death, returning unbidden. He fought back a tear.

Dermot's voice was now level and confident. "I have suffered at the hands of the Romans. I have lost two who meant more to me than my own life. I know others in this hall have also lost people close to them. The suffering our tribe has endured must not happen again."

There were nods of sympathy from around the hall.

"The Romans have left our lands. But have they left the lands of the Trinovantes? Are the Duroteges free of the Eagle-yoke? Did the Romans withdraw from Iceni territory after raping the Warrior Queen?" He paused, his eyes meeting, one by one, the gazes of the Council. "No!" He almost shouted. "THE EAGLES EXTEND THEIR LANDS NORTHWARDS

AND WESTWARDS. ONE BY ONE THE TRIBES OF BRITAIN ARE SUBSUMED."

Bran looked to the floor. He had been present at Boudicca's defiling. The memories of her daughters being forced to watch would never leave him.

Sergovax raised a hand to stop Dermot. "If conquest is inevitable, why do we not offer ourselves for treaty? We would then be free to offer the sword to the waters."

Bran shook his head slowly. "Much as I would avoid bloodshed, Sergovax, capitulation is not an option. The Duroteges succumbed to Rome by treaty, yet are treated as slaves. Conquest or treaty; it is all the same to the Eagles."

Sergovax raised his eyes from the floor and looked enquiringly at his king.

Caswallon nodded, giving his champion permission to speak.

"My King, learned Druids, Members of the Council. Forgive my ignorance of the gods, but I am a humble warrior. But I know that the goddesses we speak of are powerful." He paused for nods and murmurs of agreement. "If that is so, why cannot Andraste take the sword for herself? And why can she not push the Eagles back into the sea unaided? Why does Andraste need our help?"

The warrior turned his head in Bran's direction, but it was Novax who cut in to speak. "Sergovax, there is no doubt that you are correct. The gods are powerful. But not all-powerful." He looked to Bran, and the Archdruid gave reluctant support with a gentle nod. "You will be aware, Sergovax, how Andraste was wounded by the throw of a mortal spear at the battle of the Ford of the Forked Pole?"

Sergovax nodded. All Celts knew the stories of their forefathers.

"Well," continued Sergovax. "This and other stories from our people's history show that Andraste has her weaknesses. In some ways she is very mortal—as are all the gods. The story of her wounding proves that. If she were to try to take the sword by force... our guards could cut her down, as they could a man."

"If they don't run away first," broke in Caswallon.

Novax glared his response to his king's immaturity before continuing. "And, remember, we fight the Romans and their gods. Powerful though Andraste is, she cannot take on gods and men at the same time. She needs us to defeat the Romans in war—although she will help—while she struggles with Mars, their own Wargod."

Sergovex nodded his understanding.

"Novax gives a good account," Bran admitted. "The gods need mortals to do their will on earth, almost as much as we need the gods to send the sun and to grow our crops, to ensure our safety, and to grant us

- 85 -

victory in war." A raindrop found its way through the thatch to smack the table in front of him. "But with the magic sword she would not need mortals. Its power, combined with her own, would give her all the strength she needs. She could force a rule of blood and death. Even the other gods combined would struggle to stop her."

Caswallon sighed and shifted uncomfortably. "The Ordovices are undecided. It seems the final decision must be mine."

All faces turned towards the king. Bran caressed his chin; the discussion had been even, and The Sight gave him no indication of which way the king would lean.

"I have the most impossible of choices. Do I ignore the rumblings of the Waters, and risk further floods? Or do I disregard the call of war, and consign the tribe to the depravations of Rome? Should the Ordovices die by war or starvation?" He spread his arms. "Bran paints a picture of suffering under Andraste. But would the slow deaths of famine and disease if we do not please Boann be any worse? I propose we give the sword to neither Boann nor Andraste."

"Neither?"

"Neither. Let us cast the weapon to the pool without favour. Let her who wants it most take it."

The silence in the hall could almost be felt.

Bran wrapped his white cloak tighter around him as his hands buried his head. His closed eyes saw the warrior-lambs at his sacred pool, bloodied on their meal of Roman flesh. The memories refused to be flung aside.

But the dispute was decided. The Archdruid's staff helped him from his seat and he walked with leaden feet to lay a conciliatory hand on the king's shoulder. "I know losing the sword will hurt your heart. I know how many generations of your line have guarded it jealously. But the time has come to relinquish your grip on its hilt. Let the gods know what you are prepared to sacrifice for your people. And for Britain."

Wearily, the king spoke. "Let us do it as soon as the formalities allow. I don't want time to change my mind." He turned and snapped at Dermot. "And I don't want to hear any more songs of the Rainbow Sword. I don't want to be reminded of the weapon of Fergus mac Roy. I want Britain to forget I ever owned it."

Dermot bowed to the king and cast a nervous glance to Novax before retreating, as if his self-assurance was used up by his debate-deciding speech.

Bran felt a pang of hurt.

He should have looked for reassurance from me. His father. Not from my enemy.

Caswallon's unusually authoritative voice broke the silence. "Bran, Segovax, we'll continue this discussion outside. I need air."

The Champion and the Archdruid obediently followed their king outside, wrapping their cloaks around them against the weather. Caswallon called for the sword. The other members of the Council celebrated their dismissal by shouting for more mead.

Except for Novax, whose eyes clung to the Archdruid like resin until he left the hall.

On the stone ramparts a crow ignored the rain to busy herself with a piece of offal.

The sword was hurriedly brought to the king. "Bran, Segovax, I brought you outside because I want to speak to the both of you, an expert in the ways of the gods, and the finest warrior of the Ordovices, alone. I want your honesty. You don't need to tact while we are alone. Can we win the war and please two gods at the same time?"

Bran's responded. "You have no need to drag me into the rain, Caswallon. I will say no different from when I spoke in the Council. We must have the wargods on our side if we are to defeat the Eagles. Remember the Battle of the Sacred Isle, when the gods deserted us. With the sword and the gods, the tribes can triumph. But if Boann of the waters is not pleased..."

Segovax's brow knotted. "I fought the Romans ten summers ago with the Silurian army. The Eagles are strong, disciplined fighters. Not as good as the Britons in the first charge, it is true, but they fight as a team, not as individuals. They have the stamina of oxen. The Iceni and the Trinovantes will fight bravely, but even if the Ordovices join them we will not be strong enough to defeat them. I could not advise a king to fight against such odds."

Bran set his face hard. "The Duroteges are on the edge of revolt and will provide a diversion. But their lands are occupied and they will not send men as far as Iceni territory. It is true that the Silures, broken by Caradoc's defeat, will not join us, but the other kingdoms of the west and north are ready to fight. The Demetae and the Cornovii may be persuaded to send armies."

The champion threw his cloak and jacket to the floor, exposing his head and torso to the biting elements. He thrust out his chest and threw his arms apart. "If that is the case... if a large coalition can be found, and with the backing of the gods, I believe Britain can triumph. I am ageing, Caswallon," he said gravely as the rain ran in rivulets down his body. "I have one good campaign left in me. May the bards sing of my part in pushing the Eagles back into the sea." He was almost shouting as passion took him. "BY THE GODS, I AM READY FOR WAR. LET THE ORDOVICES TAKE OUR PLACE IN THE BATTLELINE!"

Caswallon's face mirrored his champion's excitement, and his voice rose to a screech. He raised the sword toward the heavens. "Let us prepare to fight!"

The moment the king lifted the blade, the rain stopped.

Without warning the sky parted and a fine ray of sunlight, no wider than a man's fist, broke through and struck the Rainbow Sword. For the time it takes to put one foot in front of the other, Tre'r Ceiri was enveloped by the sword's dull green light.

As quickly as they had parted, the heavens closed in again. There was a flash to the south, and the trio turned to watch a thunderbolt smite the mountains of Ereri. Heartbeats later there was a roar from the skies.

"By the Gods, which demon from the Otherworld threatens us?" demanded Sergovax, his eyes dancing around the fort and searching for monsters behind every hut.

Bran laughed loudly. "Have you never seen a sign from the heavens before? Did you see the way the sword was lit by Lugh of the Sun? The gods want the sword. And they want it delivered to my Sacred Pool, where their lightning hit the ground."

As he finished speaking, the rains returned, and Bel, the Thundergod, continued to bellow his approval of the Archdruid's interpretation.

Chapter 11

Johnny Davis stirred.

There was no light coming through his curtains, so he knew it must be the middle of the night.

He wanted to roll over and get back to sleep, but something nagged at the back of his young mind. Through half closed eyes, he questioned his surroundings. In the dim light he saw his toys and books on his new shelves, and the greying white paint which daddy had promised to replace with football wallpaper.

An action toy gazed passively from the bedside table.

Johnny was in his new home in the mountains. In his own bed. He snuggled down into his quilt. He was safe.

Or was he?

His room was different. But in a way his dulled senses couldn't place.

He was nervous. He buried his face in the bed, lying still in the hope that whatever night-monster night lay in the shadows would pass by and leave him unnoticed.

Johnny wanted to cry out to his father, to his brother or sister, but he dared not. The monster would hear him and know he was there.

He knew deep down, in the pit of his stomach, that monsters did not exist. He kept telling himself, over and over again, that there were no monsters. But the knowledge that something was out there would not go away. A nervous sweat soaked his pyjamas.

Lying still, he listened out for any sound that would betray the monster.

Nothing.

But fear still fear enveloped Johnny Davis like a shroud.

It was hard to breathe beneath the quilt. He needed air.

He risked a slow movement, edging his mouth to the side of his bed so that he could breathe the cool night. He was sure the monster would be able to hear the sound of his pyjamas moving over his sheets. His slow movement was surely the loudest noise ever made. It was certain to give him away.

But his face was at the edge of the quilt now. He squeezed his eyes shut, afraid of what they might see. He took clean air into his body, the fear bringing his breaths in small gulps. Breaths which Johnny knew were loud enough to give him away to the monster.

The monster that isn't there, he reminded himself.

Monsters don't exist.

He risked opening his eyes. The off-white wall looked blandly back at him.

But it wasn't white. The dull light was making it a mild pink.

What dull light? Johnny clenched his eyes firmly shut.

It was the middle of the night. There shouldn't be any lights. Daddy always turned everything off when he went to bed. There were no street lamps outside. The house was in the middle of the mountains. And the pink light certainly wasn't the moon.

Nervously, slowly, he opened his eyes again.

Yes. The wall was bathed in pink. But this time Johnny studied it for as long as he dared. The lower part of the wall was in dark shadow. He could see the outline of the top of his pillow, and the bump he formed under the quilt.

He knew what the shadows meant.

The light was coming from somewhere on the other side of his bed.

If he wanted to know what was making the pink light he would have to roll over.

But moving would give his presence away to the monster.

Ripples crawled up his neck. For the first time, his mind told him this was no silly midnight fear. And this wasn't a bad dream. Johnny *knew* something was wrong.

He gulped one last, big breath of air into his lungs and buried his sweaty face back into his quilt. And clamped his eyes closed again.

He listened. No noise. But *something* was there. He didn't know how he knew.

But he *knew.*

Drying clammy hands against the quilt, he prepared to slowly roll over. He wanted to throw the quilt off so that he could bathe his hot body in the cool mountain night. But he couldn't. That would expose his body to the monster. The quilt may be flimsy, but he felt safe under it.

No, he didn't feel safe under the quilt.

Just *safer.*

Slowly, inch by inch, he moved. He still wanted to hide, but he knew the monster would have seen him by now. It wasn't dark. There was the strange red light.

Another thought assaulted his mind.

Aliens!

The red light was unearthly. Had they come to take him away and do experiments on him? That was what aliens did. One of the kids at school back in Swindon had said so. His big brother had seen it on the television.

Tears welled up in Johnny's closed eyes. For a few moments he lay rigid, too terrified even to breathe. He felt a tear fall.

His heart thumped against his ribs.

I don't want to be an experiment.

Slowly, he opened his eyes. He was facing into the room, but the quilt was in the way. He knew he must move it to see the alien. But the red glow was still there.

As quietly and smoothly as he could, Johnny moved until he was at the edge of the bed.

This was the moment.

Johnny knew that when he opened his eyes, he would see whatever was in the room. Monster or alien.

He told himself there wouldn't be anything there. He told himself it was all his imagination, that the red glow was a trick of the light; maybe a warning light on a radiator. If there *was* anyone—any*thing*—in his room he would have heard it by now. Or it would have eaten him. He took in a deep breath.

He opened his eyes.

And for the first time in his life knew pure terror.

He wanted to scream, but something held the sound in his throat.

He should have called out earlier, while his voice was still working.

Daddy would have got rid of her.

The ugliest woman Johnny had seen in his life. She was old. So old that her wrinkled skin seemed ready to fall from her body. Pus-oozing warts punctured her face. Grey hair escaped from her scalp like an unruly mass of cobwebs. Her cracked lips parted in an evil leer, revealing a mouthful of black or missing teeth. Expressionless brown eyes regarded him.

Her body was thin and wrinkled, her long black dress torn and fading. He could see a withered bosom through a tear. Her hands and bare feet were as old as her face, with gnarled joints swollen by arthritis.

And in those ancient hands, the woman held a sword. She sat on his wooden toy box, grinning at him, idly fingering the blade as she watched him.

It was the sword giving off the red glow.

The word 'witch' went through his mind. He waited for her to cast a spell on him.

I don't want to be turned into a frog.

He tried to say something. He tried to scream. But only a low gurgle came out. He tried to move, but his body stayed still.

She remained expressionless.

Johnny didn't know whether he should smile at her. That might make her like him.

But the muscles in his face refused to move.

He imagined the pain of being cut to ribbons, and waited for her to stand up and plunge the weapon into his defenceless body. An overwhelming thought was that he wasn't going to be able to say goodbye to his family before he died.

The old woman ran a finger down the blade of the glowing sword.

But she didn't attack him. Instead, she grinned as the weapon drew blood from her index finger. She lifted the wound to within a few inches of her nose and watched, seemingly transfixed, as a scarlet trickle ran to the palm of her hand.

Turning her eyes to Johnny and grinning, the old woman extended a yellowing tongue and licked at her fingers. At first the action was slow and delicate, but as another red drop seeped from the wound she sucked at it greedily, as if it were clear spring water and she had not drunk for a week.

Blood was soon smeared around her chapped lips. She licked them clean. Then she sucked at her finger again.

She rose and held the sword at Johnny's throat. The red glow coming from it was warm, like the bars on an electric heater. He could feel the sharp point. He thought it *wanted* to bury itself into his flesh.

She's going to drink my blood now.

He managed to give his head a slight shake, pleading with her not to kill him. That was the nearest he could manage to speaking. He wanted her to take the sword from his neck. It was hurting, the way it dug in.

He wanted to scream. He wanted to scream more than anything he had ever wanted in his life. He wanted to yell to his father, to his sister, to his brother. They were lying only yards away, sleeping peacefully. It wouldn't take a very loud shout to wake them.

But he still couldn't force a sound from his throat.

Johnny breathed a deep sigh as the blade was removed from his windpipe. At least he would live for a few more seconds.

But she still held the sword towards him. Her brow furrowed. As if she was still deciding whether to kill him.

She ran a gnarled hand through her white hair.

She returned to Johnny's toybox and gently patted its lid, as if inviting him to join her.

When Johnny didn't move she returned to the bed and leaned over him. He pulled the quilt over his head and slammed his eyes shut, not wanting to see the swordblow coming. He desperately he wanted to hug his family one last time. He winced as the fingers, feeling bony even through the quilt, lifted him. Still wrapped in his bedding, he opened his eyes. He was sitting on her lap, only inches from her face.

Something smelled.

Her breath.

But he couldn't immediately think of why he knew the horrible smell. Then he recognised it. It smelled like the dead cat he had found in their garden, back in Swindon one day when they had all come home from a holiday. The cat had just been a mass of crawly things feeding on flesh. The stink had been horrible. The smell of death.

He took a sharp intake of breath.

Her breath smelled of death.

The old woman looked directly into his eyes. He clasped his own shut.

For a long time.

After a while he couldn't feel her holding him any more. But he didn't open his eyes to see if she had gone.

Not for a long time.

But when he did, at last, summon the bravery to open an eyelid, she was gone.

Johnny wrapped himself up tightly in his quilt. He screamed as he had never screamed before in his life.

Chapter 12

The Celtic world disappeared back into time, but not before it had left Tre'r Ceiri with the sound of screaming.

Not, this time, the yells of agony from the twisted mouth of a dying Roman which had consumed the Sacred Isle. This was a childlike wail of fear, born of the winds themselves. A scream of dark, primitive terror pulled along in the air. Bran stood silent on the ramparts of slate, his existence dimming but ears open to the breeze, searching for the source. But the sound was from everywhere and nowhere, distant yet nearby.

Caswallon and Sergovax cowered against the stone wall of a nearby hut. Even the Archdruid found the pit of his stomach filled with dread.

A screaming wind was surely an omen sent by the gods.

Bran struggled to give the sound a meaning. But even his knowledge of the Otherworld would not give him an understanding.

But there was one thing which was certain.

The sound was born of evil.

He listened, caressing his beard, as the scream faded. Not a sudden ceasing, nor a lessening of anguish.

Just a ceasing.

The wail diminished, as if the source and the world were becoming distant. Bran was left only to puzzle the significance of the omen, questioning even whether he had imagined the sound. But the fear of Caswallon and Sergovax as they cowered against the stone ramparts, and the perspiration tickling his body in the cool night, were certain signs he had heard something real.

But unnatural.

* * * *

Peter Davis stirred from his sleep. He had kicked his quilt away is quilt as he dreamed, leaving it crumpled on the floor. Through an open window, mountain air cooled his room. As consciousness returned he felt tears for the Ordovices stinging in his eyes.

But the screaming hadn't stopped. So deeply had he been immersed in the past, he didn't realise the sound had continued into his waking moments until he heard noises outside his door.

- 95 -

"JOHNNY! JOHNNY! WHAT IS IT?" Was Lucy's almost panic-stricken cry as her footsteps passed Peter's room. Their father followed close behind. And the screaming continued. Not the still-sleepy cries of a child suffering a nightmare, but the continuous, terror-stricken yells of a boy scared out of his senses.

And it wasn't getting quieter. Whatever had woken Johnny was still frightening him.

Peter ripped his dressing gown from its hook and reached his brother's room only a second or two after Lucy had flicked the light.

His brother was curled up in a corner, back against the wall and feet flat on the floor, as if he were trying to push his way through the brickwork. His quilt was pulled tightly around him, eyes wide open and staring, jumping around the room as they wildly looked for safety—or whatever nightmare had woken him. His lips were pulled back into a snarl as he took a breath into his lungs for yet another scream, features distorted into a mask. He was bathed in a torrent of sweat which held his hair and football pyjamas to his body.

Alun knelt facing his son. "Johnny, Johnny, it's okay. Daddy's here," he cajoled.

The boy, showing no hint of recognition, hooked his fingers into a claw and took a swipe at his father. Taken by surprise, Alun failed to dodge and received a graze to his left temple. Before he could put a hand to the wound, Johnny's other arm swung back in preparation for a second blow. This time Alun was ready and managed to duck before the makeshift talon flew past him. Johnny wrapped his quilt even tighter around himself and glared at his father, as if daring Alun to try to take it from him.

"Lucy, go and call a doctor," Alun ordered, turning to her. He withdrew a couple of feet, out of range of another blow.

"Which one?" She clutched her pink dressing gown around her, her mind seemingly numbed as she stared blankly at the scene in front of her.

"I DON'T CARE," Alun shouted. "Ring the first one in the 'phone book. Tell them we haven't registered because we've only just moved here. JUST GET ONE! Tell them we've got a boy here who's having a fit or something."

She left the room with moisture showing in her eyes.

Johnny screamed again. Peter moved slowly toward his brother, gently whispering the six-year-old's name in an attempt to calm him.

Peter was kneeling, his face level with Johnny's and only a couple of feet away.

"Careful, Peter," whispered Alun. Peter didn't need his father's warning, and was ready when the blow came. With a reflex action, Peter grabbed Johnny's fist as it swung towards him. His brother responded by letting a snarl escape his twisted lips. His eyes glared angrily into Peter's.

Almost without thinking Peter slapped the child's cheek. Not too hard—he didn't want to hurt the boy—but hard enough, he hoped, to bring him to his senses.

The screaming stopped. Johnny's face drained of terror. His mouth dropped open and his eyes blanked. His muscles slackened.

Tipsy's muffled barking rose from the kitchen before Johnny gave a sob. "It's okay, Jon-Jon, it's okay. I'm here and daddy's here. Tell us all about it." Peter's arms enveloped his brother. The quivering body felt small and vulnerable. The boy clung back and tried to speak, but couldn't force out more than a syllable out before another sob would take him.

"It's okay. We're all here. We're looking after you."

Johnny looked up into his Peter's eyes. His face still showed fear, but began to soften in the comfort of his brother's embrace.

From downstairs came Lucy's voice, harsher than usual, as she demanded service from an unfortunate night receptionist. "...I don't care... no, it's more than an ordinary nightmare. It's like the kid's scared shitless... out of his wits by something. He needs a sedative or something. *Please* send a doctor."

Peter shared a look with his father and whispered "Warm milk." Alun nodded for Peter to continue comforting Johnny while he left the room. Peter had at least managed to quiet his brother, and hoped that by being alone, one-to-one, the task of fully calming him would be easier.

"It's all right, Jon-Jon. It's all right now," he soothed. His brother's eyes were still wide open and jumping around the room. "Are you going to tell me what the matter is? Have you had a bad dream?"

Johnny opened his mouth, but had to loose couple more sobs before words would come from between his quivering lips.

"Old lady." It was no more than a whisper, as if to say it louder would invite the horror to return.

"An old lady? You dreamed about an old lady? Are you going to tell me about her?"

"No. I wasn't dreaming, Peetie. She was here." He flung his eyes around the room again, as if expecting her to reappear. His eyes searched out every possible hiding place in turn.

"Do you think it may have been a shadow that looked like an old lady?" Peter asked calmly, sure that Johnny must have mistaken innocent shapes in the dark for something more sinister.

"No. She was here. I saw her. But she was horrible!"

"What did she say? And what did she do?"

"She was over there watching me." He pointed a shaking finger towards his toybox.

"Tell me what she looked like."

"She was horrible. I could see her in the light of her sword. The light was red. Her skin was all wrinkly and her hair was all grey and sticking out. She looked horrible." The renewed outburst of crying, which had been simmering under the surface, broke loose. "She looked horrible," he repeated.

Light of her sword!

Red light of her sword!

A panic rose in Peter as Johnny's words sank in. Something stabbed at him. Something from Archdruid Bran's mind.

"Doctor's on his way," interrupted Lucy. "Daddy's coming with some warm milk. Come on, Johnny, let's get you cleaned up." She hugged her brother and lifted him onto the bed to change him out of his wet pyjamas.

"The old lady isn't in here any more, is she?" asked Peter.

Johnny looked around him again before replying with an unconvincing shake of his head.

"Would you like me to go outside to see if I can see the old lady? If I find her I'll chase her away."

Johnny responded with a nod and another sob. Peter was pleased to hear him break into mild laughter as Lucy found a bare armpit.

He left the room and passed his father on the landing.

"How is he?" asked Alun, clutching a mug of milk.

"Better, I think. He says there was an old lady in his room, so I said I'd go outside and see if she's still there. I just hope I can find the torch in all the packing cases."

Alan nodded as Peter padded on down the stairs. He groped for a light switch and heard another sob from Johnny's room.

He managed to find the torch, but felt faintly ridiculous wearing a coat and trainers with his dressing gown. He made a mental note to wear them back into the house. Lucy would tease him unmercifully.

Looking like this, though, I might give Johnny a laugh.

In fact, the whole family could probably do with a laugh right now.

He opened the front door. The house and garden were bathed in silver, but where the moon's sweep couldn't reach there were shadows of thick blackness. In this setting, Peter could almost believe in Johnny's old lady. In fact, he could almost believe everything Bran believed. There was something eerie about the night, the way the dark walls of the mountains enveloped him, roofed only by the purple velvet of the sky. Friendly winks from the stars above gave little comfort.

His torch pushed into the shadows, but showed nothing unexpected. Rocks formed sinister shapes as they pushed from the ground; trees groaned gently in the breeze, and a sheep bleated nearby. A knot formed in the pit of Peter's stomach. He didn't want to step out of the door and into the night.

He remembered Johnny's description of the glowing red sword Johnny had described. *Just like the sword of Fergus mac Roy.*

"Don't be stupid." The words were whispered under his breath. He kept telling himself there wouldn't be anyone here. An intruder would have run away by now. And even if there was an old woman lurking he would surely have no trouble overpowering her.

But something nagged at him.

He took a deep breath, welcoming the soothing night air in his lungs, before crossing the threshold and starting to search the area. Now he was outside, alone in the dark, this seemed less of a good idea than it had upstairs, with the light blazing and his family around him. Upstairs he hadn't believed in the old lady.

He pulled his coat around him. It was cold. He didn't realise it could get so cold in the mountains in the middle of summer.

Peter's footfall crunched the gravel at the front of the house. In the silence of the night the sound seemed magnified a thousandfold as it echoed around the valley. He knew he was being stupid. He *knew* there wasn't anyone there. He *knew* Johnny had just had a vivid dream. But he still retreated from the gravel and walked silently on the grass. He flicked the torch off, using the moonlight to guide his way. Just in case.

But Johnny had described Fergus's sword, he reminded himself.

How the hell could he know about Fergus's sword?

And how was it connected to his own dreams?

Slowly, Peter started to circle the house. He had turned left out of the front door, meaning he wouldn't have to face the ancient remains until his circuit was about two thirds complete. He didn't want to get to the cairn any sooner than he had to. Not in the dark. The cairn and the stone circle had a presence that he wanted to avoid. Especially at night.

He reached the corner of the house. He wanted to stop, to peer round the slate walls to make sure the way was clear. *This is stupid*, he told himself again as he walked around the side of the house with a forced confidence.

He flicked the torch back on.

Nothing.

A sigh of relief, which had been held in, escaped his lips. He walked to the next corner, a little more quickly, flashing his light more confidently around the garden. Johnny's bedroom was almost above him; he could hear Alun's gentle tone trying to soothe the boy, although the voice was too quiet for Peter to make out any words. Johnny was still replying with sobs, but with longer between them than when Peter had been in the house.

He bought himself back to the task in hand. He forced himself around the next corner of slate.

And Peter froze as the torch lit a pair of deep, expressionless brown eyes. He felt his stomach churn.

"Baaa."

He leaned against the whitewashed wall of the house as relief swept over him.

Just an escaped sheep!

But his heart pounded as the animal fled back to its flock. He turned the torch off again.

He entered the shadow where the moon's comforting presence was hidden behind the building. He forced his eyes to the middle distance, towards the cairn.

Something lurched inside him.

There was movement. Something atop the cairn had moved.

Another sheep, he hoped.

He forced his eyes deep into the moonlight. The thought of turning the torch on was more than his bravery could manage. But he knew it couldn't have been an old woman on the remains. No pensioner would be fit enough to climb the stones. Not with the rocks ready to give way and send her tumbling. Even if she had managed to get to the top, he would have heard the stones settling beneath her feet.

He lurched from nightmare to nightmare as various scenarios passed into his thoughts. Anything from another stray sheep to a night-summoned spirit.

Maybe I'm getting like Bran?

It was just an animal, he told himself. Or a pattern cast by a shadow as the moon broke through the nearby oaks.

But Peter knew he had to investigate. He *had* to know if it was an intruder. His clammy hand tightened around the torch, but he didn't have the nerve to throw light on the cairn. Not yet. But the torch was heavy. It would be a useful weapon. *If necessary.*

He told himself once more he was being stupid, that there was a rational, harmless explanation. Told himself he wouldn't need a weapon.

He still bent down to pick up a small rock from the ground. But even having something to throw gave him little comfort.

His heart stopped. Peter felt the hairs on the back of his neck rise from his skin.

There was movement again. And a sound.

There is an explanation. You've been dreaming about ancient gods too much.

Using every ounce of willpower, Peter forced himself, step by step, to place one foot in front of the other.

Slowly, he neared the cairn. But he still couldn't bring himself to turn the torch on.

He was afraid of what he might see.

There it was again. Movement. Something black. Flapping. He shifted the rock to his right hand and moved the torch to his left. He raised the stone, ready to throw. He flicked the switch of the torch with his left thumb.

An eye glinted back at him. There was a rasping cackle.

A raven sat atop the mound of stones. Staring at him. *Laughing* at him?

Before Peter could even think of what to do next, the night was punctured by the sound of an engine and wheels crunching the long gravel drive. A moment later twin beams of light lit the bird completely. With a final cackle it took to its wings and faded into the night.

Peter had never been so pleased to see a doctor's car in his life.

Peter thought about the raven. *Bran believed ravens were signs from the Gods.* No. *Bran thought ravens were gods.*

He thought about the frightening old lady Johnny thought he had seen.

An uneasy shiver passed through him.

* * * *

Johnny took a mild sedative and within an hour was sleeping calmly again. Lucy and Peter returned to bed. Alun, concern etched over his features, chose to stay at his son's bedside for the rest of the night, despite the doctor's advice to treat the incident as nothing more than a particularly vivid nightmare.

Something, though, tugged at Peter. He tried to believe Johnny's fear was the result of a nightmare.

But there was too much happening. His own constant dreams about Bran. His picture. He hadn't painted it as a horror picture. And it had turned back, to the way he had finished it. And the raven on the cairn. Much of it seemed to have the ties of connection linking it all, but he couldn't begin to understand how.

He rolled over and tried to get comfortable, not really expecting to return to sleep. His mind was too full: the tragedy of Kyra and Conor; Johnny's nightmare; his painting; and the raven outside.

* * * *

Peter was pleased to have Morgan in bed beside him. She lay with only long, deep breaths to break the silence; it didn't matter that she was asleep. Just holding her in the darkness was a comfort. Her head lay on his right shoulder; her breathing tickled his chest. Her knees pressed lightly against his thighs as he pulled her closer. She was petite in his arms.

Cute.

A tingle of pleasure rippled through him as the mound of a breast pushed against his ribs.

Gently, trying not to wake her, he let his right hand gently caress her long hair, enjoying its silky texture. He breathed heavily, taking in the scent of wild flowers which enveloped her.

Peter let his right hand leave behind the flowing softness of her hair to trace the line formed by her backbone. His index finger started between her shoulders and gently smoothed its way down the gentle bumps of her spine. Her skin was soft and smooth and flawless. He stopped briefly in the small of her back to enjoy the gentle inward curve, but his hand was impatient to continue on its journey down her body. He teased himself by pausing on her coccyx before allowing himself to continue to her buttocks. His breath locked in his throat as he anticipated the feel of her firm rear in his hand.

As he prepared to caress her rump, Morgan stirred. She gave the deep groan of one content in a deep sleep, then nestled back into him. Her right hand rested on his chest and she was still again.

Finally and at last he allowed his right hand to find the firm suppleness of her buttocks. He felt his own body responding to the soft, firm flesh, and slowly and gently, so as not to wake her, he caressed and massaged the smooth, gentle mounds.

He wished he could roll over and change position. That way he would be able to glide his left hand over the flat surface of her stomach and hold a silken-skinned breast.

But that would mean waking her.

He wanted Morgan to stay asleep. He wanted this moment to last forever.

He kissed the top of her head, enjoying again the taste of flowers in her flowing hair.

She stirred.

Peter stilled.

But it was too late. With a low sigh of pleasure, she slowly stretched out her body.

Her lips found Peter's chest, and her tongue lazily tickled him.

Peter wanted to do the same to her, but for the moment he was content to lie back and enjoy her caress.

Still kissing his chest, she lifted herself into a kneeling position. Her hand found his stomach and gently kneaded it in a circular motion with her palm. Peter tensed as her fingers worked their way lower with each circle, teasing him and expertly increasing his need by stopping short of the area he wanted her to find.

Now she was awake, he took a breast in each hand. They were small but firm and soft, and the nipples hardened as he brushed them with his thumbs. His right hand moved lower, to the flatness of her stomach. He felt her wince slightly as his light touch tickled, and his fingers left her tummy to continue their journey.

Very soon a light moan escaped her lips as he found his goal.

He swallowed as his own body enjoyed the way she massaged his stomach. Instinctively he dug his heels into the sheets and inched himself up the bed, nearer to Morgan's probing hand.

But she teased him, always keeping her fingers out of reach. Then she tweaked a hair.

"Ouch."

"Sorry." Followed by a playful giggle which suggested she wasn't.

She had brilliantly loosened the mood, he realised.

What a fantastic woman.

Peter Davis sweated as anticipation overtook him. He felt his explosion nearing and hoped he would be able to hold out long enough to satisfy her. He found himself crushing her breasts and loosened his grip, not wanting to hurt her as passion threatened to overcome him.

But quicker, shallow breaths and a gentle writhing around his probing fingers signalled her own nearing climax. He was about to beg for his own release, but, almost as if sensing his need, she gently closed her thighs, forcing his fingers from her. She held his hand in hers and kissed it.

He willingly allowed her to straddle his hips and sink him into her moist body.

He let his hands move over her, enjoying the way they slid over her perspiring skin as he prepared for release. He didn't know whether to hold her breasts or clasp her rear.

Her head appeared from the quilt above him, at the same instant as the first ray of dawn pushed through his curtain. Peter paused to admire her raw beauty as, eyes closed and lips pursed, she prepared to climax.

She was beautiful.

Suddenly, she gasped and tensed. Her thighs squeezed his hips.

Instinctively, he squeezed her breasts. A thousand stars exploded across his eyes.

"You happy?" she asked.

He nodded.

"Want this again? Want this all the time?"

"Yeah," he gasped.

"Will you help me?"

"Yeah."

"Anything?"

"Anything."

Peter gasped. He would do anything for Morgan. Anything to keep her. The thought of not doing as she asked, not giving her every little thing she craved, refused to enter his head.

"Because, if you don't do as I bid..." She opened her eyes. In the dawn light he could see the large, dark pupils of her eyes looking down on him. Black. Like deep, deep holes.

And out of her left nostril crawled a maggot. A massive maggot. Peter watched in stricken fascination, wondering how something so large could crawl through such a small hole.

It stopped on her upper lip for a second or two, as if wondering what it should do next, before falling onto Peter's chest.

Forgetting the pleasure he had experienced only seconds earlier, he lurched from under Morgan and swiped the animal off his body.

He looked up into Morgan's grinning face.

And another maggot fell from her other nostril.

Followed by another.

Then another.

Then a couple from between her leering lips. She bit another in two before spitting out both parts.

Peter panicked, flailing his arms around as he tried to brush the animals from his body. He writhed as he felt them crawling over him, reaching for his face, trying to eat him, to suffocate him...

More maggots fell from her body until his chest was crawling with life. She picked up a handful of the bloated yellow bodies and greedily stuffed them into her mouth, pausing only to look him in the eye as she chewed slowly and swallowed. Her face was a mask of ecstasy.

"Give me Britain," whispered Morgan, her voice dripping venom. A half-eaten maggot fell from her lips. "I want Britain."

* * * *

Peter sat up, suddenly awake. Sweat dripped from his body. His breathing came in gulps.

He fell back onto his pillow.

A dream...

But her words pushed into him. And the way she had said them.

"Give me Britain..."

He was shaking, but still managed to find the switch of his bedside light.

Only a dream...

But he recoiled as he watched a maggot crawling across his pillow.

There was no way Peter Davis would be sleeping again tonight. He tossed, trying to make sense of all that had happened to him and his family, until, to his surprise, he felt fatigue overcome him. He thought of getting himself a drink of cold water, but his muscles refused to let him out of bed as, against his will, he was pulled back into the darkness. He struggled against the past as it dragged him through swirling whorls of night into the world of the Celts.

He fought, kicking out against the journey through the years until he arrived at his destination, until he stood proud and erect in his robe of pure white.

He was Bran, Archdruid of Britain.

Chapter 13

The procession reached Bran's Sacred Pool as Bel's reddening disk caressed the western peaks. This was boundary time, when the borders of day merged into night; the time when the frontiers came down and allowed the gods to cross from the Otherworld.

While Bran would lead the sword of Fergus mac Roy on its journey to the sacred waters, Caswallon had ordered Novax to remain at Tre'r Ceiri to light the fires of protection on this night of sacrifice. The citadel's fires would banish those spirits who would snatch men struggling and screaming from the land of the living. Bran's mind pictured the Ordovices, huddling around Tre'r Ceiri's flames and casting nervous glances into the shadows.

The air had darkened even since the sombre religious party had left the shepherd's huts of Nant Bran, as the village at the valley's end was becoming known. Sombre, that was, except for the Archdruid, who strode confidently forward into the dusk.

He was prepared.

His pure white robes had taken a slave girl half a day to clean to his fastidious standards. White, too, were the beads around his neck, giving him the knowledge of the stars and the heavens. Upon his head rested a crown of oak leaves, bestowing the mental strength of ancient trees.

Bran's mind, too, was ready. Had he not trained a lifetime for this very moment? Had he not fed only on sacred hazelnuts this day to further prepare him?

Others in the party looked around nervously as they walked, studying the darkness for evil spirits. The acolytes, green-clad junior priests, led chariots bearing gifts for the goddesses, and stayed as close as their duties allowed. Some bore torches of fire to provide light once Bel's disk slipped beyond the mountains.

Also in the procession were Caswallon and other dignitaries of the Ordovices, many with fear etched across their features, and there only because pride would not let them remain at Tre'r Ceiri like frightened slave girls.

The sword was strapped tightly to the king's waist.

One prisoner, a Roman legionary captured in a raid beyond the mountains, completed the group. Now, tied to the rear of a chariot, he was no longer a conquering example of Rome's might. He made no effort to free himself, but instead whimpered like a wounded dog. His eyes were emptier than dark and his face displayed death, despite the fear-dulling herbs given to him with his last meal.

Only Bran took any notice of a single raven circling high above. The bird should have made him nervous, but instead its presence filled him with iron resolve.

The last rays of the sun still tinted the air as the procession reached Bran's sacred pool. The sacred oaks and stones to one side, the darkening orange sky, and the knowledge that the gods received gifts here, combined to give the area an air of fearful mystery. The sturdy platform of logs, built for tonight by the finest craftsmen of the Ordovices, reached out over the pool, allowing the important to keep their feet clear of the marshy waters.

Bran looked toward the raven, her silhouette clear against the sunset, until she settled in an oak and shadows consumed her. An acolyte looked in her direction and quickly made a sign to ward off evil before huddling into the middle of the group.

Bran stepped onto the platform. His toe pushed a dried length of sheep dung into the reeds. He wrinkled his nose and cursed the animal which failed to respect a sacred place.

The light dimmed further. The shadowed mountains were little more than walls of darkness and the Archdruid was anxious to start proceedings. As he threw his arms wide apart and his head back, all present turned to him. It was difficult to find the right words, for he could not know which of two ladies would respond.

The Lady of War?

Or the Mistress of the Waters?

"Oh goddesses, you have found it necessary to test the devotion of your people. You have sent the rains upon us to destroy our crops and swallow our fields. You allow the Romans to fall upon Britain like wolves upon the fold. The Ordovices beseech you, accept these humble gifts as a sign of their loyalty to you."

At the flick of his wrist four acolytes unloaded gifts from the chariots and with a minimum of reverence, as if anxious to complete their task, the young priests threw them to the murky waters. Gold and jewellery were consigned to the pool; a beautifully decorated hunting horn which had taken a smith two moons to craft; a jewel-encrusted goblet traded with the Romans in more peaceful times; a shield of bronze, too flimsy for use in war, but finely wrought and made specially as a gift to whichever goddess would receive it. All these treasures and more were despatched, and the acolytes' green robes were soon dark with mud. Though the offerings were rich, the ladies acknowledged the wealth of the Ordovices with no more than a 'splash' as it disappeared beneath the surface.

When the riches were given, Bran turned to Caswallon.

"It is time. The sword."

The king slowly removed the weapon from its scabbard. Even now the blade shimmered green, and in the light of a dozen firebrands Caswallon's face crumpled and tears streaked his cheeks. The sword seemed to belong in his hand, looking as contented in his fist as a baby at its mother's breast. Caswallon was a natural father to the weapon, Bran thought.

The Archdruid placed a comforting hand on the king's shoulder.

"Throw it. Appease the ladies with your own gift." His voice was gentle but offered no compromise.

Caswallon broke the evening with a roar of anguish as loud as a battle cry and flung the weapon into the middle of the pond.

If he were expecting any acknowledgement from the Otherworld he was to be disappointed. The sword disappeared into the water with barely a ripple.

Bran felt nerves overtake him. *Are the gifts to be ignored?*

It was time for the final gift to be given. And to his dismay Bran knew it was a gift which would appeal to Andraste, not the peace-loving Goddess of the Waters.

There was a screech from above as the raven, as if unable to restrain herself a heartbeat longer, launched herself from her bough and flew excitedly overhead, her glutteral screaming giving the tense atmosphere around the pool an added air of malevolence.

"KILL, KILL."

No man could speak the language of animals, but it did not demand knowledge of the wild to know what the bird's cries meant.

Indeed, the sacred group understood her as clearly as if she had screamed the words in the British tongue.

For all men knew of Andraste.

Was she not the shapechanging Goddess of War and Death who circled the heavens above killings, encouraging men to take lives and spill blood for her feasts? Did she not revel in death and fear as she became human, then raven, and then mortal again?

The Roman briefly looked up as he was unshackled from the chariot, but his eyes had long since lost their warrior's spirit. His face was already dead.

One of the warriors loosed a vindictive fist into the prisoner's jaw as he was led past. "This'll be one less of Suetainus' whelps to deal with in battle," he taunted as the blow struck, referring to the hated Governor of Britain. "Doesn't look so fearsome now, does he?"

Bran shot the bully a reproachful glare. Another held the man back, advising him to "Let a fellow warrior die with dignity."

There were no more interruptions. The Roman recovered his balance and allowed himself to be taken to the platform without a struggle. He didn't even bother spitting out blood or broken teeth.

Two acolytes held the captive while four warriors waded into the water to await the sacrifice. At this moment the prisoner's previously deadened eyes flickered with fear. His jaw slackened.

"I thought it was to be the knife," he said, his voice pleading for a quick death.

"You are a gift for the waters," replied Bran impassively in clipped Latin. "It is the waters which must extinguish you." Bran knew a death beneath the waters would be seen as an offering to Boann, not Andraste. The slow drowning of Roman was regrettable, but was a small price to appease the bringer of rains.

The man's terror overcame him, his brain ignoring any mind-numbing drug as he understood he was to endure a slow, desperate death beneath the waters. He struggled and begged for a quick end, but was sent without mercy to the warriors who stood in the pool and held him under the surface with muscular arms. The Archdruid spoke the necessary words, offering his life to whichever goddess would have mercy on the Ordovices.

The man struggled, but gradually the waters became less frenzied.

And were still.

Two warriors were instructed to place branches over the body and weigh it down with rocks. The corpse must be consumed by the waters, not by the carrion which would enjoy a meal should his remains float to the surface.

The Pool regained its dignified calm, hiding the gifts unclaimed among the mud and reeds of the depths.

The raven circled overhead, excitement escaping her hooked beak. The men looked up at her, their faces clear in the light of the firebrands. Some withdrew their gaze; others watched intently as if afraid to let her out of her sight, as a timid maiden might with a mouse or spider. A small number of men hurled threats—or even small rocks—at the bird.

Even those without Druid training seemed to sense the creature was evil. In the dying light fear veiled the party like a shroud.

A chariot horse whinnied nervously.

"DO NOT BE ALARMED!" the Archdruid shouted earnestly. "See how the Goddess approves! Let us make our way back to the hearthfires and leave her to enjoy her gift."

Few needed a second invitation to return to the safety of walls and a roof. Nant Bran, with its beds of straw and protective fires, was a more attractive proposition for any man than a cold, dark place sanctified for the gods.

The raven flew across the valley at speed, forcing men to duck and giving an occasional shriek as she chased them on their way.

Most seemed unable to escape down the path toward the village quickly enough and the sacred party degenerated into a terrified rabble, driven on by a screeching bird diving upon them from the darkness.

But Bran snatched a torch as a frightened warrior scampered past. He remained. Although his insides coiled, he forced an outward calm and gently caressed his beard to cool his unease.

"IS THE GIFT GOOD ENOUGH FOR YOU, GODDESS?" he shouted defiantly towards her.

To his surprise, the bird gently, delicately even, alighted on the platform beside him. She cocked her head and regarded him intently, looking up and examining him as a farmer would inspect a new calf.

Bran's heart pounded as he searched for words. His years of training should have readied him for this moment. He searched for the speech he had rehearsed, but the moment took the words from him. He would have to rely on instinct.

And he felt faintly ridiculous, preparing to address a bird.

To gain a couple of heartbeats while he grasped composure, he cleared his throat and turned his head to watch the Ordovices disappear towards Nant Bran.

He turned back towards the pool and a woman stood beside him.

Even Bran, trained to show no surprise, failed to hold a gasp. The change had happened in an instant and without warning. With no blinding flash of magic or stench of brimstone. Bran was almost disappointed. It seemed so ordinary.

But he knew this was no ordinary woman.

And he wondered if there was any maiden in the Celtic lands to match her.

Black hair swirled down to her waist, shimmering with fire and ice in the lights of the torch and the moon. Her night-dark dress was loose enough to ripple delicately around her as she moved, but at the same time tight enough to show her curves, and low cut enough to betray a hint of her breasts. Her eyes were large, dark, and deep enough to drown in, complementing her hair but contrasting with her delicate skin and full lips. She wore no jewellery. She needed no trinkets.

A hint of crushed flowers drifted from her form.

"Are you happy, Goddess? Will you spare the rains?" he mocked, knowing he addressed the shapechanging Goddess of War and Death, not the mistress of the waters. He felt no fear as he spoke. Only calm. His confidence returned as he relied on instinct bred of a lifetime's training.

He did not betray any manly interest in the beauty which had appeared beside him. To Bran's surprise, the maiden's brow furrowed. Maybe she, too, was unsure of the moment.

"I am no mere fairy of the water," she chided eventually in a soft voice which reminded Bran of Dermot's harp.

"I know you are no water goddess. I know you have many names. In Britain we call you Andraste. In Ireland you are The Morrigan. Our cousins in Gaul, before falling under the yoke of Roman rule, knew you as Nemetona. You have as many names as you have forms, Goddess of War and Death." The torch was becoming heavy. He switched it to his left hand.

"You are a wise man. You are worthy of the title 'Archdruid of Britain'."

"I do not ask for flattery, Andraste. I seek only your respect."

"Respect must be earned, Archdruid. Through strength and power."

Bran changed the subject, mocking the lady once more. "Boann has chosen not to present herself to us tonight. Does she not recognise our gifts? Will she not hold the rains?"

"I do not speak for Boann. But *I* am pleased with the gifts. I cannot spare the water, but in return for what has been given tonight I can grant the Ordovices success in battle. The Shimmering Sword of Fergus mac Roy has not been sacrificed in vain."

The Druid felt his eyes narrow. He studied her in the torchlight. The flames reflected in her eyes, giving them life. Her dress fluttered in the breeze. "You are an ambitious woman, Andraste. Do not use the sword for material means."

"I have nothing more planned for it than the glory of the Ordovices."

"Would you not add that the glory of the Ordovices is entwined with your own glory?"

"You are a wise man, Druid," was her simple response.

"Do not harm the Ordovices. Evil courses through your veins, Andraste. You may be powerful, but you are only one. The Brotherhood of Druids has many members. We are a capable adversary." He turned with a confident arrogance to head back toward shelter. He did not even permit himself to look back to see if she was casting spells or curses in is direction.

"Do you not fear me, Archdruid? Do you not know how powerful I am?" she taunted.

"I do not fear you, Andrastre. I let you fear me. For you can to no more than kill me. I, though, may thwart your ambition for eternity." He retraced his steps until once more he stood on the planking. Their eyes met. "Which of us holds the stronger threat?" he asked.

"Would you not join me in triumph? Have you not thought of ruling Britain with me?"

"Have you not already offered the kingship to Caswallon, lady? It does not pay to offer one prize to many men."

"I repeat Archdruid, that you are a wise man. You will know to accept my bargain."

"And if I don't? If Britain is taken from your grasp?"

"I will bide my time. And next time we meet…"

"Lady?"

"Pah! I though Druids wise! Have you not been taught of the passage of time?"

Bran recited his learning as he struggled to understand the threat. "Time moves as a chariot wheel. As a wheel turns and takes the chariot forward, so time itself moves."

"But let us surmise that the chariot does not move forward in a straight line."

"Lady?"

"Let us surmise that one of the chariot's two horses is lame. As it limps it pulls the vehicle to one side. No matter how hard the charioteer tries to steady his course, the wounded horse will cause our chariot to move in a circle." She put a finger thoughtfully to her lips. "No… our chariot of time is not merely moving in a single circle…"

"Our chariot is tracing the path of a circle over and over, repeatedly?"

"Exactly. Meaning that, at some point of the future, the exact same part of our chariot's wheel will make contact with the exact same piece of ground. And the longer our chariot moves in this circle, the more times the same part of the wheel will hit the same part of the ground…"

"…and the wheel of time moves continually." Bran completed the sentence for the maiden, now aware of the path she was leading him down.

"Meaning that despite the passage of time the same heartbeat can be revisited." She wore no expression but looked Bran in the eye. "Should you fail me this time, Archdruid, I will defeat you instead when we meet today in the time to come. Or the time after that. Or after that. Until I am granted Britain. For be sure, Archdruid, our spirits will meet again when the chariot wheel turns on this era of revolt once more. This moment will be replayed once, twice, infinite times until the Romans are driven from our islands and I possess Britain."

"But, Andraste, how do I know our chariot of time does not move in a straight line?"

"Maybe the charioteer can steer her straight for now, Archdruid. But even a woman may cripple a mere horse if she wishes."

She spat defiantly between the priest's feet.

Bran's stomach tumbled. He wanted to sit and contemplate the new thought Andraste had placed in his mind. He saw a reason for his existence, not in this life maybe, but in a life to come.

He could almost sense a future being inside him, without Druid training, fighting against ignorance of the Ways of the Earth, unsure of everything except fear.

And, like all untrained men, the being was incapable of fighting the whim of a beautiful woman.

Bran felt fear. But not for himself.

Fear for Britain.

For Britain must surely fall.

Unable to counter her words, Bran could only nod toward the dark, still water. "Retrieve your gifts, lady. While my firebrand still presents you with light."

Silently, she turned to the pool and in a single movement slipped beneath the surface. Her entry was delicate. She barely caused a ripple.

Bran held the flaming wood over the water. A glob of burning fat fell from it and fizzed quietly away on the surface. Anxiously, he watched the shadowy form glide beneath the surface. To his disappointment, she found the weapon easily. Its silver glow gave away its hiding place amid the mud and reeds which has already closed around it.

As soon as the sacred blade was within her grasp, the dull silver glow became a pulse of red, bringing the water were alive with fire and blood.

A prophecy of the death and suffering to come, Bran's heart told him.

The maiden's head broke the surface as she sucked a breath.

And just as quickly, the Lady of Death descended.

Bran followed her outline and the red glow as Andraste swam for the drowned Roman. He watched in fascinated unease as the waters seemed to part, his torchlight giving him a view of the Goddess beneath the surface as clear as when she stood demurely at his side.

He watched her in the water as she freed the corpse of the rocks and branches weighing it down. She surfaced for another breath before working on the carcass itself. The sword was designed for stabbing, not cutting, but the blade was keen and allowed her to sever the head. The home of the soul was soon removed from its body, and the scene was bathed in red light as the blade still glared its warning of evil.

The task completed, her feet found the bottom of the pool. She stood, thigh deep in the pond, splattered by mud, weeds and blood. Even Bran couldn't help admire the form before him, her sodden dress clinging like a lover to the perfect shape of her body. He swallowed hard as his eyes feasted on her clothing, which caressed the tight outline of her hips and buttocks. He allowed his gaze to drift up her body, past the firm, flat belly to the curves of her breasts, nipples straining to push through the wet material.

She smiled at him; the innocent smile of a maiden. For a heartbeat Bran's training deserted him and he yearned to hold her.

But only for a heartbeat.

She turned to her trophies and held them to the heavens, the sword of Fergus mac Roy with its unearthly scarlet radiance in her right hand. Bran could almost feel its strength pulsating through her arm and body like waves of emotion.

In Andraste's left hand blood oozed from the head, and she held it above her, cackling joyously as blood dripped onto her face and mouth, tasting his death as it strengthened her. She bit into the flesh and destroyed his soul as she consumed it, taking the life force for her own needs.

Any lingering doubts were chased from Bran's mind.

This woman has the power to take Britain.

The night seemed to fade before the Archdruid, with the silver moonlight and the red sword combining with his firebrand into a single, all consuming mist. He shook his head to dispel the unbidden vision, but still he saw the heat of battle, the proud warriors of Britain uniting for one last effort to push the Eagles back into the sea. He saw the legions crumble amid the clamour of war; he could taste the fear and blood as Romans cried for the release of death.

He saw suffering, but he saw victory for Britain. He saw men worshipping Andraste in gratitude for delivering them from the yoke of servitude.

He saw men sacrificing their neighbours in orgies of blood to give the Goddess the strength she needed to consummate her rule of death.

The vision cleared. Still standing in the water, Andraste's contorted lips let out the savage cry of a goddess who would soon be triumphant; a scream like a banshee's that drove the animals of the night deep into their burrows; a cry that Bran had no doubt the Ordovices would hear, whether they slept in with the elite in Nant Bran, or whether they were more humble shepherds and slaves atop Tre'r Ceiri's sheer-sided fortress. The Sight showed them huddled around their fires, already nervous, hearing her cries and covering their ears in terror.

Andraste smiled at him from the water, as if knowing his thoughts.

Her dress still clung to her flesh to display her form, but Bran was no longer enchanted.

Instead, he felt the pangs of hopelessness. These people listening to her wind-borne scream were the people she would have within her grasp. And they would help her drive the Romans from their British eerie and plunder power in her name.

Bran shivered at the thought.

Chapter 14

Peter Davis rolled over for the thousandth time. For the thousandth time he glared at his clock.

Eight-thirteen. One minute later than last time he'd looked.

He wanted to get up, but didn't. He might wake Johnny.

He rolled over yet again. He curtains dulled the morning light, but for the thousandth time he checked his pillow for maggots.

For the thousandth time he told himself it was only a dream.

But he crawled across his bed to look in the bin. The dead maggot stared up at him.

At last, a sound broke his thoughts. The patter of his brother's feet, closely followed by his father's, passed his room and tread the stairs. The second step down gave a creak.

* * * *

"How did he sleep?" Peter asked his father in the kitchen.

"Like a log. As if nothing happened. And remember, the doctor told us not to mention it. Treat it as a dream."

"Yeah," Peter agreed quickly as Johnny bounded in.

He was relieved no one mentioned the painting. Not his father this morning, and no one last night. Although he had made sure everyone knew it had changed back. As if the subject had been declared taboo without anyone saying so.

Or maybe Johnny's nightmare was more important.

"Johnny, how do you fancy a day at the beach? Dad's got some work to do, so I can drive you over to Anglesey and we'll all be out of his hair for a few hours."

"Yes! The beach! The beach! Will it be a sandy one? Can I make sandcastles?"

"I should think so, titch. The sun's beginning to get hot already. How about we ask Lucy if she wants to come and leave in a few minutes?"

Alun smiled over his toast. "I don't think it'll be 'just a few minutes' if you want your sister to come as well. Miss 'Half Hour In The Bathroom' will need her hair perfect for getting it messed up in the sea."

Peter and Johnny grinned their agreement as the 'phone rang.

"I'll get it," volunteered Alun. "It might be some work. You two can get on with finding the swimming things. They're probably still in a box to be unpacked."

"I'll find them! I'll find them!"

"Oh no you won't, little boy," corrected Peter. "I know what you're like. You'll make a mess. You'll throw everything on the floor and not put it back." He ruffled Johnny's hair. "You have your breakfast. I'll find the trunks. Do you want your blue ones or the ones with leopard stripes? You can wake your sister."

Johnny's eyes opened wide in a way which reminded Peter of last night. "No way, Peetie. I'm not waking Lucy. I'll get the swimming things."

Johnny shot off and Peter followed his father into the hall. "Yes, okay, I'll give her a shout." Alun placed a hand over the mouthpiece and called upstairs. "LUCY! IT'S FOR YOU!"

"Oh God! Tell 'em I'm dead!" came a voice, only just distinguishable through a thick duvet and a closed door.

Alun cracked a grin. "Okay. I'll tell Toby Griffiths that Lucinda will ring him back when she's been resurrected, shall I?"

Feet scurried upstairs. "Don't you dare! I'm coming down."

"She'll be with you in a minute Toby," Alun said into the receiver before placing it gently down.

Lucy, clad only in a baggy pink T-shirt nightie, charged down the stairs. Her blonde mop needed a comb, and her breasts and crucifix bounced in time as her feet pounded on the stairs.

"If Toby could see how delicate and feminine you look doing that he'd be really impressed," said Peter.

"Peter! Don't tease your sister! You know she hasn't got a sense of humour!"

She stuck out a tongue at her father and brother then frowned and waved them away with her hand.

Johnny reappeared in the kitchen minutes later, holding three sets of swimming costumes and towels aloft like trophies.

"Let's go to the beach!" he squealed.

"Not 'till I've had my breakfast, changed, and done something with my hair," corrected Lucy, no longer on the 'phone but sporting a wide grin. "Yes, tough luck lads. The Lady of the House will be accompanying you."

"Told you," laughed Alun, following his daughter. "Lunch time at least." Ignoring his daughter's playful tongue, he continued. "I thought I'd give Old Aunt Gwyn a call. If she's going to be in I thought we'd pay her a visit tonight. She'd love to have visitors. No one's doing anything, are we?"

"I'm out. Toby's taking me to the pictures. Sorry," said Lucy in a tone implying she was anything but sorry.

Peter, trying to be diplomatic, ushered his sister out of the kitchen and slipped a slice of toast into her hand. "Why don't you go and get dressed, and be *very* quick about it," he suggested. "Johnny, you go and put the swimming stuff in a bag. I'll load the car up." He paused. "Don't bother making yourself presentable, sis. We'd like to be away *this* week."

"Pig."

"Bitch."

"Well, at least *I'm* not going to Old Auntie Wales, or whatever her name is," she whispered in a voice Alun wouldn't hear.'

"Bitch again," whispered Peter, but winking at his sister to show how lucky she was at missing the appointment. "But, seeing as you're coming to Anglesey…"

"Yes? You want something. Don't you?"

"Yeah. There's a couple of art shops I wouldn't mind visiting on the island. They might be interested in flogging my pictures. If you could entertain Johnny for a while so I can nip off for an hour that would be great." Lying to his sister felt awful.

Her eyes opened in horror. "What? You want me to give up valuable sunbathing time so you can wonder off?"

"Have I told you recently what a wonderful sister you are?"

"You're a smooth talking little sod, aren't you? Go on, then. Seeing as how it's for the family's good."

The front door opened. "Hi," called Rhiannon's uncertain voice. "You said to let myself in…"

"That's fine," replied Alun. "Come on in. I'll pour you a coffee."

Johnny appeared. "We're going to the beach, Bryn," he called.

"Tell you what, Rhiannon," said Peter. "Why don't you and Bryn come?"

"Because I've got to clean up here. And anyway, I should get back. Dave's a bit down. He still can't find work."

"How about we take Bryn with us, then? Johnny's got a spare pair of trunks. That okay with you, sis?"

Lucy shrugged. "Fine. The kids can amuse each other while I get in some serious sunbathing. And I'll take my mobile. It'll probably work on the island, away from the mountains. I'll be able to have a good old yak to people with *taste*."

Bryn jumped about and squealed enthusiastically.

"And I don't think my life would be worth living if I said no," agreed Rhiannon. "Although in theory *I* should be minding *your* son. But it'll be nice to spend some time alone with Dave. If you're sure…"

The matter was settled, and Peter's old car was soon loaded with clothing, towels and beach toys.   Finally, making sure no one saw, he unlocked the small shed and loaded a garden spade into the boot of his car.

Within five minutes three willing passengers were waiting impatiently. "You must be keen, sis," he teased Lucy. "I was expecting to have time for a cup of tea before you came back down."

After extending her tongue again, she ushered Johnny and Bryn into the back seat before settling into the front. She wore jeans and black T-shirt proclaiming 'Metal Loving Lady' with a picture of a rock band prancing aggressively beneath. Sunglasses shaded her eyes and a black band held her ponytail in place.

"You'll boil in that getup," Peter pointed out as he turned the key.

"I doubt it, brother dear. There's two types of blondes in this world. There's the dizzy, no-hoper sort who spend their lives in Essex nightclubs. And then there's the ice-cool types who, as the words imply, stay chilled even under the most strenuous of circumstances—like having two brothers." She lifted her sunglasses and looked knowingly at Peter. "I, brother dear, am among the latter sort. And anyway, I've got my 'kini on underneath."

They laughed as the engine stuttered into life.

And still no-one's mentioned the painting, thought Peter.

It's almost as if it never happened.

And he wasn't about to ruin the morning by talking about it.

* * * *

The mountains disappeared into Peter's mirrors, and the car headed along the coast toward the Menai Bridge. Lucy had discovered with a whoop that her mobile could receive a signal. She fidgeted her crucifix with one hand as she typed a message with the other.

Peter swallowed, saddened as always by the sight of the crucifix. He remembered how their mother, knowing she was to die, had asked a priest to bless it before handing it to Lucy.

The family had all cried. *It was like we were all beginning to say goodbye,* Peter thought.

He sighed and flicked his eyes away from the road and to his left, to the vista of southern Anglesey laid out below, beyond the slim stretch of water.

The view bought back memories.

He could see the stretch of beach where so many of the Ordovices had valiantly given their lives against the Romans. The years had worn the coast, but dunes still stood above the shore; those same dunes from which Bran had witnessed the slaughter.

Peter slowed the car, his concentration blinkered by memories of blood.

"...I've got four action toys. That's why four is my favourite number."

"My favourite number is six. Because I'm six."

"Uncle Peter, What's your favourite number? And why?"

He answered before he could stop himself. "Nine. It's the sacred triple three." He bit his tongue. That was *Bran's* answer.

"That's a bit philosophical for this early in the day, brother."

"Sorry." To his relief no-one pushed him.

"Auntie Lucy, what's your favourite number?"

She muttered under her breath before making her voice audible. "I think you can just call me Lucy. 'Auntie' makes me sound really old. As if I'm Uncle Peter's age."

"Cheers, sis."

"Pleasure, bruv."

"Okay, Lucy. What's your favourite number?"

"Er... I don't think I've got one."

"Yes you have."

She turned to look at Peter. "I do?"

"Sure you do."

"What is it, Peetie? What's Lucy's favourite number?"

"Er... Lucy's favourite number is six hundred and sixty-six."

"Pig."

Johnny's voice was puzzled. "Why?"

"Are you implying I'm a beast, brother?"

"No."

"Good."

"More of a beast*ess*."

"Pig!"

"What's six hundred and sixty-six?"

"Er... it's in some songs daddy and Lucy like."

Johnny turned to Bryn. "Lucy and daddy like *heavy metal*." In his mirror, Peter saw the corners of his brother's mouth turn down in a grimace, as if he were being force-fed swede. Johnny hated swede.

"Daddy used to grab my and Lucy's and mummy's hands when we were about your age," said Peter. "We used to form a circle and dance to heavy metal."

"You used to headbang. Daddy told me."

"Yeah, we used to headbang."

"And six-six-six is the number of an evil beast that means the end of the world. According to the bible. And there have been lots of songs about the evil beast and the end of the world." Lucy broke into tune.

Peter joined in. He knew the words like a Druid knew incantations, and found himself concentrating on the words. The lyrics came back to him above the chatter and the car's soft purr; words proclaiming power and unstoppable evil, rolling themselves over inside his mind as his thoughts turned to Morgan. *As if the words were written for her.*

His dream came flooding back, mingling with the music's threats. He could almost hear Morgan spitting the words as maggots dripped from her lips.

But how did it connect with reality? And with Bran's life, all those centuries ago? If Bran existed.

But I'll know by the end of the morning, he reminded himself. His mind turned to chariot wheels and crippled horses.

"…Pete?…Pete?"

"Huh?"

Lucy was looking at him, concerned. "You looked as if you were miles away. I was worried you were going to crash."

He looked into his mirror. The boys were chatting happily to each other, but he still reduced his voice to a whisper. "Sorry, sis. I can't help thinking about my picture."

Her eyes turned away. "Neither can I. But it's like no-one wants to talk about it. It was a helluva shock, but like you said, it just seemed to turn back. Anyone else and I'd have put it down to a sick joke. But you're not sick."

"Thanks."

"Even though you're a pratt."

"Thanks again."

"No problem."

Peter looked towards his sister. The words had been spoken with a grin her face didn't reflect.

But he had to keep pushing. There was more he needed from her. Johnny and Bryn were in their own world of action toys. He could speak without them interrupting.

Peter flicked the indicator left to take them over the bridge to the Sacred Isle… *or Anglesey,* he reminded himself.

He took a deep breath. "Lucy?"

"Hmm?" She was half dozing, lying back in her seat, sunglasses perched on her nose, with the summer sun on her face. She took a drag from a cigarette.

"You're studying Roman Britain."

She sat up and turned her head towards him. "Yeah? Why?"

"What do you know about Boudicca's revolt?"

"Why?"

"Just wondering. Humour me. Especially what was going on around here at the time."

"I'm not sure I should tell you. Mister Peter 'A History Degree Has No Relevance To Modern Life' Davis."

"Oh, for Christ's sake, Lucy! I only asked a simple question." He bit his lip. "I'm sorry. I shouldn't have snapped."

"Have you got irritable bowel, brother?"

"No. Why?"

"Then your bowel is about the only part of you that isn't. But I'll tell you what I know so I can show off how clever I am. There's just no need to be touchy. Okay?"

Peter bit his lip to stifle a retort.

"Boudicca's revolt—she was actually called Boudicca, not Boadicea—took place over the years 60 to 61 AD. It was started when her husband died." She paused. "Christ... I can't remember his name. I'll fail if it comes up in the exam. Shit."

"His name doesn't matter," cajoled Peter.

"Anyway, King Whatever-He-Was had bequeathed half his kingdom to Rome and half to his daughters, but the Romans took the whole lot. They raped Boudicca and her daughters—or did her daughters just have to watch? Christ, I need to revise."

"Well, *I'm* impressed, sis."

She smiled. "Anyway, being raped pissed Boudicca off. Not surprising, I suppose. Then the Romans settled their own people in Colchester and gave away the Iceni's—that's Boudicca's tribe's—land. That pissed off the common Britons. So now everyone's pissed off."

Peter nodded. "So what about North Wales?"

She paused to flick a cigarette butt out of the open window. "North Wales wasn't really involved in the revolt. That was down to the Iceni and the... the... er... the Trinovantes of East Anglia. But the story does move up to Anglesey, in fact."

Peter's throat dried. He swallowed, trying to keep at least half of his mind on the road as it wound along Anglesey's west coast, through the whitewashed hamlets, past the twinkling waters of deserted bays, and over ridges of low pasture. They were nearing the beach Peter had picked from a map back at the cottage.

"How does the story come up here?" asked Peter, although he—Bran—knew the answer.

"The Druids had been stirring up rebellion. The centre of their religion was Anglesey, and the Romans sent a force up here to destroy the sacred groves and the like. It worked; there's loads of archaeological evidence—offerings and that—up to the mid-first century, but it suddenly stops. The Romans defeated the Britons then ravaged the place."

"Do we know the names of any of the Druids of the Ordovices when the Romans fought them?"

Lucy shot her head towards Peter. "I didn't know you knew your Roman tribes, brother!"

He lied. "I read a little in a book before we came up here. Wanted to know a bit about the place."

"No, we don't know the names of any of the Druids. And we don't even know it was the Ordovices who the Romans fought. There were other tribes up here as well… Christ, Pete. Why do you need to know this? You've never been the least bit interested in history before."

He brushed off the question. "But why did the revolt fail?"

"In a nutshell?"

"In a nutshell."

"In a nutshell, Boudicca ballsed it."

"Ballsed it?"

"Yup. Ballsed it. She had Roman Britain at her mercy, and after sacking London the Brits were within striking distance of the rich villas around Kent and Sussex. At the time the Roman conquest was only a few years old, and most of them still lived in the south-east."

"So what went wrong?"

"She didn't head south to the unprotected villas. She turned north, straight into the path of just about the only Roman army in Britain. The one coming back from Anglesey."

"Why?"

Lucy shrugged. "No-one seems to know. Even my Professor has no idea. Maybe Boudicca didn't know the army was there. Maybe she was badly advised."

"Badly advised? By who?"

She shrugged again. "Her Druids I suppose. She worshipped this war goddess. Maybe the Druids saw some sign that said she should go north. They relied on stupid things like birsdsongs and that to tell the future. No wonder they lost. The Druids sound like total pillocks!"

Peter took the comment as an insult but ignored it. "Goddess? What sort of goddess?"

"Like I said, a war goddess. Andraste they called her. We don't know anything about Andraste, but it seems to be reckoned she's the same as an evil Irish goddess whose name became Anglicised and she appears in the King Arthur's legends as Morgan le Fey. She could change into different shapes, but was usually either a beautiful woman or a raven or an old hag."

Instinctively, Peter slammed on the brakes.

There was commotion from the back. And fury from Lucy.

But Peter didn't care. His head swum. There was too much going through his mind.

Goddess... Morgan... beautiful... old... woman... raven... Andraste...
Things were beginning to make sense.
And soon he would prove it.

Chapter 15

The green wall of Snowdonia became more distant with each mile. At last Peter's car crested a hill, and laid out before him was a bay between two rocky cliffs, its small car park and yellow sand undisturbed except for a white ice cream van.

For the first time, Peter asked himself how he knew this beach was here. Yes, he'd seen it on a map. But how did he know it would look so inviting?

"Here okay?" he asked, pushing more sinister thoughts to the back of his mind.

"Looks gorgeous," said his sister.

"I want to stay here! I want an ice cream! I'm going to build a massive castle!" agreed Johnny.

Bryn joined in with a screech of delight as Peter parked the car. Inside the ice cream van a teenager looked up from a magazine, watched the car with disinterest and dropped his head back to his reading.

He looked up again when Lucy got out.

"I think you've got an admirer, sis," pointed out Peter.

"What's he look like? Johnny, wait for Peter to unlock the boot," she chided as the youngster fought eagerly to get his hands on his bucket and spade. "I can't look back in case he takes it as a sign of interest."

"Not your sort. No muscles. Maybe a year or so too young."

"Yeah, but he might have hidden depths. And it might not work out with Toby tonight… what say I cheer him up? Fifty pence says I can get us free ice creams."

"Don't you think it's a bit extreme to sell your body for a couple of cornets?" asked Peter as he unlocked the boot. Johnny and Bryn grabbed the beach things. Peter was relieved they didn't question his spade. "It's not as if we're paupers."

"Don't be silly. My body's priceless," she said, strutting round to Peter's side of the car, where she was in full view of the van. In one swift, expert movement of her right hand she pulled the black band from her hair, and with a toss of her head her blonde hair was falling around her shoulders, glinting in the morning sun. "Haven't you ever fluttered your eyelids to get something from a bloke?"

"Er… no."

"You ought to try it sometime," she teased, reaching to her waist and the bottom of her black T- shirt. Crossing her arms over, in one more quick movement her shirt was over her head. She tossed her hair back in place, and thrust her chest out slightly. Her breasts strained against her white bikini cups. Her golden crucifix plunged between her breasts and caught the sun.

Even Peter has to admit to himself that she was a bit of a looker. Even though she was his sister. *Not up to Morgan's standard, though*, he quickly reassured himself.

His stomach knotted.

"Is he still watching?" Lucy asked, nodding almost imperceptibly towards the ice cream van.

"Yup. Eyes out on organ stops. A bit like Bryn's," Peter laughed.

The youngster blushed and started talking obviously to Johnny about action toys.

"I don't think I'll do my jeans. It's hard to wriggle out of skin-tight trousers and still look sexy."

She pulled her purse from her pocket. "Anyone for an ice-cream?"

Johnny and Bryn squealed with delight, but Peter declined. "Thanks sis, but I want to get along to the art shop. Maybe I'll take you up on it when I get back.'"

She ushered the youngsters towards the van, fussing over them as they made a choice. They returned with Lucy glowering as if she'd been force-fed vinegar.

"'Problems, sis?"

"Bastard."

"What have I done now?"

"No, not you. Not this time, anyway." She paused, pointing her thumb back over her shoulder. "'That... that *bastard* made me pay."

"So... let me get this straight. You went to buy some ice creams... and you had to pay?"

"Yeah. *Bastard*. I virtually expose myself, and he *still* makes me pay. And he had *acne*. I kept thinking one of his zits would explode. Then we'd have yellow topping on our cornets. *Ugh!*"

"So you lose the bet then? Don't worry. You can keep your fifty pence."

"Thank you. So generous."

Peter said his goodbyes and climbed into the car. As he left, the boys disappeared among the dunes and tufts of coarse grass as they charged for the sea, ice creams in one hand, buckets in the other. Lucy juggled a blanket, beach bag, handbag, picnic hamper and ice cream as she followed behind.

Peter was relieved to be back in the car and driving again. The morning had dragged, but it was good to be alone and able to work on a hunch at last. He would either prove his dreams of Bran were real history. Or disprove them.

Either way, the answer would raise more questions.

He was near the king's palace at Abberffraw. Or rather, he reminded himself, near its site. Instinctively, he turned inland. He had never been down this road before, but he knew he was heading in the right direction. It was different being in the car to being on foot as Bran had been, but the road layout followed the ancient tracks across the island which the Archdruid knew so well. They kept to the high ground and skirted the valleys which crossed the island, and which had, in Bran's day, been treacherous bogs.

Boggy and infertile. Thanks to the rains sent by the Goddess Boann, Lady of the Waters.

Peter told himself not to be stupid. *The Celtic gods were nothing more than figments from the imaginations of superstitious, unscientific men.*

But was begging favour from a multitude of gods any more unreasonable than a Christian asking forgiveness from Christ?, he asked himself.

The path had changed in two thousand years. What had been a muddy path was now a seldom-used ribbon of tarmac with weeds pushing through. Tall hedges enclosed the road, where once horsemen had interrupted views over the island.

But it was the same path that he had seen in his dream. The dream when Dermot had half dragged, half carried the Roman legionnaire to his death. There was no doubt.

And the hill was there, rising in front of him. Bit it had changed. And not only with the trees, brambles and cows scattered across it. It was so *ordinary*. Gone was the aura of magical power which had seemed to consume a windswept hilltop, bare but for the grey monolith standing dominating its low peak.

But it was *the* hill. He had no doubt.

Peter suppressed a shiver as he remembered the agonising death the legionnaire had suffered on its summit all those years ago.

No, he reminded himself. The same hill where he had *dreamed* the Roman soldier had met his death, all those years ago.

He stopped the car as near to the hill as he could, in one of the few passing spaces on the single-track road.

Peter got out and peered up at the hill through a gap in the thick hedge. He stepped back and leaned back against the car, trying to take in the atmosphere. He didn't know whether to be relieved or disappointed when all he could feel was the heat of the sun and a trace the sea on the light breeze.

He pulled his attention from the hill, and grabbed the spade from the boot and swapped his trainers for wellington boots. Finally, he slammed the boot shut and locked the car before walking a few yards along the road and, checking no-one was about, vaulting a gate into the field. He was grateful for the thick hedge and the trees atop the hill. He would not be seen.

A few cows turned their thick necks to watch him take the slope, but none paid much heed to a human with nothing but a spade and a jaw set by determination.

Peter felt a tingling of anticipation. Nerves reached out to his limbs until he was worried he would drop the spade. Once at the top, he pushed his way through the undergrowth, hardly noticing that the brambles he pushed aside left blood on his hands.

And there it was, sitting in front of him. Half hidden by overhanging branches, and cloaked by a film of lichen.

But it was the stone.

The stone.

Peter could still hear the screams of the dying Roman filling the air as Dermot's blade excavated his eye sockets.

Anxiously, Peter's unsteady hand reached out. His fingers trembled, unwilling to touch the ancient grey slate, remembering their experience the day Peter's family had looked around the farmhouse for the first time.

It had felt like an electric shock. And the sky had bled.

He looked away, taking in his surroundings as he put off the moment when he must explore his dreams.

Before him, Aberffraw was laid out, gently enjoying the warm morning. The town had changed; whitewashed brick houses had replaced the circular huts of wood and thatch. Parked cars cluttered the once lonely streets which had known only the occasional horseman.

But the river still ran lazily. Peter could make out the spot where he had picked little Conor's body out of the water.

The back of his hand wiped memories from this eyes.

He forced his fingers back to the stone. He had come this far. He needed to know.

Nothing.

Just a slippery feeling as his fingers slid along an uneven surface of lichen and moss.

More confidently now, and with his heart beating in his throat, Peter ran his hand along the edge of the stone. His trembling fingers explored through the monolith's surface through the lichen, searching for telltale grooves carved along the side of the monolith.

He wanted to withdraw his hand from the rock.

But he had come this far. He needed to know.

Then, the sensation of a dagger entering his ribs. He struggled for breath. His burning fingers and wide eyes explored the spot.

Yes. There they were. He explored them again, needing to make sure.

Four grooves. And four more beneath them. The double 'K' Bran had carved all those years ago for Kyra and Conor.

He had found them.

Peter didn't stop to consider the implications. His mind refused to register. He became a daze of thoughts.

Dig, dig, dig.

In a frenzy, he thrust the spade into the earth next to the stone, pushing the blade deep, deep into the earth, over and over again. He turned over the soil, making a small pile next to the stone and pushing the brambles to one side. He felt his heart pound.

He stopped to pull a thorn from his thumb. He wiped sweat from his brow and palms. It was a hot day. And he had hit tree roots running below the soil and protecting the ground from the inquisitive. He found himself using all his strength to sever thick roots with his spade as he dug for his past.

But he knew exactly where he was digging. To the front of the stone, but a little to the right.

Every time the spade met resistance his heart tugged. Until the blockage was confirmed as just another root.

He realised he was pleased not to be here at night. Even in daylight he wondered if he could feel spirits closing around him. The slopes were regaining the brooding atmosphere of the past.

And as he shivered his spade hit something. But something different to a root. Dropping the spade, he knelt down on the soft earth and scraped at the soil with his bare hands.

Within seconds Peter had uncovered something which gleamed back at him. Without uncovering more of it he knew exactly what he had found.

What he was looking for.

But he carried on digging until Dermot's harp was free of the earth for the first time in two millennia.

He stood and gazed onto it.

The instrument was corroded and misshapen after two thousand years buried in the earth. The strings had long since disappeared. But it was still Dermot's harp.

In Peter's eyes, it was beautiful. As beautiful as Dermot's music which had drifted from it all those years ago.

Gently, he laid it on the ground beside the pile of soil and returned to his spade, dreading what he might find next, but knowing he must continue.

Seconds later more was exposed to the sunlight. Softened by time and stained brown by the earth, he lifted the skull from the soil. It was still intact, the perfect remains of an infant.

The tension and fear drained from Peter instantaneously as the image of Conor, laying face down and motionless in the ditch, returned to him. He cradled the head in his arms as he remembered the despair Bran had felt for the child. He remembered the little hands reaching out to grab Bran's finger that evening at Tre'r Ceiri, and the perfect face smiling and blowing bubbles up at his grandfather. He remembered the hand outstretched to him in death.

Peter wondered how the skull had survived the centuries.

Maybe it was meant to survive. For me to find.

As the memories drifted through his mind, he thought of the wasted young life, so needlessly and pitilessly extinguished.

Peter sat himself against a tree, clutched the skull to his chest, and wept for Conor and Kyra. He wept for the grief shared by Dermot and Bran.

Only later did he weep for the confused whirlwind flying around inside his head. He wasn't yet ready to contemplate the consequences of proving his dreams held the truth.

I am *Archdruid Bran.*

He had no idea how long he had been sitting crying when there was a sound from above. He wiped the tear-induced mist from his eyes to look up.

Peter Davis chilled. There, on a branch above him, sat a black raven, cackling at his despair.

Chapter 16

Guthor looked around. The sun was falling toward the west, into the forest which had been the party's constant companion since leaving the western mountains.

Guthor patted Thunder's flank reassuringly. He felt Sergovax's hand on his shoulder.

"Worried, warrior?" the old soldier asked.

"I don't like these Roman roads," Guthor admitted. "They make hooves clatter. It's an unnatural sound." He strained his eyes through the gathering murk. Up ahead he could make out the robed figure of Bran, Archdruid of Britain, on his white charger. Next to Bran rode his grieving son. The son who had uttered not a word since the party had left Tre'r Ceiri.

Further in the distance, completing the party, were two more mounted warriors.

Is this—six men—the only force the Ordovices could raise to drive the Romans from Britain?

Sergovax smiled. "And the clattering Roman cobbles will give us as much warning of the enemy's presence. No Briton would dare attack a group with a Druid, so we need only fear Romans."

Guthor touched his swordhilt. "I do not fear Romans. I fear not delivering the Archdruid safely to Queen Boudicca."

Sergovax gave a hoarse laugh. "Don't fear for the Archdruid, boy. He is more capable of looking after himself than most mighty warriors. I nearly had to twist his arm to get him to agree to an escort."

"So why did you twist his arm?"

"To get away from the Ordovices." The voice of Caswallon's champion was flat, as if inviting the next question.

"But why get away from Caswallon? You're his champion."

"And you, Guthor are loyal to Caswallon. But, bluntly, Caswallon's day is over. He was never a king. He ruled, yes. But only because he was the son of a king. He's a good, honest lad, but... no. He lacks the steel of kingship." The warrior sighed. "Defeat by the Romans, and the debacle with that festering sword... whatever faith the Ordovices had in him is lost."

"So why run away?" Guthor bit his lip. "I'm sorry. I know you are no coward."

"I must be ageing, boy. I've run a sword through men for lesser insults. But the point is a fair one." Sergovax paused and adjusted the shield which, slung on his back, had begun to slip down his swordarm. "There will be war among the Ordovices while everyone who thinks they have a claim to the kingship stakes it. The streams around Tre'r Ceiri will flow red with treachery. I've had happy years there. I don't any part of a pointless civil war. I'd rather die fighting Romans than Britons."

"I would have stayed to defend Caswallon. Had I not been ordered to escort the Archdruid."

"Well, you're a young fool." Sergovax's voice was laced with anger. "Why die in the Western Wilds? Being born in a place doesn't give you the selfish right to die there. You're a good warrior. One of the best the Ordovices can offer. That is why you have been chosen for Bran's bodyguard. Think of it as an honour."

I have been chosen, Guthor thought bitterly, *because I am just about the only warrior to come out of the battle of the Sacred Isle.* But he didn't say as much to Sergovax.

"Halt. We stay here the night," Sergovax announced.

* * * *

Guthor was excused the routine duties of cooking or collecting ferns for bedding. Instead, he was instructed to rest before his turn at guard duty.

Not that there's much use for a guard, he told himself. *All the tribes within a day's ride would have heard the hooves cracking the cursed cobbles. Even the little people wouldn't be able to weave enough magic to prevent them sounding like an army of hundreds on this road,* he thought.

The party ate in silence. Guthor refused food, insisting instead that he would wait for his watch to end before breaking bread. Hunger would keep the senses sharp, and Guthor was an ambitious warrior. It did no harm to appear committed to his task in front of an Archdruid, a bard, and the Champion of the Ordovices.

* * * *

Guthor leaned against a tree, some twenty paces from where his companions slept. There was no sound but for the occasional snore and a crackle from the dying campfire.

It was dark. The road stretched before him in both directions, but he could see nothing beyond the white outlines of his hands as they fidgeted with a twig. Even the forest beyond the road were little more than a black curtain against the sky. Clouds hid the heavens, giving him no moonlight to see by. A chill had descended, slowly, without Guthor noticing until the cold forced a shiver. He wrapped his cloak around him, the blue and green checked woollen robe bought in exchange for a calf.

Guthor sighed, wondering if he were fortunate to have first duty. He stifled a yawn, aching for something to relieve the monotony.

He looked up the road.

Nothing.

He looked down the road.

Nothing.

His foot found a clod of earth in the darkness. He kicked at it, enjoying the feeling of power as it exploded into countless fragments of dust. He looked into the black wood on the other side of the road.

Only the woods weren't black any more.

Guthor's mouth tightened. With a warrior's instinct he crouched into the undergrowth, becoming as one with the shadows. There was a slick 'swish' as he withdrew his blade from its leather scabbard.

"Sergovax!"

Silence.

His next call was louder, a whisper hissed as loudly as he dared. "Sergovax. Over here. There's something in the woods."

Within an instant the Champion was by Guthor's side, sword in hand. "What is it, lad?"

"I don't know. Some sort of fire?"

It may have been a fire, but not like one Guthor had ever seen before. Some fifty paces in the trees beyond the road, a glow the colour of blood gently lit the trees.

There was the soft sound of feet on moss behind him as the rest of the party awoke.

"I see it."

"And me."

"See, Archdruid." Sergovax's voice. "There's something strange going on."

Another footfall in the undergrowth. Bran's figure was visible as a white-robed shadow in the night.

"What is it?"

There was a sigh from Bran's direction. Guthor could almost picture the Archdruid stroking his grey beard in that calming way he had. The thought took some of the tension from him. "The work of the Otherworld," said Bran. "The gods are afoot."

Guthor shivered involuntarily and looked about him. The first glimmerings of fear manifested themselves as sweat on his palms. His fingers tightened around his swordhilt.

Sergovex's whisper broke the silence as he addressed his three fellow bodyguards. "Sital, you circle round to the left. Tuan, the centre. Guthor, the right. I'll be behind, ready to support any man who shouts."

Guthor was impressed by the old warrior's voice. It held no fear. He swallowed hard as he grasped his shield. He kissed his blade. The four warriors grasped each other's hands as a gesture of solidarity before stepping across the road.

Guthor, as ordered, circled around to the right, keeping the red glow some forty paces away. Instinctively, he moved in a crouch, ready to spring against a sudden attack. He tucked his sandals into his belt, allowing his feet to feel the undergrowth before they took his weight.

But he still paused to mutter silent oaths when his foot snapped a twig, or when his arm brushed a fern.

More than once he peered into the scarlet gloom. But he could see nothing.

A great feeling of loneliness came across him. He wished he had a colleague at his shoulder. To share the fear with. To protect his back.

The night was cool, but Guthor's body was bathed in a thin, chilling layer of sweat. At last he was level with the glow. Or he thought he was level. There was only the redness to guide him; he might have crept further round than he meant to.

It was time to close in. He listened out for sound.

Silence.

Not even the comforting scurrying of an animal to ease his worries; an owl calling to a mate; rodents hunting in the undergrowth; cattle lowing at a nearby settlement.

Just silence.

He listened again, straining his ears for a sign of his comrades.

He was met by silence.

Pure, still silence.

Evil silence.

Guthor swallowed. He ran a worried hand through his hair and pulled away a strand of bracken.

It was time to close in on the unearthly light. He kissed his swordblade and gripped the hilt tight.

The light was forty paces away.

To his relief there was moss to muffle his footfall.

Thirty-five paces. He cursed the gods silently as his left foot found a puddle. He was sure the splash must have been loud enough to summon demons from the Otherworld.

A scream.

Guthor froze.

A man screaming for mercy, pleading for his life. A man terrified out of his wits. Guthor stilled. *The voice belonged to Sital.*

The screaming stopped with a strained gurgle, as suddenly as it had started.

Then there was silence again.

Guthor would not be proven a coward in the presence of Sergovax and the Archdruid. Wiping newly formed beads of sweat for his brow, he continued.

Twenty-five paces.

Another scream.

Tual's voice, pleading for mercy in the name of the gods. It came from the direction of the red light.

Sobbing.

Guthor had lost one companion. He resolved not to lose another.

Forgetting his fear, he charged in the direction of the red glow, his sword affixed to his right hand as if by resin.

And stopped as he reached the edge of a clearing. The sight that greeted him both intrigued and terrified him.

In the centre of the clearing stood the most beautiful woman he had ever seen. Long hair ran to her waist, and perfect skin and soft, delicate features surrounded her large, soulful doe-eyes. A long, black gown of some rich material fell enticingly down her body. He recognised the sword of Fergus mac Roy sword in her right hand, but glowing the colour of blood in a way he had never seen it behave before.

He swallowed, remembering how the weapon had been given to a goddess. Cold fear caressed his flesh.

Before the woman was the trunk of a large tree. The woman's left arm held Tual's head down upon it, forcing him into a kneeling position. Tual looked at his comrade with pleading, terrified eyes. His mouth formed the word 'please', but no sound came out.

On the ground lay Sidal's body. Or what remained of it. The body had no head, which was held by one of three women standing a little back from the scene, each with raven-dark hair and clad in black, but not quite sharing the beauty of the first woman.

All four women were splattered with blood. The three to the rear were taking turns to suck the red, sticky liquid from the stump which had once been Sidal's neck.

Beneath a layer of gore, Guthor could just about make out the distorted features of Sidal's face. Features frozen to show he had met his death with pain and terror.

For a brief moment Guthor swore he saw the head blink, as if his friend had not yet succumbed to the relief of death.

Guthor wanted to vomit.

"Help me." Tuan finally managed to force sound from between his lips. The sound was quiet and dry, like the rustling of dead autumn leaves in the valleys below Tre'r Ceiri.

The beautiful woman smiled at Guthor, but said nothing. Instead, with a strength greater than her feminine arms seemed capable of possessing, she raised her sword, and placing one of the sharp edges on the nape of Tuan's neck, began to saw into the flesh.

Tuan screamed. His eyes searched out Guthor to plead, and his body thrashed helplessly against the strength of the Otherworldly woman. Beneath the screams, Guthor heard the sound of iron cleaving bone. It was a sound he had heard before in battle, but in this clearing, in the scarlet glow, the sound took on a meaning of malevolence. The woman, already covered in Sidal's blood, seemed to take delight as severed arteries splattered her arms and body. Her hair dripped scarlet.

Tuan fell silent. His body twitched spasmodically then stilled. The only sound was the sword cutting through his neck.

The three women dropped Sidal's head. Two advanced towards Guthor. He tried to run, but willpower drained from his body and he found himself powerless to resist as the creatures held him with their bloody arms and escorted him towards the tree trunk.

The third woman had bent down to pick up Tual's head. She held it above her mouth, moaning with pleasure as more blood fell onto her tongue. Some trickled over her chin and down her neck. She gasped and put her free hand to her neck, wiping blood over the flesh exposed by the low cut dress. A small dribble found her cleavage, and her groan of pleasure rose as her fingers moved inside her dress and smeared blood over her breasts.

Eyes closed, she licked her lips and shuddered. She leaned her back against a tree and climaxed.

Guthor wondered if he was imagining Tual's eyes blinking at him one last time before staring past him into space.

The beautiful woman took Guthor by the neck of his cloak. She smiled coyly at him through bloodied lips before gently, yet with a strength he could not match, forcing him down on the trunk.

Guthor prayed to Arawn, Lord of the Otherworld, reminding the God of his good deeds and bravery in battle, and asking for his acceptance into the feasting halls of the dead.

He waited to feel the cold breath of iron on his neck.

There was silence.

The beautiful woman pulled him up until their faces were level. She gazed into his eyes like a lover, but despite her beauty, he could see only evil in the brown pupils and bloodied face. "Tell Archdruid Bran the revolt must succeed." Her voice was soft and gentle, like the cooling breeze on a summer's day.

The forest went dark. Guthor was suddenly alone. He heard Sergovax's voice calling, and ran in the direction of the sound. He did not know his sword had fallen from his grip. He did not feel Sergovax trying to restrain him. He was unaware of the Archdruid; he did not remember that the thing of evil had given his a message for the white-robed man.

Guthor ran past them into the night, gibbering nonsense.

For Guthor was insane.

Chapter 17

The old woman stretched her aching bones, forcing a creak from an arthritic joint. Absentmindedly, she squeezed a boil and peered out from behind an aged oak. She could see the sacred circle where she would entice them. She could feel the power of the stones, old beyond time itself and reminding her of her own ancient potency. She felt the invigorating energy flowing around her like a river as it gave up its stamina to her. And the two souls she would soon claim would give her even more power!

And she had the sword. She caressed the blade as it were a lover's cheek, not caring that it brought a trickle of blood from her finger. But the weapon glowed red and she hid the blade in her skirts, away from prying eyes. The time for the world to see its scarlet, pulsating beacon of light would be as she feasted on the young couple's souls. She raised her cut finger to her face, enjoying the sweet aroma as blood dripped to the ground. She licked the small wound, tasting her own blood and anticipating more to come.

The old woman concentrated all five of her senses on the girl's mind until she threw her head back and laughed.

The girl had no knowledge she was being consumed. She was offering no resistance. The child's will was no longer her own.

* * * *

The thunderclouds had cleared, but still the evening sky darkened. Lucy Davis cast a quick glance towards the car's clock.

Quarter past nine.

"Looks like we chose the right time to get back," she said, breaking the stiff silence. "At least the storm's passing."

"Yeah. It was getting a bit muggy. It's not like Snowdonia to be this hot and dry—as you'll find out after a few months," said Toby.

The roadsides were flooded, and spray thrown up by the wheels glinted in the dying light like countless diamonds. The sun still peered between the mountains, though, the peaks throwing fingers of shadow, which reached out towards the summits on the other side of the valley. Darkness was descending, and it would be night by the time they got home.

"In a hurry to get back?" he enquired, glancing away from the steering wheel to flash her a smile.

"It's been a great evening, and I loved the film, but we had a broken night last night, what with Johnny's dream. And then Peter breaking down on Anglesey, leaving me with two kids and the hassle of having to get a taxi home. I'm tired. I think I need an early night."

"I understand," he said, but she picked up the tinge of disappointment in his voice.

She fell quiet, not wanting to say anything to give him hope or encouragement. In fact, she had tried to avoid giving him any encouragement the entire evening. She had even worn conservative clothes; her 'Metal Loving Lady' T-shirt, and a black skirt. One that reached below her knees.

Make-up was at a minimum.

She looked at Toby. He, on the other hand, had dressed to kill in a white shirt and cream suit. The jacket was neatly folded on the back seat and had, to her amazement, kept itself free of crumples or dirt throughout the evening. Even Toby's snazzy tie remained tight around his throat, and hadn't been loosened or discarded for comfort despite the heat.

She fumbled in her handbag and took out a pack of cigarettes, but thought better of it and dropped it back into her bag. She was sure Toby wouldn't approve of nicotine odour staining his upholstery.

Needing something to do with her hands, Lucy's fingers fidgeted with her crucifix. She glanced down and cursed as she spotted a chipped nail. She felt relief when Toby's headlights picked out the sign:

NANTBRAN
Please drive carefully through the village

"You okay?" asked Toby.

"Yeah, fine. Why?"

"You've been a bit quiet. Not getting bored I hope."

"No, I'm not bored. Just tired. I'm sorry... nothing personal, honest." She forced a yawn and fiddled absently with her crucifix.

"Yeah. It's the mountain air. It hits you when you're not used to it. At least you can sleep in tomorrow. Have a look in the glove compartment; I've got some CDs and tapes in there. No heavy metal, though," he grinned, nodding at her 'Metal Loving Lady'- clad chest.

Lucy felt herself flush, but flicked through his collection. Anything to calm her nerves. She soon decided Toby's choice in music was too bland for her taste. In fact, some of his tapes seemed decidedly feminine. She wondered of the previous occupant of the passenger seat had chosen them.

Then, not for the first time in the evening, Lucy wondered how many girls had sat in her seat before her. *A bloke of Toby's looks, money and charm could have his pick...*

She decided there must have been dozens.

I'm just another easy lay as far as he's concerned...

Lucy was beginning to dislike Toby Griffiths.

Eventually she picked a CD almost at random: 'The Sound of Welsh Myth'. "I didn't realise you liked folk music."

"Ah." Toby sounded a little embarrassed. "My father plays in a group. They do traditional stuff and songs based on Snowdonian legends. I couldn't refuse a complimentary copy."

"I suppose not." Lucy settled back into the leather as the first track started with a haunting flute solo. As the words flowed into her mind she found herself reminded her of childhood fantasies; fairies at the bottom of the garden, gallant knights felling dragons to woo her. She closed her eyes and loosed a heavy sigh, and hoped Toby would mistake it for a yawn. As she reopened her lids the car turned into Nantbran's narrow high street. Dim streetlights gave a dull light to the terraces of slate buildings.

Lucy felt calmer now. Maybe the gentle music had softened her nerves. Maybe it was Toby seeming to accept he'd only get a quick peck on the cheek. Maybe it was just that she'd had time to think things over during the drive from Bangor.

And it was a long drive. Over half an hour each way. Toby must really like her to have been willing to pick her up from her wilderness home, drive into Bangor for the film and back again, and then go home. Two hours behind the wheel, on top of the driving for his job.

They left Nantbran behind and Toby turned off onto the farmhouse's long drive. It was dark now, and the headlights pierced the night with their off-white glow, enticing insects in their hypnotic glare.

It wouldn't be fair to send him home immediately after dropping her off. Giving him a coffee couldn't hurt.

And he wasn't a bad bloke. Peter and dad were right; he fancied himself a bit. But they'd only gone to the flicks, but he had made her feel special all evening. Like a princess.

She dismissed these thought from her head. There was only one reason she wouldn't send Toby straight home tonight.

He looked good. He treated her right.

She wanted him.

She found herself humming happily along to 'March of the Men of Harlech'.

Mum had liked that song.

As she listened to the next track, Lucy sat upright. The words seemed pretty empty by themselves, but as they blended with the instruments they described a mixture of dramatic images—a world of magic, of quests and monsters, of heroes and villains, of little people and pots of gold. The song seemed so... so... *meaningful.*

She shivered. Not a shiver of cold, but a shiver that started deep, deep inside her as monsters from her nightmares found the surface of her mind, ready for vengeance after a decade or more buried beneath the detritus of adolescence. It almost felt as if the demons were being *sent* into her mind.

In an instant she was glad to be with Toby.

"Well, young lady, here we are."

She looked up at the house, cold and dark. Monsters could be hiding behind any doorway, in any cupboard. Ready to strike. "Yeah. You've got a long journey back. Do you want to break it for a few minutes?" She undid her seatbelt.

"I'm not sure that's a good idea. I don't think your family like me."

"Don't worry about that. They're out; dad's taken the Johnny to visit a distant relative. And Peter's stuck in a garage somewhere in the middle of Anglesey," she tutted.

"Well… if you're sure…"

She wanted Toby to stay. *Needed* him to stay. *Needed* him to hold her, to say that she didn't have to worry, that there were no monsters. Relief surged through her, lightening her head. "Course I'm sure. I *like* you," she replied, surprised at the playful tone in her own voice. The mountain air threw itself around her as she stepped onto the gravel, and she breathed the cool night deep into her lungs, allowing it to wrap her in its invigorating embrace. Suddenly, she could see why Peter wanted to live here. "Wait there. I'll make sure Tipsy's alright," she instructed Toby as he made to follow her through the front door. But the animal had already heard them. There was a frenzied yapping from inside. "He's okay," she muttered.

"You haven't told me why you call him Tipsy. It's an unusual name."

"We got him from an abandoned dog's home. He had some sort of ear infection which upset his balance. He fell about as if he was drunk." She smiled at the memory as she closed the door. "He did look sweet. We couldn't resist him."

"I see." He changed the subject, "Anyway, let's get inside. Now it's dark it's getting chilly."

"I don't think so."

"Why not?"

"You might take advantage."

He nodded at her T-shirt's logo and raised his palms defensively. "Wouldn't dream of taking advantage of a metal-loving maiden. Honest!"

"Fibber." *Metal-loving maiden.* She liked that. The joke put her back at ease. She felt the sudden, uncontrollable urge, driven from inside her, to enjoy herself, to banish the childhood monsters back to their pits. "Anyway," she said, gently, suggestively, placing a hand on his arm, "You don't want Tipsy jumping all over you and getting your suit messy, do you? I thought I'd show you around outside. Show you the standing stones, maybe?"

"Well, that's fine by me," he replied as she slipped her hand into his.

She didn't think he'd argue.

She led Toby into the moonlight and guided him towards the circle, stepping around puddles, which reflected the moonlight like silver saucers, and jumping over Bran's Brook, which, after the storm, was more lively than she had seen it before. They soon reached the stones.

"Well, here we are. You wanted to come up to the circle. Was there any particular stone you wanted me to see?" His voice teased.

She patted the nearest. "This one'll do."

"Do for what?"

"Ooh Toby, you beast," she giggled. She felt a girlish smile playing around the corners of her mouth   "I *do* hope you're not going to make a wicked suggestion."

From somewhere deep inside came the realisation that she had him like putty in her hands. The thought thrilled her. She felt like a cat with a mouse, toying with it at leisure, and having the power to decide when the game was over and the coup de grace should be delivered.

But the game has only just started. There's plenty of time to play.

Without waiting for more words, they held each other and kissed. Lucy explored Toby's mouth with an animal passion, enjoying the silky caress of two tongues entwining as they became more confident with each other.

He pulled away. "Where did you learn to kiss like that?"

"I didn't learn. I'm a natural." She pulled his mouth back onto hers. He responded by lowering his hands to her rear.

She gave him no reprimand.

He made his next move by sliding his palms over her T- shirt and gently cupping her breasts.

"Hey, I'm a nice girl," she chided in a tone she hoped suggested the opposite.

"Shame. I was hoping for naughty."

"Hmm.... naughty but nice. I could live with that."

His hands left her breasts and moved down and rested on her hips. He nuzzled her neck as his fingers found her belt. She felt him fumble unsuccessfully with the buckle.

"And what do you think you're playing at now?" she asked with mock severity.

"Blast this cold," he cursed. "It's making my fingers numb."

"Oh, let go, I'll do it. You are useless," she giggled, unentwining her arms from his neck and doing the job herself. They embraced again, and she winced as his hand found the small of her back.

"Sorry," he whispered in a voice half apologetic, half seeking the go-ahead to continue.

"Your hands *are* cold."

"Well, I'll have to find somewhere to warm them up then." He fumbled with her skirt button, but managed her zipper with less of a struggle.

Lucy felt a tingle of excitement as he eased her skirt over her hips, then her thighs, and then allowed it to slide gently to the ground.

She broke away from him to look down at the lifeless circle of material around her feet. Part of it had fallen in a small puddle on the uneven ground. She looked at it as glumly as she could without breaking into a fit of giggles. "Look what you've done. It's getting all wet."

"Don't worry. You won't be needing it for a while."

She looked back up, deeply, into his eyes. He returned her gaze, his face silver in the moonlight. She found herself thrilling as the cool mountain air caressed her bare thighs, and the sensation of Toby's hands massaging her rear through the soft, flimsy material of her briefs.

Lucy sighed deeply as need surged through her. Toby guided a hand around her hips and to her stomach; his fingers were still cold and felt like needles of ice as her flesh responded under her touch. She had wanted the night to be slow and sensual, but she felt an animal urge which needed satisfying.

Now.

As if in response to her call, Toby's fingers were inside the waistband of her briefs, hesitantly at first, but soon with a growing confidence and passion matching her own.

Nothing mattered except his hand between her legs. The world ceased to exist; the only thing she cared about was the need for immediate release.

Lucy writhed in answer to the call of her own flesh, pivoting on his fingers, trying to bring the moment forward. From somewhere in the distance she heard the screams of a wild animal, and didn't care that the sounds were coming from her mouth. It didn't matter that it wasn't her will to be here, but that something outside her consciousness was forcing her to do this.

Just as she thought frustration would overcome her, her whole body exploded in a climax she could never even have dreamed of.

She breathed out a deep sigh of satisfaction as she released.

"You okay?" Toby asked.

"Yeah. Sorry. Guess I got carried away. Credit to your technique."

"Thanks." He took his hand from her briefs and cupped her breast.

Her bare breast!

She looked around. Her crucifix glinted up at her from her cleavage. Her bra and T- shirt lay precariously on a low boulder. She didn't remember taking them off.

Or Toby taking them off, more likely. I must have been in some frenzy.

She made no effort to cover herself. She felt good. "You left me with my knickers, then?"

"Yeah. Black was too sexy to take off."

"Navy blue, actually."

"Ah. They seemed black in the dark. You still look great, though."

"Ta."

There was a silence.

She dropped her right hand from his neck to the zipper of his trousers. "My turn."

"Yeah."

She fell to her knees. The ground was cold and damp around her legs, but that only seemed to make the moment even better. She clasped the zipper between her teeth, and slowly lowered it. Toby stroked her hair. The zip was undone. She licked her lips to moisten them before flicking her tongue inside his trousers. She brushed her fingers across her hardened nipples.

Toby was firm. From above she heard him gasp. His body tensed. She took it as a sign of pleasure until, without warning his hands left her hair and pulled his zip up. "Who's there? Come out of the bushes, you fucking pervert," he challenged.

Passion drained from Lucy Davis in an instant. She instinctively reached for her clothes and covered her body.

Chapter 18

She fondled the swordhilt, seeking reassurance from its familiar touch.

Now, at last, she could taste fear in the lovers' mouths. Adrenaline coursed through her now, the thoughts of the double kill her only motivation. It had been many years since she had slain, and the thought filled her with a single-minded lust for blood.

* * * *

A barely whispered, "Shit," was the only sound Toby made.

Lucy, from somewhere, found some strength from her vocal cords. She let loose a night-piercing scream of raw, primeval terror. Her fingers loosed and dropped her clothes, but she didn't notice.

The old woman looked Lucy in the eye and smiled at her. A thin, lecherous smile that freed saliva to dribble from one corner of her wrinkled lips.

Lucy could only watch as gnarled fingers swung a sword above her head. Not any ordinary sword, but one that glowed red and bathed the circle of stones in its primeval light. Lucy's eyes became transfixed on the rubies illuminating the scene. In an instant, she knew Johnny's nightmare had been no dream.

"What the fuck... Jesus Christ..." Toby had found his voice, but seemed unable to do anything coherent with it.

"Who are you?" This time it was Lucy's turn to speak, terror tightening her voice. She wished her legs would move. Then she would be able to run instead of asking dumb questions.

"Who do you think I am?" was the mocking reply. "I am every nightmare, every evil vision you have ever had." Using an agility belying her appearance, she drew back the sword, ready to strike.

Lucy screamed without thought, sounds instinctively and uncontrollably tumbling from her mouth.

The old woman looked away Lucy, and fixed her stare on Toby. In one swift, expert movement she thrust the glowing sword between his ribs. He made no effort to defend himself, but with slack-jawed disbelief looked down as blood pumped out of the wound. His shirt stained dark.

In another single movement the hag pulled the sword out of Toby and slammed it back into his chest. This must have been a better blow; he looked to Lucy, eyes pleading for help before falling motionless to the ground with a throaty gurgle. The hag laughed in triumph, ignoring Lucy as she danced and screamed in triumph, hacking at Toby's neck. His throat became a bloody pulp, but still the hag slashed and stabbed at it with the sword. Twice she paused and used her dress wipe blood from the slippery hilt but each time resumed her task until, with a moan of pleasure, she put the fingers of her left hand in his mouth and pulled. There was a crack as the jaw dislocated, and a damp ripping sound as the head parted from Toby's shoulders.

Once the head was in her hand she laughed again, holding it to the sky and licking her lips as fresh blood splattered her face. Her rotting teeth clasped on an ear and pulled until it was ripped from the side of Toby's head.

She chewed. Then she paused and looked at Lucy.

Lucy couldn't even scream. She wondered why her legs still supported her if they wouldn't let her run. Something warm and wet trickled down the inside of her thigh.

Christ! I've pissed myself.

The woman held Toby's head out towards Lucy, in a gesture of offering. Toby's remaining ear faced her.

Shit! She's wants me to eat his other ear.

But Lucy couldn't move. The hag shrugged as Lucy remained motionless, seeming not to care whether she joined the feast or not. The crone stabbed a gnarled nail into one of Toby's staring eyes, and with a sigh of pleasure sucked the mess from her finger. Soon blood ran down her hands and face. She walked the few steps to the nearest stone and gently rested Toby's head on it, positioning it carefully so that the ruined face stared at Lucy. His blood trickled down the moss-covered monolith, shining in the scarlet light.

The crone knelt and muttered something in a language Lucy didn't recognise. She seemed to be making a spontaneous gesture of gratitude.

But who to?

Something snapped inside Lucy. Fear and desperation roused her to action. Shouting and screaming at the top of her voice, her naked flesh splattered with Toby's blood, she charged the old woman in a desperate attempt to live.

Lucy wondered if her attack unnerved the hag. The old woman's eyes widened with uncertainty.

Something—instinct—told Lucy to force her advantage home.

I'm damned if I'm going to let this fucking old bag kill me without a fight.

She pushed and thumped. Kicked and screamed.

She thumped hard enough to bruise her knuckles. Not that Lucy cared. The pain-driven adrenaline gave her more strength.

The old lady just laughed.

Shit. I'm not even hurting her.

And all the time the sword glowed red.

And at last the old lady readied herself to strike.

And Lucy felt the fight drain from her as a certainty descended. The scarlet blade caressed her windpipe.

I'm going to die...

She turned to look down at Toby's headless corpse. Beyond it, she could see his head adorning the rock.

I'm going to end up like that...

Lucy sank to the ground, wiping a mixture of mucus, blood and tears from her nose with the back of her hand. At last her legs gave way, and she fell on her back, propping herself up with her elbows. The ground was wet and cold beneath her.

The old lady grinned beyond the red glow. Blood and spittle drooled from her mouth as her gums parted.

Lucy could only watch, shivering, as the sword slowly traced its way down her throat towards her bare and bloodied breasts. She wondered inanely why something glowing red wasn't hot.

The swordblade stopped between her breasts. Lucy's breath locked. She waited for the splash of unbearable pain. She shivered and cried.

Just get on with it, she thought and slammed her eyes shut.

Please... The wait was unbearable.

But the thrust didn't come. Cautiously, Lucy opened her eyes.

The red glow had dulled. There was a change in the hag's face. Gone was the leer of triumph; instead her expression had tightened into concern.

But the worry in the hag's eyes dulled as the blade moved expertly between Lucy's breasts once more. With a flick like a sunbather disposing of an unwanted insect the sword yanked the chain of Lucy's crucifix. The link broke and it flew to Lucy's left before landing on the grass.

There was a cry of joy from the hag. The sword pulsed a blinding blood red in triumph.

A fleeting stab of hope swam through Lucy.

The cross! She can't cope with the cross!

Hell! I'm in the middle of some crap sixties horror movie!

Lucy lurched to her left. The sword cut her right breast as she moved suddenly, but she didn't care. She reached out a despairing hand for the crucifix.

Got it!

She rolled onto her back and thrust it above her. She squirmed off a stone which pushed into her back.

The hag hesitated. The dull glow lit up the worry in her eyes.

It's working! Jesus Christ! It's fucking working!

"GO AWAY! GO AWAY YOU EVIL OLD BAG," she screamed.

The sword withdrew a couple of inches. Grasping her courage, Lucy pushed the blade to one side and jumped to her feet. She thrust the jewellery into the hag's face. "Fuck off...Go on! Fuck off back to hell!" She held the cross firmly within an inch of the rotting nose.

The old woman stepped back and covered her eyes with her left arm.

Lucy stepped slowly forward in response, holding the crucifix outstretched before her.

The old woman took two steps backward. Her sword arm fell limp to her side.

...but it's working! It's fucking working! She can't stand the cross!

"Bitch... fucking bitch... don't like the cross, do you?" More confident now, Lucy strode forward. "Here you are, bitch. Have a closer look. Mum had it blessed before she died. You hear? It's been fucking *blessed!* By a priest!" She thrust the crucifix in the hag's face. She yelled and screamed obscenities and abuse, half in the hope someone might hear, and half to scare her enemy. At the back of her mind was the thought that, nearly naked, soaked in blood and screaming, someone might mistake her for a savage. "Fuck off! FUCK OFF! Eat shit and die, bitch." The curses rolled off her tongue.

The swordglow was dying. She was working as much by moonlight now as by the red swordlight.

Lucy kept her arm outstretched. Her face was near the hag's. The crone stank of death. Lucy ran out of obscenities, so she just screamed. She spat into the decaying face.

The old woman still moved backwards.

"That's right. Go away, you old bag. Fuck off before I fucking kill you...FUCK OFF!"

Still the hag stepped backwards, her gaze never leaving the cross.

Lucy saw her chance. The old woman was several yards way now, and the other side of a stone.

Lucy sprinted for the drive. The old woman made a half-hearted swipe at her, but Lucy was already out of range of the sword and the mouthful of spit, which flew towards her. Lucy stubbed her toe on a stone and wondered without really caring when she had taken her shoes off.

She looked back only once, to see the old woman holding the sword in her right hand and Toby's severed head in her left as her teeth ripped off chunks of his flesh in the renewed dull red glow of the sword.

Lucy ran until she reached the soft, friendly glow of Nantbran's streetamps.

* * * *

Hastily, the crone thrust the sword into the ground. It stood, buried to a hand's depth in the earth, and giving a dull red light for her to work by. She lifted the head from its stone with both hands. Her left hand had trouble grasping it by the short hair and she couldn't get a firm grip. The fingers of her right hand held the broken jaw firmly.

At last she sank her jaws into the bloodied flesh of the neck, where severed muscles dripped blood.

The fresh meat tasted good. She chewed slowly before swallowing, savouring the taste. She leaned back so she was half-sitting on one of the sacred monoliths.

She salivated.

As she feasted, she forsook her appearance, allowing her aged body to return to a more youthful appearance.

That was better.

The maiden had a full, even set of white teeth. They could chew through the man's head with more ease than the tender gums of a crone.

She paused to pull a scrap of meat from her teeth, and considered using her raven form to devour the soul. A hooked beak would sink into the flesh with ease. The sound of raven-jaws bursting the remaining, staring eyeball would give her pleasure, just as it had done countless times over the millennia.

But the lady remained as a young woman. She wanted to enjoy the feel of a head in her hands for the first time in two thousand years.

The maiden laughed as she ate.

But the cross...

Soon the symbol, the hated symbol of the belief which had swept the old gods from her people's minds, would itself be crushed.

After consuming this soul she would be strong enough to hunt outside the circle. Slowly, gaining strength with each death, she would gain control over the land of the Ordovices. Then the descendants of the tribe would rise up, and with the sword she would have the power to rule Britain at last.

The new Bran must be forced, this time, to relinquish the sword to Boudicca's uprising.

The maiden swore to rip the cross from the girl's neck herself, and consume her flesh while she screamed for release to the Otherworld.

Yes!

She licked her lips in anticipation and used her teeth to rip away a mouthful of flesh. A strip of skin came away to reveal the white skull beneath.

The taste of raw meat was wonderful.

An owl chose to settle on an oak branch. The maiden glared at the bird for interrupting her privacy. It screeched and rose into the night, leaving her alone with her meal.

She loosed her grip on the jaw to rip away the remaining ear. The shattered mouth opened and the tongue flopped out.

The tongue would be her next mouthful. She pulled at the jaw again.

The man's mouth widened grotesquely.

The maiden suppressed a giggle as more blood spurted over her. Her sodden black dress clung to the front of her body.

She loved being covered in blood. She put the ruined mouth to her own and chewed on the tongue.

The maiden tingled at the prospect of descending to Bran's village with the sword of Fergus mac Roy and taking as many souls as she wished.

She swallowed the chewed tongue and sighed, laying the gnawed head in her lap. Absent-mindedly she thrust a forefinger into a ruined eye socket. She scooped out a fingerful of brain and stuffed it into her mouth. It tasted good.

It was his soul.

She bit her bottom lip as she thought, wiping away a trickle of the man's blood with her tongue.

Yes. This time, Bran would abide by her wishes.

Her mind made up, she hungrily buried her teeth into Toby Griffiths's soul.

Chapter 19

Peter Davis stirred in his sleep. He tried to recognise his surroundings.

It was dark.

Aberffraw... I'm in Aberffraw... car broken down... cheap hotel...

He rolled over, not even bothering to inspect his watch.

His stomach was like a hollow pit. He wanted to scream out, to pull himself awake and away from the past, but he found sleep dragging him mercilessly back into the first century. Unwillingly he yawned and fell back into the pages of history.

* * * *

Boudicca, warrior queen of the Iceni, was awesome. Easily the largest woman the Archdruid had ever seen. Not fat, but built with a muscular frame any warrior would envy. She stood at least a hand width higher than most men, and even taller as she surveyed the Roman city of Camulodunum from atop her was chariot. Occasionally her concentration would be drawn to her servants as they dressed her for battle; one crone received a bloodied lip from the back of the queen's hand for catching Boudicca's flesh while fitting a golden torque around the royal neck. The queen fitted the necklace herself and refused to bow her head in response to its weight, despite the band having the width of a smith's fist.

Bran caressed his beard and glanced sideways at Dermot.

The bard, seeing the queen for the first time, gaped; his eyes wide and mouth open in an expression of awe.

Another slave, a boy too young to fight, fitted a loose cloak of russet over the queen's shoulders to protect her from the winds howling across the flat lands of the Iceni. The lad took nervous care as he fastened it with the point of a bejewelled crescent brooch. Job finished, he jumped down from the chariot, avoiding the glaze of two emerald-green eyes. Eyes shimmering with ferocity and a passion for justice rarely seen in a woman. Eyes expecting to be obeyed. The Queen tossed her head to rearrange her crimson hair, which fell to her hips like a waterfall of flame, with greying tints to add an air of authority. Boudicca, although not beautiful, was well defined and imposing.

Warriors of the Iceni and the Trinovantes swarmed like bees around her chariot, each parading warpaint and limed hair to draw attention to himself, and hoping he may be favoured.

Yes, thought Bran again as he caressed his beard. *Here is a woman with a tribe's worth of charisma and some a Druid's natural power. A woman with ten thousand men prepared to follow her to the Otherworld.* He admired the way she drew loyalty with natural ease. Her very being oozed power and confidence, from her scarlet mane to glint of danger in her eyes; from the harsh, almost masculine voice to her height and tuned muscles.

If only Caswallon had shown such authority at the Sacred Isle. Then, perhaps, the groves would not have been destroyed. If only Caswallon had but the force of personality Boudicca held in the smallest of her fingers...

If only...

If she were immortal she would be an awesome goddess.

Like Andraste.

Archdruid Bran threw the thought aside.

"Bran?"

"*Bran!*"

"My apologies, my queen. I was thinking of the battle to come."

"Archdruid. It is time for the omens. The hare."

Obediently, Bran raised his hand to a nervous acolyte.

The animal trapped in the junior priest's sack renewed its futile attempts to escape, but lad clasped the bag's neck with two clenched fists.

Boudicca stepped down from her chariot and took the bundle without acknowledgement. She would let the animal run free, hoping it would escape to the east, the direction of new life. Should it run to the west, the way of the sun's death, the failure of the revolt would be assured.

"Bran! Over there." Dermot's eyes were wild as he nodded towards the west. In that direction stood an old woman, dressed in black, with grey hair escaping from her head like strands of cobwebs. Her wrinkled face was a mass of warts and boils. But, like the queen, the hag had a presence. Her back defied the years to stand proud and erect, and despite her age and ugliness there was a look of regal power and arrogance, across the hag's features.

"A lady come to see fair play," commented Bran. But a knot formed in his stomach.

Dermot had inherited The Sight.

Of the assembled Britons, only a few of the priests, trained in the ways of the Otherworld, seemed to sense a presence and pass uneasy glances in the lady's direction.

"Andraste, I call upon you to guide the omens! Let the hare run free in the direction you choose!" Boudicca's voice was as loud, clear and deep as a man's. The queen did not have The Sight, but the conviction in her voice left little doubt she believed without question.

The warriors roared approval as the Warrior Queen opened the neck of the sack and let the terrified animal drop to the ground. Men encouraged the hare to bolt for the east with shouts and gestures.

The cheers of triumph melted into the breeze, to be replaced murmurs of concern as the animal, sensing freedom, sprinted to the west, to the way of failure. Bran turned in the queen's direction to watch her face contort into a mask of fury.

The army of Britain fell silent as Boudicca faced the Archdruid, her piercing glare blaming him for the moment.

The eyes of queen and Archdruid broke from each other in response to gasps from the army.

Dermot grabbed his father's arm. "Look! The hare, the hare," he blurted.

The animal had come upon the Goddess. It had run to within about thirty paces of the apparition and slammed to a sudden halt before rising itself on its hind feet, ears erect and nose twitching. It became fixed upon the figure in black.

Andraste met its gaze and slowly raised her arms from her side until she formed the figure of a grotesque cross. She moved her right arm in front of her and extended a bony finger to the east.

And snapped her fingers.

The animal gave a flick of its head, as if coming out of a trance. Then, without stopping to look back, it turned tail and sprinted from the lady, to the east and out of sight.

A victory roar rose from the army of Britain as the animal ran towards victory. The cheer was hesitant at first, but gained confidence as the Druids thrust their hazel staffs skyward and celebrated with their own screeches of delight.

The queen permitted her soldiers their joy before clapping her hands in a demand for silence.

As one, the Iceni and their Trinovantes allies fell still. There was not even a murmur as the army waited for Boudicca to speak.

Her voice was deep and authoritative as she threw her head back to address the heavens. She spread her arms to speak with the Goddess. "I thank you, Andraste. I call upon you as a woman speaking to a woman. I dedicate my victory to you, and beg you for liberty against the unjust and impious Eagles. May you, and you alone, be forever our leader. May you feast upon Roman souls this night!"

She lowered her head and looked at her army. Her face burned with passion. "Camulodunum is ours! Take it!"

Bran turned in response to a woman's scream. He watched in fascination as, to the west, the hag reached inside her raven-black dress and pulled Caladchlog, the rainbow sword of Fergus mac Roy from its folds. She held it reverently, right hand grasping the hilt with the blade lying in her left. She gazed down on it, wrinkled features softening, as a mother would look upon her babe.

Bran's stomach knotted. The way she held the weapon reminded him of the way it had lain comfortably in Caswallon's hands before being sacrificed to her care.

And the way Andraste regarded the sword reminded him of the way Dermot and Kyra had looked down upon Conor.

The memories hurt.

The lady raised the weapon, pointing it towards the Warrior Queen in a gesture acknowledging her words. Then, she pointed the blade skyward and gave a scream of triumph.

The warband could not see the Goddess holding the sword of Fergus mac Roy, for they lacked The Sight. But there were gasps as the weapon, pointing towards the sky, radiated its red glow. Superstition took hold, and as one, the warband took a pace back.

The Warrior Queen took immediate control and waved her own weapon above her head. "Let all men see the reddening of the air." Her voice rose to a hysterical scream. "WE HAVE BEEN SHOWN THE ROMAN BLOOD WHICH WE WILL SHED AT CAMULODUNUM. LET US ADVANCE UPON THE CITY AND DRIVE THE EAGLES FROM BRITAIN IN THE NAME OF ANDRASTE!"

The army returned to its frenzy. Screaming their warcrys and, following the chariot-borne queen, the army of Britain advanced towards the Roman city.

Amid the turmoil of an advancing warband, Dermot clasped Bran by the shoulder. "Father, you know the legends well. If the Iceni and her allies are certain of victory, why is the sword not showing green in the hands of the Goddess?"

Bran caressed his beard. "Maybe the Goddess is planning a lingering death for our captives."

Dermot's eyes closed into slits of battlelust. "Just as they denied my family a swift death."

Bran clasped his son's shoulder. "You are gifted, Dermot. You have the makings of an Archdruid. Do not let your lust for revenge lessen you as a man."

"Pah! I would willingly forsake any gift for the chance to twist the knife in the writing body of any Roman."

"The man responsible for your family's death died slowly at your hands. Rome owes you no further debt. And the sword? Do you not fear its red glow? Do you not fear a Britain at the mercy of a goddess who thrives on suffering?"

Dermot's jaw tightened. He looked into his father's eyes, giving an honesty to his answer. "Let us take countless prisoners. I could never tire of despatching Romans to the Otherworld in the name of any willing goddess."

Bran loosened his grip on Dermot's shoulder. The cries from beyond the ridge gave notice that the assault on Camulodunum was under way.

"Come, let us hasten to the battlefield," said Dermot. "There are British lives to be avenged."

Bran sighed again. At his signal a slave handed him Majestic's reins and, mounted, he ascended the crest.

He caressed his beard and surveyed the city. The River Coln offered little defence for the legions, leaving the city below at the mercy of battle-crazed Britons. Camulodunum's own defensive walls had been razed by the Romans themselves to make way for more sprawling suburbs.

Bran urged Majestic through the Coln. The horse's ears and eyes flickered in response to the clamour of battle.

"Okay, girl. I won't take you into the city. You wait here."

He dismounted and tied the animal's reins to a tree. He regretted not travelling with an acolyte. A boy would be useful now, to be stationed with his horse and act as some sort of deterrent to thieves. No superstitious warrior would be brave enough to steal a snow-white horse guarded by a priest, no matter how junior.

He ran into the undefended city as fast as his aged legs could carry him. He had to pause and lean against wattle walls twice to catch breath.

Even in the city he saw no Romans, but was not surprised. They would be preparing a stand in the Temple of Claudius, the one solid and defensible building in the entire city. Even from the outskirts, the Archdruid could see its columns rising above the skyline. The temple's stone walls contrasted with the humble wattle buildings surrounding the city, each built in a hurry to provide shelter for a growing population. But the simple wooden structures were burning, torched by Boudicca's army in their hatred of anything Roman.

The noise told Bran the direction of the battle, and acrid smoke assaulted his nostrils even before its greying shroud immersed him. The temple of Claudius was lost in its haze. He wiped his stinging eyes, but smoke-induced tears still ran down his cheeks. But he knew he must make way to the temple. He was a Druid. It was his duty to keep the slaughter to a minimum.

At last, he turned a corner. The Temple of Claudius emerged from the smoke before him, a beacon of marble columns.

He blinked the smoke from his eyes. Ascending the steps in front of him was Dermot, crazed bloodlust in his eyes, risking javelins from the barricades the Romans has put across the door.

The bard ran through the shower of weapons without receiving so much as a scratch.

But there were shadowy shapes of women around Dermot. Bran wondered if, despite The Sight, his son was too possessed by a foam-mouthed frenzy to know they were there. The black-clad maidens; Badb, Macha and Naimh, handmaidens of Andraste. With the protection of their immortal bodies, they deflected the shafts of death that were driven towards Dermot's breast. Instinctively, Bran looked up to the sky where the sun struggled to pierce the thickening layer of smoke and ash.

Would Andraste protect Dermot in battle?

Bran's heart lurched.

Here was Dermot, the boy who saw death in battle as a waste of life, sword in one hand and shield in the other, leading the charge like a man possessed. Javelins came towards him, flung from the shadows of the building, their barbed points promising an iron-tipped death until deflected by Andraste's Maidens of Death.

Ravens circled. Screeching and wailing, encouraging men onwards into battle so they could feast upon Roman souls. Warriors looked up towards the heavens in response to their calls.

One raven lowered herself onto his shoulder as the battle became fierce.

"Your son is brave, Archdruid."

Bran caressed his beard. The words were unspoken, reaching him through his mind. Bran snorted. "Dermot is battlecrazed. And who would not be brave with your handmaidens to protect him?"

The raven cackled. "He is brave. He has The Sight. He is loyal. He deserves protection."

"He is not loyal to you, Andraste. He hates the Romans. He merely shares your aims."

"But when the war is over he shall have his reward. Dermot, King of the Britons. It has a ring to it, does it not?"

"I thought Caswallon had been promised the kingship?"

The raven screeched again. "Caswallon will die before this war ends. He is nothing to me but the sword. Do you think I would seriously have offered the High Kingship to that sham of a man?"

There was a roar from the Britons in front of Bran. Roman resistance in the Temple had been broken; woad clad, lime-haired, revenge inspired Britons charged over the barricades and into the building, loosing warcrys and waving swords.

"Let us go and enjoy the carnage," screeched the raven triumphantly.

Already some birds, unable to wait for their meal, were brave enough to duck into the melee to rip a morsel from a twitching body. The crowd of warriors parted to let Bran through, in awe of an Archdruid with a raven. Battle fury ebbed from warrior's faces as the priest passed, replaced with slack-jawed awe.

Not that it matters, thought Bran bitterly. There are more than enough men still in the throes of war to slaughter every man left inside.

In one hand his staff helped him ascend the steps. The other lifted his robe from his feet. Despite the noise and clamour of war, the building held a sense of peace. The marble was serene, making everything gentle, smoother and cleaner than even the feasting halls of the Britons. And the space! The ceilings were so high and the rooms so large and airy an army could have been hidden inside. The smoke swirled, trapped by the walls and ceilings, giving a brooding atmosphere that reminded Bran of his visions of the Otherworld.

He pushed the raven from his shoulder.

The bird cackled once more. "You are too late, Archdruid," she gloated. "The bloodletting has started."

The Romans had fled from the main auditorium. Instead, the sounds of screams and weapons clashing came to him from among the many side rooms.

He stepped over the swarthy-skinned body of a Roman soldier and prepared himself.

In the first room three Romans lay slaughtered, their throats smiling at him through crimson lips. Alongside a man lay a woman and child. Probably a family slaughtered together, Bran thought, a sickening feeling rising in his stomach. Three of the woman's fingers were raw stumps, severed by warriors looting rings.

Every room held similar scenes.

Until he came to the last room but one. The curtain was torn from the door; two Trinovantes, bare to their blood-splattered chests and swords drawn, guarded the entrance. Their eyes widened when they rested on Bran, and they hesitated, seemingly drawn between unease at denying access to an Archdruid, and a wish to obey orders to let no one past.

"Who is in there?" he demanded, raising his voice as loud as the smoke grating his throat would allow. He coughed.

One of the warriors averted Bran's gaze. The other shifted his weight uneasily from foot to foot. It was the latter who eventually spoke.

"It is a man who is blessed by the gods. The man who led our charge, and no Roman weapon touched him."

"That man is my son. Let me through."

The men glanced at each other once more, but did not make way. Bran tried to listen out for what may be happening beyond the curtain, but the noise of battle blocked out the sound.

His jaw tightened. He drew himself up to his full height. "I am Bran, Archdruid of Britain. Let me pass, I say! Or do you wish to be the next sacrifices to the gods?"

The threats had the desired effect. The men stepped aside, eyes widened with fear.

Bran entered the room.

The sight greeting him brought bile to his throat. Dermot stood, bloodied sword in hand, over a dead Roman warrior. In his arms he fought a struggling woman. She wore clothes of Roman design, and her hair was bound in the Roman fashion. But she was no Roman; her pale flesh and blond locks marked her out as a Briton. She made no sound; the terror across her features spoke loud enough as she looked towards Bran, eyes pleading. Her arms shielded a crying toddler from the battle-crazed bard. The boy's hair was a mixture of British corn-gold and Roman curls.

Dermot looked around in response to Bran's arrival. Anger flashed across his face. "Leave me, Bran."

Bran forced his voice level. He stifled a cough. "No. Leave the woman alone. She is British."

"She forsook her British birthright when she became a Roman's whore." His weapon pointed towards Bran in a warning to step no nearer.

The Archdruid backed off. "Let her go, Dermot. Killing a woman and child will not win the war for Britain." The woman's pleading eyes locked onto Bran's. The child hid his face in his mother's dress.

"Killing Conor and Kyra did not win the war for Rome. I have sworn vengeance, and by the gods I will have it. I will have it now." He lifted the sword to the woman's throat. Her wide eyes fixed on the blade.

"This isn't vengeance, Dermot. This is murder. Where is the glory in killing fellow Britons in a war against Rome?"

But Dermot wasn't listening. The battlelust had returned to his eyes.

"Calm down, Dermot. Look, I am stepping backward."

But Dermot plunged the sword into the woman's heart. Bran ran forward, but too late to intervene.

Looking down at the blood spurting from her ribcage, her eyes lost all emotion. Dermot loosened his grip on her as he withdrew the blade from her body. Still holding the hysterical boy, she slumped to the floor. Blood covered the child, but still she clutched it to her dying breast, covering it with her arms in a pathetic gesture of protection.

Bran said nothing. The woman's eyes closed. He could not believe his son capable of such action. The only sound that registered to him was the screaming of a terrified child. For a moment he heard the cries Conor must have made as he was snatched from his own mother and despatched into the water.

"At least spare the child. I will take him." Bran knelt, arms outstretched, to take the boy from the arms of his dead mother.

"You are going to foster him, are you? Going to suckle him from your breast?" Dermot taunted.

"I'll find a woman who will have her. A woman who has lost her own child and would be willing to foster this one."

"Kyra would have done so." The words were spoken with a level gentleness. For a heartbeat Dermot's sword wavered, and Bran thought he recognised a glimmer of recognition in his son's eyes.

But Dermot blinked away the beginnings of compassion. He gave a humourless laugh. "I think not, Archdruid... the child is half Roman. We don't want its Eagle blood tainting Britain, do we?" In one action, he kicked away the woman's body aside, and, features glistening with hatred, thrust his sword into the terrified child.

Immediately, the screaming ceased.

Bran looked away, unable to rest his eyes upon the sight. "May the gods forgive you, my son," he whispered.

Chapter 20

Rhiannon Jones tossed her bodice ripper onto Dave's pillow and grimaced. She couldn't concentrate with heavy rock pounding the terraced walls.

She thought about getting up to close the window. That would keep out some of the noise, but she was warm and snug under the quilt, with the night breeze brushing her cheeks. Instead she flicked her bedside light on against the dying light.

But damn the noise!

Hidden amidst the sound of merrymaking, she could hear Dave treading the stairs. He pushed the bedroom door open.

"Hi, gorgeous." He grinned that bewitching smile: full, genuine and with eyes sparkling like the Irish Sea on a sunny morning. And, of course, his dimples.

"Hi, gorgeous, yourself. Not watching the football? Noise from next door too loud?"

His dimples faded. "Three-nil down after an hour. Couldn't bear to watch any more. That's the Welsh dream over for another four years." He shrugged. "Anyway, there's more to life than football. Like you and Bryn." He climbed onto the bed beside her. He smelled of beer. "As for the noise, I just turned the volume up."

"D'you think Bryn's all right? Maybe I should give mum a ring."

"Oh, Ri, you worry too much. He'll be fine. It's only for one night. He'll be sleeping better with your mother than he would here." He nodded at the pounding wall.

"Yeah. I know. I just worry when he's not with us."

He knelt on the bed and ran a comforting hand through her hair before kissing her forehead. "I said, "don't worry". She offered to have him, didn't she?" His voice changed from comforting to teasing. "Anyway, she may have been the original inspiration for the Welsh dragon, but she brought you up okay, didn't she? Well, maybe with a few faults."

"Pig," she laughed, grabbing a pillow and hitting him with it. As she did, she sat up. The quilt fell to her waist.

"No nightie, eh? You're a brazen hussy. Thankfully."

She pushed him away, but gently. "Sorry, I'd love to, but not with all that noise coming from next door."

"Nantbran, the quiet village tucked away in the mountains. Until you live next to a holiday cottage rented by drug-crazed teenagers." He tutted. "I saw them arriving this morning."

"It's a good thing Bryn's not here," she sighed. "That racket would keep him awake all night."

He pecked at her cheek. "Don't worry, darling. It's only for a week. Then it'll be back to nice quiet boring old couples again." His hand strayed back to her breast.

"I'm sorry, Davie, but I'm not in the mood. If they'd be quiet next door I'd be all for it, but the noise is giving me the hump."

"I wish you'd let me give you a hump," he leered cheerfully.

She felt a smile on her lips. "Well... if that bloody racket would shut up."

"You mean... if I go next door and ask them to shut up I may be on to a promise?"

"If you go next door and shut them up I'll promise you anything."

"Even that blonde bit who reads the news on the TV?"

"Pig."

"Don't you have to be up early in the morning?"

"No. The Davis's don't get up 'till late themselves. They aren't expecting me until about ten."

A lecherous grin creased his face.

"Dave?"

"Uh huh, my little banshee?"

"When you come back, I might have put something on."

His eyes widened. "The black stuff?"

She nodded, tracing her lips with her tongue in an exaggerated gesture.

"With the lace?"

She nodded.

"With a suspender belt."

She nodded.

"I'll be back before you even know I'm gone." He shot down the stairs.

Rhiannon smiled to herself. Eight years of marriage and he still wanted her desperately enough to have it out with a bunch of drunken teenagers!

She got out of bed, washed, and put on the clothes she had promised Dave. And hunted out one or two extras. She would let him find out about those for himself.

And the noise stopped. Suddenly. She snuggled back under the quilt, grinning to herself at the crinkling noise.

Part of Dave's treat.

The front door opened downstairs, then closed again with the comforting sound of creaking hinges.

"I'm back, Snuggles. You ready?" he called from downstairs.

"Sssh! The windows are open. Do you want the whole of Nantbran knowing our pet names?"

"I'll lean out the window and shout out to the whole of Nantbran that I love you," he threatened.

"Have you fed the hamsters?"

"Yes."

"Just come up here then." There was the sound of Dave locking up and the low clicks as he turned the lights off. "Were next door okay?" she asked as he pounded the stairs.

"Yeah, fine. Apologised for the inconvenience. They even invited us round."

"You should have said yes. We haven't had a good night out in ages."

"What? Go out when you're lying here dressed in that black flimsy stuff?"

"You can only see my bra. I might have a pair of nylon bloomers on under the quilt for all you know," she teased.

"Maybe I'd better find out."

Rhiannon smiled as he jumped onto the bed and his brow knotted.

"What's that crinkling noise?.. Hey, there's plastic under the sheet!"

"It's your added bonus for shutting those damn kids up," she purred, undoing the top two buttons of his shirt.

"Wow! Baby Oil!" His eyes widened as she took the bottle from under the duvet.

"Yes, but there's a condition." She eased him out of his shirt.

"Anything. Name it. You can have your mother over to stay. She can even live with us." He was almost panting as he took the small bottle from her and flicked open the lid.

Rhiannon wrinkled her nose. "I don't think it will be necessary to have my mother stay with us. Not necessary at all." She felt herself grimace. "Your challenge is to undo all my clasps and fasteners with slippery hands. That shouldn't be too difficult. I hope... Ow! You beast. That's cold," she complained as Dave squeezed the bottle and sent a stream of the clear liquid over her chest, covering both black bra cups.

"Bullseye!.. Or should I say Bulls*eyes*."

"Hmm, that's better," she decided as her husband began to massage it in. She took the bottle and was soon sliding her own hands into Dave's slippy torso. He didn't earn much doing casual labouring jobs, but they kept his muscles finely tuned. At night his body made up for the financial struggle.

She knelt, facing him.

Dave picked up the bottle again. "I've not finished yet," he explained, pulling at the frilly elastic at the front of her black briefs, forming a gap of about an inch between the material and her skin. He held the nozzle of the bottle just above the opening.

"You wouldn't." Hoping he would.

He did.

Rhiannon winced as the cold liquid caressed her skin, and found herself moaning gently as Dave massaged it into all the crevices he could find. She raised herself onto her knees and put her arms around his neck with her eyes closed. Their bodies skidded off each other.

Until they froze.

"What was that?" she whispered.

"The hamsters?"

Not wanting to make a sound, Rhiannon shook her head. Suddenly she felt cold and underdressed. "No. It's not the hamsters," she whispered.

"There it was again. Something moving downstairs."

They untwined.

"Stay there, Ri. I'm going down for a look."

"It's probably that cat from two doors down again, got in through an open window," she said, trying to convince herself as much as her husband. She threw him the towel she had readied for the end of their lovemaking.

He shook his head and quickly wiped the worst of the oil from his body. "I didn't have any windows open. Didn't want the football drowned out by the party next door." He pulled on his shirt and advanced to the door.

"Here, take this." She reached for her hand mirror, a heavy heirloom with a long handle, and gave it to him.

"Oh thanks. Kill an intruder by making him look at himself." He gave a quick, nervous laugh.

"Dave?"

"Yes?"

"Be careful."

He gave short nod before disappearing down the stairs. Rhiannon thought, without humour, how the oil which had dripped onto his trousers made it look as if he had wet himself.

She jumped out of bed, wiping as much of the oil from herself as she could with the towel, which was too small for the job. Especially as Dave had already used it. Her plan had been to soap the mess off in the bath together after they had finished.

She slipped into a T-shirt and shorts. They felt uncomfortable. The oil was still in every crevice. What had been raunchy and fun only a minute ago was now slimy and cold. Already, her clothes were wet and sticky with a mixture of nervous sweat and baby oil. She pulled the plastic sheet from the bed, throwing it in a crumpled mess on the floor, before jumping back under the quilt and pulling it tight for protection.

She listened intently for noises from downstairs.

Nothing.

Not even the sound of Dave moving. But he wasn't wearing shoes, so it shouldn't be difficult for him to pad about silently, she thought.

The silence was even worse than hearing a noise. It seemed deathly quiet without the constant thumping of rock music from next door.

She wiped a drop of oil or sweat from her brow.

At last, there was something from downstairs. Rhiannon strained her ear. But she couldn't make out the sound.

"Who are you? What are you doing in my house?" Dave's voice, showing no panic or hint of a threat.

"I said who are you?"

Silence.

"Shit!" Dave's voice. Panicked and concerned now. Rhiannon sat bolt upright, the quilt still wrapped around her, hands clasped around her shins. Her breath came in shallow gasps.

"RHIANNON, GET OUT. NOW... *Jesus Christ!*" Dave's voice again. Scared this time.

Fear froze Rhiannon to the bed. But she couldn't have escaped even if she'd wanted too. There was no upstairs window big enough. Except at the back. And that had a twenty-foot drop where the ground fell away.

And anyway, she wouldn't leave Dave.

The 'phone?

No. Downstairs.

Mobile?

No. In my handbag. Downstairs.

Scream?

She tried. But no sound came out.

A sound in the kitchen. A draw being opened. It rattled. Must be the cutlery draw. He imagination raced. *Christ, Dave's getting out a kitchen knife!*

Thank God Bryn's with mother. Jesus Christ! Maybe it's not Dave getting out a kitchen knife. Maybe it's the burglar.

A scream. She had never heard Dave scream before, but knew it was his voice. The sound trailed away to a gurgle.

Rhiannon pulled her arms tighter around her. Something icy caressed the back of her neck.

Silence. For a few seconds.

There were light footsteps coming up the stairs.

Her heart pounded. She thought it was going to explode. She wanted to turn the bedside light off, but her brain jumbled the thought before she could reach for the switch.

A head appeared through the open door, and Rhiannon breathed a sigh of relief. A weight fell from her shoulders. It was the head of a young woman, perhaps eighteen or nineteen years old with long, dark hair and an expression of innocence. Rhiannon relaxed her grip on her knees. Probably one of the teenagers from next door.

But she needed to know why the stranger was in her house. "What are you doing here?" she demanded, her voice returning.

The girl smiled. As she slowly ascended another stair something trickled from her mouth. Something red.

Blood.

"What have you done to yourself? And where's my husband?" Rhiannon tightened her grip on her knees again.

The black-clad girl ascended another stair. She had a grace and a poise Rhiannon found herself envying.

The girl's hands came into view. Rhiannon could see what she was carrying.

In one hand was a sword. Its blade dripped red.

In the other hand, held by its hair, was Dave's head, his eyes staring and mouth holding a twisted, silent scream of terror and agony.

The girl lifted Dave's head to her mouth. The severed neck held a few ragged chunks of flesh. The angelic lips fell back, revealing a perfect set of white teeth which ripped off a mouthful and chewed. She watched Rhiannon as she feasted, her expression showing dispassionate interest.

Rhiannon wanted to scream, to run, to ask the girl who she was and why she had killed Dave. But most of all she wanted to faint, to black out, to not know what was happening.

But her body refused to do anything. The only feeling she could find was gratitude that Bryn wasn't here.

The girl passed through the doorway and into the bedroom. Rhiannon's mind pushed away the fear, and she wondered how the girl managed to glide across the carpet. Almost as if she was floating. *So graceful...*

Rhiannon's mind refused to understand that the girl coming towards her and placing her husband's bloody head on the bed. She felt the blood seeping through the quilt, warming her toes. *Much more warm and sensual than baby oil,* she thought.

The girl had left Dave's head facing Rhiannon. His smiling eyes fixed on his wife, and she smiled back. Rhiannon wondered where his dimples were. But even without dimples he managed to reassure her. It was good to have her husband near her at a time like this.

The girl took Rhiannon's auburn hair with a gentle hand. Rhiannon obediently cocked her head to one side.

She didn't struggle as the swordpoint drove into her neck. The girl wanted her soul; it would be pedantic to disappoint her. And it was nice to share Dave's blood, to have it mingle with her own. It made her feel closer to him. But it was annoying having her own blood spurting over the quilt. She would have to wash it in the morning. The red stain would never come out completely.

The girl was having trouble. The sword only had a sharp point. The edges of the blade were blunt. It was taking her a long time.

Rhiannon Jones didn't feel pain until her spinal cord was severed. But by then her windpipe had been cut in two.

It was too late to scream.

Chapter 21

Nantbran brooded in drizzle beneath a depressed sky. Even the sun made no effort to force a way through, for this morning grey was master of the heavens.

The village seems bereft of soul, thought Peter Davis as his wounded car limped past the outlying farms.

A car came from Nantbran, headlights piercing the murk.

Peter Davis flicked his own lights on and glanced at the dashboard clock.

Eight-thirty.

He passed a couple of pensioners, backs stooped as they trudged through the atmosphere, raincoats hanging limp from aged shoulders.

They didn't even bother to look around or step to the side of the pathless road.

They don't seem to care whether or not I hit them.

Peter's heart pounded his ribcage.

Not for the first time, Peter Davis added together his dreams and his waking experiences. And his family's experiences. And the graves he had dug up yesterday, just where he had known where they would be.

He looked around, almost nervously, half expecting the human remains in the boot to have taken life and be sitting on the back seat.

Empty.

But there was still something wrong.

He couldn't place it, but he sensed something he couldn't place in the dark atmosphere.

If only I had Bran's training… The thought was unbidden, but wouldn't dislodge itself.

Peter lowered a gear as the road swung round an outcrop. He needed to get home. Gently, he squeezed more speed as the road straightened.

The engine fought back with a groan. He flicked his eyes to the dashboard.

Thirty-five miles per hour.

He eased his foot back. The car quietened.

Thirty.

"A bug in the engine", the mechanic man had called it, when he couldn't find anything wrong.

Peter wondered who had bugged it.

A raven?

He shook away the thought and looked up as he rounded a gentle corner.

NANTBRAN
Please drive carefully through the village

proclaimed the sign, beneath another warning of the thirty miles per hour speed limit.

He dropped into third gear. The engine complained until he slowed by another five. Peter touched the brake for another corner and the rows of slate-fronted houses which were the main street.

Shit!

Two police cars and a length of blue tape blocked he road. People milled around. A black and yellow sign diverted traffic down a narrow side street towards tortuous back roads. A policeman's arm encouraged drivers to obey the sign.

Peter's heart pounded again. As he turned off the main road he could have sworn he caught a television crew out of the corner of his eye.

Jesus!

Wondering what had happened, he dropped another gear, but maintained his speed as he forced the car around Nantbran's twisting back streets. The grey slate buildings glistened in the drizzle and stared dispassionately down on him as he passed.

He reached for the radio and twisted the dial.

Hissing.

Damn! No reception in the mountains!

He cursed again and slammed the brakes as a jet-black cat threw itself into the road. As the car bore down on it the animal stood motionless, its eyes wide in surprise and terror.

Peter Davis squeezed his eyelids and waited for the thud of impact.

The brakes shrieked on the wet tarmac, but there was no bump. He opened his eyes. On the edge of his vision the cat streaked into a hedge.

He held his head in his hands and, trembling, breathed a sigh of relief. He tried to remember whether a black cat crossing his path was good or bad luck, and he composed himself for a moment before turning the key in his stalled ignition.

I need to get home.

He switched the radio off, regretting not turning it on back on the Sacred Isle, where the gentle hills would have allowed him a signal. *No, not the Sacred Isle. Anglesey*, he reminded himself.

But he had wanted to keep his ears on his stricken engine.

And anyway, it was only the High Street which was cut off. No reason to assume the farmhouse was in any trouble.

So why was he terrified for his family?

He ached to get home, but Nantbran, like most villages huddled in their valleys beneath the towering Snowdonian peaks, had only one main road, an artery running through its heart. The diversion took Peter through tortuous farm tracks clinging to the sheer sides of the mountain. And he had to stop several times to make way for diverted traffic coming in the other direction.

He was only half a mile from the farmhouse's long drive before he recognised the road.

And the car had objected to every incline; every turn; every change of gear. The engine's low growl of discomfort was growing into a roar of defiance.

And Peter chilled as he saw the familiar markings of a police car blocking the entrance to the drive.

What the hell has happened?

He wished he'd rung home from the B&B this morning. But he'd left at seven o'clock. And he hadn't wanted to wake anyone.

And anyway, they all knew he'd be home this morning. Lucy would have passed on the message. He only wished he hadn't driven off, looking for Kyra...

So many 'if onlys'.

He reached the police car and stopped.

An officer handed a steaming cup to a colleague in the passenger seat. The policeman pulled his collar close around him to shut out the drizzle before striding towards Peter.

Peter wound down his window. Even in the chill of the morning his hand was slimy with sweat.

"Can I help you, sir?"

"I live here." He nodded up the drive.

"And you are?.."

"Davis... Peter Davis."

"Have you any identification, Mister Davis? I must say everyone will be pleased to see you. We couldn't be sure you were safe."

Identification? Safe? "Why? What's happened?"

The policeman's eyes widened slightly. "You don't know?"

"Know what?"

"The murders..."

Peter's throat dried. "*Murders?* What murders?"

"Er... there's been several murders in Nantbran, sir. All last night."

"My family... dad? My brother and sister?"

The policeman held up a calming hand. "I don't believe your immediate family were victims, sir. But a young local man was killed on this property last night."

"Who? And who by?"

The officer let out a deep breath before speaking, as if trying to believe the facts himself. "Er... an old lady. The witness... your sister, I believe... witnessed it. Er... she says the young man had his head cut off with a glowing sword."

A glowing sword.

Peter Davis felt his jaw fall.

He had no idea how he managed to take his car up the gravel drive.

* * * *

The front door was half open. A policeman leaned against the house, but stood to attention, arms folded defiantly, as the car ground to a halt on the gravel. He watched Peter intently.

Peter averted his eyes, uncomfortable in the officer's gaze. He locked the car and strode to the door, heart pounding.

Why should *I feel guilty? I haven't done anything.*

But he was still nervous.

"Mister Davis? Peter Davis?"

Peter replied with a nod.

The policemen wiped an accumulation of drizzle from his cheeks. "My colleague at the gate radioed me. Told me you were on your way. Better go inside, sir. Your family have been worried about you."

"Why?.. The murders... they weren't hurt?"

"But your sister was with one of the victims. And one of your relatives in the village... Mrs Jones..." His voice trailed off.

Peter grabbed at the wall. His legs lost some of their strength. "Rhiannon?"

The old lady with the glowing sword in Johnny's bedroom... Thoughts pounded his mind and merged into a blur.

"Like I said, sir. Best go in. In the lounge, I believe."

Peter was still in a daze. He had no recollection of walking down the hall, but found himself in front of the open lounge door.

A uniformed policemen stood behind the armchair. A man and a woman in plain clothes sat on the settee.

But Peter's eyes locked on his father's.

Alun stood. "Peter... thank God." Tears welled in his eyes as he hugged his son.

And Peter sat disbelieving as he was filled in on events. Seven dead. Toby Griffiths. Rhiannon and Dave. A couple of very distant relatives.

The police wondering if it was a madman's vendetta against the Davis family, a symptom of anti-English feeling in a close-knit Welsh community.

But Peter Davis knew it was no vendetta.

Facts, dreams and legends clashed and swirled, piecing together a series of events covering two thousand years. But he couldn't tell anyone. Not yet. Not without proof.

And at the moment other things were more important. Like his brother and sister.

He ventured the question. "Where are they?"

"Huh?"

"Lucy and Johnny. You said they're okay… but where are they?"

Alun shot an accusing glare at the woman, ruining the effect slightly to push his glasses up his nose.

The plain-clothes man answered defensively. "They're okay." He paused to correct himself. "Or, as okay as they can be under the circumstances. They're up in their rooms, with colleagues trained for this sort of… er… thing… I know just how stressful this must all be for your family, but you can understand how much we want to catch this madwoman."

Alun didn't look pacified. "But putting a six-year-old through all those questions. Surely there was no need to have him in tears? Or quiz my daughter about her sex life? She's just seen her boyfriend murdered for Christ's sake!"

There was a sigh of irritation. "Mister Davis, your daughter is too distressed to talk about anything at the moment. But your… er… Johnny seems to have seen the killer in his bedroom less than twenty-four hours before the murders. Of course we've got to question him. I know it must be difficult knowing she managed to get into your son's bedroom." He paused briefly. "Are you sure you can't think of anyone who might wish to harm you?" He looked towards Peter for a response.

Peter shook his head and glanced across at Alun who shrugged answering. "No. I don't think we've made any enemies. Certainly not enough to… to…"

"Hmm. I think we can probably rule out Nationalists. Some of the locals believe the English are diluting the Welsh culture and driving up house prices and forcing them to move away from the area. That would be an obvious starting point if it was just your family, but to murder locals too… and by cutting off their heads… we've got to be looking at some sort of sick ritual. My men are already quizzing some occult groups."

"We've not had any threats or anything," said Alun. "We've only been into Nantbran a couple of times, to stock up on food and buy papers. The lady in the shop seems friendly enough."

"Hmm." The inspector chewed his lip. "You haven't been to the pub or anything? The locals might think you a bit aloof."

Alun jabbed a finger at the inspector. "Are you saying it's our own fault? We haven't had time to mix yet. We've only been here a few days, for Christ's sake!"

The policemen raised his hands, palms extended. "No, Mister Davis. No one has the right to do this to your family. I was just pointing out how it looks from the local point of view."

Alun's jaw tightened, but the living room door opened before he spoke. A well dressed but greying woman stepped into the room and closed the door behind her. She was introduced her as a child psychologist. Peter didn't catch her name.

"I don't think we'll get much more out of him today, sir. The girl's sedated for a couple of hours. May as well leave these good people to themselves for the day."

"Probably a good idea. You've all been through a lot, without us traipsing around your house for any longer than we have to. Forensics will need to carry on, though, and we'll leave a couple of men outside. For your personal safety. If that's all right with you?"

Alun shrugged. His eyes and shoulders sagged in a way Peter had never noticed before. He almost looked old.

"Yes, officer. That's fine. Thank you for your consideration." Peter answered.

"Can I go and see my son now?"

"Yes, of course. But we'll probably want to question him again soon."

Alun disappeared into the hall.

The policeman turned to Peter. "I'm sorry we've had to intrude at a time of stress. But you'll understand we have to work fast."

"Yeah. And don't mind dad. He's just a bit over protective of us all since mum died." Peter changed the subject before too many memories returned. "You really have no idea who this woman is?"

"No. At least, not at this stage. A couple of my officers live pretty locally—one in Nantbran itself—and neither knows of anyone matching her description. In an area where everyone knows everyone else, that probably means we're looking for an outsider. My men will start making visits to hotels and B & Bs this afternoon."

"An old biddy with a flashing sword shouldn't be too hard to find."

He gave Peter a card. "Please ring if anything comes up. Day or night," he added. "And don't worry about the press. I've got men covering all approaches to your property, and we'll intercept all your 'phone calls. Journalists, you know... I hope your family will be left alone."

"Thanks. I—"

Raised eyebrows. "Yes?"

"Nothing," said Peter quickly. "No, it's nothing." He just managed to stop himself blurting out about his dreams. He wasn't going to make himself look a crank by suggesting a supernatural answer to Toby Griffiths' murder. But the sword the old lady had used *had* to be Caladchlog, the Rainbow Sword of Fergus mac Roy.

And he wasn't going to mention the painting. They would think him mad.

The house soon emptied of policemen. Within a couple of minutes the only officers remaining were a couple of men in a car watching the front of the house, and one more inside the stone circle, behind a flimsy barricade of blue and white tape which sealed off the murder site.

Peter retreated back down the hall. Bloodstains smeared the wall.

Peter swallowed, wondering how he had missed them when he arrived home.

I must have been in some daze...

He wondered whose blood it was, and hoped it was Toby's and not Lucy's.

It was good to get back into the fresh, warm air. He returned the nod from the bobby on duty at the stones before making for the low mound. Peter hesitated for a second before deciding not to ask whose blood was on the hall wall. He didn't want to know.

He wanted to be alone to think.

The sword Lucy had described was too like Caladchlog. In the guise of Bran he had held it in his own hand. And he had found the graves of Conor and Kyra as easily as if he had buried them himself.

Before he realised he was doing it, Peter was caressing two-day-old stubble on his chin. *Just like Bran*, he thought.

A chill passed through him, like a knife twisting his insides into a pulp as he sat on the grassy bank with its view of the house.

Did the raven want me out of the way while Andraste carried out her murders? Did she make the car break down? Was she afraid to have me nearby in case I used Bran's powers to stop her?

Peter felt the bile in this throat as another piece slotted into the ancient jigsaw.

Chapter 22

The breaking day saw Londinium lay outstretched below the Archdruid and the Bard. The low sky promised rain, but the heavens had yet to part. Behind Dermot and Bran, beyond the crest of the ridge on which they stood, the army of Boudicca awaited their queen's order to advance. But for this moment, they were alone.

A hazelnut-induced vision assaulted Bran's nostrils. He sniffed at the acrid stench of burning and turned to look for its source.

Bran could see no smoke. Not yet. But the new city's buildings were of wattle and daub, and would fire well when put to the torch.

The Archdruid took another breath and choked as fire seared his throat. He swallowed to cool his mouth. Another taste mingled with the burning; one which he recognised instantly.

The aroma of burning flesh.

Instinctively the priest spat onto the ground in attempt to cleanse his body, but the cloying stench stayed with him. He wiped his mouth with the dirty white sleeve of his robe.

"You feel it too, father?" Dermot asked with a cough.

"I do," said Bran tightly, caressing his beard. His relationship with Dermot had become cold since the slaughter at Camulodunum, but the Archdruid was patient and knew his son would slowly feel his anger replaced by grief. But Dermot had the sight, and Bran prayed once more that his son would serve Britain without revenge tainting his judgement.

Bran's greying eyes strained into the distance as he sought movement among the buildings. He saw no soldiers, just the occasional slave taking care of early morning tasks.

Londinium seemed to be awaiting catastrophe. For Paulinus, Governor of Britain, had abandoned the city to its fate. The fate he and Dermot could feel in their mouths.

British fires would raze Londinium.

Bran tensed. He could not prevent himself imagining the slaughter to come.

"The women. Spare the Roman women," ordered a female voice.

Surprised, the Archdruid turned. He had thought himself and Dermot alone.

Andraste stood behind him, her smile both innocent and evil. Her hair fluttered delicately in the breeze. Every pore oozed beauty.

But the Archdruid was not tempted. He looked sideways at Dermot, who stared at the vision almost blankly, with just a hint of recognition.

"Why should the women be spared? Your way is death," said Bran.

"My way is life. Life and power for Britain." The slightest trace of a sneer shaped on her lips. "Priests! Pah! Why must you always consider power evil?"

"Power is not evil. But I know *you* are evil. You may have charmed Caswallon with your beauty and false promises. You even tempted Cuchulain, Hound of Ulster, in the days of my father's father. But I know your ways, Andraste. I know your needs."

"My *needs* Archdruid? And what would you know of the needs of a maiden?"

"Each maiden may lust for a different need, Goddess. But I know of *your* needs. I know of your insatiable lust for power. I know you would not spare the women if you had a choice. Given a choice you would not even spare a puppy."

"So you would not spare the women of Londinium for me?"

"I would spare the women, Andraste. But not for your pleasure." As an insult, he turned his back on the Goddess. His mind tumbled as it struggled to understand why she should want Roman women to live. He glanced at Dermot, who looked almost disappointed. Did the lad want to slaughter even women that badly?

Maybe the boy did not have the makings of a Druid, after all.

Bran turned once more to address the Goddess, to warn her against corrupting the bard. But she was gone. Only the screeches of a raven circling high above broke the still air.

The Archdruid caressed his beard. Dermot avoided his father's eyes, but Bran could understand the boy's thoughts as clearly as the spoken word.

"Why does the fate of a few Latin whores concern you? When the moon is full the Roman dogs will be driven from this island. Does that not justify the needs a goddess has for their bitches?"

* * * *

They found the Warrior Queen consulting with her chieftains, sitting on a felled log to enjoy a breakfast of strawberries and goat's milk. Seeing her with the elite of her warband, Bran realised—not for the first time— how big Boudicca was. The warriors, although well built and muscular, were no taller or finely-tuned than their queen. She turned her head towards Bran and Dermot, eyebrows rising in recognition as she pulled a strawberry stalk from her teeth.

"You have been in contact with the Gods?" asked one of the warriors, who Bran recognised as Scarax, a man who refused to pray for protection before battle, preferring to put his total trust in his sword skills. His tone was a taunt, not a question.

"We have spoken with Andraste."

At the mention of the War Goddess, Boudicca's eyes narrowed. A hand brushed her flame-red hair over her shoulder. "You have spoken with Andraste? What did she say? Will we be victorious?"

"We will win today," Bran confirmed. The stench of the burning city still faintly cloyed his nostrils. "But the Goddess has one order. Spare the women."

The queen spat a mouthful of milk and strawberry to the ground. "That is what I think of Roman women. Their men had little enough mercy for me. Why should I spare the Eagles' whores?"

Bran spread his hands. "I don't know. It is a Druid's way to obey the gods, not to question them."

"Our queen needs an Archdruid who understands the gods. Not a man who seeks to deny them their rewards." Scarax pounded the palm of his right hand with his fist. "Maybe our Queen needs an Archdruid who is more willing to question." A glint appeared in his eye, and his gaze fell upon Dermot. "Here is a man both brave and blessed. I saw him at Camulodunim, the way Roman spears could not hurt him. Maybe you should make way for your son, Archdruid. Here is a man worthy of our queen's favour."

Dermot stood proud. In an instant his fuzzy boy-beard seemed to thicken into a man's mane.

But it was Bran who spoke, face dark and voice firm. "The Council of Druids voted me into my post, with each man representing the will of his king. Or queen," he added quickly after seeing Boudicca's frown. "I have no intention of leaving my post without approval from the same Council." He stared Scarax in the eye. "A Council which acts upon the wishes of the *whole* of Britain, not just one tribe."

"Pah! Our queen leads Britain. Which king will not bend his knee to her? Which man in Britain would refuse her will?" Scarax looked to Boudicca. "This woman has the whole of Britain fighting with her."

Bran felt the argument slipping from him. He made his excuses as the first of the rains hit the ground. "I am sure the queen wishes to discuss military matters. I will take care of the spiritual."

Bran turned to leave, but the queen rose with a snort. "London is unprotected. Bel's sun disk has risen. Let us take the city now."

* * * *

Bran hung back from the battle line. He had already seen enough slaughter in this campaign to turn his stomach to bile. And with the queen and the bard demanding blood, no battle-crazed warrior would heed an Archdruid preaching mercy.

Instead, he entered Londinium alone and he waited behind the front line, hiding from the drizzle in a south-facing hovel of wattle and daub. The building stank of sweat and leather, and tanner's tools hung limply from sticks wedged into the mud walls while rain dripped from the thatch. Bran ripped the hide covering from the doorway, throwing light into the earthen-floored workshop, and rested himself on a low stool of three legs facing into the street of churned mud. In the middle distance a massive thick-beamed building thrust into the skyline, dwarfing the hovels around it. He wondered at its purpose while the distant screams of war reached his ears and settled like a bad stew in the pit of his stomach.

And despite the rain, smoke drifted on the breeze towards the hovel.

But it was not the breeze bringing The Sight to Bran. The vision was unbidden, and Bran tried with all his strength to expel it from his mind. Despite his efforts, the scene of war would not leave him, and the Archdruid took his necklace of glass beads from his pouch to assist his prayers for the dying as he watched Briton inflict slaughter upon Roman. He saw the muddy streets of the fledgling city soiled scarlet with the lives of its citizens; he closed his eyes and shook his head, but still he was given no rest from watching as Roman bodies were left to eager ravens. But the Archdruid was watching only in his mind and not a clear plane of water; his imagination allowed only a blurry picture, not the sharp and detailed panorama the Archdruid was used to.

But he did not complain, for he had no wish to see the terror etched in the faces of dying children.

A spider ran across the floor and hid in a straw bed.

The slaughter was quick. Most of Londinium had lain deserted and evacuated, with only the infirm or the over-confident remaining. Those who had hopes for mercy from the British hordes had their hopes dashed, as the menfolk were despatched with more torture than mercy.

The Roman women were forced to watch as husbands, fathers and sons were slaughtered; their screams reached Bran, sitting in his hovel only an arrows' flight away, through both the Sight and the rain-drenched breeze. One woman was held, her head facing her man, as his eyes were put out with a blunt spearpoint. The agony-stricken man staggered a few paces before the blade of a sword was sliced across his stomach and he performed his own death throes amid his own entrails.

Another man was tied to his lover before being cut to ribbons by British weapons, expertly wielded to delay the moment of death. His woman was drenched in his blood before he breathed his last. She was unshackled from his corpse, and without being given a chance to regain her composure was forced into the growing melee of female prisoners.

Bran held his hands over his ears to block out the sounds of suffering, but the Gods forced the screaming through his fingers, and the panorama through his tightly squeezed lids. The Archdruid prayed to Dian Cecht, the master of healing, that he would repair their souls from the trauma of terror. He wished he had been braver, more determined. He cursed himself, knowing he had failed in his duty as a member of the priesthood.

He was a coward.

He had chosen to hide instead of use his power— waning though it was— to prevent the suffering he was witnessing.

The thought occurred to him: *Is this vision sent by Bel himself, a sign of what I should be preventing?*

Despite being given their lives, though, the women's bodies reflected terror and tears; one fell to the ground to hold a dying Roman, but, with her toga cloaked in his blood, she was pulled away as he was despatched before his eyes.

Another woman had a golden necklace ripped from her neck. The warrior looting her body looked down at her jewel-encrusted fingers. Without thought the Briton forced her wrist onto a fallen foundation brick. Too late, the noblewoman realised what was to happen; she made to rip her arm from the warrior's vicelike grip, but he was too strong. Ignoring her screams, he brought his weapon down and severed the hand from the body, leaving the woman clutching only a bloody stump. He ripped the rings from the still-twitching fingers before throwing the hand into the blood-splattered gutter.

The woman fainted and fell into the mud. But her warrior guards had been told of Andraste's orders. They would not leave any woman to bleed to death. She was kicked until she regained consciousness and dragged to her feet. Still clutching her bloodied stump, she was forced along the muddy road with her fellow Romans.

Sickened, the Archdruid turned away, trying to shake the vision. But it stayed with him unbidden as he tried to hide his eyes, clenching them closed in frustration. He ran gnarled fingers through his hair, but could not dispel The Sight.

The unknowing call The Sight a blessing, he mused. *But I would assure any man the gift is a curse.*

He coughed and opened his eyes.

Was it the sight showing him the swirling mists of the Otherworld, or was smoke filling the hovel?

The acrid stench filling his nostrils told him the answer to his question lay in this world. The Archdruid did not need to search The Sight for the flames; he forced himself to his feet and, clinging to the lintel, looked out of the doorway.

As he watched, the sky darkened. The air filled with smoke, and the breeze from the south fanned it towards the Archdruid. Soon palls of black air would hide the roof of the massive building to his front.

Even the rain could not save the city now. *For Londinuim was burning to death.*

He heard Londinium's screams, her wooden buildings complaining in agony, crackling and flaming in the heat. He heard—no, felt—the screams of the Romans as their city died around them.

And amid the sounds, there was one which stiffened Bran's back. The voice was familiar; a woman's voice, distorted by terror. But with the unmissable lisp and clipped Latin accent. The voice both imperfect yet perfect; the one voice he had loved above all others the first time he had heard it.

'Mercy. Please. Have mercy.'

The Archdruid swallowed. The tears forming in his eyes were more than those induced by smoke.

Helena! My Helena!

Bran cleared his mind and fumbled in his pouch for a hazelnut. His quivering fingers took three turns to grab one of the magical nuts. He prayed its magical properties would clear the blurred picture sent by The Sight.

He threw his head back and fully opened his eyes and ears to the world. Concentrating his mind only on The Sight, he strained to see or hear the woman among the confusion of war. As the hazelnut took effect, he peered into the herd of terrified Romans. He surveyed faces, studying each carefully before discarding it and moving to the next.

Nothing.

Only the fear etched across the features of countless women. Bran loosed a sigh of relief. He must have been mistaken. There must be scores of Roman women in Londinium alone who spoke good British with a Roman accent.

"Please...please..."

The voice again. Clear above all others.

As if the gods want me to hear this single sound.

Instinctively, the Archdruid leaned forward, trying to get closer to the terrified horde of women as the taunts and barbs of British weapons pushed them along.

Yes. A fleeting view.

The black hair was streaked with mud and grey, the features etched with time, and the waist heavier.

And her face. Streaked with tears, soot and fear.

At the prod of a spear she disappeared back into the crowd. Bran strained his eyes into The Sight once more. He needed to see her again. To be certain.

Many moons had died since he had last been here, trading trinkets and joking with these same people who were being herded like cattle to the slaughter. But Bran still recognised the streets. His knowledge of the city, and the direction of the distant screams, told him where he should head.

He licked the corners of his mouth. Before heading for the centre of the city his cracking lips and smoke-filled throat needed water. He looked around desperately for a container. But there was nothing of use in this deserted hovel.

Bran picked his staff from the floor and lifted himself to his feet. He massaged his back before stepping outside the hut, a comfort for his spine against old age, before stepping into the drizzle and smoke. Once outside he walked deliberately, his sandals sticking in the mud.

He licked his lips as the rain refreshed his face and gave a silent thanks to Boann, Mistress of the Waters. And he uttered another prayer as he found a Roman-red bowl in two pieces, thrown away after breaking, in a rubbish heap between two houses. And the rain dripped from the roof into a broken half bowl. Gratefully, the Archdruid picked it up and lifted it to his lips.

He poured the liquid down his throat in one gulp and eagerly licked the excess. It had only been a couple of mouthfuls, but Bran was refreshed. His mind was able to return to other matters.

Helena.

And scores more Roman women.

With an effort, Bran straightened his back and forced his sandals on through the mud. The cloying drizzle made his cloak uncomfortable and heavy.

But he had lives to save.

The Archdruid headed towards the sound of war, but had taken only a handful of steps before, without warning, three British warriors appeared from a side street. Two held firebrands, covering the burning wood with brightly-patterned shields to keep the drizzle off the flames. All had freshly-hewn Roman heads adorning their swordbelts, the blood trickling down their thighs. Ignoring the Archdruid, one man took his torch into a hovel and emerged from the hide-covered doorway only a heartbeat before a tongue of yellow flame licked through the roof. The fire screamed a crackled complaint as it found the rain, but its power was baulked for only a second as the wet straw succumbed.

The three warriors punched the air in joy as the building burned. They screamed Boudicca's name, promising their queen more destruction.

But at the same moment, all three set eyes on the Archdruid. As one, they stopped still, their cries locked in their throats, before looking to each other, unsure of a man so powerful.

For Bran, too, had stopped still. A season ago—maybe only a moon ago—the moment would have been his. He would have owned the situation through the respect and calmness carried on an Archdruid's shoulders. And twenty hard years of training.

But not now. Deep, deep inside, Bran knew he and Britain had been separated, as surely as a babe was severed from its mother at the breaking of the birthcord. And he was old. What had three boys, armed with keen blades and fuelled by battlelust, to fear from an old man who no longer held the esteem of their queen?

Nervously, a hand caressed his beard. The other tightened its grip on his staff.

He was no longer in control.

The biggest of the three warriors, a muscular, woad-smeared brute, took a pace forward. His sword was drawn, his shield facing the Druid. His eyes burned.

The warrior's companions adopted his pose.

Instinctively, Bran stepped backward.

"Druid?" The question was asked with menace, not respect.

"I am Bran, Archdruid of Britain." He pulled himself up to his full height. He would not be nervous.

"The man who would have us give mercy to our enemies."

"I have preached that enemies must be beaten. Not slaughtered."

The first warrior took another confident step forward. "We slaughtered the Romans at Camulodunum. We strung them up for the gods. We crucified them in their own manner." His friends nodded in agreement.

"You slaughtered women and children. There is no glory in that."

"There is glory in *victory*, Archdruid. And we must acknowledge the giver of victory."

"The gods do not demand the slaughter of children. The ravens are satisfied with the flesh of warriors."

"Pah! When the gods give us victory we thank them in whatever way they demand. Glorious or not, man or babe." He sneered. "For then we know they will give us their favour."

"And who tells you this? Or are you trained Druids?" It was Bran's turn to sneer.

"The bard tells the army. The bard who was protected by the gods at Camulodunum, so that he may lead the slaughter. Dermot, Bard to the

Ordovices, who no Roman weapon could touch. He speaks with the gods. He has the queen's ear."

Bran had no retort. Merely telling the truth, that killing at the behest of an evil entity was wrong, that a Roman-conquered Britain was better than an evil-conquered Britain, would have the same effect as ordering a bullock to stand on its hind legs and dance to the harp.

"We don't like Roman *collaborators*."

Three blades pointed menacingly at Bran. The warriors took a pace forward. The smoke and the shadow of the massive building to his right dulled the morning. He stifled a cough and thought of Helena. Dead, Bran could do nothing to help her. And dead, he could not help Britain.

But there was no escape. Three young, fit warriors would surely catch and aged Druid before he could stumble a handful of paces.

But the Archdruid would not stop still, cut down like a sacrificial lamb. He looked desperately left and then right.

The big building, with its oak beams, would offer better protection than the wattle huts scattered in its shadows. Bran took the few steps to his right, and into darkness of the building of oak.

There were no windows, and Bran took blind paces inside the building while he waited for his eyes to adjust to the gloom. His staff guided him across the rough earthen floor.

At first he thought the building empty. But no. The building was not empty.

Bran could sense the gods. Not British gods, whose presence would have filled the Archdruid with peace, but Roman gods who Bran did not know. He could feel them, feel their unseen eyes watching him, studying his every move and wondering why a Briton was invading their privacy.

"Forgive me," the Archdruid pleaded to these Roman gods he had never before addressed.

This building was a temple.

Bran's greying eyes adjusted to the low light. The massive room was empty but for a low alter, draped with red, towards the far end. Atop the altar stood a bronze statue which Bran instantly recognised as Mars, the Roman wargod. Beside Mars's likeness, a small candle of beeswax burned gently, giving off a gentle aroma and needle-thin column of smoke which rose and disappeared into the thatch.

But there was no place to hide. Bran's threw his eyes from side to side, and looked anxiously behind as the doorway shadowed.

He turned to see the three swordsmen standing before him, eager to send him to the Otherworld. Bran closed his eyes and fell to his knees. He reached into his pouch to grasp his necklace of sacred white beads, and uttered the prayer of death.

Beeswax filled his nostrils, pushing away the mixed smells of smoke and wet thatch. The burning wax filled his mouth, even though the Archdruid knew the low flame was not strong. Maybe the knowledge of imminent death heightened the senses.

He shrugged. Such detail did not matter. He was about to die; he should be praying. He realised he felt no fear, just calm. He looked forward to seeing Conor and Kyra.

But nothing happened.

The temple was silent. Bran clenched his teeth and eyelids. Heartbeats passed, but still the fatal blow refused to come.

The stench of burning beeswax began to overpower the Archdruid. He felt it tightening his throat. He wanted to cough.

But still there was silence. The nothing was worse than waiting for the blow which would end his life.

He squeezed an eye open.

And the sight before him stiffened Archdruid Bran. Had he not been trained in the ways of the gods, Bran would have tasted fear.

A cloying wall of smoke stood before him, swirling and thickening, and blocking out the light from the doorway. The solid plume, as thick as a man's body, reached up into the sky and turned solid in front of his eyes. It flickered a reflected light of reds and yellows, the colour of flames.

He turned to the source of the light mirrored in the unnatural wall, and saw the candle gushing flame and smoke like a firebrand of fresh pitch. The smoke rose and swirled into the thick thatch ceiling, and instead of dissipating through the straw it dripped down from the roof and into the thick, lung-cloying curtain of mist.

Bran pushed forward a hesitant hand to touch the unnatural wall.

It was so thick it was solid. Bran strained his eyes through the murk. But the wall would not let his vision pass.

He doubted, though, that the three warriors would have stayed in the temple once the Otherworldly wall formed. *Fled like women at the first sign of what they didn't understand,* Bran decided.

The Archdruid was safe. He sighed in relief. *But why have I been spared by the gods of the enemy?*

"Because you alone have the power to spare my Roman people."

Bran turned to the direction of the voice deep, authoritative Latin-clipped voice.

No one.

But was it his imagination, or had the statue of Mars moved slightly?

Chapter 23

For the first time since moving to Nantbran, Peter Davis woke with daylight peering through his curtains. A shaft of sunlight pierced a chink in the curtains and stabbed him in the eye. The red numbers on his alarm clock read forty-seven minutes past six. The breeze squeezing through the slightly open window cooled him, but still sweat wrapped his body. His head pounded, not with an ache, but with adrenaline and fear.

The slaughter of Roman women had taken place countless generations ago, but still the cloying stench of blood filled his nostrils. One consuming thought took Peter's mind.

I must stop Andraste.

But his insides coiled at the thought of the sacrifice needed to make.

He clenched his teeth as he dressed. Although early, there was a task he needed to start. Before his family woke.

Slowly and on tiptoe, Peter Davis descended the stairs, stepping over the two floorboards which always creaked. He donned a jacket and training shoes and grabbed his car keys.

His breath came in nervous gasps as he opened the boot of his car. Everything was as he had left it when he had returned from Anglesey. A night outside a cheap Bed and Breakfast, a thorough going-over from a mechanic, and the drive home from the island, hadn't disturbed the remains.

Peter looked up at the house, making sure the curtains were still drawn, before gently picking up the two skulls he had wrapped in his towel. He lifted the material to inspect them; the small head belonging to Conor, and Kyra's larger one. Tears welled up in his eyes as he remembered the family he—*no, Bran*, he kept reminding himself—had lost in the dim past. And Bran's future loss which must be endured if he were to save Britain. Peter looked over his shoulder, back to the house.

Still no movement.

He carried the remains to the low hill, and left them inside the rectangular ruins of the old church before returning to collect the spade and pickaxe. He looked towards the path and bank bordering the property, relieved for once that the policeman on duty was out of sight. *On a breakfast break, perhaps.*

He returned to the car a third time for Dermot's harp.

He started to dig, forming a hole in the middle of the remains. The work was easier than he had expected; there were no rocks in this man-made mound of earth. He had no trouble breaking up the layer of grass with the pick before digging a hole with the spade, and soon had to stand in the hole to dig. He stopped to cast anxious eyes over the house every few seconds, but there was still no sign of movement.

And this was something he wanted to do without discovery.

After wiping sweat from his brow he knelt down and took Kyra's skull gently in his hands. He looked into the empty eyes and raised the bone to his lips. She grinned back at him lifelessly. "Goodbye, Kyra. Rest in peace. I'm sorry I didn't protect you. The Sight deserted me." He placed the head gently in the hole and wiped tears from his cheeks with the back of his hand as he lifted Conor's skull. His stomach lurched as he remembered the small, white bundle lying dead and helpless in the shallow stream near Abberffraw. "Goodbye, grandson. I'll look on your grave and think of you every day. You would have grown up to be a man to be proud of."

Finally, Peter picked up the harp, still looking as tuneful as it had all those years ago when its music had drifted around Tre'r Ceiri's feasting hall. He let it rest gently in his hands. He would have given anything to pluck one last note, but the centuries had rotted away the strings of animal gut. Anyway, the magical sound was best left in the memory.

"Dermot, my son. I'm sorry I don't have your remains to place in this sacred spot. But it seemed fitting that I should bury your family—our family—near me. I hope your harp means I have a little of you near me too. Despite our differences, Bran never stopped loving you."

Peter said the words, but he doubted Dermot would have believed them even if he was listening.

Not after what Peter had planned for his next Roman experience.

Gently, the harp too was placed in the hole. For a couple of seconds Peter was sure he could make out the forms of Dermot, Kyra and Conor standing beside him, the two adults smiling at him, arms around each other as they held their baby.

He listened. There was something in the wind. Some sound coming from the hole beneath him as he knelt over it. The sound of voices. Kyra's voice, calling him. The words in the ancient tongue became clear, as if muffled by the mists of time which were becoming less distant. A soft, conciliatory voice. Within a second or two Peter would be able to make out words. Words from a woman who had died two thousand years ago.

"Bran, Bran—"

"Peter? What the Hell are you doing out there?" Lucy's voice broke the morning. And the spell. Peter found himself looking at nothing more than a couple of rotted skulls and a battered harp as his ancient family melted into the air.

He looked up to see his sister with her head out of her bedroom window and sporting a questioning gaze.

"Leave me alone. I'm busy."

"Doing what?"

"Mind your own business." Peter bit his lip with guilt. *I shouldn't speak to her like that. Not after what she's been through.*

"Okay, okay, don't have a fit on me. I'm coming down. Give me a minute to get dressed."

Peter ran a hand through his hair before lifting the spade and starting to dig. He wanted everything buried. Hidden. He felt anger. It wasn't the sombre burial he had planned for his ancient family.

Alun appeared at Lucy's window. "What's going on? Why are you outside? Lucy says you're up to something."

"It's personal. Right? Just leave me alone." He pulled the spade from the ground and vent his anger by thrusting it back into the earth. The blade disappeared up to its shoulder.

Lucy padded outside, wearing jeans and a blue anorak and followed by her father. Her arms were wrapped around her. She still looked pale; her face carried a permanent strain.

"Come on, Pete. What is it?" She laid a gentle hand on his shoulder.

He shrugged. "You'd never believe me."

"After the other night I think I'd believe anything."

"Why not tell the whole family?" Alun sighed.

"Okay, but you're not going to believe this." Peter sighed. He didn't know where to begin. "I've had some really strange dreams since we moved here. I dream I'm the Archdruid of Britain, who worshipped in this valley at the time of the Romans."

He looked into the faces of his father and sister. They weren't laughing at him. *Yet.*

He continued. "The Druid had an encounter with a goddess of war. Andraste."

Lucy nodded. "Boudicca made sacrifices to Andraste, dad, and asked for her help during the revolt."

"Anyway," Peter continued. "The Goddess promised Archdruid Bran she would help the Britons win the war against the Romans if she could have a magic sword, which, combined with her own magic, would be powerful enough to guarantee success."

Alun and Lucy were listening intently, but he still couldn't tell whether they believed him.

"The Britons had early success, but Bran found the slaughter and torture the Goddess demanded too much. He decided that the revolt must fail. He would rather see Britain under the Romans than free and ruled by an evil goddess, continually demanding sacrifices. He told Boudicca the

Goddess wanted the army to go north after sacking London, instead of south which the Goddess had actually decreed."

Lucy cut in with some more explanation for her father. "Some historians have wondered why Boudicca took her army right into a Roman force which had just sacked Anglesey." She paused. "So this is why you've been asking me about Roman Britain?"

"Yes."

Lucy continued. "People have asked why Boudicca didn't head south, to ravage the channel coast and the heartland of Roman Britain at that time. The south was undefended, with the legions on Anglesey." She shrugged. "The revolt failed, with the Britons crushed. They walked right into a Roman army."

Alun's brows knotted. "That's a fine tale, but is there a point to it?"

"Yes. I think the Goddess is still here. I think I'm Bran's reincarnation, and when I dream I am actually reliving Boudicca's revolt. The Goddess wants me to change history by making me—Archdruid Bran—tell Boudicca to send the army south and win the revolt. Then Britain can be hers. And what has happened to Lucy and Johnny since we moved is her way of warning me of what will happen if I don't do as she wants."

Alun shot a questioning glance at Lucy, who responded. "I... I sort of believe Pete, dad. That old woman at the stones... there was something about her. The way she ran; the way she moved and looked. And she was so single minded. All she wanted was blood. And for Johnny to describe the same person..." She paused and bit her lip. It quivered. "And Pete's been asking about Roman history. I'm the one who's studied Roman Britain, but he knows the detail better than I do. Better than my tutors, even. I know it sounds far-fetched, but it just adds up...it just fits." She looked at Peter. "Morgan? She looked so much like a younger version of the old lady."

"Yes. Morgan was... is... the Goddess, come to keep an eye on me. To make sure I... Bran... did as she wanted." He grimaced as he recalled being enchanted by her beauty. "Morrigan was the name given to her in Ireland. Morgan is the modern form."

"So Toby and Rhiannon and half of Nantbran were killed as warnings to us?" Alun's voice was disbelieving.

"No, dad. Well, yes. Partly. Andraste needs blood and souls to survive, like we need food. But they doubled as a warning to me as well."

"Peter?" Alun's voice was quiet.

"Yes?"

"Why didn't she kill Lucy?"

Lucy answered. "My crucifix. She wasn't strong enough to fight a symbol of good." She ran a trembling hand through her hair. "Dad, could you take me inside please?"

Alun put an arm around his daughter's shoulders and took her inside.

Peter waited until they had disappeared and finished a prayer to Bel. He stood quietly with his own thoughts over the newly buried remains of Bran's family, sad that he had two families being ripped in two, twenty centuries apart.

Alun came back out. "She's had another tablet. She's asleep. You'd better have damn good proof of this far-fetched tale before upsetting your sister again." Anger rose in his voice.

"I think I can prove it, dad. See the marshy area over there, where the spring comes out of the rock?"

Alun nodded.

"In my dreams—but I think they are more like experiences—that used to be a pool where offerings were made to the gods. Gold and jewels. Human sacrifices and the like. If we dig down there and we find something, will you believe me then?"

Alun frowned. "I suppose it'd be a start."

* * * *

Digging was hard work.

There was only one spade and one pick. Peter used the pick to break through the topsoil and Alun took the spade. But merely clearing the grass took an hour. Johnny woke, and the three stopped for breakfast before continuing, this time with Peter having the spade and Johnny digging out tufts of marsh grass on his own a short distance away. Alun used his hands to put the clods of earth into a wheelbarrow and take them a useful distance away.

The earth was heavy and wet, and the hole filled up with water as quickly as Peter and Alun emptied it. The stream didn't run directly into the pool, but seeped through the ground. There was always an inch or so of silty water around their feet no matter how hard they bailed. There were buried rocks which had to be dug out by hand.

After another hour they had gone down a foot. By lunch the depth had doubled. Peter was on his third shift. The sun was at its height, and he and his father were stripped to the waist. By the time they had finished eating Lucy was awake and had come out to watch. She lit up a cigarette. Alun frowned but kept silent.

Lucy seemed as convinced as Peter that they would find something.

And all the while Peter found himself nervously eyeing a raven watching the intently from the cairn.

It was Alun who was digging when the spade hit something that was neither earth nor stone. "Hey, kids. I've got something. Something hard."

Peter squeezed into the small hole beside his father. Lucy leaned over, and even Johnny interrupted his own game to watch. "I'll get out," Alun announced. "You know more what you're looking for. And anyway, it's probably about time you took another turn in the mud." He climbed out, sweat glistening on his back. His jeans and training shoes were soaked.

Peter jumped in. His feet splashed and sunk into the silt. Ignoring the water clogging his jeans, he knelt down and felt with his hands, pushing wet earth from around the object.

Whatever it was flat but made of thin material, but with bumps and grooves on it. His hand found one particular groove, and winced as his finger retreated from the raw edge. Possibly sharp from where the spade caught it, he thought.

"You all right?" asked Lucy. "What is it?"

"I don't know. But it's certainly something man made. Not a tree root or a rock. It's been carved or something. And it's metallic. And flat. A bit like a..." His voice trailed off. "Like a shield." The last words were almost whispered. The feel of the object reminded him of the oblong, finely decorated shield which had been sacrificed in this very pool. The gift to the gods he—no, Bran—had thrown in the pool only a few nights ago.

He tried to think where in the pool it had landed. Could this be the place? He couldn't remember detail in the morass of activity over the last week. And it had changed so much...

But he was confident. "I can't get it out of the mud. But it's a shield. It was made of bronze and wood, but the wood has rotted."

Alun frowned, his face still a mask of disbelief. "Let me back in." Peter jumped out to make room, and Alun prodded about. "There's hardly any of it exposed. Most of whatever it is is still under the mud. If it's what you say it is, I'll have no choice but to believe you."

"Peter may be right, dad," said Lucy, putting a lighter to another cigarette. "There was an old shield just like the one Peter's describing found in the Thames years ago. It's quite famous. The Battersea Shield."

The whole family joined in. Peter and Alun squeezed into the small hole, while Lucy helped widen it with the spade. Johnny hindered by insisting on bailing with his bucket. There was little room to work, and within minutes the whole family were splattered in mud, but ignoring it as their task took total importance. Peter cast a sideways glance at Lucy, pleased to see her old spirit back in her eyes. He looked towards the path. He was relieved not to see a policeman watching.

The work took another hour, but no-one noticed the time. Even Johnny, thinking his role important, was totally absorbed in his task of bailing. Lucy stripped off her shirt and worked in mud splattered jeans and bra. Eventually, though, there was a gurgle from the hole as something gave.

"I think I've got it. Yes! Here it is!" Alun's children stood back as he reached into the water for one last time and raised a flat oval object. Possibly a shield, but it was impossible to tell through the mass of mud covering it.

"Let's get it inside. We can put it under the tap."

"The hose might make more sense," said Alun. "We're all filthy. Let's not get any more mud inside than we have to."

"Don't do that, dad," reproved Lucy as Alun scratched away dirt from both armpits. "It makes you look like something out of the jungle!"

Alun put on a look of mock hurt. Peter smiled too. It was good to hear a joke pass his sister's lips.

The hose was agreed on, and the family gathered round. Alun turned the tap while Johnny took charge of the watering. Peter helped him gently spray the mud from the shield as it slowly took shape before their eyes.

When it was clean, Peter placed the shield against the wall and stepped back to admire it. It was bashed and bruised and corroded green. One emerald had gone, but three precious stones remained, hugged by the circular whorls of Celtic design.

The shield was beautiful.

Lucy put an arm around Peter's waist. He hugged her in return.

Alun embraced them both.

Johnny joined in and the family cried together.

"Lucy, what happened to the revolt after London?" asked Peter.

"The Britons turned north. Verulanium—St Albans—was sacked. The Britons took their families with them on the march, they were so confident of victory. They were defeated by the legions returning from Anglesey somewhere on the route of the modern A5. Possibly near Towcester. But they were all killed. Even the kids..." She looked down at Johnny with moist eyes.

"My God." Peter's heart pounded. "...and the decision to lead the Iceni and their families to the slaughter must be mine."

He turned in response to the cry of a raven circling overhead.

Chapter 24

The smoke cleared, but still the temple hung heavy with the gods.

Bran grasped his staff with two hands and rose unsteadily to his feet. He caressed his beard as he hesitated. He should step outside, to save the Roman women...

Helena.

...but unease held him back. Would every man in the army want him dead?

The Archdruid shivered. Why should he fear? He had the protection of the gods. Not British gods... but this was a *Roman* city. It seemed proper that Roman gods should defend him.

His mind made up, the Archdruid strode purposefully forward into the drizzle. He knew the army would take their prisoners to the market place, the open area in front of the planned forum. Despite the protection from the Latin gods swirling in the atmosphere around him, the Archdruid knew his path was laced with danger.

* * * *

Boudicca appeared even more fearsome than usual, for the Warrior Queen had fought alongside her warriors. Blood and gore matted her hair and clothing, and her sword still dripped red. Sweat fell from her body, and the crazed look of battle in her eyes had still to die. Her lips were drawn back in a snarl, baring yellowed teeth.

"String them up. The Goddess wants the women strung up."

The speaker was Dermot. And the warriors obeyed him without question, not even looking around for their queen to confirm the order. The forum had only its skeleton built; solid upright columns of oak reached from the gravel to support equally impressive crossbeams. Bran was reminded of the massive circle of stone on the great plain in the land of the Belgae to the west.

Ropes were thrown over the crossbeams and tied to the women's wrists, so they were forced to stand, stretching, with their arms towards the heavens.

"Dermot? Why are you doing this?" Bran had run the last few paces and his breath was shallow.

Dermot looked at Bran, a sneer of contempt across his features. "The Goddess has instructed me. Did she not speak to you too?"

Bran ignored the insult. "What has the Goddess instructed?" He turned round to watch the procession of Roman women being strung up, his eyes searching the gaggle for one woman. Some fell to their knees before they were bound, weeping and begging for mercy. Others remained brave, kicking, punching and cursing their captors until forced quiet by a clenched fist. A few, doubled up in agony, clutched wounds before they were forced to stand. One or two fell into a limp faint as they were tied, but were pulled upright by their bonds.

All knew they were to die.

Bran watched as one woman, terrified beyond endurance, collapsed, her legs unable to support her. Her captor lifted her by her perm-curled black hair. Again she fell to the ground. The warrior looked questioningly at his queen. Boudicca, watching impassively from her chariot, made a stabbing motion with her sword. The warrior slit the woman's throat, and without looking back left her to die. Other warriors merely stepped over her, or kicked her as if she were no more than a wounded dog blocking the way.

Most of the Roman women, though, looked around them with expressions of bewilderment. Most had tears rolling down their rain-spattered cheeks. Two, possibly a mother and daughter, hugged their goodbyes before being pulled apart at swordpoint.

The fires were beginning to take hold; despite the drizzle the burning buildings spilled their wisps of black smoke across the Londinium's market place.

With a wave of her hand Boudicca beckoned Dermot towards her chariot. Bran made to follow, but the queen shot him a piercing look. The Archdruid stayed still.

Bran watched uneasily as the queen spoke with his son. His insides churned. He may be Archdruid of Britain, but he felt he was in hostile hands. And Queen Boudicca had little mercy on those she did not consider totally loyal.

But Bran stood his ground, his aged ears trying without success to overhear the words spoken in front of him. He was Archdruid of Britain. He would not run from danger. The Roman gods were with him. As were the British gods.

Weren't they?

With a masculine leap the queen jumped to the ground. She swung her sword around her head as she shouted Andraste's orders which Dermot had passed on.

"Warriors of the Iceni, warriors of the Trinovantes! Listen to your queen, who has been granted victory over our enemies by the will of

Andraste." She raised her eyes and bloodied sword to the heavens. Bran, along with the warband, looked upwards in response to the cackle of a raven from overhead. There was a low murmur from the warriors. "As I am a woman, so is our Goddess, and she has given me victory, woman to woman."

"Very clever," Bran muttered to himself. She was claiming that victory was given to her only because she was a woman. No man would dare wrest Britain from her now.

The queen continued. "As the Romans ravished my body, the Goddess has demanded revenge on my behalf." She swept a hand towards the Roman women, their arms tied above their heads to the unfinished skeleton of the forum. "Men, tear their clothes from their bodies."

There were screams from among the scores of women. Bran caressed his beard and mused that there must have been many more women in London. Many must have already succumbed to British weapons. Those left alive, he had no doubt, would soon be wishing that they too had received a quick end.

Togas and cloaks were pulled away by the Britons without consideration. The luckiest of the captives were spared the hands of their captors, but most suffered grasped breasts or groins during the process. Most screamed, their eyes swivelling between woad-splattered warriors ogling their Latin bodies, and the one powerful woman who showed no mercy even towards her own sex.

Bran's eyes scoured the lines of terrified women, but they would not find the one figure they searched for.

Bran wanted to pace among them, to hunt for his Helena.

But he knew the warriors would let him no nearer. Dermot was Briton's Man of the Spirits now. Bran bore little weight.

A gasp went up from the warriors as a raven alighted on Dermot's right shoulder. It seemed to be speaking in the bard's ear. Bran felt a pang of jealousy, especially when his son whispered back.

She should be speaking with me. I am an Archdruid.

The Warrior Queen spoke. "Andraste, you have given us the greatest of victories." She looked at the bird. "Just as you have given us the blood of the Roman warriors, we commend their women to you, women to woman. Let us know your will." A wisp of smoke was blown across the Queen by the breeze. She gave a series of loud, deep coughs as her lungs fought against it, then spat a mouthful of phlegm onto the gravel.

Dermot, raven still atop his shoulder, slowly walked the few paces to his queen's chariot and bowed lightly. The two spoke. After what could only have been a few heartbeats, but which seemed like an eternity to the watching Bran, she rose her bloodied sword to the skies once more, and spoke. "Andraste, our victory goddess has spoken. These Roman *women*"—she spat out the word— "These women are to be sacrifices to her name, as our thanks to her work for us on this day." Her eyes left the heavens and rested on her men. "Brave warriors of the Iceni, draw your swords."

There was the smooth sound of metal upon leather. Women screamed or moaned. Some fainted.

Boudicca's face hardened. Now was the moment the prisoners would learn their fate. Death was certain, but its speed and discomfort had yet to be pronounced. The queen spoke in British first, then immediately repeated the phrase in a rusty, yet understandable Latin.

"Warriors of Britain! Cut off their breasts! Rape them with your spearpoints! Let them have no part of their womanhood left!"

Women screamed as their fate was translated into their own tongue. Others whimpered or fainted. Others involuntarily voided bowels or bladders, their humiliation soiling their naked thighs.

The British warriors, weapons bared, prepared to inflict Boudicca's revenge. Battlelust returned to their eyes. There was to be no mercy, for Andraste would spare no pain or violation.

Bran's eyes were drawn to the raven as it flew from Dermot's shoulder to circle above the carnage and scream encouragement.

* * * *

Peter Davis roused in his sleep. As so often in recent nights, despite the cool mountain breezes which brushed through his open window after dark, a thick layer of sweat glued his T-shirt and shorts to his flesh. He held his head between his hands and tried not to vomit. Lucy had told him atrocities were committed by Boudicca's army, but to experience them first-hand brought the suffering too close. He would watch no more. Even in his state of semi-consciousness, he knew he must take action to ensure failure of the revolt. It would mean his hands would run with British blood, and he would gain the hatred of an evil entity.

But he could not risk Britain falling into Andraste's hands.

* * * *

Bran turned, unease creeping into his mind. He had not asked his body to look away from the carnage, but he felt the will of some other being wresting away his control.

But there was no feeling of malevolence. Whatever force was coming over him was acting for good. And he would not fight it.

His only regret was that it had not manifested itself earlier. Maybe it would have prevented the torture going on behind him.

Not knowing in what direction he was being taken, but in prayer to The Daghdha, overseer of Druids, Bran allowed himself to be led away from the place of death. Helena's suffering consumed his mind, but he knew her pain was minute compared to the future of Britain. And the warriors would never allow him to help her. It wasn't until he had been taken to the outskirts of the city he noticed a lifting in the atmosphere, where the twin stenches of blood and smoke left his nostrils. The distant screams of feminine agony still assaulted his ears, but the air was freer. It no longer hung heavy with death.

He wasn't sorry to leave the half-built forum. He had been powerless to help the Roman women, and had no wish to be a party to what would certainly be slow deaths.

At the command of the being, he lay down and allowed himself to sleep in the porch of a wattle hovel.

Bran had no idea how long he remained alone. When he awoke, the sun was past its zenith; maybe he had slept for a quarter of daylight. With his staff, he struggled to his feet, cursing the gods who allowed him to suffer the fatigue of age. Something glinted in the mud. Someone had left a dagger on the doorway. Absentmindedly, he picked it up and fingered its intricately carved hilt. Its form was Roman.

He sensed, rather than saw, a presence nearby. He turned, grabbing the weapon tightly, half expecting to see a fugitive Roman seeking revenge.

But it was the Goddess who stood before him. Her black dress and pale skin were splattered with blood. She held the Rainbow Sword, blade pointing to the ground, in her right hand. Its hilt glowed red. The same colour as the sticky liquid dripping from it.

"Morgan?" The word came unbidden to his lips. Bran wondered why he had used the Irish version of her name.

The maiden laughed. "So you have discovered you have the power to alter the past, Peter Davis?"

Bran had no knowledge of the language the Goddess used. His soul felt empty; he knew it was being used by another. An entity which was one with him, helping him. And, through the benevolent invader of his soul, he could understand every word. He replied in the same language, "What do you want with me?"

"The army must go south. Take the army south and I will free your family to live your lives in peace."

Peter's mind struggled. He thought of his family. He loved them. But he would not stand aside and watch Britain being torn in two by evil. If he must now chose between the safety of his family and the safety of Britain...

He knew he must choose Britain.

Inside Peter Davis, Bran began to understand. He picked up some of the thoughts of the being inside him. Someone wanting to help Britain. He became merged with the name 'Peter Davis'; he knew Lucy, Johnny and their father. The man inside him was struggling to protect these people.

"Why have you taken Dermot?" The question came from the Archdruid, not Peter Davis.

"He is mine. He shares a passion to see Britain a land free of the Eagles. And he shares my need for the blood of revenge." Her beautiful face contorted into a sneer. "He will make a good Archdruid."

"He does not have the training. It takes twenty years of study to make a Druid."

She threw her head back and laughed. "You think Boudicca will reward him with tutors? No, the lad has earned power. He is the people's man. Boudicca will make him Archdruid in a bid to stop him claiming the kingship."

"It takes the Council of Druids to make an Archdruid. The Council must remain free of politics."

She laughed again. "Britain will be in Boudicca's pocket after the revolt. What Boudicca wants, she will get, politics or no. And Dermot will know who he owes his success to." She raised the Rainbow Sword to the sky. "At Boudicca's and Dermot's command the whole of Britain will worship me."

His fingers caressed the Roman blade. His flesh felt its razor edge.

"These islands will run with blood." Andraste licked her delicate lips. "Yes! Rivers of blood will flow through Britain as her people rejoice in my name! Now, I must leave you. I have left the slaughter too long."

She cackled and disappeared. Bran watched a raven fly back towards the market place.

Without warning, Dermot appeared before Bran and Peter. The battlelust was gone from his eyes, but victory stained his tunic red. He no longer held a sword. He looked surprisingly pleased to see his father. "The Goddess told me I should find you here."

"And what else did the Goddess tell you?"

"The army marches south."

"Have you told Boudicca?" Peter's question.

"No." He looked puzzled. "I thought to tell you first. The queen is preparing to thank her warriors."

The part of Bran which was Peter Davis lurched. He could help save Britain from more slaughter in one act. One swift moment which would prevent the history books being written in blood. He could stop evil ruling Britain down the ages, even until his own day. Peter's voice became a horse whisper. "Forgive me, Bran."

Grasping the Roman dagger, he made to hug Dermot. The boy prepared to reciprocate, his recently hardened eyes softening as he prepared to receive his father's embrace.

Dermot could never have expected the thrust of a dagger into his ribs.

The boy gave a throaty gasp. His eyes widened, in surprise more than pain. Blood and foam appeared from his mouth.

The front of his robe was wet. Bran didn't need to look down to know he was soaked in his son's blood.

"Do you hate me that much, father?"

Tears found the corners of Bran's eyes. "No, my son. I love you more than you could ever know. But I love Britain too. I could not allow you to send the army south."

But Dermot was dead before his father had finished speaking. Bran laid the body on the ground, closed Dermot's eyes and laid his arms across his chest to ease his passage into the Otherworld. He spoke the sacred words of death over his son before pacing back to the Forum.

* * * *

The walk to the half-built Forum was not a long one, but age and worry served to slow the Archdruid. He kept a keen eye out for wandering warriors looting among the smoke and, with assistance from The Sight, on one occasion a battle-crazed Briton strode past, was able to disappear into a doorway or alley before being spotted.

Another time he failed to hide, but the lone warrior, sword drawn, backed away from the white-cloaked priest.

Just as men would have done when I had the protection of the gods, the Archdruid mused. But he still had the protection of the immortals. The only difference now was that the gods of the enemy protected him.

He felt the Roman immortals around him.

They felt different to the Celtic gods; less flamboyant, less in tune with nature. But the protection felt the same. As did the demand for loyalty.

Will I have to worship the gods of the enemy for the rest of my days?

The Archdruid was still addressing his thoughts as he reached the Forum. His nostrils filled with the stench of blood-tinted drizzle.

A warrior thought to challenge the Archdruid. But Bran's old assurance, borne of god-given protection, had returned. One glare at the soldier from beneath bushed eyebrows was enough authority for him to proceed.

As he pushed his way through the smoke Bran was met by a vision of suffering. Countless lines of women were still strung up, their arms raised and tied by rope from the beams of the Forum's skeleton, and disappearing into the smoke.

At least the beings had once been women. Now, it was only the length of the black Roman hair clinging to what was left of their upper bodies which marked them out as females.

None had breasts. Instead, each woman had two gaping, bloody circles. The sharpened blades of British knives had done their work.

And spearshafts protruded from between their legs.

Bran's instinct turned him away; even a Druid's training could not stop him gagging at the carnage before him.

But there were no screams. Many of the women were dead already, and hung limply from their bonds; one or two others twitched away the last throes of life. A few gave out low moans.

The smoke swirled around the slaughter, giving an Otherworldly air to the scene of death.

Bran felt his stomach knot.

Helena!

His eyes tried to pierce the smoke, but he could not see her. He hoped against his instincts that she had found an escape.

He took a step forward, towards the torture.

A warrior stepped in front of him. The swordsman hesitated, avoided Bran's gaze, and let the Archdruid pass.

He knows there is nothing I can do.

Bran walked slowly along the lines of mutilation, the gravel around the Forum's foundations crunching beneath his sandals. Not one Roman had escaped the ravages of British knives and spears; some weapons failed to do their job and on occasion mutilated breasts still clung to a chest. Other individuals had been rammed with a spear which had missed their groins; the weapon protruded from a belly or buttock.

Sometimes as he passed, a woman would raise her head from a bloodied chest to gaze at him with dulled eyes, or whisper gasped but indecipherable words in his direction.

And everywhere blood. A pool of it beneath each hanging body; sometimes so much blood, swelled by rain, that pools beneath more than one woman joined to form a larger puddle.

Bran's feet were wet. He looked down, ready to step out of a puddle of rainwater.

But instead he saw a stream of blood around his sandals.

He stepped out of the blood and quickened his pace, eyes smarting and throat choking against the cloying smoke. His staff helped him along the rows of suffering bodies, while all the time he watched out for the one familiar face among the hanging corpses.

Until, in an instant, his body stopped still.

Helena!

Her naked back was to him, but there could be no mistake. The characteristic double mole on her right shoulder, just visible through the blood. The weal on her hip, a remnant scar from a childhood accident.

He was almost near enough to touch her. *For the first time in… in… ten years?*

"Helena…" The name escaped unbidden from his lips.

There was a grunt. The body twitched as it recognised its name.

She lives. Bran praised the gods. Until he walked around to her front and faced her.

This… this cannot be my Helena…

The being grunted through breasts which had been roughly sewn to its mouth with coarse twine. As the bloodied mass tried to speak one breast fell to the floor, ripping away her lower lip. Blood flowed from her mouth, dripping from her jaw and becoming lost in the raw circles of flesh where her breasts had once been.

Her eyes widened slightly in recognition.

"Bran?" The voice was barely audible, the word muffled by the breast still hanging from her upper lip.

"Helena." He reached down for the spear between her legs, meaning to pull it from her body. It was slippy with her blood.

She winced.

"I've got to get you out of here. I know medicines…"

"Kill me."

"What?"

"Kill me."

Bran sucked in. He thought of Helena's future life, even if her body were to survive. *A disfigured cripple, her insides ruined by an arm's length of spear. Constant pain.*

His hands trembled as he reached for the Roman dagger in his belt. It would put a quick end to her suffering.

He placed its blade against her throat and prepared himself to cut into her flesh.

She whispered through her mutilated mouth. He couldn't make out the words.

"Say it again?"

"Our son?"

Bran bit his lower lip and avoided her gaze.

"Dead?"

He nodded.

"He knew his mother loved him." But Bran didn't add that Helena's son had ordered this slaughter. Instead he whispered a goodbye into her ear, kissed her on the cheek and quickly put an end to her suffering with the Roman knife.

Bran wondered aimlessly among the dying until he reached the end of the rows of tied woman.

Boudicca, atop her chariot, appeared to him from the mist.

"Well? Where is Dermot?" she demanded without formality, but with some respect.

Bran knew the queen could sense the gods. He wondered if the respect was bought about by the presence of his Roman protector.

He wiped a tear. This one was not bought to his eyes by the smoke. "He is dead, my queen."

"Dead? How?" There was no flicker in her eye, just the steel of a warrior who has seen too many deaths to worry about one more.

"A Roman dagger. I held him as he died." Bran hoped she would not see in his eyes that he held back.

"So what of the revolt? The one man who can advise me is dead."

"I speak with the gods," Bran reminded her.

"And what has the Goddess told you?" she spat. "To go home and use our swords to till our fields?"

"No, my queen." His voice was level, despite knowing what he was putting at risk by lying. "The army must go north."

* * * *

Peter Davis sat upright. He had sent the British army into the jaws of the Roman legions.

And his actions had sacrificed his family.

Chapter 25

"I think you should leave." Peter broke the strained silence.

"Huh?" Alun looked up from his cornflakes. He rested his spoon in his bowl and pushed his glasses up his nose.

"You, Lucy and Johnny. I don't think you're safe."

"Why? There's a horde of police camping on our doorstep. We're probably safer here than anywhere else."

"But, dad, after everything that's happened…"

"All that has happened is that some sadistic old woman is running amok."

"All the more reason to get out."

Alun leaned back and looked his son in the eye. "Peter, the only thing I care about is my family. Since your mother died… if anything happened to any of you kids…"

"*Exactly*, dad. And you'd all be safer if you left."

"No. We're safer here. We've been promised a twenty-four hour guard until this woman is caught. If were not safe with half the North Wales Constabulary hanging about, then we won't be safe anywhere."

"But, dad, the shield. I *knew* where to find it! My dreams—"

"I said no. We stay here. I need more than a battered antique to persuade me that we're being stalked by a supernatural pensioner. I know you mean well, but—"

"I want to go, dad." Lucy stood in the doorway.

"Sis? I didn't hear you come downstairs. How are you? The doctor said not to wake you until midday."

"I didn't bother with the pills. They gave me nightmares. I'd rather be awake." Her chin quivered.

Peter pulled out a chair for his sister. Her shoulders slumped ahead of her as she sat. Her features hung from her face. Her eyes were red through tears and lack of sleep.

She hadn't bothered to change out of her nightie and pink dressing gown.

"I want to leave, dad. You didn't *see* her. Her eyes… she's *evil*… and that sword…" Lucy looked up, moist eyes pleading. "*Please*, dad. Don't make me stay here." Her face filled her hands and her voice lowered to a whisper. "I'm scared. I'm afraid she'll come back for me."

"And I'm sure Johnny won't want to stay any longer than he has to," added Peter.

Alun leaned back in his chair and let out a sigh, a gesture he always made when he was losing an argument. Then, hesitantly, he laid his hand on Lucy's shoulder. "Okay, kids. We'll leave. Where do you want to go? Swindon?"

"I'm not going, dad."

A crack of thunder from outside broke the silence.

"Please, Pete. I don't want you staying here... not alone... she nearly killed me." Lucy's hand touched his arm. "'The bitch nearly *killed* me," she sobbed.

Another thundercrack held back Peter's reply. The first spots of rain patted against the window. "It's *me* she wants—Morgan, or Andraste, or whatever we want to call her. But either way, she'll happily... er... hurt either of you or Johnny to get at me." He thought of his brother, lying in a drugged sleep upstairs, policewoman at his side.

"Peter, Peter, for crying out loud! How long do we have to put up with this superstitious stuff? There's a murderer around."

"Dad, I believe Peter. You didn't see this... this... *thing*. She wasn't like us. She wasn't *human*. But I don't want to leave Pete alone with her." She forced a watery smile at her brother.

"But if we all go to Swindon she'll only follow us. At least if I stay behind I'll be the only one in danger."

"No, please don't leave us. I *saw* her Pete. And she couldn't take on my cross!" She fingered the crucifix. "And you reckon she only came to life or whatever it was because you're in the area..."

"Yes, but—"

"Don't you *see*, Pete? If all this Celtic stuff you've talked about is true, she's only here because of you! If you left Nantbran she wouldn't be able to draw on your strength or whatever it is she gets from you. I wonder if she *needs* you." Her eyes pleaded.

Alun pushed his chair back. "I'm going to check on Johnny. And I'll ask the police if we can go. Just leave me out of your voodoo." He paused as if about to say more, but instead shook his head sharply and left the room. He didn't look back, and a few seconds later his footsteps pounded the stairs and landing.

"Don't mind dad, sis. He really cares, but he nearly lost you and Johnny. With mum going only a few months ago... he's come close to having his whole life destroyed."

Peter took his sister's hand as tears welled in her eyes. Gently, he brushed a strand of hair from her face. "I'll come with you, sis. I don't know if it'll do any good, but it'll give us some time to see what happens. But if she carries on... killing, I'll have to come back and face her."

"Yeah."

"I honestly hadn't thought that she might go away if I left. I thought I'd have to stay here and fight her."

"Yeah, well I'm a woman, y'know. Maybe I just understand how she thinks."

'But you're not evil."

"I could list a few ex-boyfriends who might disagree."

A crack of thunder interrupted their nervous laughter.

* * * *

"Everyone ready?"

Peter raised his thumbs and climbed behind Lucy into the back of his father's car. He slammed the door and shook the rain from his denim jacket. He wiped condensation from the window and looked back at he house, its slate walls merging with the mountain in the thunder-ridden afternoon.

And he looked at his own stricken car, reluctantly left behind in the gravel parking area, unlikely to make the tortuous route through Snowdonia to the English border.

Beside him, Johnny didn't even complain at the drenching, but yawned as another sleeping pill took effect.

Tipsy squealed from his basket at Peter's feet.

Peter looked through the rain-streaked window once more, searching for a circling raven.

Nothing.

Just the view ahead of the gravel drive crossing a gentle lower slope of the mountains, and a copse of firs in the valley.

Above him sheer slate walls reached into the cloud.

The family raised a hand to acknowledge the nod of the duty policeman, who scurried back inside the house, eager to take up Alun's offer of guarding from the inside while the storm raged. The man's eyes lingered on Lucy before he disappeared from view.

For once, neither his father or Lucy seemed to care.

Alun turned the key in the ignition and the car roared into life.

Peter breathed a sigh of relief. He had half expected the car to die as his own had done on the Sacred Isle... *no, Anglesey...* a victim of two thousand year-old hatred.

"Thank goodness," muttered Lucy, echoing her brother's thoughts. But there was not even a groan of discontent from the engine, which purred smoothly as Alun took the vehicle down the gravel track.

Peter threw his head back. He stretched and even had to stifle a yawn borne of sleepless nights. He closed his eyes, not even bothering to look back at the house, which had bought so much misery in only a few short days.

Peace. Nothing but the hum of the gentle hum of the engine over the gentle slap of rain on the windows. He realised how tired he was.

Until Lucy screamed. Alun swore.

The car's brakes argued with the drive and slid on the wet gravel. The engine stalled.

Peter's eyes shot open. Fear pierced his heart.

The road ahead was moving.

But not just the road. The whole hillside was falling noiselessly like a liquid into the gentle valley.

It only took a couple of seconds. As soon as it had started, everything was still. There was no hillside, only a wall of earth ahead of them. A loosened rock bounded down the newly formed surface.

"Shit," said Lucy as Alun got out of the car. Peter joined his father after making sure Johnny was still asleep. The boy had opened his eyes before succumbing again to his drugged sleep.

"Landslip," shrugged Alun simply, not seeming to notice the downpour soaking his check shirt. "Maybe the sudden rains after the dry spell loosened the earth."

"Yeah, maybe."

"Whatever. There's no way we're getting out of Nantbran tonight."

Peter pulled his denim collar around his neck and took a couple of steps forward. He found himself rubbing his chin. Nervously, he leaned over the edge.

To his surprise, the landslip had only sunk the road by a couple of feet, but it was enough to make the ground impassable.

Alun grabbed his arm. "Best come away. There's no telling if the rest will go."

"So what do we do now?"

"Well, short of hiring a helicopter I think our only choice is to stay here. I'll reverse the car back up the drive, and I guess you get your wish."

"Huh?"

Alun's eyes narrowed. "You're the one who didn't want to leave."

"Yeah. But, what about the house? What if that falls down the slope?"

"I reckon the house should be safe enough. It's on quite a flat area. This is the only part of the drive which is on a slope. I'd be surprised if it was in any danger."

"I hope you're right."

"I never reckoned an A-Level in Geology would have been of any practical use. But with any luck I remember enough to be relatively sure. I don't think there's a problem. And anyway, like I said, we don't really have any choice."

Alun started back towards the car and shrugged as he passed Lucy, who had braved the rain. She had a brown leather jacket on, pulled around her neck to keep the rain out. She stood at the edge of the break in the road and, supporting herself on her brother's shoulders, leaned over. "We're not going to be driving out." She seemed happy to take a couple of steps back and tuck her pigtail inside her collar.

"Yeah. Dad thinks we're stuck here. But we'll hire a car or something in the morning."

"Can't we still go tonight?"

"I doubt it. The earth probably isn't safe to walk over. Especially with all our stuff. And we'll be covered in mud. And you should get back in the car. The doctor told you to keep warm."

"Sod the doctor. I'm in more danger from this madwoman of yours than I am from a chill. And anyway, I'll have to supervise you and dad unpacking the car." She raised her eyes to the heavens, but her smile was forced. "*Men.* You're all useless."

"Tell dad I'll walk back. I want look at the landslip."

"Why?"

"Dunno... just a feeling I've got."

"Be careful. If the rest of it gives way..."

"Yeah."

"You... you don't think this was an accident, do you?"

"I... I don't know, sis. I just want to look around."

Lucy's eyes narrowed. Even her forced smile drained from her face. "You think it was the mad ancient woman, don't you?... Morgan. Or Andraste."

"Like I said earlier, I think she wants to keep me here."

"Pete?"

"Yeah?"

"Be careful."

Peter didn't even look around as the Lucy slammed the car door shut. The car roared as Alun started to reverse up the long drive.

Peter sniffed. The rain thickened the atmosphere, lying over it like a blanket. He strained, trying to use all Bran's experience to search the air for a sign. He had no idea what he searched for, but he *knew* something laced the rain. The way the wind rustled the trees. Something *she* was using the thunder to disguise. He could *feel* it.

He dug deep, searching into his consciousness for Bran's knowledge. He felt his mind engaging wisdom as old as the earth itself, taking him back to the time when the gods had loved and warred among the sacred standing monoliths of the ancestors. His mind took him into the edges of a world blurred with his own, where entities of the unknown toyed with the sacred spirals of life.

But the vision dimmed. Bran could give him nothing.

He could almost hear the Archdruid's gentle voice, see the weathered hand caressing the grey beard. *"It takes two decades to learn the secrets. Even if you have the gift."*

He took his hand from his chin and punched the air in frustration. Shaking the rain from his head, he turned to follow the drive to the farmhouse. His trainers crunched the gravel.

The car's lights shimmered at him from the middle distance. The wind hurled itself along the valley, pushing the rain into his face, stinging him like countless needle-sized javelins hurled by the miniature warriors of the *sidhe*.

He wiped water from his watchface. Not five o'clock yet, but the low sky hiding the peaks was thick enough to darken the afternoon into dusk.

Peter looked to his right. Darkness consumed the woods down the gentle slope. His imagination took him back to his childhood, and the monsters living in dark places.

"Great Bel, help me in my hour of need."

And something caught the corner of his vision. A wisp of something lighter from the depths of the wood. He stopped still. Even squinting through the rain he had no idea what he was looking at.

But he *knew* it was evil. He felt his heart pulse.

Instinct told Peter Davis to ignore whatever lay half seen amid the boughs. Instinct told him to run. He fought the urge to sprint his way to the safety of the slate-walled farmhouse. He would not run from battle like a woman.

But still the hairs on the back of his head rose from his flesh.

Peter knew he must look. Four walls and an unarmed policeman would not save his family from the forces Andraste could unleash upon them.

With a deep breath Peter turned and faced the wood.

Something moved among the foliage. Something lighter than the surrounding trees. Once more he wiped the rain from his eyes. He took a step forward and peered into the gloom.

A bare arm?

The half seen... *thing* moved— *waved?*—as if drawing its presence to Peter's attention. He squinted away the rain.

Yes. An arm. *A bare arm.* It retreated into the trees, teasing and enticing him.

He swallowed hard and looked up the drive. In the distance Alun had halted in the middle of the gravel parking space. A concerned policeman walked toward the car. No one paid him attention. No-one looked toward the trees.

No one was touched by his fear.

Peter knew he had to investigate the wood, despite his fear of Andraste's trap. Heart pounding, he readied himself. Then, locking his breath, Peter forced himself forward. He took a step into the boggy ground and his trainer sunk into the wet grass. Water soaked his sock.

He took a couple more paces. Water clogged his other trainer. His steps were uncertain; Peter didn't know whether to watch his footing in the boggy ground or to keep his eyes firmly fixed on the woods. After a few paces he began to pause between each step to survey the trees.

And at the seventh step his breath was taken from his body as a familiar figure stepped from the shadows and stood before him.

Rhiannon?

He wiped the rain from his eyes to clear his vision, trying to convince himself that in the rain and thunder-darkness he had been mistaken. She looked different. She wore the long, checked costume of Celtic women which Peter recognised from his dreams. Her wet hair clung to her scalp. She moved awkwardly, but with an arrogance he had never seen in his relative. And her head... It bobbled from side to side atop a neck ringed by a necklace of blood which seeped from her flesh. It reddened the rain to stain her yellow and orange checked dress with pink. And her face was different. The carefree grin Peter remembered from his childhood was gone; even the happiness which had remained in the corners of her mouth as an adult was banished. She still smiled, but with blank eyes.

Her face bore malice.

The light was dim. Peter tried to tell himself he was mistaken. That this vision could not be not be Rhiannon.

He shook his head and looked once more, convincing himself that this being was nothing more than a part of his imagination.

He looked up again, hoping she would be gone. But, this time, there was no doubt.

Rhiannon placed her hands on her hips and regarded him. She tilted her head to one side like an inquisitive child. It wobbled precariously before falling inelegantly back into place.

Her pallid face stared at him with staring eyes. Not her dancing eyes.

Dead eyes.

Peter's attention was caught by something beyond his dead relative. Movement among the trees.

And he was not surprised when Andraste stepped into the rain. And Peter instantly recognised the scabbard hanging from the belt around her black dress.

Caladchlog, the Rainbow Sword of Fergus mac Roy.

Andraste smiled. In answer to his thought she clasped the hilt in her right hand and pulled it from its leather sheath.

Immediately the sword saw daylight, it released its pulsating scarlet glow into the air. It shone brighter than Peter — and even Bran — had seen it glow before, and with a power bearing more than just a blood-red light.

It lit Peter's eyes; he slammed them shut, but it burned into him even through his closed lids.

But Peter's attention was stripped from the Goddess by a scream from the house.

LUCY!

He raised his hands to his face to block out the swordlight and strained his neck towards his sister's yell.

Even half-blinded he recognised the figure lurching towards his family before his sister screamed the name.

"TOBY!"

The Goddess stared impatiently at Peter and aimed the blade into the ground. Half buried, its light was dimmed.

And as the sword slammed into the loose earth Peter felt a pounding beneath his feet. The gentle slope quivered gently, almost imperceptibly at first. But the movement built up, and he felt himself swaying, waving his arms as he fought to keep his balance on the moving ground. The earth jolted and he took as step to the right in an attempt to prevent his fall, but his foot found only nothing and he fell into the wet ground.

Before him, Rhiannon stood, her bare arms outstretched to greet him as he was carried towards her. Peter found himself wondering why she wasn't falling backwards towards the trees. Panicking, he looked around for something to grab.

But everything within reach was moving with him down the slope and towards whatever horrors remained unseen in the black woods.

The earth crashed above him. He turned his head upwards, but was too late. Before he could throw up his arms to protect himself a boulder smashed into his head.

There was a blinding stab of pain and to Peter's relief the world around him blanked.

Chapter 26

The mountains of slate dwarfed Bran's white-clad frame. The wooden planking around the Sacred Pool bit into his knees, even through his linen cloak. The morning mist, trapped between the peaks, swirled around him, and he was unable to suppress a shiver as the chill bit.

His chest ached.

He caressed his beard as he contemplated the scene of battle with which the gods had rewarded his prayers. In his pool's clear waters, the Archdruid could clearly see the emerald green hill and the glint of British spearpoints in the valley below.

Behind the Iceni's battleline, countless wagons gave a grandstand view to the women and children, come to witness a final slaughter upon the Eagles.

Atop the rise, a hundred paces from the British line and with flanks protected by thick woods, Rome awaited.

And Bran was blessed with the ability to look into the eyes of both armies. The Iceni, their features contorted with hate, sneered and hurled insults. The legions set their jaws in defiance and listened to the rousing speeches of their generals.

The scene was set for carnage, and the Archdruid was grateful to be separated from the battlefield by thrice three leagues or more. Guilt stabbed at him like a dagger as his heart told him he should be at the battle to pray for the army and comfort the dying.

But Britain did not want him. He was an outcast.

The Archdruid stiffened, sensing he was not alone. It was not his training, but the waft of crushed petals on the breeze, and the dull red glow on the mist, that warned him of a presence.

Her presence.

He cursed his frail legs which had weakened even since his journey from Londinium. Placing a hand upon the pain in his ribs, he grasped his staff to steady himself as he rose.

Bran turned around.

The maiden's beauty was untarnished, a vision of demure innocence decorating her soft features. Her right hand clasped the sword of Fergus mac Roy.

Bran felt no fear. "Forsaken your people, Goddess?"

"My people have been torn from the path I have set. I cannot deliver them from the wilderness when they reject my guidance. Let them rot under the Roman yoke."

"You could at least enjoy a feast of British souls on the battlefield?"

"I shall return and feast when the time is right. Britain may be defeated, but I am not."

"No, Goddess?"

"Pah," she spat. "You celebrate victory over me as you prepare to lose your own battle."

"Lady?" Bran coughed and gasped as a need for breath overcame him. His chest ached.

"You are dying, Archdruid. Age will never touch me, but the years have finally defeated you." She circled Bran's wracked from.

He coughed again. His legs burned, but he clung to his staff and refused to fall to his knees. The cold air bit his flesh, but his lungs would not take it into his body.

His chest stabbed pain.

"Feeling the onset of age, Archdruid? What would you not give now for the healing powers of a goddess? Had you given yourself to me, you need not have feared death. Indeed, I had prepared to reward you with those things you desire beyond all else."

Despite himself, Bran raised his head as hope touched him. "My lady?"

"Your family and your health, Archdruid. Your family and your health." She paced triumphantly around his sick body. "Only a moon ago you had all you desired. Now you have nothing... *nothing*." She taunted him with a jab from the magic sword. "I could have given you everything. *Everything*, Archdruid. Dermot; Kyra; Conor... and Helena. Yes, Archdruid. *Helena*. Even now you could be holding your Helena to your chest."

Finally, Barn sucked in a breath. "You would give me nothing but empty promises, lady. Go now. Leave the land of the living. Like mine, your time is finished."

Her mouth turned upward. "Oh, no, Archdruid. There will come a time, many generations from now, when your soul, in the body of another, will return to this valley." She swept her arm around her. "I will return from my sleep when your soul calls mine." Her voice rose to a shout and she raised the weapon triumphantly. "MY PEOPLE WILL HAVE ANOTHER CHANCE TO BEND TO MY WILL. AND I HAVE THE SWORD. THE SACRED SWORD OF FERGUS MAC ROY. GOODBYE, ARCHDRUID BRAN. UNTIL OUR SOULS MEET AGAIN."

She laughed, and without waiting for a response stepped gracefully over the soft, stony ground. Bran was breathing easier now, and found himself wondering whether she was indeed walking, or whether she was floating a handswidth above the earth. The opening into the ancient cairn was half her height, but she seemed to enter without breaking her stride, without even bending her body to fit into the hole.

And then she was gone.

Bran followed, but at the steadier pace permitted by age and pain. His staff sunk into the earth as he leaned his body upon it, and he had to pause to pull it from the soft ground between each step.

He remembered the voices of the ancestors who had called to him from the gaping hole, and feared hearing them once more. For this time he was not prepared. He had not readied his will against their summons with sacred hazelnuts.

But Bran knew, for the good of Britain, he must gulp back his fear. Trembling, and with aching back, he curled his fingers around the fallen entrance stone. He had expected the massive slab of slate to outmatch his strength, but, with prayers to the gods and intermittent curses, he found it rising in his hands.

"Come to me, Bran. Come and hold your grandson." Kyra's words came from nowhere and everywhere, from all directions of the wind.

He silenced his ears. But he could not sustain the effort of fending off the voices and lifting the stone at the same time. His chest stung with the effort.

The rock slipped from his grasp and fell to the ground with a thump. He could not take on the voices.

"Leave the stone on the ground, Bran. Come to your grandson."

Bran pulled himself straight, massaged his complaining back, and paced back to the centre of his stone circle. Even here, Kyra's pleading carried to him as clearly as notes from a harp.

His knees found the indentations in the centre of the circle which they had carved over the years. His hands rose to the heavens. "Great Lord Bel, help me! This summer I have fought evil unaided for the good of Britain. Do not let me fail in my final task. I beg you, help me raise the stone."

The whispering stopped. Silence surrounded the Archdruid. A silence so quiet the priest could almost feel it; no birds welcomed the morning; no stray lambs begged for their mother; even the breeze ceased its gentle brushing of his sacred oaks. The stillness pressed against him.

Slowly, the silence was replaced with a sound. Quiet and indistinct at first as it was dragged from distance over the peaks into his valley. The noise was chaotic at first, but as more parts of the sound found themselves squeezed between the mountains it became steadily louder and more clear.

Soon, there was no mistaking the sound. Men screamed. Iron clashed with iron and ripped flesh. Horses snorted.

The Iceni's final battle had commenced.

Instinctively, Bran turned his head towards his sacred pool and the scene of battle. Then his head turned back to the cairn. Its black, open hole yawned at him, ready to spit forth evil.

Sealing the stone was more important than watching the destruction of the Iceni. Wearily, he rose to his feet once more and, grasping his staff, returned to the cairn.

The weight of the stone numbed his fingers, but despite the growing, spreading pain beneath his ribs the Druid refused to accept defeat. Slowly, with all the force of his failing body, he forced the weathered monolith until it leaned against the cairn, blocking the entrance as it had done since the earth was young. Breathing heavily but unwilling to rest until his task was completed, the Archdruid picked up clods of damp earth and wedged them in around the stone, leaving not even the slightest hole for evil to permeate.

His task done, Bran raised himself to his feet and leaned against the pile of stones, gasping for breath. He grasped at his chest, enjoying the feel of the cool air taking the aching pain from his lungs.

But his heart still hurt.

Bran had done all he could. He praised Bel for bestowing him with strength and returned to his sacred pool. Half sitting and half lying on his wooden platform, watched the battle. As the slaughter unfolded Bran took his first meal of the day; springwater collected in a simple mug, and a loaf of bread bestowed by a shepherd in exchange for a yesterday's blessing on a sick daughter.

The carnage matched for ferocity any he had witnessed on The Sacred Isle, at Camulodunum, or at Londinium. Bran watched, tears glistening on white whiskers, as the British attack uphill petered out, leaving the Eagles to charge down into the disordered ranks of the Iceni. The battle was decided, with the proud warriors of Britain becoming a rabble as they were forced backwards down the slope.

Bran's sacred pool tinted red, but still he could see the British army being pushed ever backwards down the hill until they were packed against their wagons. The front ranks retreated until each man was crushed so tightly against his neighbour that no Briton had room to raise his sword arm.

The Iceni and their allies were cut down as easily as scythes razed wheatstalks to the ground.

Bran leaned forward as his eyes found a familiar face amid the carnage.

Sergovax!

The grey streaked hair was splattered with blood now, but there was no mistaking his finely tuned form, muscular even among his fellow warriors. The Champion made no effort to avoid the slaughter, but led the front line and refused to retreat even a single step. The old warrior's face was a mask of effort and concentration, but his eyes held the tint of death Bran had seen so often in men who knew their time was over.

"Sergovax."

Bran whispered the name only softly, but the warrior paused, listening.

The moment was fatal. Bran's eyes widened as Sergovax's lapse cost him his life. The warrior's deathscream was cut short by a surge of blood from his mouth. He tried to steady himself on a friend, but his comrade was forced back a step by the attack of two mail-clad Romans. Sergovax slipped from Bran's sight among the feet of two armies.

Bran's view cut away from his dying friend as among the noises of battle came a new sound. The high-pitched screaming of women and children, bought along to enjoy a victory, but now watching their menfolk slaughtered. Some jumped from the wagons and ran to escape death, leaving everything except the occasional child clutched to a chest. Only Bran, from his vantage point among the circling ravens, could see the force of Roman cavalry lying in a wood behind the British lines. Waiting for prey.

Other women grabbed weapons and hacked aimlessly into the melee below before being picked off by Roman archers.

Still more women and children stood shocked, screaming hysterically or shivering in bewilderment as they saw a husband or father cut down. As the Roman line burst through the warriors and reached the wagons, women succumbed to mutilation before being despatched to join their menfolk in the Otherworld.

The Archdruid coughed and spat out a mouthful of blood. The sudden movement burned his chest.

Silence and the shadows of the mountains reigned in on his sacred pool once more. A toad croaked from the reeds.

But Archdruid Bran did not contemplate the beauty of nature around him. His mind was too full of slaughter, and his chest too full of pain. Shaking hands took a hazelnut from his pouch, trusting in its pain-numbing properties.

I caused this... I alone sent the Iceni northwards.

Bran felt empty, reminding himself over and over again that the Iceni had been wiped out for the good of Britain.

To ensure an island free of evil.

He first saw the fog, thicker than the mists of morning, as tendrils reaching out to him from between the stones of his sacred circle. On his knees, he opened his arms to embrace it as it enveloped him, thickening around him until he could feel it pressing into him, so thick that even the ground faded into the mist beneath his knees.

He sensed, rather than heard, their presence. But this time he was not afraid. There was no malevolence attached to his family.

"Father, I am here. I have brought Kyra and your grandson."

Dermot's voice, calling to him as musically as the boy's harp had ever done. A juvenile giggle and a motherly "Shhh" betrayed the rest of his family.

"What are you doing here?" Bran asked. But he already knew the answer.

"Your task is complete. It is time for you to join us in our world of happiness."

"Come, Bran." Helena's voice.

Bran contemplated. His actions had resulted in the destruction of Celtic Britain. The island would soon be Roman. He had no wish to live under Roman rule, much as he had striven for Boudicca's revolt to fail.

He had no friends in Britain.

"Dermot, take me to the Otherworld."

The pain left his chest as he crossed the boundary.

Chapter 27

Brigit had never seen the Archdruid's stones at night. Her breath locked as she ignored the bramble scratching her ankle and peered through the undergrowth. Lady Moon's silver light bathed the monoliths in her own colour, giving their dew-damp bodies a shimmering reflection and defining them like statues against the dank black walls of the mountains. The rocks stood proud of the uneven, sheep-cropped grass to remind Brigit of Fomorian monsters, emerging from the sea like an invasion of evil.

They almost *breathed*.

"Scared?" chided Megan from behind her, but in a whispered voice betraying her older sister's own unease.

"Of course not", said Brigit, too quickly to convince even herself. Her voice dropped. "What if *he's* here?"

"Who?.. The Druid?"

"Shhh. He'll hear us. Yes, the Druid."

"No-one's seen him for days. Word is he's gone back east to make peace with the Romans."

"But he'll know we've been here."

"How? He's with the Romans."

"The animals will tell him. The birds or the rabbits."

Megan laughed. That infuriating, teasing laugh "Poor little Brigit. After fifteen summers she still believes priests talk with animals."

"I don't." Brigit shrugged away her sister's patronising arm.

"You do too. It's just an old-fashioned story mothers tell their children to make them behave. I even tell your nephews. "Don't tell tales", I say. "The crows will hear and tell the Druids who will turn us into lizards."

Brigit fell silent. She didn't *want* to believe. Not if Megan said it were untrue.

"Come on, Biddy. The stones. The Maiden Stone."

Brigit followed her sister towards the circle with hesitant paces. Her new leather sandals squeaked as she walked. As they left the undergrowth behind she felt very exposed, sure the noise was loud enough to rouse the ancestors from their drunken slumbers in the Otherworld.

Visiting the circle was no longer the good idea it had seemed in the roundhouse at Nant Bran, giggling girlish giggles around the hearth. The pilfered mead had given her a bravery, which had long since sobered away.

It was cold. It was lonely. And this was a place where the gods would watch her.

Brigit's insides coiled in distaste.

"Come on, Biddy. Here's the stone." Megan patted the top of a megalith.

"Couldn't we…"

"Couldn't we what?"

"The pool?"

"You want to *swim* with the Gods?"

"No. In idol… a carving…"

"Of what?"

"Of me. A wooden carving of me. With a lump on my belly. To make me with child."

"So you want to pray to the ladies of childbirth and give them a gift?"

"Yes."

Megan's face was hidden in shadow, but her snort was clear against the silence. "But why? Prayers may not be answered. The stone gives child every time."

Brigit paused. She didn't want to be here. She didn't want to be naked in this place, where anyone—or any*thing* might be watching. A vision of the Archdruid, hidden among the darkened oaks, enveloped her. She felt her lips curl down as she pictured the old man, caressing his beard in that way he had, and licking his lips as he watched her remove her check dress and rub her body against the stone. She pictured him speaking with the animals, discussing her body with them as he leered.

She started to shiver, but whether because of the cooling breeze or because of fear she could not tell.

She wanted to be at home.

"*Brigit!* Stop dawdling and come here!"

"Shhh. Someone might hear." Tears formed. Her lower lip quivered.

"Who?" teased Megan. "Oh, I forgot. The Druid's *animals*. They'll tell him to turn us into lizards."

The taunt slapped Brigit around the face. She felt her cheeks flush. Fear drained from her like water from a newly thatched roof, to be replaced by anger rising like fire and scalding her breath. "Don't tease. I'm coming." Her response dripped venom. "Treat me kindly, sister, lest I make an effigy of you, with grains of corn pushed into the head. Maybe a facefull of warts would make you more humble!"

"And I will make an effigy of you with breasts as large as burial mounds. They will drag on the floor as you walk."

"And then I will make an effigy of you with no breasts. I pity you, Megan, all warts and no breasts!"

The girls laughed. Peace was restored, the savagery of the moment turned to honey.

The honey disappeared as reality came back to Brigit, but with grim determination she strode the final paces towards where her sister stood, hand resting upon the Maiden Stone. She did not even pause to wipe the embryo tears from the corners of her eyes, but instead hoped the shadows across her face would hide them from Megan.

For her sister must not think her afraid.

Brigit brushed a cloud of midges from her face, spitting out one, which flew into her mouth. She looked up, into Megan's moon-shadowed face.

Megan patted the stone again. "Here it is, Biddy."

Cautiously, like a child reaching for forbidden butter, Brigit reached out and rested her palm on the sacred megalith. It was cold and hard. Like any other stone.

It felt so *ordinary*. Her mind swayed between relief and disappointment.

"Now, take off your dress."

"Now?" Brigit looked around her, afraid of prying eyes.

Or a Druid.

Instinctively, although still clothed, she covered herself with her arms.

"Yes. Now. While Lady moon is above us, at the height of her powers."

"But…"

"No buts. You're the one who wanted to use the stone."

"But…"

"You don't want to be barren for the rest of your life, do you?"

"No…"

"You *do* want to marry Boru, don't you?"

"Yes, but…"

"So you must bear a child. Then he cannot discard you. For everyone knows you lie with him, and him alone." She paused to loose a couple of tuts. "And the gods alone know how much scolding you've taken from mother because of him."

Brigit used the first excuse that came into her mind. "But it's cold."

"But it's cold," mimicked her sister. "What's the chattering of a few teeth against a lifetime with Boru?"

The thought of a wart-faced, flat-chested sister seemed appealing once more. "I suppose…" Brigit gave one final look around her. The land was still. The bushes stood silent, giving no hint of prying eyes among their shadows. With her excuses exhausted, Brigit gave a sigh of resignation, closed her eyes and, biting her lip, counted to three. On the third count, she grabbed her checked woollen dress and hauled it above her head.

She dropped it to the ground and, naked, covered herself with her hands. She opened her eyes and scanned the valley once more.

And squealed at sudden sound among the Archdruid's sacred oaks. "What was that?"

"Night animals. You're jumpy tonight, little sister."

"You'd be jumpy if you were the one with no clothes on and wondering if the gods were leering at you." Brigit pressed her arms closer against her, but readied herself to crouch down and grab her dress. She scanned the bushes again.

Megan just laughed. Not, this time, a laugh of cruelty. A laugh of humour.

The sound put Brigit at ease. She almost stopped shivering. She still instinctively covered herself, though. One hand across her groin, the other arm over her breasts. "What now?"

Megan nodded town at monolith. "The stone."

"What do I do with it?"

Megan's gentle laugh again. "Hug it."

"*Hug* it?"

"Get down on your knees and hug it. You'll see what I mean. Just get on with it. I'll just hang around. I won't watch. Honest." She crossed moon-silver fingers in front of Brigit's face to confirm the promise.

"You'll keep a look out?"

"Who for? No one's seen the old Druid since the moon was young. He's in the east, appeasing the Romans." Brigit heard her sister spit on the floor at mention of the enemy. "And no-one else would come here with the moon at its height."

"Why not?"

"They're all afraid the animals will tell the Druid they've been here."

They both laughed.

"Megan?"

"Yes?"

"What do you think a Roman looks like?"

Megan paused. In the darkness, Brigit imagined her screwing her face up in that way she had. "I saw the prisoner the men bought back here for sacrifice before the Sacred Isle battle. The priests tried to keep him a secret, but I snuck a look. He had short black hair and sort of... sort of wood coloured skin. And always scared. He didn't really look like us. They're not *human*, you know. And anyway, they're idiots."

"Idiots?"

"Yeah. They live in *square* houses."

Brigit had to accept that square houses were unusual. "But why does that make them stupid."

"Square houses have corners. And corners are places for spiders and dust and spirits to hide. Now, stop changing the subject. The stone…"

Brigit conceded to herself that Romans must, indeed, be simple folk. *Square* houses, indeed. She snorted to herself, and realised she had forgotten she was naked.

As her sister turned away, Brigit reached out for the stone. It was cold against her palms. She had expected to feel chilly and a little afraid. Instead, reaching out to grab a big stone, she just felt silly. She reminded herself that the area was sacred; that she was here for a special reason; that this stone could help the barren receive.

She knelt in front of the waist-high monolith. The grass was wet with dew. To her surprise, she found a couple of dents in the ground, just right to slip her knees into. She reasoned that thousands of barren women had knelt in this very spot for countless generations before her.

Including Megan.

The thought calmed her, and she found herself gazing at the sacred, childgiving stone. It stood motionless before her, but Brigit couldn't brush away the feeling that the rock was staring back at her, regarding her and considering whether she was worthy of its powers. It seemed to breathe. And live.

Don't be stupid, she chided herself.

But all people knew that some sacred rocks were capable of thought. The stories of the ancestors said so. And out here, in the middle of the moonbathed night, it was possible to believe even the most childlike of tales.

She reached her arms around the stone. It was much thicker than her body and her fingers only just met around the other side. She was gentle with the rock. Respecting it. For it was old as the mountains, and wise as a Druid.

A Druid… Brigit was forced to pause for a heartbeat to regain her composure.

She brushed as little as possible of her bare flesh against the Maiden Stone. By stretching, she was able to wrap her arms a little over half the way round. To her surprise there seemed to be blemishes in the rock she could use as handholds. Placed very conveniently.

By the ancient priests who had this rock crafted at the whim of the gods?

Hesitantly, still grasping the stone, she leaned back.

Yes. Her grip would keep her attached. She would not fall backwards onto the damp ground.

Hesitating again, she held on tightly and pulled herself forward, towards the great slab of rock. When her back was straight, her eyes were level with the top of the stone.

So what do I do now? It had seemed so straightforward back at Nant Bran, giggling in the depths of their family's roundhouse. But out here, in the cold night air, it was different. Thoughts ran unbidden like rats among a rubbish heap.

What if the stone impregnates me with a monster? Her body threatened to buckle at the thought, but her memory was unable to find any stories of maidens bearing beasts at the whim of magical monoliths.

Many maidens, though, had been turned to rock themselves for such insignificant sins as collecting firewood on sacred days.

But I'm not gathering wood on a God's feast day. I have no reason to fear punishment.

Once more, she steadied her body and fought an urge to run.

"Hug the stone, Biddy. Hold it to you! Are you waiting for dawn to give a free show to the shepherds?"

"All right! Don't scream like a banshee! You're not kneeling here stark naked like a temptress."

"By The Goddess, girl! I've knelt in exactly the same spot as you and prayed for the stone to make me fertile! All you have to do is..." Megan broke off.

"What is it?"

"Don't worry about me, Biddy. I'll go and have a look at that bunch of rags over on the Archdruid's platform. We might be able to use them to patch our clothes. You just concentrate on the stone."

Brigit turned back to the rock, grateful for her sister's company— she certainly wouldn't have been brave enough to come all the way to this magic place on her own, but still she found herself relaxing a little knowing Megan's eyes were away from her.

Gently, readying herself for a shock of cold, she moved her torso towards the stone. She winced as the tips of her nipples found the rough, moon-drenched surface.

But it wasn't cold.

The stone made her breasts tingle a little. It was nice. She pushed them harder onto the stone.

Her nipples hardened. She tingled some more. The stone seemed to be sending a buzz, like a bee in flight, vibrating through her.

Brigit wanted more.

She moved her knees back, making it easier to move the rest of her body forward.

She took an arm from the stone to remove a bead of sweat from her forehead before clinging back onto the monolith.

Without thinking, she thrust her belly onto the stone.

The surge of… of… *power* pulsed through her entire body. It raced up and down her, shaking her up and down, inside and out until even her teeth tingled. She wanted at the same time to both let go of the stone and to cling tightly to it, keeping the power close to her… no, she wanted to keep it *inside* her.

The power was *inside* her belly.

Putting a baby there.

She could stay here for eternity, not needing to eat or drink, but instead gaining sustenance from the rock itself.

She kicked off her sandals and dug her toes into the ground.

She gasped, biting her lip as she thrust forwards and back onto the stone, preparing herself for climax. She heard grunting and stifled screams of pleasure, before realising that they came from her own lips.

She took a hand from the rock and cupped a breast, gently fingering a taught nipple, then eased her fingers down her body, lower, lower, caressing her flat, sweat-dampened belly, then between her thighs, where—

"BIDDY!"

Megan's scream ripped through the night, tearing the current of power from Brigit. She lurched for her dress and pulled it over her head. For a heartbeat she was angry with her sister for taking away the surge of power.

Until she turned around and anger turned to concern. And then fear.

"BIDDY!"

"Megan, ssh! You'll wake the Gods!" But in truth Biddy was more concerned about her sister's cries drifting back to Nantbran and relatives who thought them sleeping. She ran to Megan's side.

Megan ceased her screaming, but stood as still as the ancient stones, staring down onto the rags. They smelled. The stench of rotting flesh, like when one of Nantbran's dogs had hidden a stolen joint of meat in the woodpile during last summer's heat.

Brigit failed to hold onto a gasp.

The rags were alive!

They moved. Not the gentle movement of wind rustling the material. Something different.

Brigit leaned down, her eyes focusing in the moonlight. And she knew why the Archdruid had not been seen since the moon had renewed itself.

Maggots!

Instinctively, she gasped and took a step backwards. Her foot found only air, and within a heartbeat the water of Bran's Sacred Pool had taken her.

She tried to scream, a mixture of the sudden cold, shock of the maggot-ridden corpse, and the terror of falling into the water where the Gods moved between worlds.

She took in a gulp of air as her head broke the surface, and instinct borne of years splashing in the *Afon Gwyrfai* helped her paddle like a dog toward the planking.

Megan knelt above her, reaching out a hand.

Brigit held out her own arm, accepting her sister's help. The cold water had stolen her senses, but she didn't think she was hurt. She would check for damage when she was on solid ground. And away from the Archdruid's stinking body.

She hoped the baby was all right.

My baby. She smiled inwardly.

And something brushed against her foot as she swam. She froze and swallowed a mouthful of cold, black water.

She jerked her foot upwards.

The... the *thing*... brushed against her other leg. She pulled that one up, too, and found herself rolling back in the water.

Brigit's head broke the surface. Above her, Megan said something blurred by the splashing of water, her voice concerned. But Brigit wasn't listening. She screamed. The thing—a hand?—wrapped itself around her foot. Was Boann, Lady of the Waters, taking her in sacrifice?

By the Gods, by the Gods! Why did I ever come here, to the Druid's place? The ancestors are pulling me down into the Otherworld!

She felt Megan's hand grab her arm, pulling her upward. Pulling against the tug of the ancestors below her.

Will I drown first, or will they kill me in sacrifice? she wondered, trying to kick away the grip on her left ankle.

But it just tightened.

And Brigit panicked. She thrashed her legs, kicking out at the thing pulling her down. She threw her arms around in the water, splashing at the unseen monster. She snatched breaths at random intervals, sometimes when her head was above the surface, sometimes when it was below. Water filled her lungs, and breathing became harder. Her woollen dress joined forces with the Ancestors, weighing her down and tying itself around her, pulling her into the depths.

She heard Megan scream from somewhere above her, but her sister no longer held her hand.

She thrashed around.

The pool tasted of blackness. Blackness and mud.

Her head rose above the water yet again. She tried to pull in a breath, but could only choke on water. Water inside her lungs weighed her down now. The air itself seemed black, as black as the depths of the pool from which she had risen. She threw a hand out for Megan to grab, but her sister's cries came from too far away.

She was in the middle of the pool.

And still the ancestors grabbed at her legs. She could feel their grip, tightening around her left foot and pulling her from life once more.

Brigit gave up. She had no strength left, and allowed herself to be dragged without fighting downwards into the Otherworld.

* * * *

"*Ouch!*"

The bee sting on Brigit's cheek was sharp and sudden. Her eyes opened. It was dark. Instinctively, she put her hand to her face to brush away the insect.

The bee had gone. But the pain remained, only it wasn't a bee sting. It felt like a slap.

And there was a moment of panic as Brigit realised she couldn't breathe. She rolled over and vomited.

"Good girl."

Megan's voice. *Was Megan in the Otherworld too?*

"Thank the gods, Brigit. I thought you dead."

"Am I not?" She coughed up another mouthful of water.

Megan laughed. A nervous, relieved laugh. "No, you're not. But you owe me a debt of thanks. It took me an age to drag you out of the water."

"Did the ancestors not try to pull you down too? They pulled at my foot. They dragged me under..." Her voice trailed away into sobs.

"You felt them grab your leg?"

Brigit could only nod.

Megan laughed. "You mistake a hunting horn for the pull of the ancestors? My poor, baby sister."

As Brigit's eyes adjusted to the moonlight once more, she focussed on the richly decorated horn her sister held out to her.

She took it, and held it gently, for it was sacred. A gift, given by the people to the water.

Gold and silver reflected gently in Lady Moon's soft glow.

It was beautiful.

Megan clasped the horn's thick leather strap. "This was tight around your leg. Did you mistake this for the grasp of the ancestors?"

Suddenly, Brigit felt very silly. "I suppose I must have done."

"No harm, Biddy. So, out of tonight you've got a baby and a treasure rich enough to feed it for a year when it comes off your milk. All you have to do is keep it hidden until you can trade it. Come, sister. We've had enough adventure for one night. Let us go home."

Brigit studied the warhorn. She had never held one before. It was heavy. No wonder she had let it drag her under as she panicked.

And in the Archdruid's sacred pool, it was no surprise that she had mistaken the strap tied around her foot for the grip of the ancestors.

She shivered. And not because of the cold.

"I don't think so, Megan." With an effort, she despatched the gift to the gods once more. It disappeared quietly.

Brigit had interfered with the Gods more than enough for her liking.

Chapter 28

His head ached.

He put a hand to his right temple, where every pulse of blood sent a skull-pounding thud through his head. His eyes were closed, and he had no wish to open them to the clamour beyond their lids. Lights swirled beyond, his world of blackness mingling with the sounds coming from all around him. Pigskin drums thumped out a rhythm, while warhorns screamed their primitive accompaniment. Lilting voices in pure Celtic chanted praises to the Mother of Death.

The noise of celebration was laced with evil.

He knew the Mother of Death was familiar to him, but his aching head refused to recall her.

He spat earth from his mouth. His skull throbbed to the beat of the drums.

He slammed his eyes further closed and clamped his palms against his ears. The world was not inviting. He had no wish to let it in.

But still the noise invaded him, driving into his body through every pore.

He closed his mind in an effort to drift away again. As his thoughts wandered through the blackness towards oblivion, he wondered whether he was Peter Davis, or Bran, Archdruid of Britain. He asked whether the voices, Celtic and English together, meant he had taken the long journey over the Bridge of Souls to the Otherworld, the Land of the Ancestors.

Am I dead? A new fear overtook him, and it was with relief that he drifted back into the safety of his nightmares.

* * * *

Chill water slapped him in the face. Instinctively, his eyes snapped open.

Darkness. Darkness with flames jumping around him in yellows, oranges and reds. He threw an arm across his face to protect his eyes from the sudden glare.

Noise. Drums and chanting. The sounds, fires and pain in his head combined into one.

Shouting, a mixture of abuse hurled toward him in both modern and ancient tongues. Spittle landed on his face.

His eyes adjusted. He was in the stone circle, its megaliths crooked or fallen, suffocated in their cloaks of lichen and moss. The woad and check-clad crowd mingled just outside the stones, dancing sacred dances. They seemed afraid to enter a Druid's sanctuary, but brave enough to taunt him with words and spit. Amid the screaming he caught a word here, an oath there, and the chanted words of the Old Language which he knew like the calluses on Bran's hands, accompanied by the thumping of a drum or blasts from a warhorn.

Many of the throng held firebrands to light the darkness. Flames caught a bronze brooch, or an iron daggerblade. Their fires threw the shadows of the few still-erect stones toward him, in his mind reaching to grab him and pull him into the Otherworld.

The figures dancing around the circle came into focus as Peter's eyes adjusted to the firelight.

And the breath was driven from his body. Alun, Lucy and Johnny stood—no, were bound upright— tied to three of the taller rocks forming the sacred circle, their bodies hanging limp over the ropes binding them to the stones. All three were unconscious, although Alun's bloodied head swung gently from side to side, a sign he was trying to fight his way from the darkness. Figures danced behind them, taunting from beyond the magic of the monoliths.

Peter was reminded of his vision, the one which had assaulted him unbidden on his first visit to the valley, what seemed like months ago but could have been no more than a few days.

He was relieved that, unlike in his vision, his family had not yet been stripped naked.

But he knew his Celtic lore. Naked or not, his family would soon be sacrifices to the Lady of Death.

Around their feet lay scattered the bloody remains of an animal... a badger?.. a fox?.. no. The coarse white fur was matted red.

Tipsy.

Or what had once been Tipsy before being torn to pieces.

Peter's mind recalled Bran's vision, back in the days before the Roman war, of the sheep fighting to destroy Roman bodies in his sacred pool. Ripping at bare, defenceless flesh with their bared teeth.

He looked down at his clothes. Jeans and denim jacket.

I am Peter Davis. Not Archdruid Bran.

A hand grabbed him by the hair; a blurred voice in the Old Language taunted him. "See, Britain's traitor awakes. Let the sacrifice to the Lady of War and Death begin!" The hand let go of his hair and slapped Peter around the face. The blow stung.

He recognised the voice, but amid the confusion and pain he could not place it. But he knew the arrogance in the tone.

A fist grabbed at his scalp, twisting and pulling his hair without mercy until he gasped. His brave assailant—one of the few who seemed willing to risk stepping inside the circle of power—pulled him upward until he stood groggily on his feet.

He looked into the face of his tormentor as others found their voices and goaded him in the Old Language.

"Toby? Toby Griffiths!"

Even in the swirling, jumping lights and shadows of the firebrands there was no mistaking the face of Lucy's dead lover.

Or the remains of his face. Gone were both eyes, replaced by empty sockets sinking deep, deep into his skull like night shadows. Dried blood, black in the halflight, caked itself around his features. Blurred sounds emerged from his tongueless mouth. The dark, fussily styled hair straggled around the few places where has scalp remained on his skull.

Other rips and flaps of skin showed where Toby's flesh had been torn from his bones by vicious teeth.

Or a raven's hooked beak.

And a circle of red ran around his neck, where his head had been severed from his body.

The bare arms below Toby's checked Celtic tunic sported a black raven tattoo. The pattern still seeped blood, a sign it had been finished only this night.

Questions poured through Peter Davis's mind. But he could not answer even one.

The grip on his hair was released as Toby's unseeing eyes sockets bore into him, staring blankly at him. Dead breath caressed Peter's cheeks.

But he was looking beyond Toby now, into the chanting throng. He gazed into each of the hate-twisted faces as the flames danced over them for a moment, then thrust them into the darkness as the low breeze took the fires to illuminate a neighbour.

But after what seemed like hours, his eyes settled on the face he searched for. Toby Griffiths let blurred taunts fly like bile from his mouth, but Peter Davis did not hear.

Instead he looked into the stare of Rhiannon Jones.

Or what had once been Rhiannon Jones, but was still the blank-faced demon who had attacked him in earlier... *today?... Yesterday?*

Time didn't seem to matter any more.

Toby Griffiths thrust a firebrand into Peter's face. He saw it coming late, but was able to pull his face back to avoid the jerky, uncoordinated blow. The flame was hot as it brushed against his flesh. Smoke stung his eyes.

But he did not see the fist, which rammed into his stomach. Peter coiled, clutching his middle as he fell to his knees. He swallowed back vomit.

Once more his hair was grasped and, despite the pain pounding beneath him, he allowed himself to be dragged to his feet. He held his stomach and blinked back tears.

Peter called to his cousin.

"Rhiannon?"

She looked back at him. Unmoving. Uncaring. Unrecognising.

"Rhiannon! It's me. Pete. Peter Davis."

Nothing. No flicker of recognition. Just a blank stare reaching beyond his eyes.

Like Andraste's gaze.

He threw a glance towards his family. Lucy and Johnny still slumped forwards over their bonds. Alun was still semi-conscious, eyes half open and groaning quietly.

Peter felt a twinge of relief. They were not suffering.

"Where is Andraste?" Peter asked Toby.

What had once been Toby Griffiths looked blankly back at him.

"Your queen. Where is she?"

"She gives us life. Without her we would be dead." It was difficult to make out his tongueless sounds.

Peter snorted. "She killed you!"

A fist pounded his jaw. Peter stumbled.

"She gives us life," Toby insisted.

"ANDRASTE! ANDRASTE! WHERE ARE YOU? COME AND GET ME!" Peter's shout cut the moonless night.

As one, the crowd fell to their knees in supplication, their heads bowed. A silence descended.

"I am here, Peter Davis," responded a familiar, innocent female voice.

"Peter! Peter! For Christ's sake do something!" Lucy's scream stabbed at him like a spear.

Peter spun around. "Okay, Andraste. Here I am. Come and get me!" He held his arms wide, buying time.

But he had no idea what to do.

Silence. The crowd rose from their knees to stand as motionless as the stones surrounding Peter, parting only to let their Lady move into the circle, her bare feet making no mistake on the rough ground.

The valley sides rose into the night, silhouetted in black against the purple velvet background of the clouds and broken only where occasional moonbeams of silver broke the blackness. And it was a stray streak of moonlight that rested upon the maiden's form, following her like a spotlight as she delicately approached him.

And although Peter's eyes had feasted upon her before, her beauty still sucked the breath from his lungs.

Her hair remained black and silken, but instead of falling unhindered to her waist it was skilfully tied up by a small silver clip to reveal her slender neck. Not a single strand had been allowed to escape; each single hair stayed immaculately in place.

Her large, dark eyes carried their usual depth as firelight danced across them; the large lips around her small mouth were given colour by a deep red juice from a forest berry; her eyes and lips contrasted sensually with her skin, its pale hue tinted by flame.

Her low-cut, ankle length black dress clung to her like a skin, clutching at every curve of her body, but still managing to flow gently as it followed her delicate movements.

For the first time, she wore enhancements. A discreet silver chain hung around her neck, plunging between the soft mounds of her breasts. He right wrist also bore silver, a twisted torque no thicker than a babe's finger.

All Peter could do was gasp.

He forced himself to address her. "You've failed, Andraste. I've beaten you. Boudicca was defeated. Don't you want your revenge?" he goaded with false confidence. The goddess must not know him afraid.

Peter stood motionless and waited for his words to die on the breeze.

The maiden, too, stood silent.

The night was silent.

The crowd was still.

The only sound was the occasional crack from a firebrand. Peter glanced over to his family. Only Lucy was conscious, quiet, but even in the dull light the terror etched across her features was unmissable. He realized just how cold the Snowdonian nights were, and shivered through his damp jacket and sweater. But sweat still greased his palms.

He looked evil straight in her eyes. They jumped with flame, reflecting the torchlight. He had vanquished her once, two thousand years ago, and tonight he must defeat her once more.

But how?

She stepped forward again. They were no more than half a dozen paces apart. She looked perfect in the gold and silver lights of the fires and the moon.

"Come to meet me, have you, Goddess?" He tried to sound contemptuous.

Another cloud broke. The moon squeezed through, touching more of the valley with its sweep of silver.

"Have you come only to taunt me? Would you really approach me in anger?" she asked, forming her lips into a pout and looking up at him with wide, soulful eyes. She spread her hands in a gesture of disbelief.

Peter could say nothing. He felt the surge rising from deep within him, a primeval need for the disguise of innocent perfection before him. But he knew he must resist, just as the mighty warrior Cuchulain had fought off her charms over two millennia ago.

He tried to speak, to move, but could feel his willpower slowly draining from his body. Instead, a buzz of excitement enveloped him, pulsing through him, pumping through his veins until he was consumed in a passion of need. His body urged his mind to give in to its needs, to forget the danger, just to take the woman offering herself to him. He forgot the countless semi-dead Celts holding murderous blades and torches only yards away.

He even forgot his family, tied to the stones to await their sacrifice to the one standing delicately before him.

The beauty standing an arm's length from him was the only thing that mattered.

It would take only one swift, simple movement to take her in his embrace and succumb to her love. Somewhere in the recess of his mind, Peter wondered at her power and asked himself how she was manipulating his will to fulfil her every desire.

She is evil.

She is evil.

She is evil... Peter Davis fought back, repeating the words in his head until they became little more than meaningless sounds and he grasped at reality with the small, decreasing portion of his mind which was still left to him.

And with a jolt he knew. *He was inside the circle of stone.*

He was not blessed with the training to take the magic of the slate megaliths for himself, so could not turn the stones against his tormentor. *No. She* was using their power against *him.* He knew the Goddess was taking the current that was flowing around them, using it to give her strength, to sap his resistance.

He was scared.

"Don't you want me, Peter? Don't you like what you see?" Her voice had hardened. She took a step towards him. "Let me show you what you're missing," she purred. "I know you want me. And I want you just as much." Her hands found her low-cut dress, and with an effortless movement gave the material a gentle rip to reveal yet more cleavage. The soft curves of her breasts held a sheen of silver as they took the moon, their shape emphasized by the dark shadow diving between them.

She took the final step forward, and reached up on her toes to embrace him.

The last vestiges of willpower drained from Peter as their lips met. He could only grunt in frustration as his hands found her waist.

"I'm glad you have decided not to resist." Her voice was the coy, feminine purr of the temptress once more.

He had to do something. He knew that if he surrendered his family would be slaughtered as he watched, their souls becoming hers to feed on for eternity.

Lucy screamed, a piercing, wordless sound of raw terror.

Andraste paused and turned to glare at Peter's stricken sister. As she did so the soft beauty of her features hardened into a mask of hate.

For a second Peter felt her power wane as she concentrated on his sister. In that moment the Goddess released a portion of his will.

His mind returned, Peter used every last piece of energy he could muster and, urged on by fear, forced himself to jump backwards. The leap didn't take him far, and he winced with pain as he landed on his back, a jagged edge of rock puncturing his denim jacket and the flesh beneath. His teeth bit into his lip and he found himself looking up at Andraste.

"Peter, Peter, don't be naughty," she scolded, waving a finger. "Come back to me." She stretched out a hand, encouraging him to reach up to her. Her eyes fixed on his, locking the two of them together.

But she had not yet regained his will. He could still feel himself fending her off.

Peter threw himself backwards across the damp grass once more, then again, in a desperate effort to escape her. The crowd found their voices and murmured among themselves, unsure of events, and their ranks parted as he forced himself backwards.

Quickly, he looked around. He saw the one remaining upright stone to his right, its silhouette a husk of reflected firelight against the background of shadow.

He was out of the circle.

The Goddess' power was lessened. The buzz of excitement died within him. His lust for the maiden lessened.

"I hope you're not going to disappoint me, my warrior." She moved effortlessly towards him, her bare feet moving without hesitation over the broken ground. "Am I going to have to give you a bit more encouragement?" She cupped her breasts in her hands.

Peter wanted to watch, anticipating a glimpse of her body. But his mind recognized the trap she had set. He forced his eyes closed. "NO! NO! NO! I WILL *NOT* SUCCUMB."

His scream pierced the still night, and with his eyes still slammed shut he forced himself backwards yet again, crawling on his heels and elbows.

He forced his body over wickedly protruding rocks and scraped his lower back raw in the process, even through his jacket and jeans. He wiped the mixture of muddy water and blood from his cut hands.

Peter opened his eyes. Pitch black. He looked upwards, trying to find Lady Moon, but she had hidden herself, behind a thickening layer of cloud. A question raised itself in his mind. *Had the Goddess used her powers to part the cloud while within the circle? Was she now unable to prevent the heavens covering the face of the silver orb now she had stepped outside the ancient rocks?*

Did that mean her power has waned?

Lucy renewed her wordless, primeval screaming. Peter turned his head; she stood tied against the tallest of the stones, arching her back and filling her lungs to loose one more yell, but it came from her mouth as little more than a choked wail as sobs overtook her.

But her eyes pleaded with her brother.

But Peter Davis had no words of comfort. He was grateful that Alun and Johnny were still unconscious.

And where was Andraste?

The valley was still and silent again. He looked around, into the fire-flickering faces of the crowd.

But she had not hidden herself among her people.

Peter blinked as suddenly and without warning, a pulsating scarlet light forced its way into his eyes, blinding him. It came from nowhere but everywhere, filling his mind and his eyes, to the point where nothing else existed. Slowly, it withdrew from his head and stood still in the air an arm's length above him.

His mind was as numbed as he tried to recognize scarlet light.

Then Calachalog, The Rainbow Sword, came into focus.

The Goddess held the blade above him, ready to plunge it deep into his chest, to taste his blood as life oozed from his body.

But this was no beauty standing above him; the Goddess had contorted into her picture of evil. Graying hair leaped from her head at crazed angles, countless warts gave her face the swollen appearance of countless beestings. A sickly grin of malice dribbled from her mouth. Age had taken her body, and her ragged black dress gaped enough holes to show wrinkled skin and weathered breasts falling to her waist.

There was no doubt in Peter's mind that this was the being who had visited Johnny in his bedroom.

And the being that had butchered Toby Griffiths. And Rhiannon Jones. And now she prepared to despatch Peter Davis to the Otherworld.

Chapter 29

The swordblade's burning glow reflected in the hag's features, giving a scarlet twist to her malarranged face.

"Don't you still want me, lover?" she cackled, licking her upper lip as she stood astride him. "Come with me, Peter Davis. Satisfy me and let us spend eternity's embrace together."

"No!" In this guise the Goddess was easy to refuse. Peter felt hope and adrenaline coursing through his veins once more, giving him a glimmer of confidence. He knew that now, outside the circle, she lacked the power to overwhelm him. She had to work with her own skills now, without strength taken from the rocks.

"Well then, my sweet, I'll just have to take you for myself. As I drink your blood." With a dry laugh, she raised the sword to strike.

Peter lurched himself to one side, rolling over and away from the blade. He heard the weapon pass through the air, then a dull thud as it hit the earth where his chest had been. There was an unearthly scream as the Goddess vented her frustration, followed by another from Lucy as she found her voice once more.

While the Goddess cursed the heavens, Peter crawled backwards, still unable to raise the strength to stand. Andraste had managed to wrest the sword from the ground, and now she raised the pulsating red blade above her head once more. And again Peter pushed himself away from the blow; again the weapon was bought down only inches from his head. This time it smote a small rock, and red sparks flew as if from an anvil, only to fizzle away on the wet grass.

Peter found his hand clasping a small rock, and using instinct alone flung it at Andraste's face.

She spat her contempt onto his chest as the stone flew past her head, not even forcing her to take evasive action.

He hauled himself away with one last effort, drained and unable to move further. His will was dissipated. He vaguely knew head had hit a rock, but the pain didn't seem to matter. He was only seconds from death anyway. He could do no more than watch as the Goddess again raised the weapon and laughed in triumph. As she cackled, her eyes locked into Peter's. He saw nothing in them except hate. There was no pity in her mask of loathing, no inkling of mercy in her withered features.

Peter knew there was no point in pleading for mercy. The weapon was raised above him, waiting to be thrust into his chest in an orgy of scarlet light. Even Lucy's screams were merely distant noises, failing to matter as Peter awaited the inevitable like a fallen warrior.

He looked into Andraste's deep eyes and met her passionless gaze. He refused to die cowering like a slave woman.

Pain registered across the Goddess' features. Her left hand reached out for something on her throat. She let out a strangled cry as her eyeballs greyed and bulged from widened sockets.

The red glow from the sword died, being slowly replaced by a neutral moonlight radiance.

Peter raised his head to look around him. *The church!* They were on the small rise; the stone he had cracked his head on was part of the ruin of the church! He could feel his strength returning as the Goddess continued to grapple with the unseen powers assailing her. She flailed her arms and slashed the sword randomly, fighting away an assault. Peter wondered if, now and again as the lights took them, he could see small beings flying around Andraste, before they became as one with the blackness again.

Angels? The Celtic fairies, the Sidhe*?*

The questions could wait. The crowd murmured their unease. As one, the throng took a step backwards. Then another step. And another, until the mass of people swayed as a single body.

The sword fell noiselessly to the ground as she loosed her grip. Its red glow faded to black.

Peter grasped the weapon. Almost immediately a green light emanated from it. He felt the sword vibrating in his hand slightly, as if an electric current was pulsing through it.

"YOU CAN'T TAKE IT, CAN YOU ANDRASTE?" He shouted triumphantly. "YOU CAN'T BEAR CONSECRATED GROUND!"

The Goddess dropped to her knees. She held up an arm to ward him, and countless unseen beings, from her.

But Peter Davis was filled with the bloodlust of the Celts of old. *He hated.*

He looked at Lucy, tied and struggling with her bonds, letting out whimpers.

As he watched his sister's uneven struggle he felt no pity for the Goddess. He saw the valley through a haze. He wanted to kill. Using all the force he could find, he bought the weapon down. He had never held a sword in anger before, and was surprised at just how natural he felt. It seemed that the sword *wanted* to strike a blow.

The weapon *wanted* to kill.

It felt good.

There was a scream as the sword struck home. The weapon celebrated its strike with a rainbow of dancing lights.

The Goddess clutched her wounded arm, cradling the broken bone as blood flowed from the severed flesh.

Somewhere in the depths of his consciousness Peter registered surprise that even a goddess could bleed.

He could only watch, transfixed, as the apparition metamorphosed before his eyes. Her black dress changed first, leaving behind the texture of ragged cloth. It moulded itself closely around her and took the form of a layer of skin. It changed once more, to the texture of thick black feathers. It became a covering, a part of the old woman's body. Her nose lengthened and sharpened, taking with it her mouth, becoming a long, hooked beak. The flesh on her arms became soft and downy as it darkened before it, too, became as one with her dress and became feathered wings.

Her arms metamorphosed into wings, and her legs into talons.

The Goddess had changed into her raven form.

She still screamed in pain, but the sound left her beak as a glutteral screech. Her broken wing trailed pathetically along the ground as she sought to fly, to get herself away from the confines of consecrated ground. The crowd parted to let her through as she cursed their cowardice in the language of the birds.

Peter looked to his family. For the first time that evening Lucy's features registered hope in the firelight. But tears still glistened on her cheeks.

"I'VE BEATEN YOU, ANDRASTE!" Peter screamed as he raised the sword once more, but the bird half hopped, half jumped, away from him. "THIS ONE'S FOR JOHNNY!" he shouted as he bought the blade down, slicing tail feathers as his enemy leaped painfully ahead of him. 'This one's for Lucy!" he cried with his next thrust, as his sister screamed once more. "AND FOR KYRA. AND CONOR. AND DERMOT. AND EVERYONE WHO HAS DIED FOR YOUR DREAMS!"

Peter was frenzied now, not knowing or caring what he was saying. He wanted only to destroy the bird flapping in the green light before him. She just managed to keep far enough in front of his murderous blade to keep herself safe.

He cursed his luck as the raven eluded him across the broken ground. Its damaged wing still trailed across the grass and rocks except for the few occasions when it managed to raise itself into the air for a couple of yards. Feathers scattered. He chased the bird, slashing and chopping at it at every opportunity until they reached the entrance to the tomb. The raven stopped to look round at him, hatred glinting in its almost human eyes, before disappearing inside.

"THAT'S IT, ANDRASTE! RUN BACK TO YOUR OTHERWORLD!" Peter screamed as his enemy was consumed by the darkness. He stood poised at the entrance, sword raised above his head, ready to strike should his enemy venture out of the tomb.

Nothing.

He relaxed his stance, and stooped to look into the cavern. It was dark. Black. He lowered the sword until it lit the interior with its low green light.

Still nothing. Just the stench from centuries of darkness and enclosed air.

Not wanting to take his eyes off the tomb in case his enemy reappeared, Peter ventured a half-turn of his head. But he ensured he could still see the entrance from the corner of an eye.

The sacred area was empty of the snarling, chanting throng. None remained; the crowd had slipped away into the night like beaten slaves.

Even the firebrands were extinguished.

The only sound was the low sobbing escaping from Lucy. "Peter! Peter! Untie me!"

"No. I can't leave the cairn. I can't let her escape." He hated ignoring his sister's pleas.

Not wanting to put down the sacred weapon, but aware that he must seal the tomb, Peter laid the blade gently down beside him as he knelt on the moist ground. He curled his fingers around the massive entrance slab.

It was heavy. Peter strained, but his only reward was aching muscles. He took a deep breath and tried again. For a moment there was hope as the stone raised a fraction, only for that hope to be dashed as the monolith slipped from his grasp and laid itself back on the earth with a thick thud.

Peter Davis spat on the stone. And then again. And a third time.

In the sword's green light he put his finger into his spittle, and drew a spiral on the flat slab with the wet fluid. Then another, and another until the three whorls were joined.

He had no idea of the meaning of the words of the Old Tongue he chanted, but he knew they held a sacred significance. They summoned the energy of the gods. He had no idea why he sung, but he would not fight the instinct.

He finished his sacred Celtic chant and once more put his hand to the stone. Repeating the ancient verse in the Old Tongue, he pulled the slab upward as hard as his body would let him.

The stone moved beneath his hands. Encouraged, with clenched teeth he urged his body to greater effort. The monolith continued to rise, yet still he demanded more from his screaming muscles.

And the stone rose. As he lifted the slab's end moving it became easier. He still had to strain, but once it was vertical Peter had no difficulty in easing it into place across the gaping hole. Before allowing his body to relax he tore mud from the wet ground and wedged it into the gaps, promising himself that the entrance would be fully sealed with concrete before it saw another sunset.

The Goddess must not be permitted to escape.

And even in his state of battlelust, with adrenaline coursing through him, Peter Davis knew he had received help from the gods to move a slate slab of such size.

He leaned against the tomb, allowing the tension to drain from him. He had defeated his enemy. The crowd had gone.

Silence ruled where only minutes ago evil had once reigned.

"Oi! Brother! Remember me?" Lucy's voice was confident and demanding now.

Peter couldn't prevent a smile. *Back to the old Lucy!*

Casting anxious glances behind him at the cairn and, clutching the sword by its hilt, he sprinted to the stones and untied his family. Lucy was conscious. Alun soon woke, holding his head and looking dazed. Johnny regained consciousness as Lucy laid him on the damp ground. The boy said nothing, but clung tight to his sister.

No one had the heart to tell Johnny that Tipsy had been slaughtered.

But there was more Peter needed to do. He must deal with Cadalchalog, The Rainbow Sword of Fergus mac Roy. The Goddess had returned from the tomb once to wreak havoc with the magical weapon. He shivered at the prospect of her re-emerging at some future time, seeking to be reunited with the blade. And he knew that in whatever desolate place he laid it, Andraste would not rest until she had found it.

It was a beautiful piece of craftsmanship, but Peter knew he had to destroy it. The weapon's green glow faded, as if anticipating its destruction. Peter felt desolation rising within him as he prepared the weapon's death. As if it were a member of his family.

But how could he destroy it? He looked around as Lucy and his father comforted Johnny.

His car!

Without thinking of the consequences, he rushed to his car. *Keys!* A quick search of his clothes found them, still in his pocket from the last time he had driven. He placed the sword on the passenger seat and forced the key into the ignition. Remembering how the engine had collapsed on the Sacred Isle, Peter breathed a sigh of relief as it burst into life.

There was no Goddess to throw her malignant influence into the engine now.

He threw the gearstick into first and forced the car forward.

He had no idea how easy it would be to drive over the rough, stony ground, but he knew the vehicle had to be forced to the church and onto the sacred mound. And the wet ground made his task more difficult as he risked sticking in pockets of mud or on protruding rocks.

"What the hell are you doing?"

Peter took his foot off the accelerator as he asked his father to repeat the question. He held up the sword in response. "Got to destroy it, dad. Got to stop her using it again." He waited his father's response. Would Alun believe him now?

"I don't know what's going on, Peter." He waved his arm in the direction of the stones. "But I'll help you. Let me push."

Alun disappeared to the back of the car before Peter could thank him.

And avoiding the rocks was difficult, even with the headlights on full beam. Insects danced in front of the lights. The car rocked from side to side as it circumnavigated the boulders and the uneven ground, but with Alun pushing he crawled nearer and nearer the rise. There was swearing as the rear wheel wedged itself. Lucy joined in the pushing and encouraged Johnny to help, maybe to take the youngster's mind off events.

A crunch of metal meeting rock bought him to a halt. He tried accelerating.

Nothing.

He threw the car into reverse.

Only the roar of the engine as it fought the blockage. Behind him, he heard Alun urge Lucy and Johnny on to greater efforts.

Peter slammed his fist onto the passenger seat in frustration. Swearing under his breath, he got out and slammed the door behind him. He grabbed the sword, and using its dying green light as a torch, looked underneath the vehicle.

He found himself cursing the gods as he saw the jagged boulder lifting the front axle from the ground. And he was only a few short, frustrating yards from the church. He kicked out at a tyre.

"Got to get it onto the mound, dad."

Alun shook his head and looked confused, but made no attempt to question.

The two men grabbed the front bumper and lifted. With Johnny and Lucy encouraging them, they hauled it off the stone with no great trouble, and even managed to drag the vehicle to one side of the rock where it had a clear path to its goal.

Johnny didn't look upset. He seemed to be enjoying the adventure now. Peter was reminded of the phrase *'resilience of youth'.*

He jumped back into the driver's seat and turned the ignition once more. The engine roared as the car burst into life again. He urged it forward.

Slowly, gently, Peter glided the car the last few yards to the old walls. The ride became bumpier as he drove over rocks which had fallen from the church over the centuries. He was at the edge of the rise when the time came to be rough. He slammed his foot down as far as it would go, urging the vehicle to ram the church, to send the car as far onto the mound as possible.

The upward lurch and the sound of rock wrestling with metal told him he had hit the broken wall. He revved the engine again, but the car refused to budge. Quickly, Peter threw the door open, and, grabbing the sword, jumped from the driver's seat to the ground. The car was stuck firm on the rocky wall.

But it was well onto the sanctified rise.

Fire! He needed fire!

"Lucy! Have you got your lighter?"

She shot a guilty glance at her father before replying. "Yeah. Here in my pocket." She fumbled in her jeans and tossed the cheap plastic to her brother before returning her attention to comforting Johnny.

Ignoring his father's questions, he ran to the side of the house, into the tool shed—*thanking the gods it wasn't locked*—and ripped out a bucket and a pair of garden shears. He used the shears to cut away a length of hose before sprinting back to the car with the bucket and hose.

The twin beams from the headlights pointed aimlessly into the night. Moths and flies danced in their glow, but he ignored them. Instead he leaned through the still open door and flicked a lever to open the petrol tank. With his fingers trembling, he placed a length of the hose into the petrol tube, and sucked. It was hard work, but he put his finger over the end of the hose and sucked again. He coughed as the bitter, foul smelling fluid filled his mouth. But he was still thinking clearly enough to put his finger over the end of the tube to stop the flow until he placed it in the bucket and watched the dark liquid pouring gently out.

Lucy still comforted Johnny, telling him everything would be fine, that the old lady was gone now.

She didn't mention Tipsy.

Alun looked on, flapping his arms helplessly, obviously not knowing how he could help.

The bucket was about half full when Peter ripped the hose out of the hole. He lifted the bucket and threw the contents over the inside of the car. His hands trembled, but he had no trouble bringing the lighter to life. He stretched his arm out, and nervously inched it towards the saturated front seat. After what seemed like minutes the petrol-laden seat caught light and immersed the air in a sudden heat. A yellow light lit up the car, and Peter involuntarily took a pace backwards and lifted his arm to protect his face.

As he looked down at the weapon in his right hand, Peter thought. He thought of all those who had died through its misuse; *Conor, Kyra, Dermot, and countless thousand others during the revolt of Boudicca. And, in the last few days, Toby Griffiths, Rhiannon and her husband. And the terror felt by Johnny and Lucy.*

"KEEP BACK," he shouted to his family.

Peter waited until everyone had retreated before pulling his arm back and throwing the sword into the flaming car. He turned and ran to safety himself. An explosion of white light behind him rent the valley, blowing him from his feet. He thanked the gods he landed on a patch of long grass. For a moment he felt searing heat beating against has back. Although stunned, Peter forced himself to his knees to look at the fireball, mushrooming up to the heavens and lighting up the night. The flames were a mixture of colour; one instant a deep red; the next a friendly, and seemingly cooler, green; the next a surreal silver.

The cackles of the fire from the burning car were joined by a roar like the wind on a winter's day. Not the blast he would have expected from an explosion.

Now the fire had taken control there was no heat coming from the car. Peter wondered if the sword were consuming the passionate flames itself. Indeed, despite the nearly full tank of petrol, the fire was not so much getting stronger as quickly dying. The flames flickered and faded before his eyes, although the remains of the vehicle still seemed illuminated in a glow which varied between red, green and silver.

The family stood still, transfixed by the dying car.

Peter slowly approached the smouldering, shimmering remains of the vehicle which lay on the rise, little more than a skeleton of charred metal. Still there was no heat, but a strong light illuminating the valley. Cautiously, he reached out a finger to touch the remains, half expecting to be stung by a burn to his flesh. Alun tried to hold him back but Peter shrugged himself free, knowing he was safe now.

Nothing. The burned-out wreck was cold.

He looked inside for the sword, which he had thrown onto the passenger's seat.

It was no longer there. There was the occasional piece of melted iron on the floor, as if the sword had been melted by an all-consuming heat. As Peter had hoped. Maybe that was why he had found the fire cool; destroying the sword had taken up the magical power of the flames.

A sudden thought pinched at his heart. *What if the sword wasn't there, if it had escaped its funeral pyre on this sacred sanctuary, untouchable by the Goddess?*

His heart missed a beat.

On the floor of the vehicle, in front of him, was a scattering of gems. He reached down to pick them up; the rubies and emeralds twinkling in the supernatural light still being given off by the smouldering wreck. Looking at them, he knew his family would not want for anything in their home in the mountains.

He looked up sharply as movement caught his gaze. Was it his imagination, or was there a shimmering figure watching events from within the broken circle of stones? *A white-robed, white-bearded man?* The figure shimmered and rippled, as if struggling to maintain his presence as he caressed his soft beard.

The figure met Peter's gaze with eyes both soft and steely. His lips formed a tight smile and he nodded gently at Peter in a gesture of approval.

"Bran! Wait! There's so much for us to talk about!" Pete clasped his hands around the gems and bounded towards the circle.

But by the time he had reached the spot where the Druid had stood the figure had melted back into the atmosphere. Peter slumped down against a standing stone, the injuries and tensions of the night catching up with him. He had learned much over the last few days.

Lucy hugged him.

"It's all over now," he whispered.

Chapter 30

Peter Davis swung himself out of his father's car, closely followed by Alun and Johnny. The winter chill bit after the car's heater. He shivered.

The dull red student flats gazed down at him, an uninspiring throwback to another era. As always when visiting his sister, Peter was reminded of a Victorian workhouse or prison.

Only iron bars on the windows were missing.

Alun looked bored. Johnny's head was still buried in his game console.

"Be nice to him, dad. Lucy says he's different to all her other boyfriends."

"Humph," Peter's father grunted. A grunt implying the young man was unlikely to be given a chance.

Johnny manoeuvred himself into line between his brother and father without taking his eyes from his game. He gave a low squeal of delight as a cartoon character manoeuvred a maze, followed by a groan of disappointment as Alun told him to save the game and leave it in the car.

Peter led the way through the building, his rubber soles squeaking on the linoleum-carpeted stairs.

He stopped outside Lucy's door. "Here we are. Flat eleven." He lifted Johnny off the ground so the youngster could ring the bell.

Nothing.

"Bell's bust, Pete," stated Johnny.

"Really?" Peter grinned. He banged the door and took a step backward.

There was movement from inside. Lucy's head appeared, and with a smile and a "Hi!" let them in.

She had had her haircut short six months ago, but Peter couldn't get used to the new style.

Craig—at least Peter assumed it was Craig—stood looking embarrassed in the centre of the small flat's main room. His hands fidgeted nervously both inside and outside his pockets, seemingly unable to decide where they should be placed. He squinted at the visitors through thick spectacles.

Lucy introduced them.

"Er… pleased to meet you, Mister Davis," stammered Craig unsurely. He offered Alun a hand before greeting Peter and then Johnny. "I'm sorry to be unsociable, Mister Davis," he apologised almost immediately, picking up a bright orange rucksack from the couch. 'University Climbing Club', it proclaimed in black lettering. "I've got a lecture in half an hour. Still, it's been good to meet you."

Craig shook three hands once more, before lingering as if wondering whether he should give Lucy a kiss. He looked towards Alun and blushed slightly. "See you later, 'Cinda."

Lucy broke the awkward moment by offering him a cheek which was obediently pecked.

"Half an hour? You're leaving early," commented Alun.

"It's a two mile walk."

There was a short silence.

"I can give you a lift."

Craig's eyes widened for a second. He hesitated before accepting.

Johnny insisted on going as well, promising to "…squish monsters quietly in the back."

* * * *

"Why did dad want to give Craig a ride?" asked Lucy as she flicked the kettle.

"To get to know him. Encourage him."

"But dad usually tries to *discourage* my boyfriends. Remember Carlos?"

"Yeah. But Carlos offered dad marijuana."

She bit her bottom lip but failed to stifle a giggle.

"And Craig called you Lucinda. You used to say that was a hanging offence."

"Yeah. Well, life's too short. Anyway, it's my name."

"What I'm trying to say, sister dear, is that Craig isn't your usual sort. Is he?"

She spread her arms before picking up a packet of biscuits. "I have absolutely no idea what you mean, brother." She grinned a grin which showed she knew exactly what Peter meant and bit into a chocolate biscuit.

"Last summer you wouldn't have touched him. He's polite, well spoken, and wears glasses. And he washes. Not your sort at all."

"Humph."

"Yes," continued Peter, getting into a flow. "His hair's about a foot shorter than you usually like and seems acquainted with a comb, he doesn't smell, we've known him for five minutes and he hasn't used an F-word, and he's lost the uniform."

"Uniform, brother?"

"The t-shirt and denim jacket. Preferably unwashed. Along with its wearer."

Lucy placed her hands on her hips and frowned. She reached into her jeans and lit a cigarette. Her eyes were moist.

"I'm sorry, sis. I was only winding you up." He remembered how vulnerable she had looked, tied to a rock as a sacrifice and regretted teasing her.

"He *cares* about me."

"Craig?"

"Yeah. Craig. He cares about *me*. Not that I look... you know... okay." She stepped towards Peter and hugged him, holding her cigarette at an angle away from him. Sobs shook her body.

"We all care about you, sis."

"But you're miles away. Craig's here where I need him. The first week of term we had a lecture on Boudicca's revolt. And I just broke down."

"My poor sister."

"I ran out of the lecture hall. And do you know what? Not *one* person followed me out to see how I was. Not one."

"Except Craig?"

"He was just walking down the corridor. But he stopped and asked if I was alright. And wouldn't take yes for an answer. He just stayed with me until I calmed down. Then he came round later to make sure I was still okay. He *cares* about me."

Peter took his sister's head in his hands and looked her in the eyes.

"You've grown up, sis. What's happened to the fun-loving kid I knew before... before..." He trailed off, not knowing how to describe the summer.

"Before Andraste." Her crying had stopped; she wiped her eyes, composed. "If it wasn't for you, and dad and Craig I'd either be dead or in a loony bin. They—you—are sort of people I need right now."

"Blimey."

"You've lost your wild child little sister. Miss her?"

"A bit. But I like the new adult big sister too. And you weren't *that* wild."

She took a drag of her cigarette. A grin took a corner of her mouth. "You don't know the half of it."

"Tell me."

"And give you ammunition to blackmail me with dad? Maybe some other time."

"I've grown up too, sis."

The door opened. With a Druid's instinct, Peter swung around.

"It was unlocked," explained Alun.

"That was quick."

Alun looked dubious. "Craig asked me to drop him off. Said he needed some paper."

"Yeah," confirmed Lucy. "He said he needed to buy some notepaper before lectures. He ran out."

"Oh. I thought he just wanted to get away from me."

"He's nice," broke in Johnny enthusiastically. He's got the same game as me so he showed me how to play it better."

"Good."

"Dad's girlfriend is nice too, Lucy."

"Is he now?" Lucy shot a questioning glance at her father.

He shuffled and avoided her gaze.

"Dad didn't want to say anything. In case it didn't work out."

"So, who is she?"

"Kath. Kathleen Wyatt."

Lucy's eyes widened. "The archaeologist? I thought you swore to keep out of her way? And the rest of "them ruddy history buffs.""

Alun pushed his glasses up his nose. "Yeah, well. All this stuff that was found in that pool place— where we dug up that shield. She insisted on explaining it all to me. And I sort of found it interesting, and we got talking about things other than history, and just hit it off."

"Well, well. My father the dark horse. And what about my brothers?"

"Eh?"

"Any love on the horizon."

"Johnny still fancies that piece off Children's telly."

"No I don't, no I don't," protested the youngster, covering his scarlet face.

"Peter? Not found a young nymph in the trenches among Kathy Wyatt's minions?"

"No. I've been too busy helping Kath herself. Showing her where the platform was and the like. I think the rest of them think I'm some kind of freak or something, telling them where to dig. It's interesting though. She sometimes lends me a trowel. Maybe I could be an archaeologist."

"He's just being modest," said Alun. "Kath's been amazed by his accuracy. She hasn't questioned anything, though. She knows about the murders, obviously, and I think she thinks there's something fishy about Peter—"

"Don't we all!"

"I think she wants to know... you know... but hasn't plucked up the courage to ask yet."

"And Lucy, they've found an old Celtic body," burst in Johnny.

"A body, little brother? Tell me about it." Lucy brought herself down to her brother's height.

"It was… it was…" He took a deep breath and furrowed his brow in concentration. "It was… un-articled."

"Unarticled?"

"Disarticulated," corrected Alun.

"Unarticled means it was in bits," continued Johnny. "The bones weren't joined together."

Her nose screwed up. "Sounds gruesome."

"Celtic tradition," explained Peter. "They laid out their dead to decompose naturally. Then buried the bones—if there were any left after the scavengers."

"Where was it?"

"In the mound, just near the church. Someone had dug a hole and put the bones in. Probably with quite a ceremony."

"How old?"

"They got the carbon dating results a couple of days ago. About the first or second century." Peter faltered, feeling his eyes welling. "He was about sixty. Suffered from mild arthritis. Would have needed a staff to walk any distance. And he was probably quite important. There was a decorated Roman dagger buried with him."

"You think it was *you*. The Archdruid."

"Bran? Yeah. Maybe."

But there was no "maybe". Peter *knew*.

Lucy hugged her brother. "It's all over, Pete,"

"Yes, Lucy. It's all over."

But the raven flapping its wings outside the window made Peter wonder if it was, indeed, all over.

Epilogue

I am not evil.

Yes, I have caused suffering. Yes, I have gained pleasure from the death and blood shed in my name.

But I needed those lives to continue my existence. And I cannot be named 'Evil' for taking what I need.

Would you punish the thief who steals bread to fill the mouth of a starving child? No?

Then do not condemn me for taking the blood I need to satisfy my stomach.

And my prison...this mound of hollow stones.

In the depths of the tomb I will search until I find a way into the Otherworld, the home of shadows and spirits.

And the Otherworld has many paths into your world. As many as there are stars above your head when you look up to the heavens.

And I would wager your soul that you do not know where such holes meet your existence.

I watch you as you sleep, thinking your children safe in your beds. Do you not know that the sprits have only to reach out an arm to pluck your kin into another realm?

But I digress...

I am not defeated. When the Archdruid knows I have returned, I shall already have a tribe under my control. When he finds me I shall have consumed countless souls.

I will be ready to defeat him and have Britain for my own...

~ ~ ~

About the Author

Andrew Richardson lives in Wiltshire, England, where he works as an administrator. When not writing or working, Andrew can be found visiting local historical sites, following his favourite football team, and enjoying the company of his family. His other interests of horror fiction and Celtic myth have often been combined as the subject matter of the several short stories he has had published.

Visit us on the World Wide Web at www.darkrealmpress.com. Read books in ebook formats on your computer, smart phone or handheld device. New books added frequently.

Printed in the United Kingdom
by Lightning Source UK Ltd.
106074UKS00003B/82